PENGUIN BOOKS

THESE TWAIN

Arnold Bennett was born in 1867 in the 'Potteries' – the region of England about which almost all his best novels were written. After studying art for a time, he began to prepare for his father's profession, that of solicitor; and at twenty-one he left Staffordshire to work in the office of a London firm.

He wrote a novel called *A Man from the North*, having meanwhile become assistant editor of a woman's weekly. Later he edited this paper, and noticed that the serial stories which were offered to him by a literary syndicate were not as good as they should be. He wrote a serial and sold it to the syndicate for £75. This sale encouraged him to write another, which became famous. It was *The Grand Babylon Hotel*.

He also wrote much serious criticism, and a serious novel, *Anna of the Five Towns;* and at last decided to give up his editorship and devote himself wholly to writing. This decision took him to Paris, where in the course of the next eight years he wrote a number of novels, several plays, and, at length, *The Old Wives' Tale*, which was an immediate success throughout the English-speaking world.

Subsequently Bennett wrote many other books, ranging from the farce of *The Card* to the elaborate documentation of *Imperial Palace*. *Clayhanger*, which was published in 1910, is the first novel of a trilogy: it was followed by *Hilda Lessways* (1911), and *These Twain*, which appeared during the First World War. Arnold Bennett died, a much-loved figure, in 1931.

Also available in Penguins are *Anna of the Five Towns*, *The Grand Babylon Hotel*, *The Card*, *Clayhanger*, and *Hilda Lessways*.

ARNOLD BENNETT

THESE TWAIN

PENGUIN BOOKS

Penguin Books Ltd, Harmondsworth, Middlesex, England
Penguin Books Australia Ltd, Ringwood, Victoria, Australia
Penguin Books Canada Ltd, 41 Steelcase Road West, Markham, Ontario, Canada
Penguin Books (N.Z.) Ltd, 182–190 Wairau Road, Auckland 10, New Zealand

—

First published by Methuen & Co. 1916
Published in Penguin Books 1975

—

Made and printed in Great Britain by
Richard Clay (The Chaucer Press), Ltd,
Bungay, Suffolk
Set in Monotype Times

CONTENTS

BOOK I

THE WOMAN IN THE HOUSE

CHAPTER 1

THE HOUSE

I

IN the year 1892 Bleakridge, residential suburb of Bursley, was still most plainly divided into old and new, – that is to say, into the dull red or dull yellow with stone facings, and the bright red with terracotta gimcrackery. Like incompatible liquids congealed in a pot, the two components had run into each other and mingled, but never mixed.

Paramount among the old was the house of the Member of Parliament, near the top of the important mound that separates Hanbridge from Bursley. The aged and widowed Member used the house little, but he kept it up, and sometimes came into it with an unexpectedness that extremely flattered the suburb. Thus you might be reading in the morning paper that the Member had given a lunch in London on the previous day to Cabinet Ministers and ladies as splendid as the Countess of Chell, and – glancing out of the window – you might see the Member himself walking down Trafalgar Road, sad, fragile, sedately alert, with his hands behind him, or waving a gracious hand to an acquaintance. Whereupon you would announce, not apathetically: 'Member's gone down to MacIlvaine's!' (MacIlvaine's being the works in which the Member had an interest) and there would perhaps be a rush to the window. Those were the last great days of Bleakridge.

After the Member's house ranked such historic residences as those of Osmond Orgreave, the architect (which had the largest, greenest garden and the best smoke-defying trees in Bleakridge), and Fearns, the Hanbridge lawyer; together with Manor 'Cottage' (so called, though a spacious house), where lived the mechanical genius who had revolutionized the pottery industry and strangely enough made a fortune thereby, and the dark abode of the High Church parson.

Next in importance came the three terraces, – Manor Terrace, Abbey Terrace, and Sneyd Terrace, – each consisting of three or four houses, and all on the west side of Trafalgar Road, with long back gardens and a distant prospect of Hillport therefrom over the Manor fields. The terraces, considered as architecture, were unbeautiful, old-fashioned, inconvenient, perhaps paltry, as may be judged from the fact that rents ran as low as £25 a years but they had been wondrous in their day, the pride of builders and owners and the marvel of a barbaric populace. They too had histories, which many people knew. Age had softened them and sanctioned their dignity. A gate might creak, but the harsh curves of its ironwork had been mollified by time. Moreover the property was always maintained in excellent repair by its landlords, and residents cared passionately for the appearance of the windows and the front steps. The plenary respectability of the residents could not be impugned. They were as good as the best. For address, they would not give the number of the house in Trafalgar Road, but the name of its terrace. Just as much as the occupiers of detached houses, they had sorted themselves out from the horde. Conservative or Liberal, they were anti-democratic, ever murmuring to themselves as they descended the front steps in the morning and mounted them in the evening: 'Most folks are nobodies, but I am somebody.' And this was true.

The still smaller old houses in between the terraces, and even the old cottages in the side streets (which all ran to the east), had a similar distinction of caste, aloofness, and tradition. The least of them was scornful of the crowd, and deeply conscious of itself as a separate individuality. When the tenant-owner of a cottage in Manor Street added a bay window to his front room the event seemed enormous in Manor Street, and affected even Trafalgar Road, as a notorious clean-shaven figure in the streets may disconcert a whole quarter by growing a beard. The congeries of cottage yards between Manor Street and Higginbotham Street, as visible from certain high back bedrooms in Trafalgar Road, – a crowded higgledy-piggledy of plum-coloured walls and chimneys, blue-brick pavements, and slate roofs, – well illustrated the grand Victorian epoch of the Building Society, when eighteenpence was added weekly to eighteenpence, and land haggled over by the foot, and every brick counted, in the grim, long effort to break away from the mass.

The traditionalism of Bleakridge protected even Roman Catholicism in that district of Nonconformity, where there were at least three Methodist Chapels to every church and where the adjective 'popish' was commonly used in preference to 'papal'. The little 'Catholic Chapel' and the priest's house with its cross-keys at the top of the mound were as respected as any other buildings, because Roman Catholicism had always been endemic there, since the age when the entire hamlet belonged to Cistercian monks in white robes. A feebly endemic Catholicism and a complete exemption from tithes were all that remained of the Cistercian occupation. The exemption was highly esteemed by the possessing class.

Alderman Sutton, towards the end of the seventies, first pitted the new against the old in Bleakridge. The lifelong secretary of a first-class Building Society, he was responsible for a terrace of three commodious modern residences exactly opposite the house of the Member. The Member and Osmond Orgreave might modernize their antique houses as much as they liked, – they could never match the modernity of the Alderman's terrace, to which, by the way, he declined to give a name. He was capable of covering his drawing-room walls with papers at 3s. 6d. a roll, and yet he capriciously preferred numbers to a name! These houses cost £1,200 each (a lot of money in the happy far-off days when good bricks were only £1 a thousand, or a farthing apiece), and imposed themselves at once upon the respect and admiration of Bleakridge. A year or two later the Clayhanger house went up at the corner of Trafalgar Road and Hulton Street, and easily outvied the Sutton houses. Geographically at the centre of the residential suburb, it represented the new movement in Bleakridge at its apogee, and indeed was never beaten by later ambitious attempts.

Such fine erections, though nearly every detail of them challenged tradition, could not disturb Bleakridge's belief in the stability of society. But simultaneously whole streets of cheap small houses (in reality, pretentious cottages) rose round about. Hulton Street was all new and cheap. Oak Street offered a row of

pink cottages to Osmond Orgreave's garden gates, and there were
three other similar new streets between Oak Street and the Catholic Chapel. Jerry-building was practised in Trafalgar Road itself,
on a large plot in full view of the Catholic Chapel, where a specu-
lative builder, too hurried to use a measure, 'stepped out' the
foundations of fifteen cottages with his own bandy legs, and when
the corner of a freshly constructed cottage fell into the street
remarked that accidents would happen and had the bricks replaced. But not every cottage was jerry-built. Many, perhaps
most, were of fairly honest workmanship. All were modern and
relatively spacious, and much superior in plan to the old. All had
bay windows. And yet all their bay windows together could not
produce an effect equal to one bay window in ancient Manor
Street, because they had omitted to be individual. Not one showy
dwelling was unlike another, nor desired to be unlike another.

The garish new streets were tenanted by magic. On Tuesday the
paperhangers might be whistling in those drawing-rooms (called
parlours in Manor Street), – on Wednesday bay windows were
curtained and chimneys smoking. And just as the cottages lacked
individuality, so the tenants were nobodies. At any rate no traditional person in Bleakridge knew who they were, nor where they
came from, except that they came mysteriously up out of the
town. (Not that there had been any shocking increase in the
birthrate down there!) And no traditional person seemed to care.
The strange inroad and portent ought to have puzzled and
possibly to have intimidated traditional Bleakridge: but it did not.
Bleakridge merely observed that 'a lot of building was going on',
and left the phenomenon at that. At first it was interested and
flattered; then somewhat resentful and regretful. And even Edwin
Clayhanger, though he counted himself among the enlightened
and the truly democratic, felt hurt when quite nice houses, copy-
ing some features of his own on a small scale, and let to such
people as insurance agents, began to fill up the remaining empty
spaces of Trafalgar Road. He could not help thinking that the
prestige of Bleakridge was being impaired.

II

Edwin Clayhanger, though very young in marriage, considered that he was getting on in years as a householder. His age was thirty-six. He had been married only a few months, under peculiar circumstances which rendered him self-conscious, and on an evening of August 1892, as he stood in the hall of his house awaiting the commencement of a postponed and unusual At Home, he felt absurdly nervous. But the nervousness was not painful; because he himself could laugh at it. He might be timid, he might be a little gawky, he might often have the curious sensation of not being really adult but only a boy after all, – the great impressive facts would always emerge that he was the respected head of a well-known family, that he was successful, that he had both ideas and money, and that his position as one of the two chief master-printers of the district would not be challenged. He knew that he could afford to be nervous. And further, since he was house-proud, he had merely to glance round his house in order to be reassured and puffed up.

Loitering near the foot of the stairs, discreetly stylish in an almost new blue serge suit and a quite new black satin tie, with the light of the gas on one side of his face, and the twilight through the glazed front door mitigating the shadow on the other, Edwin mused pleasingly upon the whole organism of his home. Externally, the woodwork and metalwork of the house had just been repainted, and the brickwork pointed. He took pleasure in the thought of the long even lines of fresh mortar, and of the new sage-tinted spoutings and pipings, every foot of which he knew by heart and where every tube began and where it ended and what its purpose was. The nice fitting of a perpendicular spout into a horizontal one, and the curve of the joint from the eave to the wall of the house, and the elaborate staples that firmly held the spout to the wall, and the final curve of the spout that brought its orifice accurately over a spotless grid in the ground, – the perfection of all these ridiculous details, each beneath the notice of a truly celestial mind, would put the householder Edwin into a sort of contemplative ecstasy. Perhaps he was comical. But such inner experiences were part of his great interest in life, part of his large general passion.

Within the hall he regarded with equal interest and pride the
photogravure of Bellini's 'Agony in the Garden', from the
National Gallery, and the radiator which he had just had installed.
The radiator was only a half measure, but it was his precious toy,
his pet lamb, his mistress; and the theory of it was that by warming
the hall and the well of the staircase it softly influenced the whole
house and abolished draughts. He had exaggerated the chilliness
of the late August night so that he might put the radiator into
action. About the small furnace in the cellar that heated it he
was both crotchety and extravagant. The costly efficiency of the
radiator somewhat atoned in his mind for the imperfections of the
hot-water apparatus, depending on the kitchen boiler. Even in
1892 this middle-class pioneer and sensualist was dreaming of an
ideal house in which inexhaustible water was always positively
steaming, so that if a succession of persons should capriciously
desire hot baths in the cold middle of the night, their collective
fancy might be satisfied.

Bellini's picture was the symbol of an artistic revolution in
Edwin. He had read somewhere that it was 'perhaps the greatest
picture in the world'. A critic's exhortation to 'observe the loving
realistic passion shown in the foreshortening of the figure of the
sleeping apostle' had remained in his mind; and, thrilled, he
would point out this feature of the picture alike to the comprehending and the uncomprehending. The hanging up of the
Bellini, in its strange frame of stained unpolished oak, had been
an epochal event, closing one era and inaugurating another. And
yet, before the event, he had not even noticed the picture on a
visit to the National Gallery! A hint, a phrase murmured in the
right tone in a periodical, a glimpse of an illustration, – and the
mighty magic seed was sown. In a few months all Victorian
phenomena had been put upon their trial, and most of them
condemned. And condemned without even the forms of justice!
Half a word (in the right tone) might ruin any of them. Thus was
Sir Frederick Leighton, P.R.A., himself overthrown. One day his
'Bath of Psyche' reigned in Edwin's bedroom, and the next it had
gone, and none knew why. But certain aged Victorians, such as
Edwin's Auntie Hamps, took the disappearance of the licentious
engraving as a sign that the beloved queer Edwin was at last
coming to his senses – as, of course, they knew he ultimately

would. He did not and could not explain. More and more he was growing to look upon his house as an island, cut off by a difference of manners from the varnished barbarism of multitudinous new cottages, and by an immensely more profound difference of thought from both the cottages and the larger houses. It seemed astounding to Edwin that modes of thought so violently separative as his and theirs could exist so close together and under such appearances of similarity. Not even all the younger members of the Orgreave family, who counted as his nearest friends, were esteemed by Edwin to be meet for his complete candour.

The unique island was scarcely a dozen years old, but historical occurrences had aged it for Edwin. He had opened the doors of all three reception-rooms, partly to extend the benign sway of the radiator, and partly so that he might judge the total effect of the illuminated chambers and improve that effect if possible. And each room bore the mysterious imprints of past emotion.

In the drawing-room, with its new orange-coloured gas-globes that gilded everything beneath them, Edwin's father used to sit on Sunday evenings, alone. And one Sunday evening, when Edwin, entering, had first mentioned to his father a woman's name, his father had most terribly humiliated him. But now it seemed as if some other youth, and not Edwin, had been humiliated, so completely was the wound healed . . . And he could remember leaning in the doorway of the drawing-room one Sunday morning, and his sister Clara was seated at the piano, and his sister Maggie, nursing a baby of Clara's, by her side, and they were singing Balfe's duet 'Excelsior', and his father stood behind them, crying, crying steadily, until at length the bitter old man lost control of himself and sobbed aloud under the emotional stress of the women's voices, and Clara cheerfully upbraided him for foolishness; and Edwin had walked suddenly away. This memory was somehow far more poignant than the memory of his humiliation . . . And in the drawing-room too he had finally betrothed himself to Hilda. That by comparison was only yesterday; yet it was historical and distant. He was wearing his dressing-gown, being convalescent from influenza; he could distinctly recall the feel of his dressing-gown; and Hilda came in – over her face was a veil . . .

The dining-room, whose large glistening table was now covered with the most varied and modern 'refreshments' for the At Home, had witnessed no event specially dramatic, but it had witnessed hundreds of monotonous tragic meals at which the progress of his father's mental malady and the approach of his death could be measured by the old man's increasing disability to distinguish between his knife and his fork; it had seen Darius Clayhanger fed like a baby. And it had never been the same dining-room since. Edwin might transform it, repaper it, refurnish it, – the mysterious imprint remained . . .

And then there was the little 'breakfast-room', inserted into the plan of the house between the hall and the kitchen. Nothing had happened there, because the life of the household had never adjusted itself to the new, borrowed convention of the 'breakfast-room'. Nothing? But the most sensational thing had happened there! When, with an exquisite passing timidity, she took posses-sion of Edwin's house as his wife, Hilda had had a sudden gust of audacity in the breakfast-room. A mature woman (with a boy aged ten to prove it), she had effervesced into the naïve gestures of a young girl who has inherited a boudoir. 'This shall be my very own room, and I shall arrange it just how I like, without asking you about *anything*. And it will be my very own.' She had not offered an idea; she had announced a decision. Edwin had had other notions for the room, but he perceived that he must bury them in eternal silence, and yield eagerly to this caprice. Thus to acquiesce had given him deep and strange joy.

He was startled, perhaps, to discover that he had brought into his house – not a woman, but a tripartite creature – woman, child, and sibyl. Neither Maggie nor Clara, nor Janet Orgreave, nor even Hilda before she became his wife, had ever aroused in him the least suspicion that a woman might be a tripartite creature. He was married, certainly – nobody could be more legally and respectably married than was he – but the mere marriage seemed naught in comparison with the enormous fact that he had got this unexampled creature in his house and was living with her, she at his mercy, and he at hers. Enchanting escapade! Solemn doom! . . . By the way, she had yet done nothing with the breakfast-room. Yes, she had stolen a 'cabinet' gold frame from the shop, and put his photograph into it, and stuck his picture on the mantelpiece; but that was all. She would not permit him to worry her about her secret designs for the breakfast-room. The breakfast-room was her affair. Indeed the whole house was her affair. It was no longer his house, in which he could issue orders without considering another individuality – orders that would infallibly be executed, either cheerfully or glumly, by the plump spinster, Maggie. He had to mind his 'p's and 'q's; he had to be wary, everywhere. The creature did not simply live in the house; she pervaded it. As soon as he opened the front door he felt her.

III

She was now upstairs in their joint bedroom, dressing for the At Home. All day he had feared she might be late, and as he looked at the hall clock he saw that the risk was getting acute.

Before the domestic rearrangements preceding the marriage had been fully discussed, he had assumed, and Maggie and Clara had assumed, and Auntie Hamps had absolutely assumed, that the husband and wife would occupy the long-empty bedroom of old Darius, because it was two-foot-six broader than Edwin's, and because it was the 'principal' bedroom. But Hilda had said 'No' to him privately. Whereupon, being himself almost morbidly unsentimental, he had judiciously hinted that to object to a room because an old man had died in it under distressing circumstances was to be morbidly sentimental and unworthy of her. Whereupon she had mysteriously smiled, and called him sweet bad names, and kissed him, and hung on his neck. *She* sentimental! Could not the great stupid see without being told that what influenced her was not an aversion for his father's bedroom, but a predilection for Edwin's? She desired that they should inhabit *his* room. She wanted to sleep in *his* room; and to wake up in it, and to feel that she was immersing herself in his past . . . (Ah! The exciting flattery, like an aphrodisiac!) And she would not allow him to uproot the fixed bookcases on either side of the hearth. She said that for her they were part of the room itself. Useless to argue that they occupied space required for extra furniture! She would manage! She did manage. He found that the acme of convenience for a husband had not been achieved, but convenience was naught in the rapture of the escapade. He had 'needed shaking up', as they say down there, and he was shaken up.

Nevertheless, though undoubtedly shaken up, he had the male wit to perceive that the bedroom episode had been a peculiar triumph for himself. Her attitude in it, imperious superficially, was in truth an impassioned and outright surrender to him. And further, she had at once become a frankly admiring partisan of his theory of bedrooms. The need for a comfortable solitude earlier in life had led Edwin to make his bedroom habitable by means of a gas-stove, an easy-chair, and minor amenities. When teased by hardy compatriots about his sybaritism, Edwin was apt sometimes to flush and be 'nettled', and he would make offensive un-English comments upon the average bedroom of the average English household, which was so barbaric that during eight months of the year you could not maintain your temperature in it unless you were either in the bed or running about the room, and that even in summer you could not sit down therein at ease because there was nothing easy to sit on, nor a table to sit at, nor even a book to read. He would caustically ask to be informed why the supposedly practical and comfort-loving English were content with an Alpine hut for a bedroom. And in this way he would go on. He was rather pleased with the phrase 'Alpine hut'. One day he had overheard Hilda replying to an acquaintance upstairs: 'People may say what they like, but Edwin and I don't care to sleep in an Alpine hut.' She had caught it! She was his disciple in that matter! And how she had appreciated his easy-chair! And as for calm deliberation in dressing and undressing, she could astonishingly and even disconcertingly surpass him in the quality. But it is to be noted that she would not permit her son to have a gas-stove in his bedroom. Nor would she let him occupy the disdained principal bedroom, her argument being that that room was too large for a little boy. Maggie Clayhanger's old bedroom was given to George, and the principal bedroom remained empty.

CHAPTER 2

HILDA ON THE STAIRS

I

ADA descended the stairs, young, slim, very neat. Ada was one of Hilda's two new servants. Before taking charge of the house Hilda had ordained the operation called 'a clean sweep', and Edwin had approved. The elder of Maggie's two servants had been a good one, but Hilda had shown no interest in the catalogue of her excellences. She wanted fresh servants. Maggie, like Edwin, approved, but only as a general principle. In the particular case she had hinted that her prospective sister-in-law was perhaps unwise to let slip a tested servant. Hilda wanted not merely fresh servants, but young servants agreeable to behold. 'I will not have a lot of middle-aged scowling women about my house,' Hilda had said. Maggie was reserved, but her glance was meant to remind Hilda that in those end-of-the-century days mistresses had to be content with what they could get. Young and comely servants were all very well – if you could drop on them, but supposing you couldn't? The fact was that Maggie could not understand Hilda's insistence on youth and comeliness in a servant, and she foresaw trouble for Hilda. Hilda, however, obtained her desire. She was outspoken with her servants. If Edwin, after his manner, implied that she was dangerously ignoring the touchiness of the modern servant, she would say indifferently: 'It's always open to them to go if they don't like it.' They did not go. It is notorious that fool-hardy mistresses are often very lucky.

As soon as Ada caught sight of her master in the hall she became self-conscious; all the joints of her body seemed to be hung on very resilient springs, and, reddening slightly, she lowered her gaze and looked at her tripping toes. Edwin seldom spoke to her more than once a day, and not always that. He had one day visited the large attic into which, with her colleague, she dis-appeared late at night, and from which she emerged early in the morning, and he had seen two small tin trunks and some clothes behind the door, and an alarm-clock and a portrait of a fireman on the mantelpiece. (The fireman, he seemed to recollect, was her brother.) But she was a stranger in his house, and he had no sustained curiosity about her. The days were gone when he used to be the intimate of servants – of Mrs Nixon, for example, sole prop of the Clayhanger family for many years, and an entirely human being to Edwin. Mrs Nixon had never been either young, slim, or neat. She was dead. The last servant whom he could be said to have known was a pert niece of Mrs Nixon's – now somebody's prolific wife and much changed. And he was now somebody's husband, and bearded, and perhaps occasionally pompous, and much changed in other ways. So that enigmatic Adas bridled at sight of him and became intensely aware of themselves. Still, this Ada in her smartness was a pretty sight for his eyes as like an aspen she trembled down the stairs, though the coarseness of her big red hands, and the vulgarity of her accent were a surprising contrast to her waist and her fine carriage.

He knew she had been hooking her mistress's dress, and that therefore the hooking must be finished. He liked to think of Hilda being attired thus in the bedroom by a natty deferential wench. The process gave to Hilda a luxurious, even an Oriental quality, which charmed him. He liked the suddenly impressive tone in which the haughty Hilda would say to Ada, 'Your master', as if mentioning a sultan.

He was more and more anxious lest Hilda should be late, and he wanted to ask Ada:

'Is Mrs Clayhanger coming down?'

But he discreetly forbore. He might have run up to the bedroom and burst in on the toilette – Hilda would have welcomed him. But he preferred to remain with his anxiety where he was, and meditate upon Hilda bedecking herself up there in the bedroom – to please him; to please not the guests, but him.

Ada disappeared down the narrow passage leading to the kitchen, and a moment later he heard a crude giggle, almost a scream, and some echo of the rough tones in which the servants spoke to each other when they were alone in the kitchen. There were in fact two Adas; one was as timid as a fawn with a voice like a delicate invalid's; the other a loud-mouthed hoity-toity girl such as rushed out of potbanks in flannel apron at one o'clock. The Clayhanger servants were satisfactory, more than satisfactory, the subject of favourable comment for their neatness among the mistresses of other servants. He liked them to be about; their presence and their official demeanour flattered him; they perfected the complex superiority of his house, – that island. But when he overheard them alone together, or when he set himself to imagine what their soul's life was, he was more than ever amazed at the unnoticed profound differences between modes of thought that in apparently the most natural manner could exist so close together without producing a cataclysm. Auntie Hamps's theory was that they were all – he, she, the servants – equal in the sight of God!

II

Hilda's son, George Edwin, sidled surprisingly into the hall. He was wearing a sailor-suit, very new, and he had probably been invisible somewhere against the blue curtains of the drawing-room window – an example of nature's protective mimicry. George was rather small for his ten years. Dark, like his mother, he had her eyes and her thick eyebrows that almost met in the middle, and her pale skin. As for his mind, he seemed to be sometimes alarmingly precocious and sometimes a case of arrested development. In this and many other respects he greatly resembled other boys. The son of a bigamist can have no name, unless it be his mother's maiden name, but George knew nothing of that. He had borne his father's name, and when at the exciting and puzzling period of his mother's marriage he had learnt that his surname would in future be Clayhanger he had a little resented the affront to his egoism. Edwin's explanation, however, that the change was for the convenience of people in general had caused him to shrug his shoulders in concession and to murmur casually: 'Oh, well then –!' He seemed to be assenting with loftiness: 'If it's any particular use to the whole world, I don't really mind.'

'I say, uncle,' he began.

Edwin had chosen this form of address. 'Stepfather' was

preposterous, and 'father' somehow offended him; so he constituted himself an uncle.

'Hello kid!' said he. 'Can you find room to keep anything else in your pockets besides your hands?'

George snatched his hands out of his pockets. Then he smiled confidently up. These two were friends. Edwin was as proud as the boy of the friendship, and perhaps more flattered. At first he had not cared for George, being repelled by George's loud, positive tones, his brusque and often violent gestures, and his intense absorption in himself. But gradually he had been won by the boy's boyishness, his smile, his little, soft body, his unspoken invocations, his resentment of injustice (except when strict justice appeared to clash with his own interests), his absolute impotence against adult decrees, his touching fatalism, his recondite personal distinction that flashed and was gone, and his occasional cleverness and wit. He admitted that George charmed him. But he well knew that he also charmed George. He had a way of treating George as an equal that few children (save possibly Clara's) could have resisted. True, he would quiz the child, but he did not forbid the child to quiz. The mother was profoundly relieved and rejoiced by this friendship. She luxuriated in it. Edwin might well have been inimical to the child; he might through the child have shown a jealousy of the child's father. But, somewhat to the astonishment of even Edwin himself, he never saw the father in the child, nor thought of the father, nor resented the parenthood that was not his. For him the child was an individual. And in spite of his stern determination not to fall into the delusions of conceited parents, he could not help thinking that George was a remarkable child.

'Have you seen my horse?' asked George.

'Have I seen your horse? . . . Oh! . . . I've seen that you've left it lying about on the hall table.'

'I put it there so that you'd see it,' George persuasively excused himself for the untidiness.

'Well, let's inspect it,' Edwin forgave him, and picked up from the table a piece of cartridge-paper on which was a drawing of a great cart-horse with shaggy feet. It was a vivacious sketch.

'You're improving,' said Edwin, judicially, but in fact much impressed. Surely few boys of ten could draw as well as that! The design was strangely more mature than certain quite infantile watercolours that Edwin had seen scarcely a year earlier.

'It's rather good, isn't it?' George suggested, lifting up his head so that he could just see over the edge of the paper which Edwin held at the level of his watch-chain.

'I've met worse. Where did you see this particular animal?'

'I saw him down near the Brewery this morning. But when I'm doing a horse, I see him on the paper before I begin to draw, and I just draw round him.'

Edwin thought:

'This kid is no ordinary kid.'

He said:

'Well, we'll pin it up here. We'll have a Royal Academy and hear what the public has to say.' He took a pin from under his waistcoat.

'That's not level,' said George.

And when Edwin had readjusted the pin, George persisted boldly:

'That's not level either.'

'It's as level as it's going to be. I expect you've been drawing horses instead of practising your piano.'

He looked down at the mysterious little boy, who lived always so much nearer to the earth's surface than himself.

George nodded simply, and then scratched his head.

'I suppose if I don't practise while I'm young I shall regret it in after life, shan't I?'

'Who told you that?'

'It's what Auntie Hamps said to me, I think . . . I say, uncle.'

'What's up?'

'Is Mr John coming tonight?'

'I suppose so. Why?'

'Oh, nothing . . . I say, uncle.'

'That's twice you've said it.'

The boy smiled.

'You know that piece in the Bible about if two of you shall agree on earth – ?'

'What of it?' Edwin asked rather curtly, anticipating difficulties.

'I don't think two *boys* would be enough, would it? Two grown-ups might. But I'm not so sure about two boys. You see in the very next verse it says two *or three*, gathered together.'

'Three might be more effective. It's always as well to be on the safe side.'

'Could you pray for anything? A penknife, for instance?'

'Why not?'

'But could you?' George was a little impatient.

'Better ask your mother,' said Edwin, who was becoming self-conscious under the strain.

George exploded coarsely:

'Poh! It's no good asking mother.'

Said Edwin:

'The great thing in these affairs is to know what you want, and to *want* it. Concentrate as hard as you can, a long time in advance. No use half wanting!'

'Well, there's one thing that's poz [positive]. I couldn't begin to concentrate tonight.'

'Why not?'

'Who could?' George protested. 'We're all so nervous tonight, aren't we, with this At Home business? And I know I never could concentrate in my best clothes.'

For Edwin, the boy with his shocking candour had suddenly precipitated out of the atmosphere, as it were, the collective nervousness of the household, made it into a phenomenon visible, tangible, oppressive. And the household was no longer a collection of units, but an entity. A bell rang faintly in the kitchen, and the sound abraded his nerves. The first guests were on the threshold, and Hilda was late. He looked at the clock. Yes, she was late. The hour named in the invitations was already past. All day he had feared lest she should be late, and she was late. He looked at the glass of the front door; but night had come, and it was opaque. Ada tripped into view and ran upstairs.

'Don't you hear the front door?' he stopped her flight.

'It was missis's bell, sir.'

'Ah!' Respite!

Ada disappeared.

Then another ring! And no parlourmaid to answer the bell!

Naturally! Naturally Hilda, forgetting something at the last moment, had taken the parlourmaid away precisely when the girl was needed! Oh! He had foreseen it! He could hear shuffling outside and could even distinguish forms through the glass – many forms. All the people converging from various streets upon the waiting nervousness of the household seemed to have arrived at once.

George moved impulsively towards the front door.

'Where are you going?' Edwin asked roughly. 'Come here. It's not your place to open the door. Come with me in the drawing-room.'

It was no affair of Edwin's, thought Edwin crossly and uncompromisingly, if guests were kept waiting at the front door. It was Hilda's affair; she was the mistress of the house, and the blame was hers.

At high speed Ada swept with streamers down the stairs, like a squirrel down the branch of a tree. And then came Hilda.

III

She stood at the turn of the stairs, waiting while the front door was opened. He and George could see her over and through the banisters. And at sight of her triumphant and happy air, all Edwin's annoyance melted. He did not desire that it should melt, but it melted. She was late. He could not rely on her not to be late. In summoning the parlourmaid to her bedroom when the parlour-maid ought to have been on duty downstairs she had acted indefensibly and without thought. No harm, as it happened, was done. Sheer chance often thus saved her, but logically her double fault was not thereby mitigated. He felt that if he forgave her, if he dismissed the charge and wiped the slate, he was being false to the great male principles of logic and justice. The godlike judge in him resented the miscarriage of justice. Nevertheless justice miscarried. And the weak husband said like a woman: 'What does it matter?' Such was her shameful power over him, of which the unscrupulous creature was quite aware.

As he looked at her he asked himself: 'Is she magnificent? Or is she just ordinary and am I deluded? Does she seem her age? Is she a mature woman getting past the prime, or has she miraculously kept herself a young girl for me?'

In years she was thirty-five. She had large bones, and her robust body, neither plump nor slim, showed the firm, assured carriage of its age. It said: 'I have stood before the world, and I cannot be intimidated.' Still, marriage had rejuvenated her. She was marvellously young at times, and experience would drop from her and leave the girl that he had first known and kissed ten years earlier; but a less harsh, less uncompromising girl. At their first acquaintance she had repelled him with her truculent seriousness. Nowadays she would laugh for no apparent reason, and even pirouette. Her complexion was good; he could nearly persuade himself that that olive skin had not suffered in a decade of distress and disasters.

Previous to her marriage she had shown little interest in dress. But now she would spasmodically worry about her clothes, and she would make Edwin worry. He had to decide, though he had no qualifications as an arbiter. She would scowl at a dressmaker as if to say: 'For God's sake do realize that upon you is laid the sacred responsibility of helping me to please my husband!' Tonight she was wearing a striped blue dress, imperceptibly *décolletée*, with the leg-of-mutton sleeves of the period. The colours, two shades of blue, did not suit her. But she imagined that they suited her, and so did he; and the frock was elaborate, was the result of terrific labour and produced a rich effect, meet for a hostess of position.

The mere fact that this woman with no talent for coquetry should after years of narrow insufficiency scowl at dressmakers and pout at senseless refractory silks in the yearning for elegance was utterly delicious to Edwin. Her presence there on the landing of the stairs was in the nature of a miracle. He had wanted her, and he had got her. In the end he had got her, and nothing had been able to stop him – not even the obstacle of her tragic adventure with a rascal and a bigamist. The strong magic of his passion had forced destiny to render her up to him mysteriously intact, after all. The impossible had occurred, and society had accepted it, beaten. There she was, dramatically, with her thick eyebrows, and the fine wide nostrils and the delicate lobe of the ear, and that mouth that would startlingly fasten on him and kiss the life out of him.

'There is dear Hilda!' said someone at the door amid the arriving group.

None but Auntie Hamps would have said 'dear' Hilda. Maggie, Clara and even Janet Orgreave never used sentimental adjectives on occasions of ceremony.

And in her clear, precise, dominating voice Hilda with gay ease greeted the company from above:

'Good evening, all!'

'What the deuce was I so upset about just now?' thought Edwin, in sudden, instinctive, exulting felicity: 'Everything is absolutely all right.'

CHAPTER 3

ATTACK AND REPULSE

I

THE entering guests were Edwin's younger sister Clara with her husband Albert Benbow, his elder sister Maggie, Auntie Hamps, and Mr Peartree. They had arrived together, and rather unfashionably soon after the hour named in the invitation, because the Benbows had called at Auntie Hamps's on the the way up, and the Benbows were always early, both in arriving and in departing, 'on account of the children'. They called themselves 'early birds'. Whenever they were out of the nest in the evening they called themselves early birds. They used the comparison hundreds, thousands, of times, and never tired of it; indeed each time they were convinced that they had invented it freshly for the occasion.

Said Auntie Hamps, magnificent in jetty black, handsome and, above all, imposing:

'I knew you would be delighted to meet Mr Peartree again, Edwin. He is staying the night at my house – I can be so much more hospitable now Maggie is with me – and I insisted he should come up with us. But it needed no insisting.'

The old erect lady looked from Mr Peartree with pride towards her nephew.

Mr Peartree was a medium-sized man of fifty, with greying sandy hair. Twenty years before, he had been second minister in the Bursley Circuit of the Wesleyan Methodist Connexion. He was now superintendent minister in a Cheshire circuit. The unchangeable canons of Wesleyanism permit its ministers to marry, and celibacy is even discouraged, for the reason that wives and daughters are expected to toil in the cause, and their labour costs the circuit not a halfpenny. But the canons forbid ministers to take root and found a home. Eleven times in thirty years Mr Peartree had been forced to migrate to a strange circuit and to adapt his much-travelled furniture and family to a house which he had not chosen, and which his wife generally did not like. During part of the period he had secretly resented the autocracy of Superintendent Ministers, and during the remainder he had learnt that Superintendent Ministers are not absolute autocrats.

He was neither overworked nor underpaid. He belonged to the small-tradesman class, and, keeping a shop in St Luke's Square, he might well have worked harder for less money than he now earned. His vocation, however, in addition to its desolating nomadic quality, had other grave drawbacks. It gave him contact with a vast number of human beings, but the abnormal proportion among them of visionaries, bigots, hypocrites and petty office-seekers falsified his general estimate of humanity. Again, the canons rigorously forbade him to think freely for himself on the subjects which in theory most interested him; with the result that he had remained extremely ignorant through the very fear of knowledge, that he was a warm enemy of freedom, and that he habitually carried intellectual dishonesty to the verge of cynicism. Thirdly, he was obliged always to be diplomatic (except of course with his family), and nature had not meant him for the diplomatic career. He was so sick of being all things to all men that he even dreamed diplomatic dreams as a galley-slave will dream of the oar; and so little gifted for the role that he wore insignificant tight turned-down collars, never having perceived the immense moral advantage conferred on the diplomatist by a high, loose, wide-rolling collar. Also he was sick of captivity, and this in no wise lessened his objection to freedom. He had lost all youthful enthusiasm, and was in fact equally bored with earth and with heaven.

Nevertheless, he had authority and security. He was accustomed to the public gaze and to the forms of deference. He knew that he was as secure as a judge, and far more secure than a Cabinet Minister. Nothing but the inconceivable collapse of a powerful and wealthy sect could affect his position or his livelihood to the very end of life. Hence, beneath his weariness and his professional attitudinarianism there was a hint of the devil-may-care that had its piquancy. He could foresee with indifference even the distant but approaching day when he would have to rise in the pulpit and assert that the literal inspiration of the Scriptures was not and never had been an essential article of Wesleyan faith.

Edwin blenched at the apparition of Mr Peartree. That even Auntie Hamps should dare uninvited to bring a Wesleyan minister to the party was startling; but that the minister should be Mr Peartree staggered him. For twenty years and more Edwin had secretly, and sometimes in public, borne a tremendous grudge against Mr Peartree. He had execrated, anathematized, and utterly excommunicated Mr Peartree, and had extended the fearful curse to his family, all his ancestors, and all his descendants. When Mr Peartree was young and fervent in the service of heaven he had had the monstrous idea of instituting a Saturday Afternoon Bible Class for schoolboys. Abetted by parents weak-minded and cruel, he had caught and horribly tortured some score of miserable victims, of whom Edwin was one. The bitter memory of those weekly half-holidays thieved from him and made desolate by a sanctimonious crank had never softened, nor had Edwin ever forgiven Mr Peartree.

It was at the sessions of the Bible Class that Edwin, while silently perfecting himself in the art of profanity and blasphemy, had in secret fury envenomed his instinctive mild objection to the dogma, the ritual, and the spirit of conventional Christianity, especially as exemplified in Wesleyan Methodism. He had left Mr Peartree's Bible Class a convinced anti-religionist, a hater and despiser of all that the Wesleyan Chapel and Mr Peartree stood for. He deliberately was not impartial, and he took a horrid pleasure in being unfair. He knew well that Methodism had produced many fine characters, and played a part in the moral development of the race; but he would not listen to his own knowledge. Nothing could extenuate, for him, the noxiousness of Methodism. On the other hand he was full of glee if he could add anything to the indictment against it and Christianity. Huxley's controversial victories over Gladstone were then occurring in the monthly press, and he acclaimed them with enormous gusto. When he first read that the Virgin Birth was a feature of sundry creeds more ancient than Christianity, his private satisfaction was intense and lasted acutely for days. When he heard that Methodism had difficulty in maintaining its supply of adequately equipped

ministers, he rejoiced with virulence. His hostility was the more
significant in that it was concealed – embedded like a foreign
substance in the rather suave gentleness of his nature. At intervals
– decreasingly frequent, it is true – he would carry it into the
chapel itself; for, through mingled cowardice and sharp prudence,
he had not formally left the Connexion. To compensate himself
for such borings-down he would now and then assert, judicially to
a reliable male friend, or with ferocious contempt to a scandalized
defenceless sister, that, despite all parsons, religion was not a
necessity of the human soul, and that he personally had never felt
the need of it, and never would. In which assertion he was
profoundly sincere.

And yet throughout he had always thought of himself as a rebel
against authority; and – such is the mysterious intimidating
prestige of the past – he was outwardly an apologetic rebel.
Neither his intellectual pride nor his cold sustained resentment,
nor his axiomatic conviction of the crude and total falseness of
Christian theology, nor all three together, had ever sufficed to rid
him of the self-excusing air. When Auntie Hamps spoke with careful reverence of 'the Super' (short for 'superintendent minister'),
the word had never in thirty years quite failed to inspire in him
some of the awe with which he had heard it as an infant. Just as a
policeman was not an employee but a *policeman*, so a minister
was not a person of the trading class who happened to have been
through a certain educational establishment, subscribed to certain
beliefs, submitted to certain ceremonies and adopted a certain
costume, – but a *minister*, a being inexplicably endowed with
authority, – in fact a sort of arch-policeman. And thus, while
detesting and despising him, Edwin had never thought of Abel
Peartree as merely a man.

Now, in the gas-lit bustle of the hall, after an interval of about
twenty years, he beheld again his enemy, his bugbear, his loathed
oppressor, the living symbol of all that his soul condemned.

Said Mrs Hamps:

'I reminded Mr Peartree that you used to attend his Bible Class,
Edwin. Do you remember? I hope you do.'

'Oh, yes!' said Edwin, with a slight nervous laugh, blushing.
His eye caught Clara's, but there was no sign whatever of the old

malicious grin on her maternal face. Nor did Maggie's show a tremor. And, of course, the majestic duplicity of Auntie Hamps did not quiver under the strain. So that the Rev. Mr Peartree, protesting honestly that he should have recognized his old pupil Mr Clayhanger anywhere, never suspected the terrific drama of the moment.

And the next moment there was no drama . . . Teacher and pupil shook hands. The recognition was mutual. To Edwin, Mr Peartree, save for the greying of his hair, had not changed. His voice, his form, his gestures, were absolutely the same. Only, instead of being Mr Peartree, he was a man like another man – a commonplace, hard-featured, weary man; a spare little man, with a greenish-black coat and bluish-white low collar; a perfunctory, listless man with an unpleasant voice; a man with the social code of the Benbows and Auntie Hamps; a man the lines of whose face disclosed a narrow and self-satisfied ignorance; a man whose destiny had forbidden him ever to be natural; the usual snobbish man, who had heard of the importance and the success and the wealth of Edwin Clayhanger and who kowtowed thereto and was naïvely impressed thereby, and proud that Edwin Clayhanger had once been his pupil; and withal an average decent fellow.

Edwin rather liked the casual look in Mr Peartree's eyes that said: 'My being here is part of my job. I'm indifferent. I do what I have to do, and I really don't care. I have paid tens of thousands of calls and I shall pay tens of thousands more. If I am bored I am paid to be bored, and I repeat I really don't care.' This was the human side of Mr Peartree showing itself. It endeared him to Edwin.

'Not a bad sort of cuss, after all!' thought Edwin.

All the carefully tended rage and animosity of twenty years evaporated out of his heart and was gone. He did not forgive Mr Peartree, because there was no Mr Peartree – there was only this man. And there was no Wesleyan Chapel either, but only an ugly forlorn three-quarters-empty building at the top of Duck Bank. And Edwin was no longer an apologetic rebel, nor even any kind of a rebel. It occurred to nobody, not even to the mighty Edwin, that in those few seconds the history of dogmatic religion had passed definitely out of one stage into another.

Abel Peartree nonchalantly, and with a practised aplomb which was not disturbed even by the vision of George's heroic stallion, said the proper things to Edwin and Hilda; and it became known, somehow, that the parson was revisiting Bursley in order to deliver his well-known lecture entitled 'The Mantle and Mission of Elijah', – the sole lecture of his repertoire, but it had served to raise him ever so slightly out of the ruck of 'Supers'. Hilda patronized him. Against the rich background of her home she assumed the pose of the grand lady. Abel Peartree seemed to like the pose, and grew momentarily vivacious in knightly response. 'And why not?' said Edwin to himself, justifying his wife after being a little critical of her curtness.

Then, when the conversation fell, Auntie Hamps discreetly suggested that she and the girls should 'go upstairs'. The negligent Hilda had inexcusably forgotten in her nervous excitement that on these occasions arriving ladies should be at once escorted to the specially-titivated best bedroom, there to lay their things on the best counterpane. She perhaps ought to have atoned for her negligence by herself leading Auntie Hamps to the bedroom. But instead she deputed Ada. 'And why not?' said Edwin to himself again. As the ladies mounted, Mr Peartree laughed genuinely at one of Albert Benbow's characteristic pleasantries, which always engloomed Edwin. 'Kindred spirits, those two!' thought the superior sardonic Edwin, and privately raised his eyebrows to his wife, who answered the signal.

II

Somewhat later, various other guests having come and distributed themselves over the reception-rooms, the chandeliers glinted down their rays upon light summer frocks and some jewellery and coats of black and dark grey and blue; and the best counterpanes in the best bedroom were completely hidden by mantles and cloaks, and the hat-stand in the hall heavily clustered with hats and caps. The reception was in being, and the interior full of animation. Edwin, watchful and hospitably anxious, wandered out of the drawing-room into the hall. The door of the breakfast-room was ajar, and he could hear Clara's voice behind it. He knew that the Benbows and Maggie and Auntie Hamps were all in the breakfast-room, and he blamed chiefly Clara for this provincial clannishness, which was so characteristic of her. Surely Auntie Hamps at any rate ought to have realized that the duty of members of the family was to spread themselves among the other guests!

He listened.

'No,' Clara was saying, 'we don't know what's happened to him since he came out of prison. He got two years.' She was speaking in what Edwin called her 'scandal' tones – low, clipped, intimate, eager, blissful.

And then Albert Benbow's voice:

'He's had the good sense not to bother us.'

Edwin, while resenting the conversation and the Benbows' use of 'we' and 'us' in a matter which did not concern them, was grimly comforted by the thought of their ignorance of a detail which would have interested them passionately. None but Hilda and himself knew that the bigamist was at that moment in prison again for another and a later offence. Everything had been told but that.

'Of course,' said Clara, 'they needn't have said anything about the bigamy at all, and nobody outside the family need have known that poor Hilda was not just an ordinary widow. But we all thought –'

'I don't know so much about that, Clary,' Albert Benbow interrupted his wife. 'You mustn't forget his real wife came to Turnhill to make inquiries. That started a hare.'

'Well, you know what I mean,' said Clara vaguely.

Mr Peartree's voice came in:

'But surely the case was in the papers?'

'I expect it was in the Sussex papers,' Albert replied. 'You see, they went through the ceremony of marriage at Lewes. But it never got into the local rag, because he got married in his real name, – Cannon wasn't his real name; and he'd no address in the Five Towns then. He was just a boarding-house keeper at Brighton. It was a miracle it didn't get into the *Signal*, if you ask me; but it didn't. I happen to know' – his voice grew important – 'that the *Signal* people have an arrangement with the Press Association for a full report of all matrimonial cases that 'ud be likely

to interest the district. However, the Press Association weren't
quite on the spot that time. And it's not surprising they weren't,
either.'

Clara resumed:

'No. It never came out. Still, as I say, we all thought it best not
to conceal anything. Albert strongly advised Edwin not to attempt
any such thing.' ('What awful rot!' thought Edwin.) 'So we just
mentioned it quietly like to a few friends. After all, poor Hilda was
perfectly innocent. Of course she felt her position keenly when she
came to live here after the wedding.' ('Did she indeed!' thought
Edwin.) 'Edwin would have the wedding in London. We did so
feel for her.' ('Did you indeed!' thought Edwin.) 'She wouldn't
have an At Home. I knew it was a mistake not to. We all knew.
But no, she *would not*. Folks began to talk. They thought it
strange she didn't have an At Home like other folks. Many young
married women have two At Homes nowadays. So in the end she
was persuaded. She fixed it for August because she thought so
many people would be away at the seaside. But they aren't – at
least not so many as you'd think. Albert says it's owing to the
General Election upset. And she wouldn't have it in the afternoon
like other folks. Mrs Edwin isn't like other folks, and you can't
alter her.'

'What's the matter with the evening for an At Home, anyhow?'
asked Benbow the breezy and consciously broad-minded.

'Oh, of course, *I* quite agree. I like it. But folks are so funny.'

After a momentary pause, Mr Peartree said uncertainly:

'And there's a little boy?'

Said Clara:

'Yes, the one you've seen.'

Said Auntie Hamps:

'Poor little thing! I do feel so sorry for him – when he grows
up –'

'You needn't, Auntie,' said Maggie curtly, expressing her
attitude to George in that mild curtness.

'Of course,' said Clara quickly. 'We never let it make any
difference. In fact our Bert and he are rather friends, aren't they,
Albert?'

At this moment George himself opened the door of the dining-room, letting out a faint buzz of talk and clink of vessels. His mouth was not empty. Precipitately Edwin plunged into the breakfast-room.

'Hello! You people!' he murmured. 'Well, Mr Peartree.'

There they were – all of them, including the parson – grouped together, lusciously bathing in the fluid of scandal.

Clara turned, and without the least constraint said sweetly:

'Oh, Edwin! There you are! I was just telling Mr Peartree about you and Hilda, you know. We thought it would be better.'

'You see,' said Auntie Hamps impressively, 'Mr Peartree will be about the town tomorrow, and a word from *him* –'

Mr Peartree tried unsuccessfully to look as if he was nobody in particular.

'That's all right,' said Edwin. 'Perhaps the door might as well be shut.' He thought, as many a man has thought: 'My relations take the cake!'

Clara occupied the only easy-chair in the room. Mrs Hamps and the parson were seated. Maggie stood. Albert Benbow, ever uxorious, was perched sideways on the arm of his wife's chair. Clara, centre of the conclave, and of all conclaves in which she took part, was the mother of five children, and nearing thirty-five years of age. Maternity had ruined her once slim figure, but neither she nor Albert seemed to mind that, – they seemed rather to be proud of her unshapeliness. Her face was unspoiled. She was pretty, and had a marvellously fair complexion. In her face Edwin could still always plainly see the pert, charming, malicious girl of fourteen who loathed Auntie Hamps and was rude to her behind her back. But Clara and Auntie Hamps were fast friends nowadays. Clara's brood had united them. They thought alike on all topics. Clara had accepted Auntie Hamps's code practically entire; but on the other hand she had dominated Auntie Hamps. The respect which Auntie Hamps showed for Clara and for Edwin, and in a slightly less degree for Maggie, was a strange phenomenon in the old age of that grandiose and vivacious pillar of Wesleyanism and the conventions.

Edwin did not like Clara; he objected to her domesticity, her motherliness, her luxuriant fruitfulness, the intonations of her voice, her intense self-satisfaction and her remarkable duplicity;

and perhaps more than anything to her smug provinciality. He did not positively dislike his brother-in-law, but he objected to him for his uxoriousness, his cheerful assurance of Clara's perfection, his contented and conceited ignorance of all intellectual matters, his incorrigible vulgarity of a small manufacturer who displays everywhere the stigmata of petty commerce, and his ingenuous love of office. As for Maggie, the plump spinster of forty, Edwin respected her when he thought of her, but reproached her for social gawkiness and taciturnity. As for Auntie Hamps, he could not respect, but he was forced to admire, her gorgeous and sustained hypocrisy, in which no flaw had ever been found, and which victimized even herself; he was always invigorated by her ageless energy and the sight of her handsome, erect, valiant figure.

Edwin's entrance had stopped the natural free course of conversation. But there were at least three people in the room whom nothing could abash: Mrs Hamps, Clara, and Mr Peartree.

Mr Peartree, sitting up with his hands on his baggy knees, said: 'Everything seems to have turned out very well in the end, Mr Clayhanger – very well, indeed.' His features showed less of the tedium of life.

'Eh, yes! Eh, yes!' breathed Auntie Hamps in ecstasy.

Edwin, diffident and ill-pleased, was about to suggest that the family might advantageously separate, when George came after him into the room.

'Oh!' cried George.

'Well, little jockey!' Clara began instantly to him with an exaggerated sweetness that Edwin thought must nauseate the child, 'would you like Bert to come up and play with you one of these afternoons?'

George stared at her, and slowly flushed.

'Yes,' said George. 'Only –'

'Only what?'

'Supposing I was doing something else when he came?'

Without waiting for possible developments George turned to leave the room again.

'You're a caution, you are!' said Albert Benbow; and to the adults: 'Hates to be disturbed, I suppose.'

'That's it,' said Edwin responsively, as brother-in-law to brother-in-law. But he felt that he, with a few months' experience of another's child, appreciated the exquisite strange sensibility of children infinitely better than Albert were he fifty times a father.

'What is a caution, Uncle Albert?' asked George peeping back from the door.

Auntie Hamps good-humouredly warned the child of the danger of being impertinent to his elders:

'George! George!'

'A caution is a caution to snakes,' said Albert. 'Shoo!' Making a noise like a rocket, he feinted to pursue the boy with violence.

Mr Peartree laughed rather loudly, and rather like a human being, at the word 'snakes'. Albert Benbow's flashes of humour, indeed, seemed to surprise him, if only for an instant, out of his attitudinarianism.

Clara smiled, flattered by the power of her husband to reveal the humanity of the parson.

'Albert's so good with children,' she said. 'He always knows exactly . . .' She stopped, leaving what he knew exactly to the listeners' imagination.

Uncle Albert and George could be heard scuffling in the hall. Auntie Hamps rose with a gentle sigh, saying:

'I suppose we ought to join the others.'

Her social sense, which was pretty well developed, had at last prevailed.

The sisters Maggie and Clara, one in light and the other in dark green, walked out of the room. Maggie's face had already stiffened into mute constraint, and Clara's into self-importance, at the prospect of meeting the general company.

III

Auntie Hamps held back, and Edwin at once perceived from the conspiratorial glance in her splendid eyes that in suggesting a move she had intended to deceive her fellow-conspirator in life, Clara. But Auntie Hamps could not live without chicane. And she was happiest when she had superimposed chicane upon chicane in complex folds.

She put a ringed hand softly but arrestingly upon Edwin's arm, and pushed the door to. Alone with her and the parson, Edwin felt himself to be at bay, and he drew back before an unknown menace.

'Edwin, dear,' said she, 'Mr Peartree has something to suggest to you. I was going to say "a favour to ask", but I won't put it like that. I'm sure my nephew will look upon it as a privilege. You know how much Mr Peartree has at heart the District Additional Chapels Fund –'

Edwin did not know how much; but he had heard of the Macclesfield District Additional Chapels Fund, Bursley being one of the circuits in the Macclesfield District. Wesleyanism finding itself confronted with lessening congregations and with a shortage of ministers, the Macclesfield District had determined to prove that Wesleyanism was nevertheless spiritually vigorous by the odd method of building more chapels. Mr Peartree, inventor of Saturday Afternoon Bible Classes for schoolboys, was one of the originators of the bricky scheme, and in fact his lecture upon the 'Mantle and Mission of Elijah' was to be in aid of it. The next instant Mr Peartree had invited Edwin to act as District Treasurer of the Fund, the previous treasurer having died.

More chicane! The parson's visit, then, was not a mere friendly call, inspired by the moment. It was part of a scheme. It had been planned against him. Did they (he seemed to be asking himself) think him so ingenuous, so simple, as not to see through their dodge? If not, then why the preliminary pretences? He did not really ask himself these questions, for the reason that he knew the answers to them. When a piece of chicane had succeeded Auntie Hamps forgot it, and expected others to forget it, – or at any rate she dared, by her magnificent front, anybody on earth to remind her of it. She was quite indifferent whether Edwin saw through her dodge or not.

'You're so good at business,' said she.

Ah! She would insist on the business side of the matter, affecting to ignore the immense moral significance which would be attached to Edwin's acceptance of the office! Were he to yield, the triumph for Methodism would ring through the town. He read all her thoughts. Nothing could break down her magnificent front.

She had cornered him by a device; she had him at bay; and she counted on his weak good-nature, on his easy-going cowardice for a victory.

Mr Peartree talked. Mr Peartree expressed his certitude that Edwin was 'with them at heart', and his absolute reliance upon Edwin's sense of the responsibilities of a man in his, Edwin's, position. Auntie Hamps recalled with fervour Edwin's early activities in Methodism – the Young Men's Debating Society, for example, which met at six o'clock on frosty winter mornings for the proving of the faith by dialectics.

And Edwin faltered in his speech.

'You ought to get Albert,' he feebly suggested.

'Oh, no!' said Auntie. 'Albert is grand in his own line. But for this, *we want a man like you*.'

It was a master-stroke. Edwin had the illusion of trembling, and yet he knew that he did not tremble, even inwardly. He seemed to see the forces of evolution and the forces of reaction ranged against each other in a supreme crisis. He seemed to see the alternative of two futures for himself – and in one he would be a humiliated and bored slave, and in the other a fine, reckless ensign of freedom. He seemed to be doubtful of his own courage. But at the bottom of his soul he was not doubtful. He remembered all the frightful and degrading ennui which when he was young he had suffered as a martyr to Wesleyanism and dogma, all the sinister deceptions which he had had to practise and which had been practised upon him. He remembered his almost lifelong intense hatred of Mr Peartree. And he might have clenched his hands bitterly and said with homicidal animosity: '*Now* I will pay you out! And I will tell you the truth! And I will wither you up and incinerate you, and be revenged for everything in one single sentence!' But he felt no bitterness, and his animosity was dead. At the bottom of his soul there was nothing but a bland indifference that did not even scorn.

'No,' he said quietly, 'I shan't be your treasurer. You must ask somebody else.'

A vast satisfaction filled him. The refusal was so easy, the opposing forces so negligible.

Auntie Hamps and Mr Peartree knew nothing of the peculiar

phenomena induced in Edwin's mind by the first sight of the legendary Abel Peartree after twenty years. But Auntie Hamps, though puzzled for an explanation, comprehended that she was decisively beaten. The blow was hard. Nevertheless she did not wince. The superb pretence must be kept up, and she kept it up. She smiled, and, tossing her curls, checked Edwin with cheerful, indomitable rapidity.

'Now, now! Don't decide at once. Think it over very carefully, and we shall ask you again. Mr Peartree will write to you. I feel sure . . .'

Appearances were preserved.

The colloquy was interrupted by Hilda, who came in excited, gay, with sparkling eyes, humming an air. She had protested vehemently against an At Home. She had said again and again that the idea of an At Home was abhorrent to her, and that she hated all such wholesale formal hospitalities, and could not bear 'people'. And yet now she was enchanted with her situation as hostess – delighted with herself and her rich dress, almost ecstatically aware of her own attractiveness and domination. The sight of her gave pleasure and communicated zest. Mature, she was yet only beginning life. And as she glanced with secret condescension at the listless Mr Peartree, she seemed to say: 'What is all this talk of heaven and hell? I am in love with life and the senses, and everything is lawful to me, and I am above you.' And even Auntie Hamps, though one of the most self-sufficient creatures that ever lived, envied in her glorious decay the young maturity of sensuous Hilda.

'Well,' said Hilda, 'what's going on *here*? They're all gone mad about missing words in the drawing-room.'

She smiled splendidly at Edwin, whose pride in her thrilled him. Her superiority to other women was patent; she made other women seem negative. In fact, she was a tingling woman before she was anything else – that was it! He compared her with Clara, who was now nothing but a mother, and with Maggie, who had never been anything at all.

Mr Peartree made the mistake of telling her the subject of the conversation. She did not wait to hear what Edwin's answer had been.

She said curtly and with finality:

'Oh, no! I won't have it!'

Edwin did not quite like this. The matter concerned him alone, and he was an absolutely free agent. She ought to have phrased her objection differently. For example, she might have said: 'I hope he has refused.'

Still, his annoyance was infinitesimal.

'The poor boy works quite hard enough as it is,' she added, with a delicious caressing intonation of the first words.

He liked that. But she was confusing the issue. She always would confuse the issue. It was not because the office would involve extra work for him that he had declined the invitation, as she well knew.

Of course Auntie Hamps said in a flash:

'If it means overwork for him I shouldn't dream . . .' She was putting the safety of appearances beyond doubt.

'By the way, Auntie,' Hilda continued, 'what's the trouble about the pew down at chapel? Both Clara and Maggie have mentioned it.'

'Trouble, my dear?' exclaimed Auntie Hamps, justifiably shocked that Hilda should employ such a word in the presence of Mr Peartree. But Hilda was apt to be headlong.

To the pew originally taken by Edwin's father, and since his death standing in Edwin's name, Clara had brought her husband; and although it was a long pew, the fruits of the marriage had gradually filled it, so that if Edwin chanced to go to chapel there was not too much room for him in the pew, which presented the appearance of a second-class railway carriage crowded with season ticket holders. Albert Benbow had suggested that Edwin should yield up the pew to the Benbows, and take a smaller pew for himself and Hilda and George. But the women had expressed fear lest Edwin 'might not like' this break in an historic tradition, and Albert Benbow had been forbidden to put forward the suggestion until the diplomatic sex had examined the ground.

'We shall be only too pleased for Albert to take over the pew,' said Hilda.

'But have you chosen another pew?' Mrs Hamps looked at Edwin.

'Oh, no!' said Hilda lightly.

'But –'

'Now, Auntie,' the tingling woman warned Auntie Hamps as one powerful individuality may warn another, 'don't worry about us. You know we're not great chapel-goers.'

She spoke the astounding words gaily but firmly. She could be firm and even harsh in her triumphant happiness. Edwin knew that she detested Auntie Hamps. Auntie Hamps no doubt also knew it. In their mutual smilings, so affable, so hearty, so appreciative, apparently so impulsive, the hostility between them gleamed mysteriously like lightning in sunlight.

'Mrs Edwin's family were Church of England,' said Auntie Hamps in the direction of Mr Peartree.

'No great church-goers, either,' Hilda finished cheerfully.

No woman had ever made such outrageous remarks in the Five Towns before. A quarter of a century ago a man might have said as much, without suffering in esteem – might indeed have earned a certain intellectual prestige by the declaration; but it was otherwise with a woman. Both Mrs Hamps and the minister thought that Hilda was not going the right way to live down her dubious past. Even Edwin in his pride was flurried. Great matters, however, had been accomplished. Not only had the attack of Auntie Hamps and Mr Peartree been defeated, but the defence had become an onslaught. Not only was he not the treasurer of the District Additional Chapels Fund, but he had practically ceased to be a member of the congregation. He was free with a freedom which he had never had the audacity to hope for. It was incredible! Yet there it was! A word said, bravely, in a particular tone, – and a new epoch was begun. The pity was that he had not done it all himself. Hilda's courage had surpassed his own. Women were astounding. They were disconcerting too. His manly independence was ever so little wounded by Hilda's boldness in initiative on their joint behalf.

'Do come and take something, Auntie,' said Hilda, with the most winning, the most loving, inflection.

Auntie Hamps passed out.

Hilda turned back into the room: 'Do go with Auntie, Mr

Peartree. I must just –' She affected to search for something on the mantelpiece.

Mr Peartree passed out. He was unmoved. He did not care in his heart. And as Edwin caught his indifferent eye, with that 'it's-all-one-to-me' glint in it, his soul warmed again slightly to Mr Peartree. And further, Mr Peartree's aloof unworldliness, his personal practical unconcern with money, feasting, ambition, and all the grosser forms of self-satisfaction, made Edwin feel somewhat a sensual average man and accordingly humiliated him.

As soon as, almost before, Mr Peartree was beyond the door, Hilda leaped at Edwin, and kissed him violently. The door was not closed. He could hear the varied hum of the party.

'I had to kiss you while it's all going on,' she whispered. Ardent vitality shimmered in her eyes.

CHAPTER 4
THE WORD

I

ADA was just crossing the hall to the drawing-room, a telegram on a salver in her red hand.

'Here you are, Ada,' said Edwin, stopping her, with a gesture towards the telegram.

'It's for Mr Tom Swetnam, sir.'

Edwin and Hilda followed the starched and fussy girl into the drawing-room, in which were about a dozen people, including Fearns, the lawyer, and his wife, the recently married Stephen and Vera Cheswardine, several Swetnams, and Janet Orgreave, who sat at the closed piano, smiling vaguely.

Tom Swetnam, standing up, took the telegram.

'I never knew they delivered telegrams at this time o' night,' said Fearns sharply, looking at his watch. He was wont to keep a careful eye on the organization of railways, ships, posts, and other contrivances for the shifting of matter from one spot to another. An exacting critic of detail, he was proud of them in the mass, and called them civilization.

'They don't,' said Tom Swetnam naughtily, glad to plague a man older than himself, and the father of a family. Tom was a mere son, but he had travelled, and was, indeed, just returned from an excursion through Scandinavia. 'Observe there's no deception. The envelope's been opened. Moreover, it's addressed to Ben Clewlow, not to me. Ben's sent it up – I asked him to. Now, we'll see.'

Having displayed the envelope like a conjurer, he drew forth the telegram, and prepared to read it aloud. One half of the company was puzzled; the other half showed an instructed excitement. Tom read the message:

'"Twenty-seven pounds ten nine. Philosophers tell us that there is nothing new under the sun. Nevertheless it may well be doubted whether the discovery of gold at Barmouth, together with two earthquake shocks following each other in quick succession in the same district, does not constitute, in the history of the gallant little Principality, a double event of unique –"' He stopped.

Vera Cheswardine, pretty, fluffy, elegant, cried out with all the impulsiveness of her nature:

'Novelty!'

'Whatever is it all about?' mildly asked Mrs Fearns, a quiet and dignified, youngish woman whom motherhood had made somewhat absent-minded when she was away from her children.

'Missing-word competition,' Fearns explained to her with curt, genial superiority. He laughed outright. 'You do go it, some of you chaps,' he said. 'Why, that telegram cost over a couple of bob, I bet!'

'Well, you see,' said Tom Swetnam, 'three of us share it. We get it thirty-six hours before the paper's out – fellow in London – and there's so much more time to read the dictionary. No use half-doing a thing! Twenty-seven pounds odd! Not a bad share this week, eh?'

'Won anything?'

'Rather. We had the wire about the winning word this morning. We'd sent it in four times – that makes about £110, doesn't it? Between three of us. We sent in nearly two hundred postal orders, which leaves £100 clear. Thirty-three quid apiece, net.'

He tried to speak calmly and nonchalantly, but his excitement was extreme. The two younger Swetnams regarded him with awe. Everybody was deeply impressed by the prodigious figures, and in many hearts envy, covetousness, and the wild desire for a large, free life of luxury were aroused.

'Seems to me you've reduced this game to a science,' said Edwin.

'Well, we have,' Tom Swetnam admitted. 'We send in every possible word.'

'It's a mere thousand per cent profit per week,' murmured Fearns, 'at the rate of fifty thousand per cent per annum.'

Albert Benbow, entering, caught the last phrase, which very properly whetted his curiosity as a man of business. Clara followed him closely. On nearly all ceremonial occasions these two

had an instinctive need of each other's presence and support; and
if Albert did not run after Clara, Clara ran after Albert.

II

Then came the proof of the genius, the cynicism and the insight of
the leviathan newspaper-proprietor who had invented the dodge
of inviting his readers to risk a shilling and also to buy a coupon
for the privilege of supplying a missing word, upon the understanding that the shillings of those who supplied the wrong word
should be taken for ever away from them and given to those who
supplied the right word. The entire company in the Clayhanger
drawing-room was absorbed in the tremendous missing-word
topic, and listened to Swetnam as to a new prophet bearing the
secret of eternal felicity. The rumour of Swetnam's triumph drew
people out of the delectable dining-room to listen to his remarks;
and among these was Auntie Hamps. So it was in a thousand, in
ten thousand, in hundreds of thousands of homes of all kinds
throughout the kingdom. The leviathan journalist's readers
(though as a rule they read nothing in his paper save the truncated
paragraph and the rules of the competition) had grown to be
equivalent to the whole British public. And he not only held them
but he had overshadowed all other interests in their minds. Upon
honeymoons people thought of the missing word amid caresses,
and it is a fact that people had died with the missing word on their
lips. Sane adults of both sexes read the dictionary through from
end to end every week with an astounding conscientiousness. The
leviathan newspaper-proprietor could not buy enough paper, nor
hire sufficient presses, to meet the national demands. And no
wonder, seeing that any small news-agent in a side street was liable
at any moment to receive an order from an impassioned student
of periodical literature for more copies of one issue of the journal
than the whole town had been used to buy before the marvellous
invention of the missing word. The Post Office was incommoded;
even the Postmaster-General was incommoded, and only by
heroical efforts and miraculous feats of resourcefulness did he
save himself from the ignominy of running out of shilling postal
orders. Post-Office girls sold shilling postal orders with a sarcastic

smile, with acerbity, with reluctance, – it was naught to them that the revenue was benefited and the pressure on taxpayers eased. Employers throughout the islands suffered vast losses owing to the fact that for months their offices and factories were inhabited, not by clerks and other employees, but by wage-paid mono- maniacs who did naught but read dictionaries and cut out and fill up coupons. And over all the land there hung the dark incredible menace of an unjust prosecution under the Gambling Laws, urged by interfering busybodies who would not let a nation alone.

'And how much did you make last week, Mr Swetnam?' judicially asked Albert Benbow, who was rather pleased and flattered, as an active Wesleyan, to rub shoulders with frank men of the world like Tom. As an active Wesleyan he had hitherto utterly refused to listen to the missing word, but now it seemed to be acquiring respectability enough for his ears.

Swetnam replied with a casual air:

'We didn't make much last week. We won something, of course. We win every week; that's a mathematical certainty – but some- times the expenses mount up a bit higher than the receipts. It depends on the word. If it's an ordinary word that everybody chooses, naturally the share is a small one because there are so many winners.' He gave no more exact details.

Clara breathed a disillusioned 'Oh!' implying that she had known there must be some flaw in the scheme – and her husband had at once put his finger on it.

But her husband, with incipient enthusiasm for the word, said:

'Well, it stands to reason they must take one week with another, and average it out.'

'Now, Albert! Now, Albert!' Edwin warned him. 'No gambling.'

Albert replied with some warmth:

'I don't see that there's any gambling in it. Appears to me that it's chiefly skill and thoroughness that does the trick.'

'Gambling!' murmured Tom Swetnam shortly. 'Of course it's not gambling.'

'No!'

'Well,' said Vera Cheswardine, 'I say "novelty". "A double event of unique novelty." That's it.'

'I shouldn't go nap on "novelty", if I were you,' said Tom Swetnam, the expert.

Tom read the thing again.

'"Novelty",' Vera repeated. 'I know it's "novelty". I'm always right, aren't I, Stephen?' She looked round. 'Ask Stephen.'

'You were right last week but one, my child,' said Stephen.

'And did you make anything?' Clara demanded eagerly.

'Only fifteen shillings,' said Vera discontentedly. 'But if Stephen had listened to me we should have made lots.'

Albert Benbow's interest in the word was strengthened.

Fearns, leaning carefully back in his chair, asked with fine indifference:

'By the way, what is this week's word, Tom? I haven't your secret sources of information. I have to wait for the paper.'

'"Unaccountably",' said Tom. 'Had you anything on it?'

'No,' Fearns admitted. 'I've caught a cold this week, it seems.'

Albert Benbow stared at him. Here was another competitor – and as acute a man of business as you would find in the Five Towns!

'Me, too!' said Edwin, smiling like a culprit.

Hilda sprang up gleefully, and pointed at him a finger of delicious censure.

'Oh! You wicked sinner! You never told me you'd gone in! You deceitful old thing!'

'Well, it was a man at the shop who would have me try,' Edwin boyishly excused himself.

III

Hilda's vivacity enchanted Edwin. The charm of her reproof was simply exquisite in its good nature and in the elegance of its gesture. The lingering taste of the feverish kiss she had given him a few minutes earlier bemused him and he flushed. To conceal his inconvenient happiness in the thought of his wife he turned to open the new enlarged window that gave on the garden. (He had done away with the old garden entrance of the house, and thrown the side corridor into the drawing-room.) Then he moved towards Janet Orgreave, who was still seated at the closed piano.

'Your father isn't coming, I suppose?' he asked her quietly.

The angelic spinster, stylishly dressed in white, and wearing as usual her kind heart on her sleeve, smiled with soft benignity, and shook her head.

'He told me to tell you he was too old. He *is*, you know.'

'And how's your mother?'

'Oh, pretty well, considering . . . I really ought not to leave them.'

'Oh, yes!' Edwin protested. The momentary vision of Mr and Mrs Orgreave in the large house close by, now practically deserted by all their children except Janet, saddened him.

Then a loud voice dominated the general conversation behind him:

'I say, this is a bit stiff. I did think I should be free of it here. But no! Same old missing word everywhere! What is it this week, Swetnam?'

It was Johnnie Orgreave, appreciably younger than his sister, but a full-grown man of the world, and somewhat dandiacal. After shaking hands with Hilda he came straight to Edwin.

'Awfully sorry I'm so late, old chap. How do, Jan?'

'Of course you are,' Edwin quizzed him like an uncle.

'Where's Ingpen?'

'Not come.'

'Not come! He said he should be here at eight. Just like him!' said Johnnie. 'I expect he's had a puncture.'

'I've been looking out for him every minute,' Edwin muttered.

In the middle of the room Albert Benbow, stocky and vulgar, but feeling himself more and more a man of the world among men and women of the world, was proclaiming, not without excitement:

'Well, I agree with Mrs Cheswardine. "Novelty"'s much more likely than "interest". "Interest"'s the wrong kind of word altogether. It doesn't agree with the beginning of the paragraph.'

'That's right, Mr Benbow,' Vera encouraged him with flirtatious dimples. 'You put your money on me, even if my own husband won't.' Albert as a dowdy dissenter was quite out of her expensive sphere, but to Vera any man was a man.

'Now, Albert,' Clara warned him, 'if you win anything, you must give it to me for the new perambulator.'

('Dash that girl's infernal domesticity!' thought Edwin savagely.)

'Who says I'm going in for it, missis?' Albert challenged.

'I only say *if* you do, dear,' Clara said smoothly.

'Then I *will*!' Albert announced the great decision. 'Just for the fun of the thing, I will. Thank ye, Mrs Cheswardine.'

He glanced at Mrs Cheswardine as a knight at his unattainable mistress. Indeed the decision had in it something of the chivalrous; the attention of slim provocative Vera, costliest and most fashionably dressed woman in Bursley, had stirred his fancy to wander far beyond its usual limits.

'Albert! Well, I never!' exclaimed Mrs Hamps.

'You don't mind, do you, Auntie?' said Albert jovially, standing over her.

'Not if it's not gambling,' said Mrs Hamps stoutly. 'And I hope it isn't. And it would be very nice for Clara, I'm sure, if you won.'

'Hurrah for Mrs Hamps!' Johnnie Orgreave almost yelled.

At the same moment, Janet Orgreave, swinging round on the music-stool, lifted the lid of the piano, and, still with her soft, angelic smile, played loudly and dashingly the barbaric, Bacchic, orgiastic melody which had just recently inflamed England, Scotland, Ireland, Wales, and the Five Towns – the air which was unlike anything ever heard before by British ears, and which meant nothing whatever that could be avowed, the air which heralded social revolutions and inaugurated a new epoch. And as the ringed fingers of the quiet, fading spinster struck out the shocking melody, Vera Cheswardine and one or two others who had been to London and there seen the great legendary figure, Lottie Collins, hummed more or less brazenly the syllables heavy with mysterious significance:

> Tarara-boom-deay!
> Tarara-boom-deay!
> Tarara-boom-deay!
> Tarara-boom-deay!

Upon this entered Mr Peartree, like a figure of retribution, and silence fell.

'I'm afraid . . .' he began. 'Mr Benbow.'

They spoke together.

A scared servant-girl had come up from the Benbow home with the affrighting news that Bert Benbow, who had gone to bed with the other children as usual, was not in his bed and could not be discovered in the house. Mr Peartree, being in the hall, had chosen himself to bear the grievous tidings to the drawing-room. In an instant Albert and Clara were parents again. Both had an idea that the unprecedented, incomprehensible calamity was a heavenly dispensation to punish them for having trifled with the missing word. Their sudden seriousness was terrific. They departed immediately, without ceremony of any sort. Mrs Hamps said that she really ought to go too, and Maggie said that as Auntie Hamps was going she also would go. The parson said that he had already stayed longer than he ought, in view of another engagement, and he followed. Edwin and Hilda dutifully saw them off and were as serious as the circumstances demanded. But those who remained in the drawing-room sniggered, and when Hilda rejoined them she laughed. The house felt lighter. Edwin, remaining longest at the door, saw a bicyclist on one of the still quaint pneumatic-tyred 'safety' bicycles, coming along behind a 'King of the Road' lamp. The rider dismounted at the corner.

'That you, Mr Ingpen?'

Said a blithe voice:

'How d'ye do, host? When you've known me a bit longer you'll earn that I always manage to arrive just when other people are leaving.'

CHAPTER 5
TERTIUS INGPEN

I

TERTIUS INGPEN was the new District Factory Inspector, a man of about thirty-five, neither fair nor dark, neither tall nor short. He was a native of the district, having been born somewhere in the aristocratic regions between Knype and the lordly village of Sneyd, but what first struck the local observer in him was that his speech had none of the local accent. In the pursuit of his vocation he had lived in other places than the Five Towns. For example, in London, where he had become acquainted with Edwin's friend, Charlie Orgreave, the doctor. When Ingpen received a goodish appointment amid the industrial horrors of his birth, Charlie Orgreave recommended him to Edwin, and Edwin and Ingpen had met once, under arrangement made by Johnnie Orgreave. It was Johnnie who had impulsively suggested in Ingpen's presence that Ingpen should be invited to the At Home. Edwin, rather intimidated by Ingpen's other-worldliness, had said: 'You'll run up against a mixed lot.' But Ingpen, though sternly critical of local phenomena, seemed to be ready to meet social adventures in a broad and even eager spirit of curiosity concerning mankind. He was not uncomely, and he possessed a short silky beard of which secretly he was not less proud than of his striking name. He wore a neat blue suit, with the trousers fastened tightly round the ankles for bicycle-riding, and thick kid gloves. He took off one glove to shake hands, and then, having leisurely removed the other, and talking all the time, he bent down with care and loosed his trousers and shook them into shape.

'Now what about this jigger?' he asked, while still bending. 'I don't care to leave it anywhere. It's a good jigger.'

As it leaned on one pedal against the kerb of Hulton Street, the strange-looking jigger appeared to be at any rate a very dirty jigger. Fastened under the saddle were a roll of paper and a mackintosh.

'There are one or two ordinaries knocking about the place,' said Edwin, 'but we haven't got a proper bicycle-house. I'll find a place for it somewhere in the garden.' He lifted the front wheel.

'Don't trouble, please. I'll take it,' said Ingpen, and before picking up the machine blew out the lamp, whose extinction left a great darkness down the slope of Hulton Street.

'You've got a very nice place here. Too central for me, of course!' Ingpen began, after they had insinuated the bicycle through narrow paths to the back of the house.

Edwin was leading him along the side of the lawn farthest away from Trafalgar Road. Certainly the property had the air of being a very nice place. The garden with its screen of high rustling trees seemed spacious and mysterious in the gloom, and the lighted windows of the house produced an effect of much richness – especially the half-open window of the drawing-room. Fearns and Cheswardine were standing in front of it chatting (doubtless of affairs) with that important adult air which Edwin himself could never successfully imitate. Behind them were bright women, and the brilliant chandelier. The piano faintly sounded. Edwin was proud of his very nice place. 'How strange!' he thought. 'This is all mine! These are my guests! And my wife is mine!'

'Well, you see,' he answered Ingpen's criticism with false humility, 'I've no choice. I've got to be central.'

Ingpen answered pleasantly:

'I take your word for it; but I don't see.'

The bicycle was carefully bestowed by its groping owner in a small rustic arbour which, situated almost under the wall that divided the Clayhanger property from the first cottage in Hulton Street, was hidden from the house by a clump of bushes.

In the dark privacy of this shelter Tertius Ingpen said in a reflective tone:

'I understand that you haven't been married long, and that this is a sort of function to inform the world officially that you're no longer what you were?'

'It's something like that,' Edwin admitted with a laugh.

He liked the quiet intimacy of Ingpen's voice, whose delicate inflections indicated highly cultivated sensibilities. And he thought:

'I believe I shall be friends with this chap.' And was glad, and faith in Ingpen was planted in his heart.

'Well,' Ingpen continued, 'I wish you happiness. It may seem a strange thing to say to a man in your position, but my opinion is that the proper place for women is – behind the veil. Only my personal opinion, of course! But I'm entitled to hold it, and therefore to express it.' Whatever his matter, his manner was faultless.

'Yes?' Edwin murmured awkwardly. What on earth did Ingpen expect by way of reply to such a proposition? Surely Ingpen should have known that he was putting his host in a disagreeable difficulty. His new-born faith in Ingpen felt the harsh wind of experience and shivered. Nevertheless, there was a part of Edwin that responded to Ingpen's attitude. 'Behind the veil.' Yes, something could be said for the proposition.

They left the arbour in silence. They had not gone more than a few steps when a boy's shrill voice made itself heard over the wall of the cottage yard.

'O Lord, Thou 'ast said, "If two on ye sh'll agray on earth as touching onything that they sh'll ask it sh'll be done for them of My Father which is in 'eaven. For where two or three are gathered together i' My name theer am I in th' midst of 'em." O Lord, George Edwin Clay'anger wants a two-bladed penknife. We all three on us want Ye to send George Edwin Clay'anger a two-bladed penknife.'

The words fell with impressive effect on the men in the garden.

'What the – ?' Edwin exclaimed.

'Hsh!' Ingpen stopped him in an excited whisper. 'Don't disturb them for anything in the world!'

Silence followed.

Edwin crept away like a scout towards a swing which he had erected for his friend George before he became the husband of George's mother. He climbed into it and over the wall could just see three boys' heads in the yard illuminated by a lamp in the back window of the cottage. Tertius Ingpen joined him, but immediately climbed higher on to the horizontal beam of the swing.

'Who are they?' Ingpen asked, restraining his joy in the adventure.

'The one on the right's my stepson. The other big one is my sister Clara's child, Bert. I expect the little one's old Clowes' the gravedigger's kid. They say he's a regular little parson – probably to make up for his parents. I expect they're out somewhere having a jollification.'

'Well,' Ingpen breathed. 'I wouldn't have missed this for a good deal.' He gave a deep, almost soundless giggle.

Edwin was startled – as much as anything by the extraordinary deceitfulness of George. Who could possibly have guessed from the boy's demeanour when his Aunt Clara mentioned Bert to him, that he had made an outrageous rendezvous with Bert that very night? Certainly he had blushed, but then he often blushed. Of course, the Benbows would assert that George had seduced the guileless Bert. Fancy them hunting the town for Bert at that instant! As regards Peter Clowes, George, though not positively forbidden to do so, had been warned against associating with him – chiefly because of the bad influence which Peter's accent would have on George's accent. His mother had said that she could not understand how George could wish to be friendly with a rough little boy like Peter. Edwin, however, inexperienced as he was, had already comprehended that children, like Eastern women, have no natural class bias; and he could not persuade himself to be the first to inculcate into George ideas which could only be called snobbish. He was a democrat. Nevertheless he did not like George to play with Peter Clowes.

The small Peter, with uplifted face and clasped hands repeated urgently, passionately:

'O God! We all three on us want Ye to send George Edwin Clay'anger a two-bladed penknife. Now lads, kneel, and all three on us together!'

He stood between the taller and better-dressed boys unashamed, fervent, a born religionist. He was not even praying for himself. He was praying out of his profound impersonal interest in the efficacy of prayer.

The three boys, kneeling, and so disappearing from sight behind the wall, repeated together:

'O God! Please send George Edwin Clayhanger a two-bladed penknife.'

Then George and Bert stood up again, shuffling about. Peter Clowes did not reappear.

'I can't help it,' whispered Ingpen in a strange moved voice, 'I've got to be God. Here goes! And it's practically new, too!'

Edwin in the darkness could see him feeling in his waistcoat pocket, and then raise his arm, and, taking careful aim, throw in the direction of the dimly lighted yard.

'Oh!' came the cry of George, in sudden pain.

The descending penknife had hit him.

There was a scramble on the pavement of the yard, and some muttered talk. The group went to the back window where the lamp was and examined the heavenly penknife. They were more frightened than delighted by the miracle. The unseen watchers in the swing were also rather frightened, as though they had inter- fered irremediably in a solemn and delicate crisis beyond their competence. In a curious way they were ashamed.

'Yes, and what about me?' said the voice of fat Bert Benbow sulkily. 'This is all very well. But what about me? Ye tried without me and ye couldn't do anything. Now I've come and ye've done it. What am I going to get? Ye've got to give me something instead of a half-share in that penknife, George.'

George said:

'Let's pray for something for you now. What d'you want?'

'I want a bicycle. Ye know what I want.'

'Oh, no, you don't, Bert Benbow!' said George. 'You've got to want something safer than a bike. Suppose it comes tumbling down like the penknife did! We shall be damn well killed.'

Tertius Ingpen could not suppress a snorting giggle.

'I want a bike,' Bert insisted. 'And I don't want nothing else.'

The two bigger boys moved vaguely away from the window, and the little religionist followed them in silence, ready to supplicate for whatever they should decide.

'All right,' George agreed. 'We'll pray for a bicycle. But we'd better all stand as close as we can to the wall, under the spouting, in case.'

The ceremonial was recommenced.

'No,' Ingpen murmured, 'I'm not being God this time. It won't run to it.'

Footsteps were heard on the lawn behind the swing. Ingpen slid down and Edwin jumped down. Johnnie Orgreave was approaching.

'Hsh!' Ingpen warned him.

'What are you chaps –'

'Hsh!' Ingpen was more imperative.

All three men walked away out of earshot of the yard, towards the window of the drawing-room – Johnnie Orgreave mystified, the other two smiling but with spirits disturbed. Johnnie heard the story in brief; it was told to him in confidence, as Tertius Ingpen held firmly that eavesdroppers, if they had any honour left, should at least hold their tongues.

II

When Tertius Ingpen was introduced to Hilda in the drawing-room, the three men having entered by the French window, Edwin was startled and relieved by the deportment of the Orientalist who thought that the proper place for women was behind the veil. In his simplicity he had assumed that the Orientalist would indicate his attitude by a dignified reserve. Not at all! As soon as Ingpen reached Hilda's hospitable gaze his whole bearing altered. He bowed, with a deferential bending that to an untravelled native must have seemed exaggerated; his face was transformed by a sweet smile; his voice became the voice of a courtier; he shook hands with chivalrous solicitude for the fragile hand shaken. Hilda was pleased by him, perceiving that this man was more experienced in the world than any of the other worldly guests. She liked that. Ingpen's new symptoms were modified after a few moments, but when he was presented to Mrs Fearns he reproduced them in their original intensity, and again when he was introduced to Vera Cheswardine.

'Been out without your cap?' Hilda questioned Edwin, lifting her eyebrows. She said it in order to say something, for the entry of this ceremonious personage, who held all the advantages of the native and of the stranger, had a little overpowered the company.

'Only just to see after Mr Ingpen's machine. Give me your cap, Mr Ingpen. I'll hang it up.'

When he returned to the drawing-room from the hat-stand, Ingpen was talking with Janet Orgreave, whom he already knew.

'Have you seen George, Edwin?' Hilda called across the drawing-room.

'Hasn't he gone to bed?'

'That's what I want to know. I haven't seen him lately.'

Every one, except Johnnie Orgreave and a Swetnam or so, was preoccupied by the thought of children, by the thought of this incalculable and disturbing race that with different standards and ideals lived so mysteriously in and among their adult selves. Nothing was said about the strange disappearance of Bert Benbow, but each woman had it in mind, and coupled it with Hilda's sudden apprehension concerning George, and imagined weird connections between the one and the other, and felt forebodings about children nearer to her own heart. Children dominated the assemblage and, made restless, the assemblage collectively felt that the moment for separation approached. The At Home was practically over.

Hilda rang the bell, and as she did so Johnnie Orgreave winked dangerously at Edwin, who with sternness responded. He wondered why he should thus deceive his wife, with whom he was so deliciously intimate. He thought also that women were capricious in their anxieties, and yet now and then their moods – once more by the favour of hazard – displayed a marvellous appositeness. Hilda had no reason whatever for worrying more about George on this night than on any other night. Nevertheless this night happened to be the night on which anxiety would be justified.

'Ada,' said Hilda to the entering servant. 'Have you seen Master George?'

'No'm,' Ada replied, almost defiantly.

'When did you see him last?'

'I don't remember, m'm.'

'Is he in bed?'

'I don't know, m'm.'

'Just go and see, will you?'

'Yes'm.'

The company waited with gentle concealed excitement for the returning Ada, who announced:

'His bedroom door's locked, m'm.'

'He *will* lock it sometimes, although I've positively forbidden him to. But what are you to do?' said Hilda smilingly to the other mothers.

'Take the key away, obviously,' Tertius Ingpen answered the question, turning quickly and interrupting his chat with Janet Orgreave.

'That ought not to be necessary,' said Fearns, as an expert father.

Ada departed, thankful to be finished with the ordeal of cross-examination in a full drawing-room.

'Don't *you* know anything about him?' Hilda addressed Johnnie Orgreave suddenly.

'Me? About your precious? No. Why should I know?'

'Because you're getting such friends, you two.'

'Oh! Are we?' Johnnie said carelessly. Nevertheless he was flattered by a certain nascent admiration on the part of George, which was then beginning to be noticeable.

A quarter of an hour later, when several guests had gone, Hilda murmured to Edwin:

'I'm not easy about that boy. I'll just run upstairs.'

'I shouldn't,' said Edwin.

But she did. And the distant sound of knocking, and 'George, George', could be heard even down in the hall.

'I can't wake him,' said Hilda, back in the drawing-room.

'What do you want to wake him for, foolish girl?' Edwin demanded.

She enjoyed being called 'foolish girl', but she was not to be tranquillized.

'Do you think he *is* in bed?' she questioned, before the whole remaining company, and the dread suspicion was out!

After more journeys upstairs, and more bangings, and essays with keys, and even attempts at lock-picking, Hilda announced that George's room must be besieged from its window. A ladder was found, and interested visitors went into the back entry, by the kitchen, to see it reared and hear the result. Edwin thought that the cook in the kitchen looked as guilty as he himself felt, though she more than once asseverated her belief that Master George was safely in bed. The ladder was too short. Edwin mounted it and tried to prise himself on to the window-sill, but could not.

'Here, let me try!' said Ingpen, joyous.

Ingpen easily succeeded. He glanced through the open window into George's bedroom, and then looked down at the upturned faces, and Ada's apron, whitely visible in the gloom.

'He's here all right.'

'Oh, good!' said Hilda. 'Is he asleep?'

'Yes.'

'He deserves to be wakened,' she laughed.

'You see what a foolish girl you've been,' said Edwin affectionately.

'Never mind!' she retorted. '*You* couldn't get on the window. And you were just as upset as anybody. Do you think I don't know? Thank you, Mr Ingpen.'

'Is he really there?' Edwin whispered to Ingpen as soon as he could.

'Yes. And asleep, too!'

'I wonder how the deuce he slipped in. I'll bet anything those servants have been telling a lot of lies for him. He pulls their hair down and simply does what he likes with them.'

Edwin was now greatly reassured, but he could not quite recover from the glimpse he had had of George's capacity for leading a double life. Sardonically he speculated whether the heavenly penknife would be brought to his notice by its owner, and if so by what ingenious method.

III

The final sensation was caused by the arrival, in a nearly empty drawing-room, of plump Maggie, nervous, constrained, and somewhat breathless.

'Bert has turned up,' she said. 'Clara thought I'd better come along and tell you. She felt sure you'd like to know.'

'Well, that's all right then,' Hilda replied perfunctorily, indicating that Clara's conceited assumption of a universal interest in her dull children was ridiculous.

Edwin asked:

'Did the kid say where he'd been?'

'Been running about the streets. They don't know what's come over him – because, you see, he'd actually gone to bed once. Albert is quite puzzled; but he says he'll have it out of him before he's done.'

'When he does get it out of him,' thought Edwin again, 'there will be a family row and George will be indicted as the corrupter of innocence.'

Maggie would not stay a single moment. Hilda attentively accompanied her to the hall. The former and the present mistress of the house kissed with the conventional signs of affection. But the fact that one had succeeded the other seemed to divide them. Hilda was always lying in wait for criticism from Maggie, ready to resent it; Maggie divined this and said never a word. The silence piqued Hilda as much as outspoken criticism would have annoyed her. She could not bear it.

'How do you like my new stair-carpet?' she demanded defiantly.

'Very nice! Very nice, I'm sure!' Maggie replied without conviction. And added, just as she stepped outside the front door, 'You've made a lot of changes.' This was the mild, good-natured girl's sole thrust, and it was as effective as she could have wished.

Everybody had gone except the two Orgreaves and Tertius Ingpen.

'I don't know about you, Johnnie, but I must go,' said Janet Orgreave when Hilda came back.

'Hold on, Jan!' Johnnie protested. 'You're forgetting those duets you are to try with Ingpen.'

'Really?'

'Duets!' cried Hilda, instantly uplifted and enthusiastic. 'Oh, do let's have some music!'

Ingpen, by arrangement with the Orgreaves, had brought some pianoforte duets. They were tied to his bicycle. He was known as an amateur of music. Edwin, bidding Ingpen not to move, ran out into the garden to get the music from the bicycle. Johnnie ran after him through the French window.

'I say!' Johnnie called in a low voice.

'What's up?' Edwin stopped for him.

'I've a piece of news for you. About that land you've set your heart on, down at Shawport! . . . It can be bought cheap – at least the old man says it's cheap – whatever his opinion may be worth. I was telling him about your scheme for having a new printing works altogether. Astonishing how keen he is! If I'd had a plan of the land I believe he'd have sat down and made sketches at once.'

Johnnie (with his brother Jimmie) was in partnership with old Orgreave as an architect.

'"Set my heart on"?' Edwin mumbled, intimidated as usual by a nearer view of an enterprise which he had himself conceived and which had enchanted him from afar. '"Set my heart on"?'

'Well, had you, or hadn't you?'

'I suppose I had,' Edwin admitted. 'Look here, I'll drop in and see you tomorrow morning.'

'Right!'

Together they detached the music from the bicycle, and, as Edwin unrolled it and rolled it the other side out to flatten it, they returned silently through the dark wind-stirred garden into the drawing-room.

There were now the two Orgreaves, Tertius Ingpen, and Hilda and Edwin in the drawing-room.

'We will now begin the evening,' said Ingpen, as he glanced at the music.

All five were conscious of the pleasant feeling of freedom, intimacy, and mutual comprehension which animates a small company that by self-selection has survived out of a larger one. The lateness of the hour aided their zest. Even the more staid among them perceived, as by a revelation, that it did not in fact matter, once in a way, if they *were* tired and inefficient on the morrow, and that too much regularity of habit was bad for the soul. Edwin had brought in a tray from the dining-room, and rearranged the chairs according to Hilda's caprice, and was providing cushions to raise the bodies of the duet-players to the proper height. Janet began to excuse herself, asserting that if there was one member of her family who could not play duets, she was that member, that she had never seen this Dvorak music before, and that if they had got her brother Tom, or her elder sister Marion, or even Alicia, – etc. etc.

'We are quite accustomed to these formal preliminaries from duet-players, Miss Orgreave,' said Ingpen. 'I never do them myself, – not because I can play well, but because I am hardened. Now shall we start? Will you take the treble or the bass?'

Janet answered with eager modesty that she would take the bass.

'It's all one to me,' said Ingpen, putting on spectacles, 'I play either equally badly. You'll soon regret leaving the most import-ant part to me. However . . .! Clayhanger, will you turn over?'

'Er – yes,' said Edwin boldly. 'But you'd better give me the tip.'

He knew a little about printed music, from his experiences as a boy when his sisters used to sing two-part songs. That is to say, he had a vague idea 'where a player was' on a page. But the enter-prise of turning over Dvorak's 'Legends' seemed to him critically adventurous. Dvorak was nothing but a name to him; beyond the correct English method of pronouncing that name he had no knowledge whatever of the subject in hand.

Then the performance of the 'Legends' began. Despite halts, hesitations, occasional loud insistent chanting of the time, explanations between the players, many wrong notes by Ingpen, and a few wrong notes by Janet, and one or two enormous mis-apprehensions by Edwin, the performance was a success, in that it put a spell on its public, and permitted the loose and tender genius of Dvorak to dominate the room.

'Play that again, will you?' said Hilda, in a low dramatic voice, at the third 'Legend'.

'We will,' Ingpen answered; 'and we'll play it better.'

Edwin had the exquisite sensation of partially comprehending music whose total beauty was beyond the limitations of his power to enjoy – power, nevertheless, which seemed to grow each moment. Passages entirely intelligible and lovely would break at intervals through the veils of general sound and ravish him. All his attention was intensely concentrated on the page. He could hear Ingpen breathing hard. Out of the corner of his eye he was aware of Johnnie Orgreave on the sofa making signs to Hilda about drinks, and pouring out something for her, and something for himself, without the faintest noise. And he was aware of Ada coming to the open door and being waved away to bed by her mistress.

'Well,' he said, when the last 'Legend' was played. 'That's a bit of the right sort – no mistake.' He was obliged to be banal and colloquial.

Hilda said nothing at all. Johnnie, who had waited for the end in order to strike a match, showed by two words that he was an expert listener to duets. Tertius Ingpen was very excited and pleased. 'More tricky than difficult, isn't it – to read?' he said privately to his fellow-performer, who concurred. Janet also was excited in her fashion. But even amid the general excitement Ingpen had to be judicious.

'Delightful stuff, of course,' he said, pulling his beard. 'But he's not a great composer, you know, all the same.'

'He'll do to be going on with,' Johnnie murmured.

'Oh, yes! Delightful! Delightful!' Ingpen repeated warmly, removing his spectacles. 'What a pity we can't have musical evenings regularly!'

'But we can!' said Hilda positively. 'Let's have them here – every week!'

'A great scheme!' Edwin agreed with enthusiasm, admiring his wife's initiative. He had been a little afraid that the episode of George had upset her for the night, but he now saw that she had perfectly recovered from it.

'Oh!' Ingpen paused. 'I doubt if I could come every week. I could come once a fortnight.'

'Well, once a fortnight then!' said Hilda.

'I suppose Sunday wouldn't suit you?'

Edwin challenged him almost fiercely:

'Why won't it suit us? It will suit us first class.'

Ingpen merely said, with quiet delicacy:

'So much the better . . . We might go all through the Mozart fiddle sonatas.'

'And who's your violinist?' asked Johnnie.

'I am, if you don't mind.' Ingpen smiled. 'If your sister will take the piano part.'

Hilda exclaimed admiringly:

'Do you play the violin, too, Mr Ingpen?'

'I scrape it. Also the tenor. But my real instrument is the clarinet.' He laughed. 'It seems odd,' he went on with genuine scientific unegotistic interest in himself, 'but d'you know, I thoroughly enjoy playing the clarinet in a bad orchestra whenever I get the chance. When I happen to have a free evening I often wish I could drop in at a theatre and play rotten music in the band. It's better than nothing. Some of us are born mad.'

'But, Mr Ingpen,' said Janet Orgreave anxiously, after this speech had been appreciated, 'I have never played those Mozart sonatas.'

'I'm glad to hear it,' he replied, with admirable tranquillity. 'Neither have I. I've often meant to. It'll be quite a sporting event. But of course we can have a rehearsal if you like.'

The project of the musical evenings was discussed and discussed until Janet, having vanished silently upstairs, reappeared with her hat and cloak on.

'I can go alone if you aren't ready, Johnnie,' said she.

Johnnie yawned.

'No. I'm coming.'

'I must also go – I suppose,' said Ingpen.

They all went into the hall. Through the open door of the dining-room, where one gas-jet burned, could be seen the rich remains of what had been 'light refreshments' in the most generous interpretation of the term.

Ingpen stopped to regard the spectacle, fingering his beard.

'I was just wondering,' he remarked, with that strange eternal curiosity about himself, 'whether I'd had enough to eat. I've got to ride home.'

'Well, what have you had?' Johnnie quizzed him.

'I haven't had anything,' said Ingpen, 'except drink.'

Hilda cried:

'Oh, you poor sufferer! I am ashamed!' and led him familiarly to the table.

IV

Edwin was kept at the front door some time by Johnnie Orgreave, who resumed, as he was departing, the subject of the proposed new works, and maintained it at such length that Janet, tired of waiting on the pavement, said that she would walk on. When he returned to the dining-room, Ingpen and Hilda were sitting side by side at the little table, and the first words that Edwin heard were from Ingpen:

'It cost me a penknife, but it was dirt cheap at the price. You can't expect to be the Almighty for much less than a penknife.' Seeing Edwin, he added, with a nonchalant smile: 'I've told Mrs Clayhanger all about the answer to prayer. I thought she ought to know.'

Edwin laughed awkwardly, saying to himself:

'Ingpen, my boy, you ought to have thought of my position first. You've been putting your finger into a rather delicate piece of mechanism. Supposing she cuts up rough with me afterwards for hiding it from her all this time! . . . I'm living with her. You aren't.'

'Of course,' Ingpen added, 'I've sworn the lady to secrecy.'

Hilda said:

'I knew all the time there was something wrong.'

And Edwin thought:

'No, you didn't. And if he hadn't happened to tell you about the thing, you'd have been convinced that you'd been alarming yourself for nothing.'

But he only said, not certain of Hilda's humour, and anxious to placate her:

'There's no doubt George ought to be punished.'

'Nothing of the kind! Nothing of the kind!' Ingpen vivaciously protested. 'Why, bless my soul! The kids were engaged in a religious work! They were busy with some one far more important than any parents.' And after a pause, reflectively: 'Curious thing the mentality of a child! I doubt if we understand anything about it.'

Hilda smiled, but said naught.

'May I inquire what there is in that bottle?' Ingpen asked.

'Benedictine.'

'Have some, Mr Ingpen?'

'I will if you will, Mrs Clayhanger.'

Edwin raised his eyebrows at his wife.

'You needn't look at me!' said Hilda. 'I'm going to have some.'

Ingpen smacked his lips over the liqueur.

'It's a very bad thing late at night, of course. But I believe in giving your stomach something to think about. I never allow my digestive apparatus to boss me.'

'Quite right, Mr Ingpen.'

They touched glasses, without a word, almost instinctively.

'Well,' thought Edwin, 'for a chap who thinks women ought to be behind the veil . . .!'

'Be a man, Clayhanger, and have some.'

Edwin shook his head.

With a scarcely perceptible movement of her glass, Hilda greeted her husband, peeping out at him as it were for a fraction of a second in a glint of affection. He was quite happy. They were all seated close together, Edwin opposite the other two at the large table. The single gas-jet by the very inadequacy with which it lighted the scene of disorder, produced an effect of informal homeliness and fellowship that warmed the heart. Each of the three realized with pleasure that a new and promising friendship was in the making. They talked at length about the Musical Evenings, and Edwin said that he should buy some music, and Hilda asked him to obtain a history of music that Ingpen described with some enthusiasm, and the date of the first evening was settled, – Sunday week. And after uncounted minutes Ingpen remarked that he presumed he had better go.

'I have to cycle home,' he announced once more.

'Tonight?' Hilda exclaimed.

'No. This morning.'

'All the way to Axe?'

'Oh, no! I'm three miles this side of Axe. It's only six and a half miles.'

'But all those hills!'

'Pooh! Excellent for the muscles of the calf.'

'Do you live alone, Mr Ingpen?'

'I have a sort of housekeeper.'

'In a cottage?'

'In a cottage.'

'But what do you *do* – all alone?'

'I cultivate myself.'

And Hilda, in a changed tone, said:

'How wise you are!'

'Rather inconvenient, being out there, isn't it?' Edwin suggested.

'It may be inconvenient sometimes for my job, but I can't help that. I give the State what I consider fair value for the money it pays me, and not a grain more. I've got myself to think about. There are some things I won't do, and one of them is to live all the time in a vile hole like the Five Towns. I won't do it. I'd sooner be a blooming peasant on the land.'

As he was a native he had the right to criticize the district without protest from other natives.

'You're quite right as to the vile hole,' said Hilda with conviction.

'I don't know –' Edwin muttered. 'I think old Bursley isn't so bad.'

'Yes. But you're an old stick-in-the-mud, dearest,' said Hilda. 'Mr Ingpen has lived away from the district, and so have I. You haven't. You're no judge. We know, don't we, Mr Ingpen?'

When, Ingpen having at last accumulated sufficient resolution to move and get his cap, they went through the drawing-room to the garden, they found that rain was falling.

'Never mind,' said Ingpen, lifting his head sardonically in a mute indictment of the heavens. 'I have my mack.'

Edwin searched out the bicycle and brought it to the window, and Hilda stuck a hat on his head. Leisurely Ingpen clipped his trousers at the ankle, and unstrapped a mackintosh cape from the machine, and folded the strap. Leisurely he put on the cape, and gazed at the impenetrable heavens again.

'I can make you up a bed, Mr Ingpen.'

'No thanks. Oh, no thanks! The fact is, I rather like rain.'

Leisurely he took a box of fusees from his pocket, and lighted his lamp, examining it as though it contained some hidden and perilous defect. Then he pressed the tyres.

'The back tyre'll do with a little more air,' he said thoughtfully. 'I don't know if my pump will work.'

It did work, but slowly. After which, gloves had to be assumed.

'I suppose I can get out this way. Oh! My music! Never mind, I'll leave it.'

Then, with a sudden access of ceremoniousness, he bade adieu to Hilda; no detail of punctilio was omitted from the formality.

'Good-bye. Many thanks.'

'Good-bye. Thank *you!*'

Edwin preceded the bicyclist and the bicycle round the side of the house to the front gate at the corner of Hulton Street and Trafalgar Road.

In the solemn and chill nocturnal solitude of rainswept Hulton Street, Ingpen straddled the bicycle, with his left foot on one raised pedal and the other on the pavement; and then held out a gloved hand to Edwin.

'Good-bye, old chap. See you soon.'

Much goodwill and appreciation and hope was implicit in that rather casual handshake.

He sheered off strongly down the dark slope of Hulton Street in the rain, using his ankles with skill in the pedal-stroke. The man's calves seemed to be enormously developed. The cape ballooned out behind his swiftness, and in a moment he had swerved round the flickering mournful gas-lamp at the bottom of the mean new street and was gone.

CHAPTER 6

HUSBAND AND WIFE

I

'I'M upstairs,' Hilda called in a powerful whisper from the head of the stairs as soon as Edwin had closed and bolted the front door.

He responded humorously. He felt very happy, lusty, and wide-awake. The evening had had its contretemps, its varying curve of success, but as a whole it was a triumph. And, above all, it was over – a thing that had had to be accomplished, and that had been accomplished, with dignity and effectiveness. He walked in ease from room to lighted empty room, and the splendid waste of gas pleased him, arousing something royal that is at the bottom of generous natures. In the breakfast-room especially the gas had been flaring to no purpose for hours. '*Her* room, her very own room!' He wondered indulgently when, if ever, she would really make it her own room by impressing her individuality upon it. He knew she was always meaning to do something drastic to the room, but so far she had got no further than his portrait. Child! Infant! Wayward girl! . . . Still the fact of the portrait on the mantelpiece touched him.

He dwelt tenderly on the invisible image of the woman up-stairs. It was marvellous how she was not the Hilda he had married. The new Hilda had so overlaid and hidden the old, that he had positively to make an effort to recall what the old one was, with her sternness and her anxious air of responsibility. But at the same time she was the old Hilda too. He desired to be splendidly generous, to environ her with all luxuries, to lift her clear above other women; he desired the means to be senselessly extravagant for her. To clasp on her arm a bracelet whose cost would keep a working man's family for three years would have delighted him. And though he was interested in social schemes, and had a social conscience, he would sooner have bought that bracelet, and so purchased the momentary thrill of putting it on her capricious arm, than have helped to ameliorate the lot of thousands of victimized human beings. He had Hilda in his bones and he knew it, and he knew that it was a grand and a painful thing.

Nevertheless he was not without a considerable self-satisfaction, for he had done very well by Hilda. He had found her at the mercy of the world, and now she was safe and sheltered and beloved, and made mistress of a house and home that would stand comparison with most houses and homes. He was proud of his house; he always watched over it; he was always improving it; and he would improve it more and more; and it should never be quite finished.

The disorder in it, now, irked him. He walked to and fro, and restored every piece of furniture to its proper place, heaped the contents of the ash-trays into one large ash-tray, covered some of the food, and locked up the alcohol. He did this leisurely, while thinking of the woman upstairs, and while eating two chocolates, – not more, because he had notions about his stomach. Then he shut and bolted the drawing-room window, and opened the door leading to the cellar steps and sniffed, so as to be quite certain that the radiator furnace was not setting the house on fire. And then he extinguished the lights, and the hall-light last of all, and his sole illumination was the gas on the first-floor landing inviting him upstairs.

Standing on the dark stairs, eager and yet reluctant to mount, he realized the entity of the house. He thought of the astounding and mysterious George, and of those uncomprehended beings, Ada and the cook in their attic, sleeping by the side of the portrait of a fireman in uniform. He felt sure that one or both of them had been privy to George's unlawful adventures, and he heartily liked them for shielding the boy. And he thought of his wife, moving about in the bedroom upon which she *had* impressed her individuality. He went upstairs . . . Yes, he should proceed with the enterprise of the new works. He had the courage for it now. He was rich, according to Bursley ideas, – he would be far richer . . . He gave a faint laugh at the memory of George's objection to Bert's choice of a bicycle as a gift from heaven.

II

Hilda was brushing her hair. The bedroom seemed to be full of her and the disorder of her multitudinous things. Whenever he asked why a particular item of her goods was in a particular spot – the spot appearing to him to have been bizarrely chosen – she always proved to her own satisfaction, by a quite improvised argument – that that particular spot was the sole possible spot for that particular item. The bedroom was no longer theirs – it was hers. He picnicked in it. He didn't mind. In fact he rather liked the picnic. It pleased him to exercise his talent for order and organization, so as to maintain his own comfort in the small spaces which she left to him. Tonight the room was in a divine confusion. He accepted it with pleasure. The beds had not been turned down, because it was improper to turn them down when they were to be used for the deposit of strangers' finery. On Edwin's bed now lay the dress which Hilda had taken off. It was a most agreeable object on the bed, and seemed even richer and more complex there than on Hilda. He removed it carefully to a chair. An antique diaphanous shawl remained, which was unfamiliar to him.

'What's this shawl?' he asked. 'I've never seen this shawl before. What is it?'

Hilda was busy, her bent head buried in hair.

'Oh, Edwin, what an old fusser you are!' she mumbled. 'What shawl?'

He held it up.

'Someone must have left it.'

He proceeded with the turning down of his bed. Then he sat on a chair to regard Hilda.

When she had done her hair she padded across the room and examined the shawl.

'What a precious thing!' she exclaimed. 'It's Mrs Fearns's. She must have taken it off to put her jacket on, and then forgotten it. But I'd no idea how good it was. It's genuine old. I wonder how it would suit me?'

She put it round her shoulders, and then stood smiling, posing, bold, provocative, for his verdict. The whiteness of her *déshabillé* showed through the delicate pattern and tints of the shawl, with a strange effect. For him she was more than a woman; she was the incarnation of a sex. It was marvellous how all she did, all her ideas and her gestures, were so intensely feminine, so sure to perturb or enchant him. Nervously he began to wind his watch. He wanted to spring up and kiss her because she was herself. But he could not. So he said:

'Come here, chit. Let me look at that shawl.'

She obeyed. She knelt acquiescent. He put his watch back into his pocket and fingered the shawl.

Then she said:

'I suppose one'll be allowed to grumble at Georgie for locking his bedroom door.' And she said it with a touch of mockery in her clear, precise voice, as though twitting him, and Ingpen too, about their absurd theoretical sense of honour towards children. And there was a touch of fine bitterness in her voice also, – a reminiscence of the old Hilda. Incalculable creature! Who could have guessed that she would make such a remark at such a moment? In his mind he dashed George to pieces. But as a wise male he ignored all her implications and answered casually, mildly, with an affirmative.

She went on:

'What were you talking such a long time to Johnnie Orgreave about?'

'Talking a long time to Johnnie Orgreave? Oh, d'you mean at the front door? Why, it wasn't half a minute! He happened to mention a piece of land down at Shawport that I had a sort of a notion of buying.'

'Buying? What for?' Her tone hardened.

'Well, supposing I had to build a new works?'

'You never told me anything about it.'

'I've only just begun to think of it myself. You see, if I'm to go in for lithography as it ought to be gone in for, I can't possibly stay at the shop. I must have more room, and a lot more. And it would be cheaper to build than to rent.'

She stood up.

'Why go in more for lithography?'

'You can't stand still in business. Must either go forward or go back.'

'It seems to me it's very risky. I wondered what you were hiding from me.'

'My dear girl, I was not hiding anything from you,' he protested.

'Whose land is it?'

'It belongs to Tobias Hall's estate.'

'Yes, and I've no doubt the Halls would be very glad to get rid of it. Who told you about it?'

'Johnnie.'

'Of course it would be a fine thing for him too.'

'But I'd asked him if he knew of any land going cheap.'

She shrugged her shoulders, and shrugged away the disinterestedness of all Orgreaves.

'Anyone could get the better of you,' she said.

He resented this estimate of himself as a good-natured simpleton. He assuredly did not want to quarrel, but he was obliged to say:

'Oh! Could they?'

An acerbity scarcely intentional somehow entered into his tone. As soon as he heard it he recognized the tone as the forerunner of altercations.

'Of course!' she insisted, superiorly, and then went on: 'We're all right as we are. We spend too much money, but I dare say we're all right. If you go in for a lot of new things you may lose all we've got, and then where shall we be?'

In his heart he said to her:

'What's it got to do with you? You manage your home, and I'll manage my business! You know nothing at all about business. You're the very antithesis of business. Whatever business you've ever had to do with you've ruined. You've no right to judge and no grounds for judgement. It's odious of you to asperse any of the Orgreaves. They were always your best friends. I should never have met you if it hadn't been for them. And where would you be now without me? Trying to run some wretched boarding-house and probably starving. Why do you assume that I'm a d—d fool? You always do. Let me tell you that I'm one of the most common-sense men in this town, and everybody knows it except you. Anyhow, I was clever enough to get you *out* of a mess . . . You knew I was hiding something from you, did you? I wish you wouldn't talk such infernal rot. And, moreover, I won't have you interfering in my business. Other wives don't, and you shan't. So let that be clearly understood.' In his heart he was very ill-used and very savage.

But he only said:

'Well, we shall see.'

She retorted:

'Naturally, if you've made up your mind, there's no more to be said.'

He broke out viciously:

'I've not made up my mind. Don't I tell you I've only just begun to think about it?'

He was angry. And now that he actually was angry, he took an almost sensual pleasure in being angry. He had been angry before, though on a smaller scale, with less provocation, and he had sworn that he would never be angry again. But now that he was angry again, he gloomily and fiercely revelled in it.

Hilda silently folded up the shawl, and, putting it into a drawer of the wardrobe, shut the drawer with an irritatingly gentle click. . . Click! He could have killed her for that click . . . She seized a dressing-gown.

'I must just go and look at George,' she murmured, with cool, clear calmness, – the virtuous, anxious mother; not a trace of coquetry anywhere in her.

'What bosh!' he thought. 'She knows perfectly well George's door is bolted.'

Marriage was a startling affair. Who could have foretold this finish to the evening? Nothing had occurred . . . nothing . . . and yet everything. His plans were all awry. He could see naught but trouble.

She was away some time. When she returned, he was in bed, with his face averted. He heard her moving about.

'Will she, or won't she, come and kiss me?' he thought.

She came and kissed him, but it was a meaningless kiss.

'Good night,' she said aloofly.

'Night.'

She slept, but he could not sleep. He kept thinking the same thought: 'She's no right whatever . . . I must say I never bargained for this . . .' etc.

CHAPTER 7
THE TRUCE

I

NEARLY a week passed. Hilda, in the leisure of a woman of fashion after dinner, was at the piano in the drawing-room. She had not urgent stockings to mend, nor jam to make, nor careless wenches to overlook, nor food to buy, nor accounts to keep, nor a new dress to scheme out of an old one, nor to perform her duty to her neighbour. She had nothing to do. Like Edwin she could not play the piano, but she had picked up a note here and a note there in the course of her life, and with much labour and many slow hesitations she could puzzle out a cord or a melody from the printed page. She was now exasperatingly spelling with her finger a fragment of melody from one of Dvorak's 'Legends', – a fragment that had inhabited her mind since she first heard it, and that seemed to gather up and state all the sweet heart-breaking intolerable melancholy implicit in the romantic existence of that city on the map, Prague. On the previous day she had been a quarter of an hour identifying the unforgettable, indismissible fragment amid the multitude of notes. Now she had recognizably pieced its phrases together, and as her stiff finger stumbled through it, her ears heard it once more; and she could not repeat it often enough. What she heard was not what she was playing, but something finer – her souvenir of what Tertius Ingpen had played; and something finer than that, something finer than the greatest artist could possibly play – magic!

It was in the nature of a miracle to her that she had been able to reproduce the souvenir in physical sound. She was proud of herself as a miracle-worker, and somewhat surprised. And at the same time she was abject because she 'could not play the piano'. She thought that she would be ready to sacrifice many happinesses in order to be able to play as well as even Georgie played, that she would exchange all her own gifts multiplied by a hundred in order to be able to play as Janet Orgreave played, and that to be a world-renowned pianist dominating immense audiences in European capitals must mean the summit of rapture and glory. (She had never listened to a world-renowned pianist.) Meanwhile, without the ennui and slavery of practice, she was enchanting herself; and she savoured her idleness, and thought of her young pretty servants at work, and her boy loose and at large, and her husband keeping her, and of the intensity of beautiful sorrow palpitating behind the medieval façades of Prague. Had Ingpen overheard her, he might have demanded: 'Who is making that infernal noise on the piano?'

Edwin came into the room, holding a thick green book. He ought long ago to have been back at the works (or 'shop', as it was still called, because it had once been principally a shop), keeping her.

'Hello!' she murmured, without glancing away from the piano. 'I thought you were gone.'

They had not quarrelled; but they had not made peace; and the open question of lithography and the new works still separated them. Sometimes they had approached each other, pretending amiably or even affectionately that there was no open question. But the reality of the question could not be destroyed by any pretence of ignoring it.

While gazing at the piano, Hilda could also see Edwin. She thought she knew him, but she was always making discoveries in this branch of knowledge. Now and then she was so bewildered by discoveries that she came to wonder why she had married him, and why people do marry – really! The fact was that she had married him for the look in his eyes. It was a sad look, and beyond that it could not be described. Also, a little, she had married him for his bright untidy hair, and for that short oblique shake of the head which, with him, meant a greeting or an affirmative. She had not married him for his sentiments nor for his goodness of heart. Some points in him she did not like. He had a tendency to colds, and she hated him whenever he had a cold. She often detested his terrible tidiness, though it was a convenient failing. More and more she herself wilfully enjoyed being untidy, as her mother had been untidy . . . And to think that her mother's untidiness used to annoy her! On the other hand, she found pleasure in humouring Edwin's crotchetiness in regard to the details of a meal. She did not like his way of walking, which was ungainly, nor his way of standing, which was infirm. She preferred him to be seated. She could not but regret his irresolution and his love of ease. However, the look in his eyes was paramount, because she was in love with him. She knew that he was more deeply and helplessly in love with her than she with him, but even she was perhaps tightlier bound than in her pride she thought.

Her love had the maladies of a woman's love when it is great; these may possibly be also the maladies of a man's love. It could be bitter. Certainly it could never rest from criticism, spoken or unspoken. In the presence of others she would criticize him to herself, if not aloud, nearly all the time; the ordeal was continuous. When she got him alone she would often endow him at a stroke with perfection, and her tenderness would pour over him. She trusted him profoundly; and yet she had constant misgivings, which weakened or temporarily destroyed her confidence. She would treat a statement from him with almost hostile caution, and accept blindly the very same statement from a stranger! Her habit was to assume that in any encounter between him and a stranger he would be worsted. She was afraid for him. She felt that she could protect him better than he could protect himself – against any danger whatever. This instinct to protect him was also the instinct of self-protection; for peril to him meant peril to her. And she had had enough of peril. After years of disastrous peril she was safe and George was safe. And if she was passionately in love with Edwin, she was also passionately in love with safety. She had breathed a long sigh of relief, and from a desperate self-defender had become a woman. She lay back, as it were, luxuriously on a lounge, after exhausting and horrible exertions; she had scarcely ceased to pant. At the least sign of recurring danger all her nerves were on the *qui vive*. Hence her inimical attitude towards the project of the new works and the extension of lithography in Bursley. The simpleton (a moment earlier the perfect man) might ruin himself – and her! In her view he was the last person to undertake such an enterprise.

Since her marriage, Clara, Maggie, and Auntie Hamps had
been engaged in the pleasant endless task of telling her all about
everything that related to the family, and she had been permitted
to understand that Edwin, though utterly admirable, was not of
a creative disposition, and that he had done nothing but conserve
what his father had left. Without his father Edwin 'would have
been in a very different position'. She believed this. Every day,
indeed, Edwin, by the texture of his hourly life, proved the truth
of it . . . All the persons standing to make a profit out of the new
project would get the better of his fine ingenuous temperament –
naturally! She knew the world. Did Edwin suppose that she did
not know what the world was? . . . And then the interminable
worry of the new enterprise – misgivings, uncertainties, extra
work, secret preoccupations! What room for love, what hope of
tranquillity in all that? He might argue – But she did not want
to argue; she would not argue. She was dead against the entire
project. He had not said to her that it was no affair of hers, but
she knew that such was his thought, and she resented the attitude.
No affair of hers? When it threatened her felicity? No! She would
not have it. She was happy and secure. And while lying luxuriously back in her lounge she would maintain all the defences of
her happiness and her security.

II

Holding the green book in front of her, Edwin said quietly:
  'Read this!'
  'Which?'
  He pointed with his finger.
  She read:

I think I could turn and live with animals, they are so placid and
self-contained.
  I stand and look at them long and long.
  They do not sweat and whine about their condition.
  They do not lie awake in the dark and weep for their sins.
  They do not make me sick discussing their duty to God.
  Not one is dissatisfied, not one is demented with the mania of owning
things.

Not one kneels to another, nor to his kind that lived thousands of years ago.

Not one is respectable or unhappy over the whole earth.

Edwin had lately been exciting himself, not for the first time, over Walt Whitman.

'Fine, isn't it?' he said, sure that she would share his thrill.

'Magnificent!' she agreed, with quiet enthusiasm. 'I must read more of that.' She gazed over the top of the book through the open blue-curtained window into the garden.

He withdrew the book and closed it.

'You haven't got that tune exactly right, you know,' he said, jerking his head in the direction of the music.

'Oh!' She was startled. What did he know about it? He could not play the piano.

'Where are you?' he asked. 'Show me. Where's the confounded place on the piano? Well! At the end you play it like this' – he imitated her – 'whereas it ought to be like this.' He played the last four notes differently.

'So it ought!' She murmured with submission, after having frowned.

'That bit of a tune's been running in my head, too,' he said.

The strange beauty of Whitman and the strange beauty of Dvorak seemed to unite, and both Edwin and Hilda were uplifted, not merely by these mingled beauties, but by their realization of the wondrous fact that they both took intense pleasure in the same varied forms of beauty. Happiness rose about them like a sweet smell in the spaces of the comfortable impeccable drawing-room. And for a moment they leaned towards each other in bliss – across the open question . . . Was it still open? . . . Ah! Edwin might be ingenuous, a simpleton, but Hilda admitted the astounding, mystifying adroitness of his demeanour. Had he abandoned the lithographic project, or was he privately nursing it? In his friendliness towards herself was there a reserve, or was there not? She knew . . . she did not know . . . she knew . . . Yes, there was a reserve, but it was so infinitesimal that she could not define it, – could not decide whether it was due to obstinacy of purpose, or merely to a sense of injury, whether it was resentful or condescending. Exciting times! And she perceived that her new life was gradually getting fuller of such excitements.

'Well,' said he, 'it's nearly three. Quarter-day's coming along. I'd better be off down and earn a bit towards Maggie's rent.'

Before the June quarter-day he had been jocular in the same way about Maggie's rent. In the division of old Darius Clayhanger's estate Maggie had taken over the Clayhanger house, and Edwin paid rent to her therefore.

'I wish you wouldn't talk like that,' said Hilda, pouting amiably.

'Why not?'

'Well, I wish you wouldn't.'

'Anyhow, the rent has to be paid, I suppose.'

'And I wish it hadn't. I wish we didn't live in Maggie's house.'

'Why?'

'I don't like the idea of it.'

'You're sentimental.'

'You can call it what you like. I don't like the idea of us living in Maggie's house. I never feel as if I was at home. No, I don't feel as if I was at home.'

'What a kid you are!'

'You won't change me,' she persisted stoutly.

He knew that she was not sympathetic towards the good Maggie. And he knew the reasons for her attitude, though they had never been mentioned. One was mere vague jealousy of Maggie as her predecessor in the house. The other was that Maggie was always very tepid towards George. George had annoyed her on his visits previous to his mother's marriage, and moreover Maggie had dimly resented Edwin's interest in the son of a mysterious woman. If she had encountered George after the proclamation of Edwin's engagement she would have accepted the child with her customary cheerful blandness. But she had encountered him too soon, and her puzzled gaze had said to George: 'Why is my brother so taken up with you? There must be an explanation, and your strange mother is the explanation.' Edwin did not deny Maggie's attitude to George, but he defended Maggie as a human being. Though dull, she was 'absolutely the right sort', and the very slave of duty and loyalty. He would have liked to make Hilda see all Maggie's excellences.

'Do you know what I've been thinking?' Hilda went on. 'Suppose you were to buy the house from Maggie? Then it would be ours.'

He answered with a smile:

'What price "the mania for owning things"? . . . Would you like me to?' There was promise in his roguish voice.

'Oh! I should. I've often thought of it,' she said eagerly. And at the same time all her gestures and glances seemed to be saying: 'Humour me! I appeal to you as a girl pouting and capricious. But humour me. You know it gives you pleasure to humour me. You know you like me not to be too reasonable. We both know it. I *want* you to do this.'

It was not the fact that she had often thought of the plan. But in her eagerness she imagined it to be the fact. She had never seriously thought of the plan until that moment, and it appeared doubly favourable to her now, because the execution of it, by absorbing capital, ought to divert Edwin from his lithographic project, and perhaps render the lithographic project impossible for years.

She added, aloud:

'Then you wouldn't have any rent to pay.'

'How true!' said Edwin, rallying her. 'But it would stand me in a loss, because I should have to pay too much for the place.'

'Why?' she cried, in arms. 'Why should Maggie ask too much just because you want it? And think of all the money you've spent on it!'

'The money spent on it only increases its value to Maggie. You don't seem to understand landlordism, my child. But that's not the point at all. Maggie won't *ask* any price. Only I couldn't decently pay her less than the value she took the house over at when we divided up. To wit, £1,800. It ain't worth that. I only pay £60 rent.'

'If she took it over at too high a value that's her look-out,' said the harsh and unjust Hilda.

'Not at all. She was a fool. Albert and Clara persuaded her. It was a jolly good thing for them. I couldn't very well interfere.'

'It seems a great shame you should have to pay for what Albert and Clara did.'

'I needn't unless I want to. Only, if I buy the house, £1,800 will have to be the price.'

'Well,' said Hilda, 'I wish you'd buy it.'

'Would she feel more at home if he did?' he seductively chaffed her.

'Yes, she would.' Hilda straightened her shoulders and smiled with bravado.

'And suppose Mag won't sell?'

'Will you allow me to mention it to her?' Hilda's submissive tone implied that Edwin was a tyrant who ruled with a nod.

'I don't mind,' he said negligently.

'Well, one of these days I just will.'

Edwin departed, leaving the book behind. Hilda was flushed. She thought: 'It is marvellous. I can do what I like with him. When I use a particular tone, and look at him in a particular way, I can do what I like with him.'

She was ecstatically conscious of an incomprehensible power. What a role, that of the capricious, pouting queen, reclining luxuriously on her lounge, and subduing a tyrant to a slave! It surpassed that of the world-renowned pianist! . . .

III

But soon she became more serious. She had a delicious glow of seriousness. She overflowed with gratitude to Edwin. His good-nature was exquisite. He was not perfect. She could see all his faults just as plainly as when she was angry with him. But he was perfect in lovableness. She adored every aspect of him, every manifestation of his character. She felt her responsibility to him and to George. It was hers to bring grace into their lives. Without her, how miserable, how uncared-for, those two would be! They would be like lost children. Nobody could do for them what she did. Money could not buy what she gave naturally, and mere invention could not devise it. She looked up to Edwin, but at the same time she was mysteriously above both him and George. She had a strange soft wisdom for them. It was agreeable, and it was proper, and it was even prudent to be capricious on occasion and to win by pouting and wiles and seductions; but beneath all that lay the tremendous sternness of the wife's duty, everlasting and intricate – a heavy obligation that demanded all her noblest powers for its fulfilment. She rose heroically to the thought of duty, conceiving it as she had never conceived it before. She desired intensely to be the most wonderful wife in the whole history of marriage. And she believed strongly in her capabilities.

She went upstairs to put on another and a finer dress; for since the disastrous sequel to the At Home she had somewhat wearied in the pursuit of elegance. She had thought: 'What is the use of me putting myself to such a lot of trouble for a husband who is insensible enough to risk my welfare unnecessarily?' She was now ashamed of this backsliding. Ada was in the bedroom finicking with something on the dressing-table. Ada sprang to help as soon as she knew that her mistress had to go out; and she openly admired the new afternoon-dress, and seemed as pleased as though she was to wear it herself. And Ada buttoned her boots and found her gloves and her parasol, and remembered her purse and her bag and her handkerchief.

'I don't quite know what time I shall be back, Ada.'

'No'm,' said Ada eagerly, as though saying: 'Of course you don't, m'm. You have many engagements. But no matter when you come back we shall be delighted to see you because the house is nothing without you.'

'Of course I shall be back for tea.'

'Oh, yes'm!' Ada agreed, as though saying: 'Need you tell me that, m'm? I know you would never leave the master to have his tea alone.'

Hilda walked regally down the stairs and glanced round about her at the house which belonged to Maggie, and which Edwin had practically promised to buy. Yes, it was a fine house, a truly splendid abode, and it seemed all the finer because it was Maggie's. Hilda had this regrettable human trait of overvaluing what was not hers and depreciating what was. It accounted in part, possibly, for her often very critical attitude towards Edwin. She passed out of the front door in triumph, her head full of wise schemes and plots. But even then she was not sure whether she had destroyed – or could ever destroy, by no matter what arts! – the huge, dangerous, lithographic project.

As soon as she was gone, Ada ran yelling to the kitchen: 'Hooray! *She's* safe.'

And both servants burst like infants into the garden, to disport themselves upon the swing.

CHAPTER 8

THE FAMILY AT HOME

WHEN Hilda knocked at the door of Auntie Hamps's house in King Street, a marvellously dirty and untidy servant answered the summons, and a smell of greengage jam in the making surged out through the doorway into the street. The servant wore an apron of rough sacking.

'Is Miss Clayhanger in?' coldly asked Hilda, offended by the sight and the smell.

The servant looked suspicious and mysterious.

'No, mum. Her's gone out.'

'Mrs Hamps, then?'

'Missis is up yon,' said the servant, jerking her tousled head back towards the stairs.

'Will you tell her I'm here?'

The servant left the visitor on the doorstep, and with an elephantine movement of the knees ran upstairs.

Hilda walked into the passage towards the kitchen. On the kitchen fire was the brilliant copper pan sacred to 'preserving'. Rows of earthenware and glass jars stood irregularly on the table.

'Her'll be down,' said the brusque servant, returning, and glared open-mouthed.

'Shall I wait in the sitting-room?'

The house, about seventy years old, was respectably situated in the better part of King Street, at the bottom of the slope near St Luke's Church. It had once been occupied by a dentist of a certain grandeur, and possessed a garden, of which, however, Auntie Hamps had made a wilderness. The old lady was magnificent, but her magnificence was limited to herself. She could be sublimely generous, gorgeously hospitable, but only upon special occasions. Her teas, at which a fresh and costly pineapple and wonderful confectionery and pickled salmon and silver plate never lacked, were renowned, but the general level of her existence was very mean. Her servants, of whom she had many, though never more than one at a time, were not only obliged to be Wesleyan Methodists and to attend the Sunday-night service, and in the week to go to class-meeting for the purpose of confessing sins and proving the power of Christ, – they were obliged also to eat dripping instead of butter. The mistress sometimes ate dripping, if butter ran short or went up in price. She considered herself a tremendous housewife. She was a martyr to her housewifely ideals. Her private career was chiefly an endless struggle to keep the house clean – to get forward with the work. The house was always going to be clean and never was, despite eternal soap, furniture polish, scrubbing, rubbing. Auntie Hamps never changed her frowsy house-dress for rich visiting attire without the sad thought that she was 'leaving something undone'. The servant never went to bed without hearing the discontented phrase: 'Well, we must do it tomorrow.' Spring-cleaning in that house lasted for six weeks. On days of hospitality the effort to get the servant 'dressed' for tea-time was simply desperate, and not always successful.

Auntie Hamps had no sense of comfort and no sense of beauty. She was incapable of leaning back in a chair, and she regarded linoleum as one of the most satisfactory inventions of the modern age. She 'saved' her carpets by means of patches of linoleum, often stringy at the edges, and in some rooms there was more linoleum than anything else. In the way of renewals she bought nothing but linoleum, – unless some chapel bazaar forced her to purchase a satin cushion or a hand-painted grate-screen. All her furniture was old, decrepit, and ugly; it belonged to the worst Victorian period, when every trace of the eighteenth century had disappeared. The abode was always oppressive. It was oppressive even amid hospitality, for then the mere profusion on the tables accused the rest of the interior, creating a feeling of discomfort; and moreover Mrs Hamps could not be hospitable naturally. She could be nothing and do nothing naturally. She could no more take off her hypocrisy than she could take off her skin. Her hospitality was altogether too ruthless. And to satisfy that ruthlessness, the guests had always to eat too much. She was so determined to demonstrate her hospitality to herself, that she would never leave a guest alone until he had reached the bursting point.

Hilda sat grimly in the threadbare sitting-room amid morocco-bound photograph albums, oleographs, and beady knick-knacks, and sniffed the strong odour of jam; and in the violence of her revolt against that widespread messy idolatrous eternal domesticity of which Auntie Hamps was a classic example, she protested that she would sooner buy the worst jam than make the best, and that she would never look under a table for dust, and that naught should induce her to to do any housework after midday, and that she would abolish spring-cleaning utterly.

The vast mediocre respectability of the district weighed on her heart. She had been a mistress-drudge in Brighton during a long portion of her adult life; she knew the very depths of domesticity; but at Brighton the eye could find large, rich, luxurious, and sometimes beautiful things for its distraction; and there was the sea. In the Five Towns there was nothing. You might walk from one end of the Five Towns to the other, and not see one object that gave a thrill – unless it was a pair of lovers. And when you went inside the houses you were no better off, – you were even worse off, because you came at once into contact with an ignoble race of slatternly imprisoned serfs driven by narrow-minded women who themselves were serfs with the mentality of serfs and the prodigious conceit of virtue ... Talk to Auntie Hamps at home of lawn-tennis or a musical evening, and she would set you down as flighty, and shift the conversation on to soaps or chapels. And there were hundreds of houses in the Five Towns into which no ideas save the ideas of Auntie Hamps had ever penetrated, and tens and hundreds of thousands of such houses all over the industrial districts of Staffordshire, Cheshire, Lancashire, and Yorkshire, – houses where to keep bits of wood clean and to fulfil the ceremonies of pietism, and to help the poor to help themselves, was the highest good, the sole good. Hilda in her mind saw every house, and shuddered. She turned for relief to the thought of her own house, and in a constructive spirit of rebellion she shaped instantaneously a conscious policy for it ... Yes, she took oath that her house should at any rate be intelligent and agreeable before it was clean. She pictured Auntie Hamps gazing at a layer of dust in the Clayhanger hall, and heard herself saying: 'Oh, yes, Auntie, it's dust right enough. I keep it there on purpose, to remind me of something I want to remember.' She looked round Auntie Hamps's sitting-room and revelled grimly in the monstrous catalogue of its mean ugliness.

And then Auntie Hamps came in, splendidly and yet soberly attired in black to face the world, with her upright, vigorous figure, her sparkling eye, and her admirable complexion; self-content, smiling hospitably; quite unconscious that she was dead, and that her era was dead, and that Hilda was not guiltless of the murder.

'This is nice of you, Hilda. It's quite an honour.' And then, archly: 'I'm making jam.'

'So I see,' said Hilda, meaning that so she smelt. 'I just looked in on the chance of seeing Maggie.'

'Maggie went out about half an hour ago.'

Auntie Hamps's expression had grown mysterious. Hilda thought: 'What's she hiding from me?'

'Oh, well, it doesn't matter,' said she. 'You're going out too, Auntie.'

'I do wish I'd known you were coming, dear. Will you stay and have a cup of tea?'

'No, no! I won't keep you.'

'But it will be a *pleasure*, dear,' Auntie Hamps protested warmly.

'No, no! Thanks! I'll just walk along with you a little of the way. Which direction are you going?'

Auntie Hamps hesitated, she was in a dilemma.

'What *is* she hiding from me?' thought Hilda.

'The truth is,' said Auntie Hamps, 'I'm just popping over to Clara's.'

'Well, I'll go with you, Auntie.'

'Oh, do!' exclaimed Mrs Hamps almost passionately. 'Do! I'm sure Clara will be delighted!' She added in a casual tone: 'Maggie's there.'

Thought Hilda:

'She evidently doesn't want me to go.'

After Mrs Hamps had peered into the grand copper pan and most particularly instructed the servant, they set off.

'I shan't be easy in my mind until I get back,' said Auntie Hamps. 'Unless you look after them all the time they always forget to stir it.'

II

When they turned in at the gate of the Benbows' house the front door was already open, and Clara, holding Rupert – her youngest – by the hand, stood smiling to receive them. Obviously they had been descried up the street from one of the bow windows. This small fact, strengthening in Hilda's mind the gradually formed notion that the Benbows were always lying in wait and that their existence was a vast machination for getting the better of other people, enlivened her prejudice against her sister-in-law. Moreover Clara was in one of her best dresses, and her glance had a peculiar self-conscious expression, partly guilty and partly cunning. Nevertheless, the fair fragility of Clara's face, with its wonderful skin, and her manner, at once girlish and maternal, of holding fast the child's hand, reacted considerably against Hilda's prejudice.

Rupert was freshly all in white, stitched and embroidered with millions of plain and fancy stitches; he had had time neither to tear nor to stain; only on his bib there was a spot of jam. His obese right arm was stretched straight upwards to attain the immense height of the hand of the protective giantess his mother, and this reaching threw the whole balance of his little body over towards the left, and gave him a comical and wistful appearance. He was a pretty and yet sturdy child, with a look indicating a nice disposition, and he had recently been acquiring the marvellous gift of speech . . . Astounding how the infantile brain added word to word and phrase to phrase, and (as though there were not enough) actually invented delicious words and graphic droll phrases! Nobody could be surprised that he became at once the centre of greetings. His grand-aunt snatched him up, and without the slightest repugnance he allowed the ancient woman to bury her nose in his face and neck.

And then Hilda embraced him with not less pleasure, for the contact of his delicate flesh, and his flushed timid smile, were exquisite. She wished for a moment that George was only two and a half again, and that she could bathe him, and wipe him, and nurse him close. Clara's pride, though the visitors almost forgot to shake hands with her, was ecstatic. At length Rupert was safely on the step once more. He had made no remark whatever. Shyness prevented him from showing off his new marvellous gift, but his mother, gazing at him, said that in ordinary life he never stopped chattering.

'Come this way, will you?' said Clara effusively, and yet conspiratorially pointing to the drawing-room, which was to the left of the front door. From the dining-room, which was to the right of the front door, issued confused sounds. 'Albert's here. I'm so glad you've come,' she added to Hilda.

Auntie Hamps murmured warningly into Hilda's ear:

'It's Bert's birthday party.'

A fortnight earlier Hilda had heard rumours of Bert's approaching birthday – his twelfth, and therefore a high solemnity – but she had very wrongly forgotten about it.

'I'm so glad you've come,' Clara repeated in the drawing-room. 'I was afraid you might be hurt. I thought I'd just bring you in here first and explain it all to you.'

'Oh! Bless me!' exclaimed Auntie Hamps, – interrupting, as she glanced round the drawing-room. 'We are grand! Well I never! We are grand!'

'Do you like it?' said Clara, blushing.

Auntie Hamps in reply told one of the major lies of her career. She said with rapture that she did like the new drawing-room suite. This suite was a proof, disagreeable to Auntie Hamps, that the world would never stand still. It quite ignored all the old Victorian ideals of furniture; and in ignoring the past, it also ignored the future. Victorian furniture had always sought after immortality; in Bursley there were thousands of Victorian chairs and tables that defied time and that nothing but an axe or a conflagration could destroy. But this new suite thought not of the morrow; it did not even pretend to think of the morrow. Nobody believed that it would last, and the owners of it simply forbore to reflect upon what it would be after a few years of family use. They contemplated with joy its first state of dainty freshness, and were content therein. Whereas the old Victorians lived in the future (in so far as they truly lived at all), the neo-Victorians lived careless in the present.

The suite was of apparent rosewood, with salmon-tinted upholstery ending in pleats and bows. But white also entered considerably into the scheme, for enamel paint had just reached Bursley and was destined to become the rage. Among the items of the suite was a three-legged milking-stool in deal covered with white enamel paint heightened by salmon-tinted bows of imitation silk. Society had recently been thunderstruck by the originality of putting a milking-stool in a drawing-room; its quaintness appealed with tremendous force to nearly all hearts; nearly every housemistress on seeing a milking-stool in a friend's drawing-room, decided that she must have a milking-stool in her drawing-room, and took measures to get one. Clara was among the earlier possessors, the pioneers. Ten years – five years – before, Clara had appropriated the word 'aesthetic' as a term of sneering abuse, with but a vague idea of its meaning; and now – such is the miraculous effect of time – she was caught up in the movement as it had ultimately spread to the Five Towns, a willing convert and captive, and nothing could exceed her scorn for that which once she had admired to the exclusion of all else. Into that mid-Victorian respectable house, situate in a rather old-fashioned street leading from Shawport Lane to the Canal, and whose boast (even when inhabited by Nonconformists) was that it overlooked the Rectory garden, the new ideals of brightness, freshness, eccentricity, brittleness, and impermanency had entered, and Auntie Hamps herself was intimidated by them.

Hilda gave polite but perfunctory praise. Left alone, she might not have been averse from the new ideals in their more expensive forms, but the influence of Edwin had taught her to despise them. Edwin's tastes in furniture, imbibed from the Orgreaves, neglected the modern, and went even further back than earliest Victorian. Much of the ugliness bought by his father remained in the Clayhanger house, but all Edwin's own purchases were either antique, or, if new, careful imitations of the pre-Victorian.

Had England been peopled by Edwins, all original artists in furniture might have died of hunger. Yet he encouraged original literature. What, however, put Hilda against Clara's drawing-room suite, was not its style, nor its enamel, nor its frills, nor the obviously inferior quality of its varnish, but the mere fact that it had been exposed for sale in Nixon's shop window in Duck Bank, with the price marked. Hilda did not like this. Now Edwin might see an old weather-glass in some frowsy second-hand shop at Hanbridge or Turnhill, and from indecision might leave it in the second-hand shop for months, and then buy it and hang it up at home, – and instantly it was somehow transferred into another weather-glass, a superior and personal weather-glass. But Clara's suite was not – for Hilda – thus transformed. Indeed, as she sat there in Clara's drawing-room, she had the illusion of sitting in Nixon's shop.

Further, Nixon had now got in his window another suite precisely like Clara's. It was astonishing to Hilda that Clara was not ashamed of the publicity and the wholesale reproduction of her suite. But she was not. On the contrary she seemed to draw a mysterious satisfaction from the very fact that suites precisely similar to hers were to be found or would soon be found in un-numbered other drawing-rooms. Nor did she mind that the price was notorious. And in the matter of the price the phrase 'hire purchase' flitted about in Hilda's brain. She felt sure that Albert Benbow had not paid cash to Nixon. She regarded the hire purchase system as unrespectable, if not immoral, and this opinion was one of the very few she shared with Auntie Hamps. Both ladies in their hearts, and in the security of their financial positions, blamed the Benbows for imprudence. Nobody, not even his wife, knew just how Albert 'stood', but many took leave to guess – and guessed unfavourably.

'Do sit down,' said Clara, too urgently. She was so pre-occupied that Hilda's indifference to her new furniture did not affect her.

They all sat down, primly, in the pretty primness of the drawing-room, and Rupert leaned as if tired against his mother's fine skirt.

Hilda, expectant, glanced vaguely about her. Auntie Hamps did the same. On the central table lay a dictionary of the English language, open and leaves downwards; and near it a piece of paper containing a long list of missing words in pencil. Auntie Hamps, as soon as her gaze fell on these objects, looked quickly away, as though she had by accident met the obscene. Clara caught the movement, flushed somewhat, and recovered herself.

'I'm so glad you've come,' she repeated yet again to Hilda, with a sickly-sweet smile. 'I did so want to explain to you how it was we didn't ask George – I was afraid you might be vexed.'

'What an idea!' Hilda murmured as naturally as she could, her nostrils twitching uneasily in the atmosphere of small feuds and misunderstandings which Clara breathed with such pleasure. She laughed, to reassure Clara, and also in enjoyment of the thought that for days Clara had pictured her as wondering sensitively why no invitation to the party had come for George, while in fact the party had never crossed her mind. She regretted that she had no gift for Bert, but decided to give him half-a-crown for his savings-bank account, of which she had heard a lot.

'To tell ye the truth,' said Clara, launching herself, 'we've had a lot of trouble with Bert. Albert's been quite put about. It was only the day before yesterday Albert got out of him the truth about the night of your At Home, Hilda, when he ran away after he'd gone to bed. Albert said to him: "I shan't whip you, and I shan't put you on bread and water. Only if you don't tell me what you were doing that night there'll be no birthday and no birthday party – that's all." So at last Bert gave in. And d'you know what he *was* doing? Holding a prayer-meeting with your George and that boy of Clowes's next door to your house down Hulton Street. Did you know?'

Hilda shook her head bravely. Officially she did not know.

'Did you ever hear of such a thing?' exclaimed Auntie Hamps.

'Yes,' proceeded Clara, taking breath for a new start. 'And Bert's story is that they prayed for a penknife for your George, and it came. And then they prayed for a bicycle for our Bert, but the bicycle didn't come, and then Bert and George had a fearful quarrel, and George gave him the penknife – made him have it – and then said he'd never speak to him any more as long as he lived. At first Albert was inclined to thrash Bert for

telling lies and being irreverent, but in the end he came to the
conclusion that at any rate Bert was telling what he thought to
be the truth . . . And that Clowes boy is so *little*! . . . Bert wanted
his birthday party, of course, but he begged and prayed us not
to ask George. So in the end we decided we'd better not, and we
let him have his own way. That's all there is to it . . . So George
has said nothing?'

'Not a word,' replied Hilda.

'And the Clowes boy is so *little*!' said Clara again. She went
suddenly to the mantelpiece and picked up a penknife and offered
it to Hilda.

'Here's the penknife. Of course Albert took it off him.'

'Why?' said Hilda ingenuously.

But Clara detected satire and repelled it with a glance.

'It's not Edwin's penknife, I suppose?' she queried, in a
severe tone.

'No, it isn't. I've never seen it before. Why?'

'We were only thinking Edwin might have overheard the boys
and thrown a knife over the wall. It would be just like Edwin,
that would.'

'Oh, no!' The deceitful Hilda blew away such a possibility.

'I'm quite sure he didn't,' said she, and added mischievously
as she held out the penknife: 'I thought all you folks believed in
the efficacy of prayer?'

These simple words were never forgiven by Clara.

The next moment, having restored the magic penknife to the
mantelpiece, and gathered up her infant, she was leading the way
to the dining-room.

'Come along, Rupy, my darling,' said she.

'Rupy!' Hilda privately imitated her, deriding the absurdity
of the diminutive.

'If you ask me,' said Auntie Hamps, determined to save the
honour of the family, 'it's that little Clowes monkey that is
responsible. I've been thinking it over since you told me about it
last night, Clara, and I feel almost sure it must have been that
little Clowes monkey.'

She was magnificent. She was no longer a housekeeper worried
about the processes of jam-making, but a grandiose figure out

in the world, a figure symbolic, upon whom had devolved the duty of keeping up appearances on behalf of all mankind.

III

The dining-room had not yet begun to move with the times. It was rather a shabby apartment, accustomed to daily ill-treatment, and its contents dated from different periods, the most ancient object of all stretching backwards in family history to the epoch of Albert's great-grandfather. This was an oak armchair, occupied usually by Albert, but on the present occasion by his son and heir, Bert. Bert, spectacled, was at the head of the table; and at the foot was his Auntie Maggie in front of a tea-tray. Down the sides of the table were his sisters, thin Clara, fat Amy, and little Lucy – the first nearly as old as Bert – and his father; two crumb-strewn plates showed that the mother and Rupert had left the meal to greet the visitors. And there were two other empty places. In a tiny vase in front of Amy was a solitary flower. The room was nearly full; it had an odour of cake, tea, and children.

'Well, here we are,' said Clara, entering with the guests and Rupert, very cheerfully. 'Getting on all right?' (She gave Albert a glance which said: 'I have explained everything, but Hilda is a very peculiar creature.')

'A1,' Albert answered. 'Hello, all you aunties!'

'Albert left the works early on purpose,' Clara explained her husband's presence.

He was a happy man. In early adolescence he had taken to Sunday Schools as some youths take to vice. He loved to exert authority over children, and experience had taught him all the principal dodges. Under the forms of benevolent autocracy, he could exercise a ruthless discipline upon youngsters. He was not at all ashamed at being left in charge of a tableful of children while his wife went forth to conduct diplomatic interviews. At the same time he had his pride. Thus he would express no surprise, nor even pleasure, at the presence of Hilda, his theory being that it ought to be taken as a matter of course. Indeed he was preoccupied by the management of the meal, and he did not conceal the fact. He shook hands with the ladies in a perfunctory style, which seemed to say: 'Now the supreme matter is this birthday repast. I am running it, and I am running it very well. Slip unobtrusively into your places in the machine, and let me continue my work of direction.'

Nevertheless, he saw to it that all the children rose politely and saluted according to approved precedents. His eye was upon them. He attached importance to every little act in any series of little acts. If he cut the cake, he had the air of announcing to the world: 'This is a beautiful cake. I have carefully estimated the merits of this cake, and mother has carefully estimated them; we have in fact all come to a definite and favourable conclusion about this cake, – namely that it is a beautiful cake. I will now cut it. The operation of cutting it is a major operation. Watch me cut it, and then watch me distribute it. Wisdom and justice shall preside over the distribution.' Even if he only passed the salt, he passed it as though he were passing extreme unction.

Auntie Hamps with apparent delight adapted herself to his humour. She said she would 'squeeze in' anywhere, and was soon engaged in finding perfection in everything that appertained to the Benbow family. Hilda, not being quite so intimate with the household, was installed with more ceremony. She could not keep out of her eye the idea that it was droll to see a stoutish, somewhat clay-dusted man neglecting his business in order to take charge of a birthday party of small children; and Albert, observing this, could not keep out of his eye the rebutting assertion that it was not in the least droll, but entirely proper and laudable.

The first mention of birthday presents came from Auntie Hamps, who remarked with enthusiasm that Bert looked a regular little man in his beautiful new spectacles. Bert, glowering, gloomy and yet proud, and above all self-conscious, grew even more self-conscious at this statement. Spectacles had been ordained for him by the oculist, and his parents had had the hardihood to offer him his first pair for a birthday present. They had so insisted on the beauty and originality of the scheme that Bert himself had almost come to believe that to get a pair of spectacles for a birthday present was a great thing in a boy's life.

He was now wearing the spectacles for the first time. On the whole, gloom outbalanced pride in his demeanour, and Bert's mysterious soul, which had flabbergasted his father for about a week, peeped out sidelong occasionally through those spectacles in bitter criticism of the institution of parents. He ate industriously. Soon Auntie Hamps, leaning over, rapped half a sovereign down on his sticky plate. Everybody pretended to be overwhelmed, though nobody entitled to prophesy had expected less. Almost simultaneously with the ring of the gold on the plate, Clara said:

'Now what do you say?'

But Albert was judiciously benevolent:

'Leave him alone, mother – he'll say it all right.'

'I'm sure he will,' his mother agreed.

And Bert said it, blushing, and fingering the coin nervously. And Auntie Hamps sat like an antique goddess, bland, superb, morally immense. And even her dirty and broken fingernails detracted naught from her grandiosity. She might feed servants on dripping, but when the proper moment came she could fling half-sovereigns about with anybody.

And then, opening her purse, Hilda added five shillings to the half-sovereign, amid admiring exclamations sincere and insincere. Beside Auntie Hamps's gold the two half-crowns cut a poor figure, and therefore Hilda, almost without discontinuing the gesture of largesse, said:

'That is from Uncle Edwin. And this,' putting a florin and three shillings more to the treasure, 'is from Auntie Hilda.'

Somehow she was talking as the others talked, and she disliked herself for yielding to the spirit of the Benbow home, but she could not help it; the pervading spirit conquered everybody. She felt self-conscious; and Bert's self-consciousness was still further increased as the exclamations grew in power and sincerity. Though he experienced the mournful pride of rich possessions, he knew well that the money would be of no real value. His presents, all useful (save a bouquet of flowers from Rupert), were all useless to him. Thus the prim young Clara had been parentally guided to give him a comb. If all the combs in the world had been suddenly annihilated Bert would not have cared,

– would indeed have rejoiced. And as to the spectacles, he would have preferred the prospect of total blindness in middle age to the compulsion of wearing them. Who can wonder that his father had not fathomed the mind of the strange creature?

Albert gazed rapt at the beautiful sight of the plate. It reminded him pleasantly of a collection-plate at the Sunday-School Anniversary sermons. In a moment the conversation ran upon savings-bank accounts. Each child had a savings-bank account, and their riches were astounding. Rupert had an account and was getting interest at the rate of two and a half per cent on six pounds ten shillings. The thriftiness of the elder children had reached amounts which might be mentioned with satisfaction even to the luxurious wife of the richest member of the family. Young Clara was the wealthiest of the band. 'I've got the most, haven't I, fardy?' she said with complacency. 'I've got more than Bert, haven't I?' Nobody seemed to know how it was that she had surpassed Bert, who had had more birthdays and more Christmases. The inferiority of the eldest could not be attributed to dissipation or improvidence, for none of the children was allowed to spend a cent. The savings-bank devoured all, and never rendered back. However, Bert was now creeping up, and his mother exhorted him to do his best in future. She then took the money from the plate, and promised Bert for the morrow the treat of accompanying her to the Post Office in order to bury it.

A bell rang within the house, and at once young Clara exclaimed:

'Oh! there's Flossie! Oh, my word, she *is* late, isn't she, fardy? What a good thing we didn't wait tea for her! ... Move up, miss.' This to Lucy.

'People who are late must take the consequences, especially little girls,' said Albert in reply.

And presently Flossie entered, tripping, shrugging up her shoulders and throwing back her mane, and wonderfully innocent.

'This is Flossie, who is always late,' Albert introduced her to Hilda.

'Am I really?' said Flossie, in a very low, soft voice, with a bright and apparently frightened smile.

Dark Flossie was of Amy's age and supposed to be Amy's particular friend. She was the daughter of young Clara's music-mistress. The little girl's prestige in the Benbow house was due to two causes. First, she was graceful and rather stylish in movement – qualities which none of the Benbow children had, though young Clara was pretty enough; and second, her mother had rather more pupils than she could comfortably handle, and indeed sometimes refused a pupil.

Flossie with her physical elegance was like a foreigner among the Benbows. She had a precocious demeanour. She shook hands and embraced like a woman, and she gave her birthday gift to Bert as if she were distributing a prize. It was a lead pencil, with a patent sharpener. Bert would have preferred a bicycle, but the patent sharpener made an oasis in his day. His father pointed out to him that as the pencil was already sharpened he could not at present use the sharpener. Amy thereupon furtively passed him the stump of a pencil to operate upon, and then his mother told him that he had better postpone his first sharpening until he got into the garden, where bits of wood would not be untidy. Flossie carefully settled her very short white skirts on a chair, smiling all the time, and inquired about two brothers who she had been told were to be among the guests. Albert informed her with solemnity that these two brothers were both down with measles, and that Auntie Hamps and Auntie Hilda had come to make up for their absence.

'Poor things!' murmured Flossie sympathetically.

Hilda laughed, and Flossie, screwing up her eyes and shrugging up her shoulders, laughed too, as if saying: 'You and I alone understand me.'

'What a pretty flower!' Flossie exclaimed, in her low, soft voice, indicating the flower in the vase in front of Amy.

'There's half a crumb left,' said Albert, passing the cake-plate to Flossie carefully. 'We thought we'd better keep it for you, though we don't reckon to keep anything for little girls that come late.'

'Amy,' whispered her mother, leaning towards the fat girl. 'Wouldn't it be nice of you to give your flower to Flossie?'

Amy started.

'I don't want to,' she whispered back, flushing.

The flower was a gift to Amy from Bert, out of the birthday bunch presented to him by Rupert. Mysterious relations existed between Bert and the benignant, acquiescent Amy.

'Oh! Amy!' her mother protested, still whispering, but shocked.

Tears came into Amy's eyes. These tears Amy at length wiped away, and, straightening her face, offered the flower with stiff, outstretched arm to her friend Flossie. And Flossie smilingly accepted it.

'It *is* kind of you, you darling!' said Flossie, and stuck the flower in an interstice of her embroidered pinafore.

Amy, gravely lacking in self-control, began to whimper again.

'*That*'s my good little girl!' muttered Clara to her, exhibiting pride in her daughter's victory over self, and rubbed the child's eyes with her handkerchief. The parents were continually thus 'bringing up' their children. Hilda pressed her lips together.

Immediately afterwards it was noticed that Flossie was no longer eating.

'I've had quite enough, thank you,' said she, in answer to expostulations.

'No jam, even? And you've not finished your tea!'

'I've had quite enough, thank you,' said she, and folded up her napkin.

'Please, father, can we go and play in the garden now?' Bert asked.

Albert looked at his wife.

'Yes, I think they might,' said Clara. 'Go and play nicely.' They all rose.

'Now quietly, quietly!' Albert warned them.

And they went from the room quietly, each in his own fashion, – Flossie like a modest tsarina, young Clara full of virtue and holding Rupert by the hand, Amy lumpily, tiny Lucy as one who had too soon been robbed of the privilege of being the youngest, and Bert in the rear like a criminal who is observed in a suspicious act. And Albert blew out wind, as if getting rid of a great weight.

IV

'Finished your greengage, Auntie?' asked Clara, after the pause
which ensued while the adults were accustoming themselves to
the absence of the children.

And it was Maggie who answered, rather eagerly:

'No, she hasn't. She left it to the tender mercies of that Maria.
She wouldn't let me stay, and she wouldn't stay herself.'

These were almost the first words, save murmurings as to cups
of tea, quantities of sugar and of milk, etc., that the taciturn
Maggie had uttered since Hilda's arrival. She was not sulky, she
had merely been devoting herself and allowing herself to be
exploited, in the vacuous manner customary to her, and listening
receptively – or perhaps not even receptively – offering no
remark. Save that the smooth-working mechanism of the repast
would have creaked and stopped at her departure, she might
have slipped from the room unnoticed as a cat. But now she
spoke as one capable of enthusiasm and resentment on behalf
of an ideal. To her it was scandalous that greengage jam should
be jeopardized for the sake of social pleasures, and suddenly it
became evident she and her auntie had had a difference on the
matter.

Mrs Hamps said stoutly and defiantly, with grandeur:

'Well, I wasn't going to have my eldest grand-nephew's
twelfth birthday party interfered with for any jam.'

'Hear, hear!' said Hilda, liking the terrific woman for an
instant.

But mild Maggie was inflexible.

Clara, knowing that in Maggie very slight symptoms had
enormous significance, at once changed the subject. Albert went
to the back window, whence, by twisting his neck, he could descry
a corner of the garden.

Said Clara, smiling:

'I hear you're going to have some *musical evenings*, Hilda . . .
on Sunday nights.'

Malice and ridicule were in Clara's tone. On the phrase
'musical evenings' she put a strange disdainful emphasis, as
though a musical evening denoted something not only

unrighteous but snobbish, new-fangled, and absurd. Yet envy also was in her tone.

Hilda was startled.

'Ah! Who told you that?'

'Never mind! I heard,' said Clara darkly.

Hilda wondered where the Benbows, from whom seemingly naught could be concealed, had in fact got this titbit of news. By tacit consent she and Edwin had as yet said nothing to anybody except the Orgreaves, who alone, with Tertius Ingpen and one or two more intimates, were invited, or were to be invited, to the first evening. Relations between the Orgreaves and the Benbows scarcely existed.

'We're having a little music on Sunday night,' said Hilda, as it were apologetically, and scorning herself for being apologetic. Why should she be apologetic to these base creatures? But she couldn't help it; the public opinion of the room was too much for her. She even added: 'We're hoping that old Mrs Orgreave will come. It will be the first time she's been out in the evening for ever so long.' The name of Mrs Orgreave was calculated by Hilda to overawe them and stop their mouths.

No name, however, could overawe Mrs Hamps. She smiled kindly, and with respect for the caprices of others; she spoke in a tone exceptionally polite, – but what she said was:

'I'm sorry . . . I'm sorry.'

The deliverance was final. Auntie Hamps was almost as deeply moved about the approaching desecration of the Sabbath as Maggie had been about the casual treatment of jam. In earlier years she would have said a great deal more – just as in earlier years she would have punctuated Bert's birthday mouthfuls with descants upon the excellence of his parents and moral exhortations to himself; but Auntie Hamps was growing older, and quieter, and 'I'm sorry . . . I'm sorry' meant much from her.

Hilda became sad, disgusted, indignant, moody. The breach which separated her and Edwin from the rest of the family was enormous, as might be seen in the mere fact that they had never for a moment contemplated asking anybody in the family to the musical evening, nor had the family ever dreamed of an invitation. It was astonishing that Edwin should be so different from the others. But after all, was he? She could see in him sometimes bits of Maggie, of Clara, and even of the Unspeakable. She was conscious of her grievances against Edwin. Among these was that he never, or scarcely ever, praised her. At moments, when she had tried hard, she felt a great need of praise. But Edwin would watch her critically, with the damnable grim detachment of the Five Towns towards a stranger or a returned exile.

As she sat in the stuffy dining-room of the Benbows, surrounded by hostilities and incomprehensions, she had a sensation of unreality, or at any rate of a vast mistake. Why was she there? Was she not tied by intimate experience to a man at that very instant in prison? (She had a fearful vision of him in prison, – she, sitting there in the midst of Maggie, Clara, and Auntie Hamps!) Was she not the mother of an illegitimate boy? Victimized or not, innocent or not, she, a guest at Bert's intensely legitimate birthday fête, was the mother of an illegitimate boy. Incredible! She ought never to have married into the Clayhangers, never to have come back to this cackling provincial district. All these people were inimical towards her, – because she represented the luxury and riches and worldly splendour of the family, and because her illegitimate boy had tempted the heir of the Benbows to blasphemous wickedness, and because she herself had tempted a weak Edwin to abandon chapel and to desecrate the Sabbath, and again because she, without a penny of her own, had stepped in and now represented the luxury and riches and worldly splendour of the family. And all the family's grievances against Edwin were also grievances against her. Once, long ago, when he was yet a bachelor, and had no hope of Hilda, Edwin had prevented his father, in dotage, from lending a thousand pounds to Albert upon no security. The interference was unpardonable, and Hilda would not be pardoned for it.

Such was marriage into a family. Such was family life . . . Yes, she felt unreal there, and also unsafe. She had prevaricated about George and the penknife; and she had allowed Clara to remain under the impression that her visit to the house was a birthday visit. Auntie Hamps and destiny, between them, would lay bare all this lying. The antipathy against her would increase. But let it increase never so much, it still would not equal Hilda's against the family, as she thrilled to it then. Their narrow ignorance, their narrow self-conceit, their detestation of beauty, their pietism, their bigotry – revolted her. In what century had they been living all those years? Was this married life? Had Albert and Clara ever felt a moment of mutual passion? They were nothing but parents, eternally preoccupied with 'oughts' and 'ought nots', and forbiddances and horrid reluctant permissions. They did not know what joy was, and they did not want anybody else to know what joy was. Even on the outskirts of such a family, a musical evening on a Sunday night appeared a forlorn enterprise. And all the families in all the streets were the same. Hilda was hard enough on George sometimes, but in that moment she would have preferred George to be a thoroughly bad rude boy and to go to the devil, and herself to be a woman abandoned to every licence, rather than that he and she should resemble Clara and her offspring. All her wrath centred upon Clara as the very symbol of what she loathed.

'Hello!' cried the watchful Albert from the window. 'What's happening, I wonder?'

In a moment Rupert ran into the room, and without a word scrambled on his mother's lap, absolutely confident in her goodness and power.

'What's amiss, tuppenny?' asked his father.

'Tired,' answered Rupert, with a faint, endearing smile.

He laid himself close against his mother's breast, and drew up his knees, and Clara held his body in her arms and whispered to him.

'Amy 'udn't play with me,' he murmured.

'Wouldn't she? Naughty Amy!'

'Mammy tired too,' he glanced upwards at his mother's eyes in sympathy.

And immediately he was asleep. Clara kissed him bending her head down and with difficulty reaching his cheek with her lips.

Auntie Hamps inquired fondly:

'What does he mean – "Mother tired too"?'

'Well,' said Clara, 'the fact is, some of 'em were so excited they stopped my afternoon sleep this afternoon. I always do have my nap, you know,' – she looked at Hilda, 'in here! When this door's closed they know mother mustn't be disturbed. Only this afternoon Lucy or Amy – I don't know which, and I didn't inquire too closely – forgot . . . He's remembered it, the little turk.'

'Is he asleep?' Hilda demanded in a low voice.

'Fast. He's been like that lately. He'll play a bit, and then he'll stop and say he's tired, and sometimes cry, and he'll come to me and be asleep in two jiffs. I think he's been a bit run down. He said he had toothache yesterday. It was nothing but a little cold; they've all had colds; but I wrapped his face up to please him. He looked so sweet in his bandage, I assure you I didn't want to take it off again. No, I didn't . . . I wonder why Amy wouldn't play with him. She's such a splendid playmate – when she likes. Full of imagination! Simply full of it!'

Albert had approached from the window.

With an air of important conviction, he said to Hilda:

'Yes, Amy's imagination is really remarkable.' As no one responded to this statement, he drummed on the table to ease the silence, and then suddenly added: 'Well, I suppose I must be getting on with my dictionary reading! I'm only at S; and there's bound to be a lot of words under U – beginning with *un*, you know. I saw at once there would be.' He spoke rather defiantly, as though challenging public opinion to condemn his new dubious activity.

'Oh!' said Clara. 'Albert's quite taken up with missing words nowadays.'

But instead of conning his dictionary, Albert returned to the window, drawn by his inexhaustible paternal curiosity, and he even opened the window and leaned out, so that he might more effectively watch the garden. And with the fresh air there entered the high, gay, inspiriting voices of the children.

Clara smiled down at the boy sleeping in her lap. She was happy. The child was happy. His flushed face, with its expression of loving innocence, was exquisitely touching. Clara's face was full of proud tenderness. Everybody gazed at the picture with secret and profound pleasure. Hilda wished once more that George was only two and a half years old again. George's infancy, and her early motherhood, had been very different from all this.

Shd had never been able to shut a dining-room door, or any other door, as a sign that she must not be disturbed. And certainly George had never sympathetically remarked that she was tired . . . She was envious . . . And yet a minute ago she had been execrating the family life of the Benbows. The complexity of the tissue of existence was puzzling.

V

When Albert brought his head once more into the room he suddenly discovered the stuffiness of the atmosphere, and with the large free gestures of a mountaineer and a sanitarian threw open both windows as wide as possible. The bleak wind from the moorlands surged in, fluttering curtains, and lowering the temperature at a run.

'Won't Rupert catch cold?' Hilda suggested, chilled.

'He's got to be hardened, Rupert has!' Albert replied easily. 'Fresh air! Nothing like it! Does 'em good to feel it!'

Hilda thought:

'Pity you didn't think so a bit earlier!'

Her countenance was too expressive. Albert divined some ironic thought in her brain, and turned on her with a sort of parrying jeer:

'And how's the great man getting along?'

In this phrase, which both he and Clara employed with increasing frequency, Albert let out not only his jealousy of, but his respect for, the head of the family. Hilda did not like it, but it flattered her on Edwin's behalf, and she never showed her resentment of the attitude which prompted it.

'Edwin? Oh, he's all right. He's working.' She put a slight emphasis on the last pronoun, in order revengefully to contrast Edwin's industry with Albert's presence during business hours at a children's birthday party. 'He said to me as he went out that he must go and earn something towards Maggie's rent.' She laughed softly.

Clara smiled cautiously; Maggie smiled and blushed a little; Albert did not commit himself; only Auntie Hamps laughed without reserve.

'Edwin will have his joke,' said she.

Although Hilda had audaciously gone forth that afternoon with the express intention of opening negotiations, on her own initiative, with Maggie for the purchase of the house, she had certainly not meant to discuss the matter in the presence of the entire family. But she was seized by one of her characteristic impulses, and she gave herself up to it with the usual mixture of glee and apprehension. She said:

'I suppose you wouldn't care to sell us the house would you, Maggie?'

Everybody became alert, and as it grew apparent that the company was assisting at the actual birth of a family episode or incident, a peculiar feeling of eager pleasure spread through the room, and the appetite for history-making leapt up.

'Indeed I should!' Maggie answered, with a deepening flush, and all were astonished at her decisiveness and at the warmth of her tone. 'I never wanted the house. Only it was arranged that I should have it, so of course I took it.' The long-silent victim was speaking. Money was useless to her, for she was incapable of turning it into happiness; but she had her views on finance and property, nevertheless; and though in all such matters she did as she was told, submissively accepting the decisions of brother or brother-in-law as decrees of fate, yet she was quite aware of the victimhood. The assemblage was surprised and even a little intimidated by her mild outburst.

'But you've got a very good tenant, Maggie,' said Auntie Hamps enthusiastically.

'She's got a very good tenant, admitted!' Albert said judicially and almost sternly. 'But she'd never have any difficulty in finding a very good tenant for that house. That's not the point. The point is that the investment really isn't remunerative. Maggie could do much better for herself than that. Very much better. Why, if she went the right way about it, she could get ten per cent on her money! I know of things . . . And I bet she doesn't get three and a half per cent clear from the house. Not three and a half.' He glanced reproachfully at Hilda.

'Do you mean the rent's too low?' Hilda questioned boldly.

He hesitated, losing courage.

'I don't say it's too low. But Maggie perhaps took the house over at too big a figure.'

Maggie looked up at her brother-in-law.

'And whose fault was that?' she asked sharply. The general surprise was intensified. No one could understand Maggie. No one had the wit to perceive that she had been truly annoyed by Auntie Hamps's negligence in regard to jam, and was momentarily capable of bitterness. 'Whose fault was that?' she repeated. 'You and Clara and Edwin settled it between you. You yourself said over and over again it was a fair figure.'

'I thought so at the time! I thought so at the time!' said Albert quickly. 'We all acted for the best.'

'I'm sure you did,' murmured Auntie Hamps.

'I should think so, indeed!' murmured Clara, seeking to disguise her constraint by attentions to the sleeping Rupert.

'Is Edwin thinking of buying, then?' Albert asked Hilda, in a quiet, studiously careless voice.

'We've discussed it,' responded Hilda.

'Because if he is, he ought to take it over at the price Mag took it at. She oughtn't to lose on it. That's only fair.'

'I'm sure Edwin would never do anything unfair,' said Auntie Hamps.

Hilda made no reply. She had already heard the argument from Edwin, and Albert now seemed to her more tedious and unprincipled than usual. Her reason admitted the force of the argument as regards Maggie, but instinct opposed it.

Nevertheless she was conscious of sudden sympathy for Maggie, and of a weakening of her prejudice against her.

'Hadn't we better be going, Auntie?' Maggie curtly and reproachfully suggested. 'You know quite well that jam stands a good chance of being ruined.'

'I suppose we had,' Auntie Hamps concurred with a sigh, and rose.

'I shall be able to carry out my plan,' thought Hilda, full of wisdom and triumph. And she saw Edwin owner of the house, with his wild lithographic project scotched. And the realization of her own sagacity, thus exercised on behalf of those she loved, made her glad.

At the same moment, just as Albert was recommencing his flow, the door opened and Edwin entered. He had glimpsed the children in the garden and had come into the house by the back way. There were cries of stupefaction and bliss. Both Albert and Clara were unmistakably startled and flattered. Indeed, several seconds elapsed before Albert could assume the proper grim, casual air. Auntie Hamps rejoiced and sat down again. Maggie disclosed no feeling, and she would not sit down again. Hilda had a serious qualm. She was obliged to persuade herself that in opening the negotiations for the house she had not committed an enormity. She felt less sagacious and less dominant. Who could have dreamt that Edwin would pop in just then? It was notorious, it was even a subject of complaint, that he never popped in. In reply to inquiries he stammered in his customary hesitating way that he happened to be in the neighbourhood on business and that it had occurred to him, etc. etc. In short, there he was.

'Aren't you coming, Auntie?' Maggie demanded.

'Let me have a look at Edwin, child,' said Auntie Hamps, somewhat nettled. 'How set you are!'

'Then I shall go alone,' said Maggie.

'Yes. But what about this house business?' Albert tried to stop her.

He could not stop her. Finance, houses, rents, were not real to her. She owned but did not possess such things. But the endangered jam was real to her. She did not own it, but she possessed it. She departed.

'What's amiss with her today?' murmured Mrs Hamps. 'I must go too, or I shall be catching it; my word I shall!'

'What house business?' Edwin asked.

'Well,' said Albert, 'I like that! Aren't you trying to buy her house from her? We've just been talking it over.'

Edwin glanced swiftly at Hilda, and Hilda knew from the peculiar constrained, almost shamefaced, expression on his features, that he was extremely annoyed. He gave a little nervous laugh.

'Oh! Have ye?' he muttered.

VI

Although Edwin discussed the purchase of the house quite calmly with Albert, and appeared to regard it as an affair practically settled, Hilda could perceive, from a single gesture of his in the lobby as they were leaving, that his resentment against herself had not been diminished by the smooth course of talking. Nevertheless she was considerably startled by his outburst in the street.

'It's a pity Maggie went off like that,' she said quietly. 'You might have fixed everything up immediately.'

Then it was that he turned on her, glowering angrily:

'Why on earth did you go talking about it without telling me first?' he demanded, furious.

'But it was understood, dear –' She smiled, affecting not to perceive his temper, and thereby aggravating it.

He almost shouted:

'Nothing of the kind! Nothing of the kind!'

'Maggie was there. I just happened to mention it.' Hilda was still quite placid.

'You went down on purpose to tell her, so you needn't deny it. Do you take me for a fool?'

Her placidity was undiminished.

'Of course I don't take you for a fool, dear. I assure you I hadn't the slightest idea you'd be annoyed.'

'Yes, you had. I could see it on your face when I came in. Don't try to stuff me up. You go blundering into a thing without the least notion – without the least notion! I've told you before, and I tell you again – I won't have you interfering in my business affairs. You know nothing of business. You'll make my life impossible. All you women are the same. You will poke your noses in. There'll have to be a clear understanding between you and me on one or two points, before we go much further.'

'But you told me I could mention it to her.'

'No, I didn't.'

'You did, Edwin. Do be just.'

'I didn't say you could go and plunge right into it at once.

These things have to be thought out. Houses aren't bought like that. A house isn't a pound of tea, and it isn't a hat.'

'I'm very sorry.'

'No, you aren't. And you know jolly well you aren't. Your scheme was simply to tie my hands.'

She knew the truth of this, and her smile became queer. Nevertheless the amiable calm which she maintained astonished even herself. She was not happy, but certainly she was not unhappy. She had got, or she was going to get, what she wanted; and here was the only fact important to her; the means by which she had got it, or was going to get it, were negligible now. It cost her very little to be magnanimous. She wondered at Edwin. Was this furious brute the timid worshipping boy who had so marvellously kissed her a dozen years earlier – before she had fallen into the hands of a scoundrel? Were these scenes what the exquisite romance of marriage had come to? . . . Well, and if it was so, what then? If she was not happy she was elated, and she was philosophic, and she had the terrific sense of realities of some of her sex. She was out of the Benbow house, she breathed free, she had triumphed, and she had her man to herself. He might be a brute – the Five Towns (she had noticed as a returned exile) were full of brutes whose passions surged and boiled, beneath the phlegmatic surface – but he existed, and their love existed. And a peep into the depth of the cauldron was exciting . . . The injustice or the justice of his behaviour did not make a live question.

Moreover, she did not in truth seriously regard him as a brute. She regarded him as an unreasonable creature, something like a baby, to be humoured in the inessentials of a matter of which the essentials were now definitely in her favour. His taunt that she went blundering into a thing, and that she knew naught of business, amused her. She knew her own business, and knew it profoundly. The actual situation was a proof of that. As for abstract principles of business, the conventions and etiquette of it, her lips condescendingly curled. After all, what had she done to merit this fury? Nothing! Nothing! What could it matter whether the negotiations were begun instantly or in a week's or a month's time? (Edwin would have dilly-dallied probably for three months or six.) She had merely said a few harmless words, offered a suggestion. And now he desired to tear her limb from limb and eat her alive. It was comical! Impossible for her to be angry, in her triumph! It was too comical! She had married an astounding personage . . . But she *had* married him. He was hers. She exulted in the possession of him. His absurd peculiarities did not lower him in her esteem. She had a perfect appreciation of his points, including his general wisdom. But she was convinced that she had a special and different and superior kind of wisdom.

'And a nice thing you've let Maggie in for!' Edwin broke out afresh after a spell of silent walking.

'Let Maggie in for?' she exclaimed lightly.

'Albert ought never to have known anything of it until it was all settled. He will be yarning away to her about how he can use her money for her, and what he gets hold of she'll never see again, – you may bet your boots on that. If you'd left it to me I could have fixed things up for her in advance. But no! *In* you must go! Up to the neck! And ruin everything!'

'Oh!' she said reassuringly. 'You'll be able to look after Maggie all right.'

He sniffed, and settled down into embittered disgust, quickening somewhat his speed up the slope of Acre Lane.

'Please don't walk so fast, Edwin,' she breathed, just like a nice little girl. 'I can't keep up with you.'

In spite of his enormous anger he could not refuse such a request. She was getting the better of him again. He knew it; he could see through the devices. With an irritated swing of his body he slowed down to suit her.

She had a glimpse of his set, gloomy, savage, ruthless face, the lower lip bulging out. Really it was grotesque! Were they grown up, he and she? She smiled almost self-consciously, fearing that passers-by might notice his preposterous condition. All the way up Acre Lane and across by St Luke's Churchyard into Trafalgar Road they walked thus side by side in silence. By strange good luck they did not meet a single acquaintance, and as Edwin had a latchkey, no servant had to come and open the door and behold them.

Edwin, throwing his hat on the stand, ran immediately up-stairs. Hilda passed idly into the drawing-room. She was glad to be in her own drawing-room again. It was a distinguished apartment, after Clara's. There lay the Dvorak music on the piano . . . The atmosphere seemed full of ozone. She rang for Ada and spoke to her with charming friendliness about Master George. Master George had returned from an informal cricket match in the Manor Fields, and was in the garden. Yes, Ada had seen to his school clothes. Everything was in order for the new term shortly to commence. But Master George had received a blow from the cricket ball on his shin, which was black and blue . . . Had Ada done anything to the shin? No, Master George would not let her touch it, but she had been allowed to see it . . . Very well, Ada . . . There was something beatific about the state of being mistress of a house. Without the mistress, the house would simply crumble to pieces.

Hilda went upstairs; she was apprehensive, but her apprehensiveness was agreeable to her . . . No, Edwin was not in the bedroom . . . She could hear him in the bathroom. She tried the door. It was bolted. He always bolted it.

'Edwin!'

'What is it?'

He opened the door. He was in his shirt-sleeves and had just finished with the towel. She entered, and shut the door and bolted it. And then she began to kiss him. She kissed him time after time, on his cheek so damp and fresh.

'Poor dear!' she murmured.

She knew that he could not altogether resist those repeated kisses. They were more effective than the best arguments or the most graceful articulate surrenders. Thus she completed her triumph. But whether the virtue of the kisses lay in their sensuousness or in their sentiment, neither he nor she knew. And she did not care . . . She did not kiss him with abandonment. There was a reserve in her kisses, and in her smile. Indeed she went on kissing him rather sternly. Her glance, when their eyes were very close together, was curious. It seemed to imply: 'We are in love. And we love. I am yours. You are mine. Life is very fine after all. I am a happy woman. But still – *each is for himself in this world*, and that's the bedrock of marriage as of all other institutions.' Her sense of realities again! And she went on kissing, irresistibly.

'Kiss me.'

And he had to kiss her.

Whereupon she softened to him, and abandoned herself to the emanations of his charm, and her lips became almost liquid as she kissed him again; nevertheless there was still a slight reserve in her kisses.

At tea she chattered like a magpie, as the saying is. Between her and George there seemed to be a secret instinctive understanding that Edwin had to be humoured, enlivened, drawn into talk, – for although he had kissed her, his mood was yet by no means restored to the normal. He would have liked to remain, majestic, within the tent of his soul. But they were too clever for him. Then, to achieve his discomfiture, entered Johnnie Orgreave, with a suggestion that they should all four – Edwin, Hilda, Janet, and himself – go to the theatre at Hanbridge that night. Hilda accepted the idea instantly. Since her marriage, her appetite for pleasure had developed enormously. At moments she was positively greedy for pleasure. She was incapable of being bored at the theatre, she would sooner be in the theatre of a night than out of it.

'Oh! Do let's go!' she cried.

Edwin did not want to go, but he had to concur. He did not want to be pleasant to Johnnie Orgreave or to anybody, but he had to be pleasant.

'Be on the first car that goes up after seven-fifteen,' said Johnnie as he was departing.

'You understand, Teddy? The first car that goes up after seven-fifteen.'

'All right! All right!'

Blithely Hilda went to beautify herself. And when she had beautified herself and made herself into a queen of whom the haughtiest master-printer might be proud, she despatched Ada for Master George. And Master George had to come to her bedroom.

'Let me look at that leg,' she said. 'Sit down.'

Devious creature! During tea she had not even divulged that she had heard of the damaged shin. Master George was taken by surprise. He sat down. She knelt, and herself unloosed the stocking and exposed the little calf. The place was black and blue, but it had a healthy look.

'It's nothing,' she said.

And then, all in her splendid finery, she kissed the dirty discoloured shin. Strange! He was only two years old and just learning to talk.

'Now then, missis! Here's the tram!' Edwin yelled out loudly, roughly, from below. He would have given a sovereign to see her miss the car, but his inconvenient sense of justice forced him to warn her.

'Coming! Coming!'

She kissed Master George on the mouth eagerly, and George seemed, unusually, to return the eagerness. She ran down the darkening stairs, ecstatic.

In the dusky road, Edwin curtly signalled to the vast ascending steam-car, and it stopped. That was in the old days, when people did what they liked with the cars, stopping them here and stopping them there according to their fancy. The era of electricity and fixed stopping-places, and soulless, conscienceless control from London had not set in. Edwin and Hilda mounted. Two hundred yards farther on the steam-tram was once more arrested, and Johnnie and Janet joined them. Hilda was in the highest spirits. The great affair of the afternoon had not been a quarrel, but an animating experience which, though dangerous, intensified her self-confidence and her zest.

CHAPTER 9

THE WEEK-END

THE events of the portentous week-end which included the musical evening began early on the Saturday, and the first one was a chance word uttered by George.

Breakfast was nearly over in the Clayhanger dining-room. Hilda sat opposite to Edwin, and George between them. They had all eaten with appetite, and the disillusion which usually accompanies the satisfaction of desire was upon them. They had looked forward to breakfast, scenting with zest its pleasing odours, and breakfast was over, save perhaps for a final unnecessary piece of toast or half a cup of chilled coffee.

Hilda did not want to move, because she did not care for the Saturday morning task of shopping and revictualling and being bland with fellow shoppers in the emporiums. The house doors were too frequently open on Saturday mornings, and errand-boys thereat, and a wind blowing through the house, and it was the morning for specially cleaning the hall – detestable and damp operation – and servants seemed loose on Saturday morning, and dinner was apt to be late. But Hilda knew she would have to move. To postpone was only to aggravate. Destiny grasped her firm. George was not keen about moving, because he had no plan of campaign; the desolating prospect of resuming school on Monday had withered his energy; he was in a mood to be either a martyr or a villain. Edwin was lazily sardonic, partly because the leisure of breakfast was at an end, partly because he hated the wage-paying slackness of Saturday morning at the shop, and partly because his relations with Hilda had remained indefinite and disquieting, despite a thousand mutual urbanities and thoughtful refinements, and even some caresses. A sense of aimlessness dejected him; and in the central caves of his brain the question was mysteriously stirring: What is the use of all these things – success, dignity, importance, luxury, love, sensuality, order, moral superiority? He foresaw thirty years of breakfasts, with plenty of the finest home-cured bacon and fresh eggs, but no romance.

Before his marriage he used to read the paper honestly and rudely at breakfast. That is to say, he would prop it up squarely in front of him, hiding his sister Maggie, and anyhow ignoring her; and Maggie had to 'like it or lump it'; she probably lumped it. But upon marriage he had become a chevalier; he had nobly decided that it was not correct to put a newspaper between yourself and a woman who had denied you nothing. Nevertheless, his appetite for newspapers being almost equal to his appetite for bacon, he would still take nips at the newspaper during breakfast, hold it in one hand, glance at it, drop it, pick it up, talk amiably while glancing at it, drop it, pick it up again. So long as the newspaper was held aside and did not touch the table, so long as he did not read more than ten lines at a time, he considered that punctilio was satisfied, and that he was not in fact reading the newspaper at all. But towards the end of breakfast, when the last food was disappearing, and he lapped the cream off the news, he would hold the newspaper in both hands – and brazenly and conscientiously read. His chief interest, just then, was political. Like most members of his party, he was endeavouring to decipher the party programme and not succeeding, and he feared for his party and was a little ashamed of it. Grave events had occurred. The substructure of the state was rocking. A newly elected supporter of the Government, unaware that he was being admitted to the best club in London, had gone to the House of Commons in a tweed cap and preceded by a brass band. Serious pillars of society knew that the time had come to invest their savings abroad. Edwin, with many another ardent Liberal, was seeking to persuade himself that everything was all right after all. The domestic atmosphere – Hilda's baffling face, the emptied table, the shadow of business, repletion, early symptoms of indigestion, the sound of a slop-pail in the hall – did not aid him to optimism. In brief, the morning was a fair specimen of a kind of morning that seemed likely to be for him an average morning.

'Can't I leave the table, mother?' asked George discontentedly.

Hilda nodded.

George gave a coarse sound of glee.

'George! . . . That's so unlike you!' his mother frowned.

Instead of going directly towards the door, he must needs pass right round the table, behind the chair of his occupied uncle. As he did so, he scanned the newspaper and read out loudly in passing for the benefit of the room:

' "Local Divorce case. Etches *v*. Etches. Painful details." '

The words meant nothing to George. They had happened to catch his eye. He read them as he might have read an extract from the books of Euclid, and noisily and ostentatiously departed, not without a further protest from Hilda.

And Edwin and Hilda, left alone together, were self-conscious.

'Lively kid!' murmured Edwin self-consciously.

And Hilda, self-consciously:

'You never told me that case was on.'

'I didn't know till I saw it here.'

'What's the result?'

'Not finished . . . Here you are, if you want to read it.'

He handed the sheet across the table. Despite his serious interest in politics he had read the report before anything else. Etches *v*. Etches, indeed, surpassed Gladstonian politics as an aid to the dubious prosperity of the very young morning newspaper, which represented the latest and most original attempt to challenge the journalistic monopoly of the afternoon *Staffordshire Signal*. It lived scarcely longer than the divorce case, for the proprietors, though Nonconformists and therefore astute, had failed to foresee that the Five Towns public would not wait for racing results until the next morning.

'Thanks,' Hilda amiably and negligently murmured.

Edwin hummed.

Useless for Hilda to take that casual tone! Useless for Edwin to hum! The unconcealable thought in both their minds was – and each could divine the other's thought, and almost hear its vibration:

'We might end in the divorce court, too.'

Hence their self-consciousness.

The thought was absurd, irrational, indefensible, shocking; it had no father and no mother, it sprang out of naught, but it existed, and it had force enough to make them uncomfortable.

The Etches couple, belonging to the great, numerous, wealthy, and respectable family of Etches, had been married barely a year.

Edwin rose and glanced at his well-tinted fingernails. The pleasant animation of his skin caused by the bath was still perceptible; he could feel it in his back, and it helped his conviction of virtue. He chose a cigarette out of his silver case – a good cigarette, a good case – and lit it, and waved the match into extinction, and puffed out much smoke, and regarded the correctness of the crease in his trousers (the vertical trouser-crease having recently been introduced into the district and insisted on by that tailor and artist and seeker after perfection, Shillitoe), and walked firmly to the door. But the self-consciousness remained.

Just as he reached the door, his wife, gazing at the newspaper, stopped him:

'Edwin.'

'What's up?'

He did not move from the door, and she did not look up from the newspaper.

'Seen your friend Big James this morning?'

Edwin usually went down to business before breakfast, so that his conscience might be free for a leisurely meal at nine o'clock. Big James was the oldest employee in the business. Originally he had been foreman compositor, and was still technically so described, but in fact he was general manager, and Edwin's majestic vicegerent in all the printing-shops. 'Ask Big James' was the watchword of the whole organism.

'No,' said Edwin. 'Why?'

'Oh, nothing! It doesn't matter.'

Edwin had made certain resolutions about his temper, but it seemed to him that such a reply justified annoyance, and he therefore permitted himself to be annoyed, failing to see that serenity is a positive virtue only when there is justification for annoyance. The nincompoop had not even begun to perceive that what is called 'right living' means the acceptance of injustice and the excusing of the inexcusable.

'Now then,' he said brusquely. 'Out with it.' But there was still a trace of rough tolerance in his voice.

'No. It's all right. I was wrong to mention it.'

Her admission of sin did not in the least placate him.

He advanced towards the table.

'You haven't mentioned it,' he said stiffly.

Their eyes met, as Hilda's quitted the newspaper. He could not read hers. She seemed very calm. He thought as he looked at her: 'How strange it is that I should be living with this woman! What is she to me? What do I know of her?'

She said with tranquillity:

'If you do see Big James you might tell him not to trouble himself about that programme.'

'Programme? What programme?' he asked, startled.

'Oh, Edwin!' she gave a little laugh. 'The musical-evening programme, of course. Aren't we having a musical evening to-morrow night?'

More justification for annoyance! Why should she confuse the situation by pretending that he had forgotten the musical evening? The pretence was idiotic, deceiving no one. The musical evening was constantly being mentioned. Reports of assiduous practising had reached them; and on the previous night they had had quite a subdued altercation over a proposal of Hilda's for altering the furniture in the drawing-room.

'This is the first I've heard of any programme,' said Edwin. 'Do you mean a printed programme?'

Of course she could mean nothing else. He was absolutely staggered at the idea that she had been down to his works, without a word to him, and given orders to Big James, or even talked to Big James, about a programme. She had no remorse. She had no sense of danger. Had she the slightest conception of what business was? Imagine Maggie attempting such a thing! It was simply not conceivable. A wife going to her husband's works, and behind his back giving orders –! It was as though a natural law had suspended its force.

'Why, Edwin,' she said in extremely clear, somewhat surprised, and gently benevolent accents. 'Whatever's the matter with you? There *is* a programme of music, I suppose?' (There she was, ridiculously changing the meaning of the word programme! What infantile tactics!) 'It occurred to me all of a sudden yesterday afternoon how nice it would be to have it printed on gilt-edged cards, so I ran down to the shop, but you weren't there. So I saw Big James.'

'You never said anything to me about it last night, nor this morning.'

'Didn't I? . . . Well, I forgot.'

Grotesque creature!

'Well, what did Big James say?'

'Oh! Don't ask me. But if he treats all your customers as he treated me . . . However, it doesn't matter now. I shall write the programme out myself.'

'What did he say?'

'It wasn't what he said . . . But he's very rude, you know. Other people think so too.'

'What other people?'

'Oh! Never mind who! Of course, *I* know how to take it. And I know you believe in him blindly. But his airs are preposterous. And he's a dirty old man. And I say, Edwin, seeing how very particular you are about things at home, you really ought to see that the front shop is kept cleaner. It's no affair of mine, and I never interfere, – but really . . .!'

Not a phrase of this speech but what was highly and deliberately provocative. Assuredly no other person had ever said that Big James was rude. (But *had* someone else said so, after all? Suppose, challenged, she gave a name!) Big James's airs were not preposterous; he was merely old and dignified. His apron and hands were dirty, naturally . . . And then the implication that Big James was a fraud, and that he, Edwin, was simpleton enough to be victimized by the fraud, while the great all-seeing Hilda exposed it at a single glance! And the implication that he, Edwin, was fussy at home, and negligent at the shop! And the astounding assertion that she never interfered!

He smothered up all his feelings, with difficulty, as a sailor smothers up a lowered sail in a high wind, and merely demanded. for the third time:

'What did Big James say?'

'I was given to understand,' said Hilda roguishly, 'that it was quite, quite, quite impossible. But his majesty would see! ... Well, he needn't "see". I see how wrong I was to suggest it at all.'

Edwin moved away in silence.

'Are you going, Edwin?' she asked innocently.

'Yes,' glumly.

'You haven't kissed me.'

She did not put him to the shame of returning to her. No, she jumped up blithely, radiant. Her make-believe that nothing had happened was maddening. She kissed him lovingly, with a smile, more than once. He did not kiss; he was kissed. Nevertheless, somehow the kissing modified his mental position, and he felt better after it.

'Don't work yourself up, darling,' she counselled him, with kindness and concern, as he went out of the room. 'You know how sensitive you are.' It was a calculated insult, but an insult which had to be ignored. To notice it would have been a grave tactical error.

II

When he reached the shop, he sat down at his old desk in the black-stained cubicle, and spied forth and around for the alleged dust which he would tolerate in business but would not tolerate at home. It was there. He could see places that had obviously not been touched for weeks, withdrawn places where the undisturbed mounds of stock and litter had the eternal character of Roman remains or vestiges of creation. The senior errand-boy was in the shop, snuffling over a blue-paper parcel.

'Boy,' said Edwin. 'What time do you come here in the morning?'

''A'-past seven, sir.'

'Well, on Monday morning you'll be here at seven, and you'll move everything – there and there and there – and sweep and dust properly. This shop's like a pigsty. I believe you never dust anything but the counters.'

He was mild but firm. He knew himself for a just man; yet the fact that he was robbing this boy of half an hour's sleep and probably the boy's mother also, and upsetting the ancient order of the boy's household, did not trouble him, did not even occur to him. For him the boy had no mother and no household, but was a patent self-causing boy that came miraculously into existence on the shop doorstep every morning and achieved annihilation thereon every night.

The boy was a fatalist, but his fatalism had limits, because he well knew that the demand for errand-boys was greater than the supply. Though the limits of his fatalism had not yet been reached, he was scarcely pleased.

'If I come at seven who'll gi' me th' kays, sir?' he demanded rather surlily, wiping his nose on his sleeve.

'I'll see that you have the keys,' said Edwin, with divine assurance, though he had not thought of the difficulty of the keys.

The boy left the shop, his body thrown out of the perpendicular by the weight of the blue-paper parcel.

'*You* ought to keep an eye on this place,' said Edwin quietly to the young man who combined the function of clerk with that of salesman to the rare retail customers. 'I can't see to everything. Here, check these wages for me.' He indicated small piles of money.

'Yes, sir,' said the clerk with self-respect, but admitting the justice of the animadversion.

Edwin seldom had difficulty with his employees. Serious friction was unknown in the establishment.

He went out by the back entrance, thinking:

'It's no affair whatever of hers. Moreover the shop's as clean as shops are, and a damned sight cleaner than most. A shop isn't a drawing-room . . . And now there's the infernal programme.'

He would have liked to bury and forget the matter of the programme. But he could not. His conscience, or her fussiness, would force him to examine into it. These was no doubt that Big James was getting an old man, with peculiar pompous mannerisms and a disposition towards impossibilism. Big James ought to have remembered, in speaking to Hilda, that he was speaking to the wife of his employer. That Hilda should give an order, or even make a request, direct was perhaps unusual, but –

dash it! – you knew what women were, and if that old josser of a bachelor, Big James, didn't know what women were, so much the worse for him. He should just give Big James a hint. He could not have Big James making mischief between himself and Hilda.

But the coward would not go straight to Big James. He went first up to what had come to be called 'the litho room', partly in order to postpone Big James, but partly also because he had quite an affectionate proud interest in the litho room. In Edwin's childhood this room, now stripped and soiled into a workshop, had been the drawing-room of the Clayhanger family; and it still showed the defect which it had always shown; the window was too small and too near the corner of the room. No transformation could render it satisfactory save a change in the window. Old Darius Clayhanger had vaguely talked of altering the window. Edwin had thought seriously of it. But nothing had been done. Edwin was continuing the very policy of his father which had so roused his disdain when he was young: the policy of 'making things do'. Instead of entering upon lithography in a manner bold, logical, and decisive, he had nervously and half-heartedly slithered into it. Thus at the back of the yard was a second-hand 'Newsom' machine in quarters too small for it, and the apparatus for the preliminary polishing of the stones; while up here in the ex-drawing-room were grotesquely mingled the final polishing process and the artistic department.

The artist who drew the designs on the stone was a German, with short fair hair and moustache, a thick neck and a changeless expression. Edwin had surprisingly found him in Hanbridge. He was very skilled in judging the amount of 'work' necessary on the stone to produce a desired result on the paper, and very laborious. Without him the nascent lithographic trade could not have prospered. His wages were extremely moderate, but they were what he had asked, and in exchange for them he gave his existence. Edwin liked to watch him drawing, slavishly, meticulously, endlessly. He was absolutely without imagination, artistic feeling, charm, urbanity, or elasticity of any sort, – a miracle of sheer gruff positiveness. He lived somewhere in Hanbridge, and had once been seen by Edwin on a Sunday afternoon, wheeling a perambulator and smiling at a young *enceinte* woman who held his free arm. An astounding sight, which forced Edwin to adjust his estimates! He grimly called himself an Englishman, and was legally entitled to do so. On this morning he was drawing a ewer and basin, for the illustrated catalogue of an earthenware manufacturer.

'Not a very good light today,' murmured Edwin.

'Eh?'

'Not a very good light.'

'No,' said Karl sourly and indifferently, bent over the stone, and breathing with calm regularity. 'My eyesight is being destroit.'

Behind, a young man in a smock was industriously polishing a stone.

Edwin beheld with pleasure. It was a joy to think that here was the sole lithography in Bursley, and that his own enterprise had started it. Nevertheless he was ashamed too, – ashamed of his hesitations, his half-measures, his timidity, and of Karl's impaired eyesight. There was no reason why he should not build a proper works, and every reason why he should; the operation would be remunerative; it would set an example; it would increase his prestige. He grew resolute. On the day of the party at the Benbows he had been and carefully inspected the plot of land at Shawport, and yesterday he had made a very low offer for it. If the offer was refused, he would raise it. He swore to himself he would have his works.

Then Big James came into the litho room.

'I was seeking ye, sir,' said Big James majestically, with a mysterious expression.

Edwin tried to look at him anew, as it were with Hilda's eyes. Certainly his bigness amounted now to an enormity, for proportionately his girth more than matched his excessive height. His apron descended from the semicircle of his paunch like a vast grey wall. The apron was dirty, this being Saturday, but it was at any rate intact; in old days Big James and others at critical moments of machining used to tear strips off their aprons for machine-rags ... Yes, he was conceivably a grotesque figure, with his spectacles, which did not suit him, his heavy breathing, his mannerisms, and his grandiose air of Atlas supporting the moral world. A woman might be excused for seeing the comic side of him. But surely he was honest and loyal. Surely he was not the adder that Hilda with an intonation had suggested!

'I'm coming,' said Edwin, rather curtly.

He felt just in the humour for putting Big James 'straight'. Still his reply had not been too curt, for to his staff he was the opposite of a bully; he always scorned to take a facial advantage of his power, often tried even to conceal his power in the fiction that the employee was one man and himself merely another. He would be far more devastating to his wife and his sister than to any employee. But at intervals a bad or careless workman had to meet the blaze of his eye and accept the lash of his speech.

'It's about that little job for the mistress, sir,' said Big James in a soft voice, when they were out on the landing.

Edwin gave a start. The ageing man's tones were so eager, so anxiously loyal! His emphasis on the word 'mistress' conveyed so clearly that the mistress was a high and glorious personage to serve whom was an honour and a fearful honour! The ageing man had almost whispered, like a boy, glancing with jealous distrust at the shut door of the room that contained the German.

'Oh!' muttered Edwin, taken aback.

'I set it up myself,' said Big James, and holding his head very high looked down at Edwin under his spectacles.

'Why?' said Edwin cautiously. 'I thought you'd given Mrs Clayhanger the idea it couldn't be done in time?'

'Bless ye, sir! Not if I know it! I intimated to her the situation in which we were placed, with urgent jobs on hand, as in duty bound, sir, she being the mistress. Ye know how slow I am to give a promise, sir. But not to do it – such was not my intention. And as I have said already, sir, I've set it up myself, and here's a rough pull.'

He produced a piece of paper.

Edwin's ancient affection for Big James grew indignant. The old fellow was the very mirror of loyalty. He might be somewhat grotesque and mannered upon occasion, but he was the soul of the Clayhanger business. He had taught Edwin most of what he knew about both typesetting and machining. It seemed not long

since that he used to call Edwin 'young sir', and to enter into
tacit leagues with him against the dangerous obstinacies of his
decaying father. Big James had genuinely admired Darius Clayhanger. Assuredly he admired Darius's son not less. His fidelity
to the dynasty was touching; it was wistful. The order from the
mistress had tremendously excited and flattered him in his secret
heart ... And yet Hilda must call him names, must insinuate
against his superb integrity, must grossly misrepresent his attitude
to herself. Whatever in his pompous old way he might have said,
she could not possibly have mistaken his anxiety to please her.
No, she had given a false account of their interview, – and Edwin
had believed it! Edwin now swerved violently back to his own
original view. He firmly believed Big James against his wife. He
reflected: 'How simple I was to swallow all Hilda said without
confirmation! I might have known!' And that he should think
such a thought shocked him tremendously.

The programme was not satisfactorily set up. Apart from
several mistakes in the spelling of proper names, the thing with
its fancy types, curious centring, and superabundance of full-
stops, resembled more the libretto of a Primitive Methodist Tea-
meeting than a programme of classical music offered to refined
dilettanti on a Sunday night. Though Edwin had endeavoured to
modernize Big James, he had failed. It was perhaps well that he
had failed. For the majority of customers preferred Big James's
taste in printing to Edwin's. He corrected the misspellings and
removed a few full stops, and then said:

'It's all right. But I doubt if Mrs Clayhanger'll care for all
these fancy founts,' implying that it was a pity, of course, that
Big James's fancy founts would not be appreciated at their true
value, but women were women. 'I should almost be inclined to
set it all again in old-face. I'm sure she'd prefer it. Do you mind?'

'With the greatest *of* pleasure, sir,' Big James heartily concurred, looking at his watch. 'But I must be lively.'

He conveyed his immense bulk neatly and importantly down
the narrow stairs.

III

Edwin sat in his cubicle again, his affection for Big James very active. How simple and agreeable it was to be a man among men only! The printing business was an organism fifty times as large as the home, and it worked fifty times more smoothly. No misunderstandings, no secrecies (at any rate among the chief persons concerned), and a general recognition of the principles of justice! Even the errand-boy had understood. And the shop clerk by his tone had admitted that he too was worthy of blame. The blame was not overdone, and commonsense had closed the episode in a moment. And see with what splendid goodwill Big James, despite the intense conservatism of old age, had accepted the wholesale condemnation of his idea of a programme! The relations of men were truly wonderful, when you came to think about it. And to be at business was a relief and even a pleasure. Edwin could not remember having ever before regarded the business as a source of pleasure. A youth, he had gone into it greatly against his will, and by tradition he had supposed himself still to hate it.

Why had Hilda misled him as to Big James? For she had misled him. Yes, she had misled him. What was her motive? What did she think she could gain by it? He was still profoundly disturbed by this deception. 'Why!' he thought, 'I can't trust her! I shall have to be on my guard! I've been in the habit of opening my mouth and swallowing practically everything she says!' His sense of justice very sharply resented her perfidy to Big James. His heart warmed to the defence of the excellent old man. What had she got against Big James? Since the day when the enormous man had first shown her over the printing-shops, before their original betrothal, a decade and more ago, he had never treated her with anything but an elaborate and sincere respect. Was she jealous of him, because of his, Edwin's, expressed confidence in and ancient regard for him, and because Edwin and he had always been good companions? Or had she merely taken a dislike to him, – a physical dislike? Edwin had noticed that some women had a malicious detestation for some old men, especially when the old men had any touch of the grotesque or the pompous . . . Well,

he should defend Big James against her. She should keep her
hands off Big James. His sense of justice was so powerful in that
moment that if he had had to choose between his wife and Big
James he would have chosen Big James.

He came out of the cubicle into the shop, and arranged his
countenance so that the clerk should suppose him to be thinking
in tremendous concentration upon some complex problem of
the business. And simultaneously Hilda passed up Duck Bank
on the way to market. She passed so close to the shop that she
seemed to brush it like a delicious, exciting, and exasperating
menace. If she turned her head she could scarcely fail to see
Edwin near the door of the shop. But she did not turn her head.
She glided up the slope steadily and implacably. And even in the
distance of the street her individuality showed itself mysterious
and strong. He could never decide whether she was beautiful or
not; he felt that she was impressive, and not to be scorned or
ignored. Perhaps she was not beautiful. Certainly she was not
young. She had not the insipidity of the young girl unfulfilled.
Nor did she inspire melancholy like the woman just beyond her
prime. The one was going to be; the other had been. Hilda was.
And she had lived. There was in her none of the detestable
ignorance and innocence that, for Edwin, spoilt the majority of
women. She knew. She was an equal, and a dangerous equal.
Simultaneously he felt that he could crush and kill the little thing,
and that he must beware of the powerful, unscrupulous, inscrutable individuality . . . And she receded still higher up Duck Bank
and then turned round the corner to the Market Place and
vanished. And there was a void.

She would return. As she had receded gradually, so she would
gradually approach the shop again with her delicious, exciting,
exasperating menace. And he had a scheme for running out to
her and with candour inviting her in and explaining to her in
just the right tone of goodwill that loyalty to herself simply
hummed and buzzed in the shop and the printing-works, and that
Big James worshipped her, and that though she was perfect in
sagacity she had really been mistaken about Big James. And he
had a vision of her smiling kindly and frankly upon Big James,
and Big James twisting upon his own axis in joyous pride.

Nothing but goodwill and candour was required to produce this bliss.

But he knew that he would never run out to her and invite her to enter. The enterprise was perilous to the point of being fool-hardy. With a tone, with a hesitation, with an undecipherable pout, she might, she would, render it absurd . . . And then, his pride! . . . At that moment young Alec Batchgrew, perhaps then the town's chief mooncalf, came down Duck Bank in dazzling breeches on a superb grey horse. And Edwin went abruptly back to work lest the noodle should rein in at the shop door and talk to him.

IV

When he returned home, a few minutes before the official hour of one o'clock, he heard women's voices and laughter in the drawing-room. And as he stood in the hall, fingering the thin little parcel of six programmes which he had brought with him, the laughter overcame the voices and then expended itself in shrieks of quite uncontrolled mirth. The drawing-room door was half open. He stepped quietly to it.

The weather, after being thunderous, had cleared, and the part of the drawing-room near the open window was shot with rays of sunshine.

Janet Orgreave, all dressed in white, lay back in an easy-chair; she was laughing and wiping the tears from her eyes. At the piano sat very upright a seemingly rather pert young woman, not laughing, but smiling, with arch sparkling eyes fixed on the others; this was Daisy Marrion, a cousin of Mrs Tom Orgreave, and the next to the last unmarried daughter of a large family up at Hillport. Standing by the piano was a young timid girl of about sixteen, whom Edwin, who had not seen her before, guessed to be Janet's niece, Elaine, eldest daughter of Janet's elder sister in London; Elaine's approaching visit had been announced. These other two, like Janet, were in white. Lastly there was Hilda, in grey, with a black hat, laughing like a child. 'They are all children,' he thought as, unnoticed, he watched them in their bright fragile frocks and hats, and in their excessive gaiety, and

in the strange abandon of their gestures. 'They are a foreign race
encamped among us men. Fancy women of nearly forty giggling
with these girls as Janet and Hilda are giggling!' He felt much
pleasure in the sight. It could not have happened in poor old
Maggie's reign. It was delicious. It was one of the rewards of
existence, for the grace of these creatures was surpassing. But at
the same time it was hysterical and infantile. He thought: 'I've
been taking women too seriously.' And his heart lightened somewhat.

Elaine saw him first. A flush flowed from her cheeks to her
neck. Her body stiffened. She became intensely self-conscious.
She could not speak, but she leaned forward and gazed with a
passion of apprehension at Janet, as if murmuring: 'Look! The
enemy! Take care!' The imploring silent movement was delightful in its gawky ingenuousness.

'Do tell us some more, Daisy,' Hilda implored weakly.

'There is no more,' said Daisy, and then started: 'Oh, Mr
Clayhanger! How long *have* you been there?'

He entered the room, yielding himself, proud, masculine,
acutely aware of his sudden effect on these girls. For even Hilda
was naught but a girl at the moment; and Janet was really a girl,
though the presence of that shy niece, just awaking to her own
body and to the world, made Janet seem old in spite of her slim-
ness and of that smoothness of skin that was due to a tranquil,
kind temperament. The shy niece was enchantingly constrained
upon being introduced to Edwin, whom she was enjoined to call
uncle. Only yesterday she must have been a child. Her marvellously clear complexion could not have been imitated by any aunt
or elder sister.

'And now perhaps you'll tell me what it's all about,' said Edwin.
Hilda replied:

'Janet's called about tennis. It seems they're sick of the new
Hillport Club. I knew they would be. And so next year Janet's
having a private club on her lawn –'

'Bad as it is,' said Janet.

'Where the entire conversation won't be remarks by girls
about other girls' frocks and remarks by men about the rotten
inferiority of other men.'

'This is all very sound,' said Edwin, rather struck by Hilda's epigrammatic quality. 'But what I ask is – what were you laughing at?'

'Oh, nothing!' said Daisy Marrion.

'Very well then,' said Edwin, going to the door and shutting it. 'Nobody leaves this room till I know . . . Now, niece Elaine!'

Elaine went crimson and squirmed on her only recently hidden legs, but she did not speak.

'Tell him, Daisy,' said Janet.

Daisy sat still straighter.

'It was only about Alec Batchgrew, Mr Clayhanger; I suppose you know him?'

Alec was the youngest scion of the great and detested plutocratic family of Batchgrew, – enormously important in his nineteen years.

'Yes, I know him,' said Edwin. 'I saw him on his new grey horse this morning.'

'His 'orse,' Janet corrected. They all began to laugh again loudly.

'He's taken a terrific fancy to Maud, my kiddie sister,' said Daisy. 'She's sixteen. Yesterday afternoon at the tennis club he said to Maud: "Look 'ere. I shall ride through the town tomorrow morning on my 'orse, while you're all marketing. I shan't take any notice of any of the other girls, but if you bow to me I'll take my 'at off to you."' She imitated the Batchgrew intonation.

'That's a good tale,' said Edwin calmly. 'What a cuckoo! He ought to be put in a museum.'

Daisy, made rather nervous by the success of her tale, bent over the piano, and skimmed *pianissimo* and rapidly through the 'Clytie' waltz. Elaine moved her shoulders to the rhythm.

Janet said they must go.

'Here! Hold on a bit!' said Edwin, through the light film of music, and undoing the little parcel he handed one specimen of the programme to Hilda and another to Janet, simultaneously.

'Oh, so my ideas *are* listened to, sometimes!' murmured Hilda, who was, however, pleased.

A malicious and unjust remark, he thought. But the next instant Hilda said in a quite friendly natural tone:

'Janet's going to bring Elaine. And she says Tom says she is to tell you that he's coming whether he's wanted or not. Daisy won't come.'

'Why?' asked Edwin, but quite perfunctorily; he knew that the Marrions were not interested in interesting music, and his design had been to limit the audience to enthusiasts.

'Church,' answered Daisy succinctly.

'Come after church.'

She shook her head.

'And how's the practising?' Edwin inquired from Janet.

'Pretty fair,' said she. 'But not so good as this programme. What swells we are, my word!'

'Hilda's idea,' said Edwin generously. 'Your mother coming?'

'Oh, yes, I think so.'

As the visitors were leaving, Hilda stopped Janet.

'Don't you think it'll be better if we have the piano put over there, and all the chairs together round here, Janet?'

'It might be,' said Janet uncertainly.

Hilda turned sharply to Edwin:

'There! What did I tell you?'

'Well,' he protested good-humouredly, 'what on earth do you expect her to say, when you ask her like that? Anyhow I may announce definitely that I'm not going to have the piano moved. We'll try things as they are, for a start, and then see. Why, if you put all the chairs together over there, the place'll look like a blooming boarding-house.'

The comparison was a failure in tact, which he at once recognized but could not retrieve. Hilda faintly reddened, and the memory of her struggles as manageress of a boarding-house was harshly revived in her.

'Some day I shall try the piano over there,' she said, low.

And Edwin concurred, amiably:

'All right. Some day we'll try it together, just to see what it *is* like.'

The girls, the younger ones still giggling, slipped elegantly out of the house, one after another.

Dinner passed without incident.

V

The next day, Sunday, Edwin had a headache; and it was a bilious headache. Hence he insisted to himself and to everyone that it was not a bilious headache, but just one of those plain headaches which sometimes visit the righteous without cause or excuse; for he would never accept the theory that he had inherited his father's digestive weakness. A liability to colds he would admit, but not on any account a feeble stomach. Hence, further, he was obliged to pretend to eat as usual. George was rather gnat-like that morning, and Hilda was in a susceptible condition, doubtless due to nervousness occasioned by the novel responsibilities of the musical evening – and a Sabbath musical evening at that! After the one o'clock dinner, Edwin lay down on the sofa in the dining-room and read and slept; and when he woke up he felt better, and was sincerely almost persuaded that his headache had not been and was not a bilious headache. He said to himself that a short walk might disperse the headache entirely. He made one or two trifling adjustments in the disposition of the drawing-room furniture – his own disposition of it, and immensely and indubitably superior to that so pertinaciously advocated by Hilda – and then he went out. Neither Hilda nor George was visible. Possibly during his rest they had gone for a walk; they had fits of intimacy.

He walked in the faint September sunshine down Trafalgar Road into the town. Except for a few girls in dowdy finery and a few heavy youths with their black or dark-blue trousers turned up round the ankles far enough to show the white cotton lining, the street was empty. The devout at that hour were either dozing at home or engaged in Sunday school work; thousands of children were concentrated in the hot Sunday schools. As he passed the Bethesda Chapel and school he heard the voices of children addressing the Lord of the Universe in laudatory and intercessory song. Near the Bethesda Chapel, by the Duke of Cambridge Vaults, two men stood waiting, their faces firm in the sure knowledge that within three hours the public houses would again be open. Thick smoke rose from the chimneys of several manufactories and thin smoke from the chimneys of many others. The scheme of a Sunday musical evening in that land presented itself to Edwin as something rash, fantastic, and hopeless, – and yet solacing. Were it known it could excite only hostility, horror, contempt, or an intense bovine indifference; chiefly the last . . . Breathe the name of Chopin in that land! . . .

As he climbed Duck Bank he fumbled in his pocket for his private key of the shop, which he had brought with him; for, not the desire for fresh air, but an acute curiosity as to the answer to his letter to the solicitor to the Hall trustees making an offer for the land at Shawport, had sent him out of the house. Would the offer be accepted or declined, or would a somewhat higher sum be suggested? The reply would have been put into the post on Saturday, and was doubtless then lying in the letter-box within the shop. The whole future seemed to be lying unopened in that letter-box.

He penetrated into his own shop like a thief, for it was not meet for an important tradesman to be seen dallying with business of a Sunday afternoon. As he went into the shutter-darkened interior he thought of Hilda, whom many years earlier he had kissed in that very same shutter-darkened interior one Thursday afternoon. Life appeared incredible to him, and in his wife he could see almost no trace of the girl he had kissed there in the obscure shop. There was a fair quantity of letters in the box. The first one he opened was from a solicitor; not the solicitor to the Hall trustees, but Tom Orgreave, who announced to Edwin Clayhanger, Esquire, dear sir, that his clients, the Palace Porcelain Company of Longshaw, felt compelled to call their creditors together. The Palace Porcelain Company, who had believed in the efficacy of printed advertising matter and expensive catalogues, owed Edwin a hundred and eighty pounds. It was a blow, and the more so in that it was unexpected. 'Did I come messing down here on a Sunday afternoon to receive this sort of news?' he bitterly asked. A moment earlier he had not doubted the solvency of the Palace Porcelain Company; but now he felt that the Company wouldn't pay two shillings in the pound, – perhaps not even that, as there were debenture-holders. The next letter was an acceptance of his offer for the Shawport land. The die was cast, then. The new works would have to be created; litho-

graphy would increase; in the vast new enterprise he would be
hampered by the purchase of Maggie's house; he had just made
a bad debt; and he would have Hilda's capricious opposition to
deal with. He quitted the shop abruptly, locked the door, and
went back home, his mind very active but undirected.

VI

Something unfamiliar in the aspect of the breakfast-room, as
glimpsed through the open door from the hall, drew him within.
Hilda had at last begun to make it into 'her' room. She had
brought an old writing-desk from upstairs and put it between
the fireplace and the window. Edwin thought: 'Doesn't she even
know the light ought to fall over the left shoulder, not over the
right?' Letter-paper and envelopes and even stamps were
visible; and a miscellaneous mass of letters and bills had been
pushed into the space between the flat of the desk and the small
drawers about it. There was also an easy-chair, with a freshly
covered cushion on it; a new hearthrug that Edwin neither
recognized nor approved of; several framed prints, and other
oddments. His own portrait still dominated the mantelpiece, but
it was now flanked by two brass candlesticks. He thought: 'If
she'd asked me, I could have arranged it for her much better
than that.' Nevertheless the idea of her being absolute monarch
of the little room, and expressing her individuality in it and by it,
both pleased and touched him. Nor did he at all resent the fact
that she had executed her plan in secret. She must have been
anxious to get the room finished for the musical evening.

Thence he passed into the drawing-room, – and was thunderstruck. The arrangement of the furniture was utterly changed,
and the resemblance to a boarding-house parlour after all
achieved. The piano had crossed the room; the chairs were
massed together in the most ridiculous way; the sofa was so
placed as to be almost useless. His anger was furious but cold.
The woman had considerable taste in certain directions, but she
simply did not understand the art of fixing up a room, whereas
he did. Each room in the house (save her poor little amateurish
breakfast-room or 'boudoir') had been arranged by himself, even

to small details, – and well arranged. Everyone admitted that
he had a talent for interiors. The house was complete before she
ever saw it, and he had been responsible for it. He was not the
ordinary inexperienced ignorant husband who 'leaves all that
sort of thing to the missis'. Interiors mattered to him; they influenced his daily happiness. The woman had clearly failed to
appreciate the sacredness of the *status quo*. He appreciated it
himself, and never altered anything without consulting her and
definitely announcing his intention to alter. She probably didn't
care a fig for the *status quo*. Her conduct was inexcusable. It
was an attack on vital principles. It was an outrage. Doubtless,
in her scorn for the *status quo*, she imagined that he would
accept the *fait accompli*. She was mistaken. With astounding
energy he set to work to restore the *status quo ante*. The vigour
with which he dragged and pushed an innocent elephantine piano
was marvellous. In less than five minutes not a trace remained
of the *fait accompli*. He thought: 'This is a queer start for a
musical evening!' But he was triumphant, resolute, and remorse-
less. He would show her a thing or two. In particular he would
show that fair play had to be practised in his house. Then,
perceiving that his hands were dirty, and one finger bleeding, he
went majestically, if somewhat breathless, upstairs to the bathroom, and washed with care. In the glass he saw that, despite his
exertions, he was pale. At length he descended, wondering where
she was, where she had hidden herself, who had helped her to
move the furniture, and what exactly the upshot would be. There
could be no doubt that he was in a state of high emotion, in which
unflinching obstinacy was shot through with qualms about disaster.

He revisited the drawing-room to survey his labours. She was
there. Whence she had sprung he knew not. But she was there.
He caught sight of her standing by the window before entering
the room.

When he got into the room he saw that her emotional excitement far surpassed his own. Her lips and her hands were twitching; her nostrils dilated and contracted; tears were in her eyes.

'Edwin,' she exclaimed very passionately, in a thick voice,
quite unlike her usual clear tones, as she surveyed the furniture,
'this is really too much!'

Evidently she thought of nothing but her resentment. No consideration other than her outraged dignity would have affected her demeanour. If a whole regiment of their friends had been watching at the door, her demeanour would not have altered. The bedrock of her nature had been reached.

'It's war, this is!' thought Edwin.

He was afraid; he was even intimidated by her anger; but he did not lose his courage. The determination to fight for himself, and to see the thing through no matter what happened, was not a bit weakened. An inwardly feverish but outwardly calm vindictive desperation possessed him. He and she would soon know who was the stronger.

At the same time he said to himself:

'I was hasty. I ought not to have acted in such a hurry. Before doing anything I ought to have told her quietly that I intended to have the last word as regards furniture in this house. I was within my rights in acting at once, but it wasn't very clever of me, clumsy fool!'

Aloud he said, with a kind of self-conscious snigger:

'What's too much?'

Hilda went on:

'You simply make me look a fool in my own house, before my own son and the servants.'

'You've brought it on yourself,' said he fiercely. 'If you will do these idiotic things you must take the consequences. I told you I didn't want the furniture moved, and immediately my back's turned you go and move it. I won't have it, and so I tell you straight.'

'You're a brute,' she continued, not heeding him, obsessed by her own wound. 'You're a brute!' She said it with terrifying conviction. 'Everybody knows it. Didn't Maggie warn me? You're a brute and a bully. And you do all you can to shame me in my own house. Who'd think I was supposed to be the mistress here? Even in front of my friends you insult me.'

'Don't act like a baby. How do I insult you?'

'Talking about boarding-houses. Do you think Janet and all of them didn't notice it?'

'Well,' he said, 'let this be a lesson to you.'

She hid her face in her hands and sobbed, moving towards the door.

He thought:

'She's beaten. She knows she's got to take it.'

Then he said:

'Do *I* go altering furniture without consulting you? Do *I* do things behind your back? Never!'

'That's no reason why you should try to make me look a fool in my own house. I told Ada how I wanted the furniture, and George and I helped her. And then a moment afterwards you give them contrary orders. What will they think of me? Naturally they'll think I'm not your wife, but your slave. You're a brute.' Her voice rose.

'I didn't give any orders. I haven't seen the damned servants and I haven't seen George.'

She looked up suddenly:

'Then who moved the furniture?'

'I did.'

'Who helped you?'

'Nobody helped me.'

'But I was here only a minute or two since.'

'Well, do you suppose it takes me half a day to move a few sticks of furniture?'

She was impressed by his strength and his swiftness, and apparently silenced; she had thought that the servants had been brought into the affair.

'You ought to know perfectly well,' he proceeded, 'I should never dream of insulting you before the servants. Nobody's more careful of your dignity than I am. I should like to see anybody do anything against your dignity while I'm here.'

She was still sobbing.

'I think you ought to apologize to me,' she blubbered. 'Yes, I really do.'

'Why should I apologize to you? You moved the furniture against my wish. I moved it against yours. That's all. You began. I didn't begin. You want everything your own way. Well, you won't have it.'

She blubbered once more:

'You ought to apologize to me.'

And then she wept hysterically.

He meditated sourly, harshly. He had conquered. The furniture was as he wished, and it would remain so. The enemy was in tears, shamed, humiliated. He had a desire to restore her dignity, partly because she was his wife and partly because he hated to see any human being beaten. Moreover, at the bottom of his heart he had a tremendous regard for appearances, and he felt fears for the musical evening. He could not contemplate the possibility of visitors perceiving that the host and hostess had violently quarrelled. He would have sacrificed almost anything to the social proprieties. And he knew that Hilda would not think of them, or at any rate would not think of them effectively. He did not mind apologizing to her, if an apology would give her satisfaction. He was her superior in moral force, and naught else mattered.

'I don't think I ought to apologize,' he said, with a slight laugh. 'But if you think so I don't mind apologizing. I apologize. There!' He dropped into an easy-chair.

To him it was as if he had said:

'You see what a magnanimous chap I am.'

She tried to conceal her feelings, but she was pleased, flattered, astonished. Her self-respect returned to her rapidly.

'Thank you,' she murmured, and added: 'It was the least you could do.'

At her last words he thought:

'Women are incapable of being magnanimous.'

She moved towards the door.

'Hilda,' he said.

She stopped.

'Come here,' he commanded, with gentle bluffness.

She wavered towards him.

'Come here, I tell you,' he said again.

He drew her down to him, all fluttering and sobbing and wet, and kissed her, kissed her several times; and then, sitting on his knees, she kissed him. But, though she mysteriously signified forgiveness, she could not smile; she was still far too agitated and out of control to be able to smile.

The scene was over. The proprieties of the musical evening
were saved. Her broken body and soul huddled against him were
agreeably wistful to his triumphant manliness. But he had had a
terrible fright. And even now there was a certain mere bravado
in his attitude. In his heart he was thinking:

'By Jove! Has it come to this?'

The responsibilities of the future seemed too complicated,
wearisome, and overwhelming. The earthly career of a bachelor
seemed almost heavenly in its wondrous freedom . . . Etches *v*.
Etches . . . The unexampled creature, so recently the source of
ineffable romance, still sat on his knees, weighing them down.
Suddenly he noticed that his head ached very badly – worse than
it had ached all day.

VII

The Sunday musical evening, beyond its artistic thrills and
emotional quality, proved to be exciting as a social manifestation.
Those present at it felt as must feel Russian conspirators in a
back room of some big grey house of a Petrograd suburb when
the secret printing-press begins to function before their eyes. This
concert of profane harmonies, deliberately planned and pouring
out through open windows to affront the ears of returners from
church and chapel, was considered by its organizers as a remarkable event; and rightly so. The Clayhanger house might have been
a fortress, with the blood-red standard of art and freedom floating
from a pole lashed to its chimney. Of course everybody pretended
to everybody else that the musical evening was a quite ordinary
phenomenon.

It was a success, and a flashing success, yet not unqualified.
The performers – Tertius Ingpen on the piano, on the fiddle, and
on the clarinet, Janet Orgreave on the piano, and very timidly
in a little song by Grieg, Tom Orgreave on the piano, and his
contralto wife in two famous and affecting songs by Schumann
and also on the piano, and Edwin, sick but obstinate, as turner-
over of pages – all did most creditably. The music was given with
ardent sympathy, and in none of it did any marked pause occur
which had not been contemplated by the composer himself. But

abstentions had thinned the women among the audience. Elaine
Hill did not come, and, far more important, Mrs Orgreave did
not come. Her husband, old Osmond Orgreave, had not been
expected, as of late (owing to the swift onset of renal disease,
hitherto treated by him with some contempt) he had declined
absolutely to go out at night; but Edwin had counted on Mrs
Orgreave. She simply sent word that she did not care to leave
her husband, and that Elaine was keeping her company. Disappointment, keen but brief, resulted. Edwin's severe sick
headache was also a drawback. It did, however, lessen the bad
social effect of an altercation between him and Hilda, in which
Edwin's part was attributed to his indisposition. This altercation
arose out of an irresponsible suggestion from somebody that
something else should be played instead of something else. Now,
for Edwin, a programme was a programme, – sacred, to be
executed regardless of every extrinsic consideration. And seeing
that the programme was printed ... ! Edwin negatived the
suggestion instantly, and the most weighty opinion in the room
agreed with him, but Hilda must needs fly out: 'Why not change
it? I'm sure it will be better,' etc. Whereas she could be sure of
nothing of the sort, and was incompetent to offer an opinion.
And she unreasonably and unnecessarily insisted, despite Tertius
Ingpen, and the change was made. It was astounding to Edwin
that, after the shattering scene of the afternoon, she should be so
foolhardy, so careless, so obstinate. But she was. He kept his
resentment neatly in a little drawer in his mind, and glanced at
it now and then. And he thought of Tertius Ingpen's terrible
remark about women at Ingpen's first visit. He said to himself:
'There's a lot in it, no doubt about that.'

At the close of the last item, two of Brahms's Hungarian Dances
for pianoforte duet (played with truly electrifying *brio* by little
wizening Tom Orgreave and his wife), both Tertius Ingpen and
Tom fussed self-consciously about the piano, triumphant, not
knowing what to do next, and each looking rather like a man who
has told a good story, and in the midst of the applause tries to
make out by an affectation of casualness that the story is nothing
at all.

'Of course,' said Tom Orgreave carelessly, and glancing at the ground, as he usually did when speaking, 'fine as those dances are on the piano, I should prefer to hear them with the fiddle.'

'Why?' demanded Ingpen challengingly.

'Because they were written for the fiddle,' said Tom Orgreave with finality.

'Written for the fiddle? Not a bit of it!'

With superiority outwardly unruffled, Tom said:

'Pardon me. Brahms wrote them for Joachim. I've heard him play them.'

'So have I,' said Tertius Ingpen lightly, but scornfully. 'But they were written originally for pianoforte duet, as you played them tonight. Brahms arranged them afterwards for Joachim.'

Tom Orgreave shook under the blow, for in musical knowledge his supremacy had never been challenged in Bleakridge.

'Surely –' he began weakly.

'My dear fellow, it is so,' said Ingpen impatiently.

'Look it up,' said Edwin, with false animation, for his head was thudding. 'George, fetch the encyclopedia B – and J too.'

Delighted, George ran off. He had been examining Johnnie Orgreave's watch, and it was to Johnnie he delivered the encyclopedia amid mock protests from his Uncle Edwin. More than one person had remarked the growing alliance between Johnnie and young George.

But the encyclopedia gave no light.

Then the eldest Swetnam (who had come by invitation at the last moment) said:

'I'm sure Ingpen is right.'

He was not sure, but from the demeanour of the two men he could guess, and he thought he might as well share the glory of Ingpen's triumph.

The next instant Tertius Ingpen was sketching out future musical evenings at which quartets and quintets should be performed. He knew men in the orchestra at the Theatre Royal, Hanbridge; he knew girl violinists who could be drilled, and he was quite certain that he could get a 'cello. From this he went on to part-songs, and in answer to scepticism about local gift for music, said that during his visits of inspection to factories he had heard spontaneous part-singing 'that would knock spots off

the Savoy chorus'. Indeed, since his return to it, Ingpen had
developed some appreciation of certain aspects of his native
district. He said that the kindly common sense with which as an
inspector he was received on pot-banks, surpassed anything in
the whole country.

'Talking of pot-banks, you'll get a letter from me about the
Palace Porcelain Company,' Tom Orgreave lifting his eyebrows
muttered to Edwin with a strange, gloomy constraint.

'I've had it,' said Edwin. 'You've got some nice clients, I must
say.'

In a moment, though Tom said not a word more, the Palace
Porcelain Company was on the carpet, to Edwin's disgust. He
hated to talk about a misfortune. But others beside himself were
interested in the Palace Porcelain Company, and the news of its
failure had boomed mysteriously through the Sabbath air of the
district.

Hilda and Janet were whispering together. And Edwin, gazing
at them, saw in them the giggling tennis-playing children of the
previous day, – specimens of a foreign race encamped among the
men.

Suddenly Hilda turned her head towards the men, and said:

'Of course *Edwin's* been let in!'

It was a reference to the Palace Porcelain Company. How
ungracious! How unnecessary! How unjust! And somehow
Edwin had been fearing it. And that was really why he had not
liked the turn of the conversation, – he had been afraid of one
of her darts!

Useless for Tom Swetnam to say that a number of business-
men quite as keen as Edwin had been 'let in'! From her disdainful silence it appeared that Hilda's conviction of the unusual
simplicity of her husband was impregnable.

'I hear you've got that Shawport land,' said Johnnie Orgreave.
The mystic influences of music seemed to have been overpowered.

'Who told ye?' asked Edwin in a low voice, once more
frightened of Hilda.

'Young Toby Hall. Met him at the Conservative Club last
night.'

But Hilda had heard.

'What land is that?' she demanded curtly.

'"What land is that?"' Johnnie mimicked her. 'It's the land for the new works, missis.'

Hilda threw her shoulders back, glaring at Edwin with a sort of outraged fury. Happily most of the people present were talking among themselves.

'You never told me,' she muttered.

He said:

'I only knew this afternoon.'

Her anger was unmistakable. She was no longer a fluttering feminine wreck on his manly knee.

'Well, good-bye,' said Janet Orgreave startlingly to him. 'Sorry I have to go so soon.'

'You aren't going!' Edwin protested, with unnatural loudness. 'What about the victuals? I shan't touch 'em myself. But they must be consumed. Here! You and I'll lead the way.'

Half playfully he seized her arm. She glanced at Hilda uncertainly.

'Edwin,' said Hilda very curtly and severely, 'don't be so clumsy. Janet has to go at once. Mr Orgreave is very ill – very ill indeed. She only came to oblige us.' Then she passionately kissed Janet.

It was like a thunderclap in the room. Johnnie and Tom confirmed the news. Of the rest only Tom's wife and Hilda knew. Janet had told Hilda before the music began. Osmond Orgreave had been taken ill between five and six in the afternoon. Dr Stirling had gone in at once, and pronounced the attack serious. Everything possible was done; even a nurse was obtained instantly, from the Clowes Hospital by the station. From reasons of sentiment, if from no other, Janet would have stayed at home and foregone the musical evening. But those Orgreaves at home had put their heads together and decided that Janet should still go, because without her the entire musical evening would crumble to naught. Here was the true reason of the absence of Mrs Orgreave and Elaine – both unnecessary to the musical evening. The boys had come, and Tom's wife had come, because, even considered only as an audience, the Orgreave contingent was almost essential to the musical evening. And so Janet, her father's especial favourite and standby, had come, and she had played, and not a word whispered except to Hilda. It was wondrous. It was impressive. All the Orgreaves departed, and the remnant of guests meditated in proud, gratified silence upon the singular fortitude and heroic common sense that distinguished their part of the world. The musical evening was dramatically over, the refreshments being almost wasted.

VIII

Hilda was climbing on to the wooden-seated chair in the hall to put out the light there when she heard a noise behind the closed door of the kitchen, which she had thought to be empty. She went to the door and pushed it violently open. Not only was the gas flaring away in an unauthorized manner, not only were both servants (theoretically in bed) still up, capless and apronless and looking most curious in unrelieved black, but the adventurous and wicked George was surreptitiously with them, flattering them with his aristocratic companionship, and eating blancmange out of a cut-glass dish with a tablespoon. Twice George had been sent to bed. Once the servants had been told to go to bed. The worst of carnivals is that the dregs of the population, such as George, will take advantage of them to rise to the surface and, conscienceless and mischievous, set at defiance the conventions by which society protects itself.

She merely glanced at George; the menace of her eyes was alarming. His lower lip fell; he put down the dish and spoon, and slunk timorously past her on his way upstairs.

Then she said to the servants:

'You ought to be ashamed of yourselves, encouraging him! Go to bed at once.' And as they began nervously to handle the things on the table, she added, more imperiously: 'At once! Don't keep me waiting. I'll see to all this.'

And they followed George meekly.

She gazed in disgust at the general litter of broken refreshments, symbolizing the traditional inefficiency of servants, and extinguished the gas.

The three criminals were somewhat the victims of her secret resentment against Edwin, who, a mere martyrized perambulating stomach, had retired. Edwin had defeated her in the afternoon; and all the evening, in the disposition of the furniture, the evidence of his victory had confronted her. By prompt and brutal action, uncharacteristic of him and therefore mean, he had defeated her. True he had embraced and comforted her tears, but it was the kiss of a conqueror. And then, on the top of that, he had proved his commercial incompetence by making a large bad debt, and his commercial rashness by definitely adopting a scheme of whose extreme danger she was convinced. One part of her mind intellectually knew that he had not wilfully synchronized these events in order to wound her, but another part of her mind felt deeply that he had. She had been staggered by the revelation that he was definitely committed to the project of lithography and the new works. Not one word about the matter had he said to her since their altercation on the night of the reception; and she had imagined that, with his usual indecision, he was allowing it to slide. She scarcely recognized her Edwin. Now she accused him of malicious obstinacy, not understanding that he was involved in the great machine of circumstance and perhaps almost as much surprised as herself at the movement of events. At any rate she was being beaten once more, and her spirit rebelled. Through all the misfortunes previous to her marriage that spirit, if occasionally cowed, had never been broken. She had sat grim and fierce against even bum-bailiffs in her time. Yes, her spirit rebelled, and the fact that others had known about the Shawport land before she knew made her still more mutinous against destiny. She looked round dazed at the situation. What? The mild Edwin defying and crushing her? It was scarcely conceivable. The tension of her nerves from this cause only was extreme. Add to it the strain of the musical evening, intensified by the calamity at the Orgreaves'!

A bell rang in the kitchen, and all the ganglions of her spinal column answered it. Had Edwin rung? No. It was the front door.

'Pardon me,' said Tertius Ingpen when she opened. 'But all my friends soon learn how difficult it is to get rid of me.'

'Come in,' she said, liking his tone, which flattered her by assuming her sense of humour.

'As I'm sleeping at the office tonight, I thought I might as well take one or two of my musical instruments after all. So I came back.'

'You've been round?' she asked, meaning round to the Orgreaves'.

'Yes.'

'What is it, really?'

'Well, it appears to be pericarditis supervening on renal disease. He lost consciousness, you know.'

'Yes, I know. But what is pericarditis?'

'Pericarditis is inflammation of the pericardium.'

'And what's the pericardium?'

They both smiled faintly.

'The pericardium is the membrane that encloses the heart. I don't mind telling you that I've only just acquired this encyclopedic knowledge from Stirling, – he was there.'

'And is it supposed to be very dangerous?'

'I don't know. Doctors never tell you anything except what you can find out for yourself.'

After a little hesitating pause they went into the drawing-room, where the lights were still burning, and the full disorder of the musical evening persisted, including the cigarette-ash on the carpet. Tertius Ingpen picked up his clarinet-case, took out the instrument, examined the mouthpiece lovingly, and with tenderness laid it back.

'Do sit down a moment,' said Hilda, sitting limply down. 'It's stifling, isn't it?'

'Let me open the window,' he suggested politely.

As he returned from the window, he said, pulling his short beard:

'It was wonderful how those Orgreaves went through the musical evening, wasn't it? Makes you proud of being English . . . I suppose Janet's a great friend of yours?'

His enthusiasm touched her, and her pride in Janet quickened to it. She gave a deliberate satisfied nod in reply to his question. She was glad to be alone with him in the silence of the house.

'Ed gone to bed?' he questioned, after another little pause.

Already he was calling her husband Ed, and with an affectionate intonation!

She nodded again.

'He stuck it out jolly well,' said Ingpen, still standing.

'He brings these attacks on himself,' said Hilda, with the calm sententiousness of a good digestion discussing a bad one. She was becoming pleased with herself – with her expensive dress, her position, her philosophy, and her power to hold the full attention of this man.

Ingpen replied, looking steadily at her:

'We bring everything on ourselves.'

Then he smiled as a comrade to another.

She shifted her pose. A desire to discuss Edwin with this man grew in her, for she needed sympathy intensely.

'What do *you* think of this new scheme of his?' she demanded somewhat self-consciously.

'The new works? Seems all right. But I don't know much about it.'

'Well, I'm not so sure.' And she exposed her theory of the entire satisfactoriness of their present situation, of the needlessness of fresh risks, and of Edwin's unsuitability for enterprise. 'Of course he's splendid,' she said. 'But he'll never push. I can look at him quite impartially – I mean in all those things.'

Ingpen murmured as it were dreamily:

'Have you had much experience of business yourself?'

'It depends what you call business. I suppose you know I used to keep a boarding-house?' She was a little defiant.

'No, I didn't know. I may have heard vaguely. Did you make it pay?'

'It did pay in the end.'

'But not at first? . . . Any disasters?'

She could not decide whether she ought to rebuff the cross-examiner or not. His manner was so objective, so disinterested, so innocent, so disarming, that in the end she smiled uncertainly, raising her thick eyebrows.

'Oh, yes,' she said bravely.

'And who came to the rescue?' Ingpen proceeded.

'Edwin did.'

'I see,' said Ingpen, still dreamily.

'I believe you knew all about it,' she remarked, having flushed.

'Pardon me! Almost nothing.'

'Of course you take Edwin's side.'

'Are we talking man to man?' he asked suddenly, in a new tone.

'Most decidedly!' She rose to the challenge.

'Then I'll tell you my leading theory,' he said in a soft, polite voice. 'The proper place for women is the harem.'

'Mr Ingpen!'

'No, no!' he soothed her, but firmly. 'We're talking man to man. I can whisper sweet nothings to you if you prefer it, but I thought we were trying to be honest. I hold a belief. I state it. I may be wrong, but I hold that belief. You can persecute me for my belief if you like. That's your affair. But surely you aren't afraid of an idea! If you don't like the mere word, let's call it *zenana*. Call it the drawing-room and kitchen.'

'So we're to be kept to our sphere?'

'Now don't be resentful. Naturally you're to be kept to your own sphere. If Edwin began dancing around in the kitchen you'd soon begin to talk about *his* sphere. You can't have the advantages of married life for nothing – neither you nor he. But some of you women nowadays seem to expect them gratis. Let me tell you, everything has to be paid for on this particular planet. I'm a bachelor. I've often thought about marrying, of course. I might get married some day. You never know your luck. If I do –'

'You'll keep your wife in the harem, no doubt! And she'll have to accept without daring to say a word all the risks you choose to take.'

'There you are again!' he said. 'This notion that marriage ought to be the end of risks for a woman is astonishingly rife, I find. Very curious! Very curious!' He seemed to address the wall. 'Why, it's the beginning of them. Doesn't the husband take risks?'

'He chooses his own. He doesn't have business risks thrust upon him by his wife.'

'Doesn't he? What about the risk of finding himself tied for life to an inefficient housekeeper? That's a bit of a business risk, isn't it? I've known more than one man let in for it.'

'And you've felt so sorry for him!'

'No, not specially. You must run risks. When you've finished running risks you're dead, and you ought to be buried. If I was a wife I should enjoy running a risk with my husband. I swear I shouldn't want to shut myself up in a glass case with him out of all the draughts! Why, what are we all alive for?'

The idea of the fineness of running risks struck her as original. It challenged her courage, and she began to meditate.

'Yes,' she murmured. 'So you sleep at the office sometimes?'

'A certain elasticity in one's domestic arrangements.' He waved a hand, seeming to pooh-pooh himself lightly. Then, quickly changing his mood, he bent and said good night, but not quite with the saccharine artificiality of his first visit – rather with the honest, friendly sincerity, in which were mingled both thanks and appreciation. Hilda jumped up responsively. And, the clarinet-case under his left arm, and the fiddle-case in his left hand, leaving the right arm free, Ingpen departed.

She did not immediately go to bed. Now that Ingpen was gone she perceived that though she had really said little in opposition to Edwin's scheme, he had at once assumed that she was a strong opponent of it. Hence she must have shown her feelings far too openly at the first mention of the affair before anybody had left. This annoyed her. Also the immense injustice of nearly all Ingpen's argument grew upon her moment by moment. She was conscious of a grudge against him, even while greatly liking him. But she swore that she would never show the grudge, and that he should never suspect it. To the end she would play a man's part in the man-to-man discussion. Moreover her anger against Edwin had not decreased. Nevertheless a sort of zest, perhaps an angry joy, filled her with novel and intoxicating sensations. Let the scheme of the new works go forward! Let it fail! Let it ruin them! She would stand in the breach. She would show the whole world that no ordeal could lower her head. She had had enough of being the odalisque and the queen, reclining on the soft couch of security. Her nostrils scented life on the wind . . . Then she heard a door close upstairs, and began at last rapidly, as it were cruelly, to put out the lights.

IX

The incubus and humiliations of a first-class bilious attack are not eternal. Edwin had not retired very long before the malignant phase of the terrible malady passed inevitably, by phenomena according with all clinical experience, into the next phase. And the patient, who from being chiefly a stomach, had now become chiefly a throbbing head, lay on his pillow exhausted but once more capable of objective thought.

His resentment against his wife on account of her gratuitous disbelief in his business faculty, and on account of her interference in a matter that did not concern her, flickered up into new flame. He was absolutely innocent. She was absolutely guilty; no excuse existed or could be invented for her rude and wounding attitude. He esteemed Tertius Ingpen, bachelor, the most fortunate of men... Women – unjust, dishonourable, unintelligent, unscrupulous, giggling, pleasure-loving! Their appetite for pleasure was infantile and tigerish. He had noticed it growing in Hilda. Previous to marriage he had regarded Hilda as combining the best feminine with the best masculine qualities. In many ways she had exhibited the comforting straightforward characteristics of the male. But since marriage her mental resemblance to a man had diminished daily, and now she was the most feminine woman he had ever met, in the unsatisfactory sense of the word. Women ... Still, the behaviour of Janet and Hilda during the musical evening had been rather heroic. Impossible to dismiss them as being exclusively of the giggling race! They had decided to play a part, and they had played it with impressive fortitude ... And the house of the Orgreaves – was it about to fall? He divined that it was about to fall. No death had so far occurred in the family, which had seemed to be immune through decades and for ever. He wondered what would have happened to the house of Orgreave in six months' time ... Then he went back into the dark origins of his bilious attack ... And then he was at inexcusable Hilda again.

At length he heard her on the landing.

She entered the bedroom, and quickly he shut his eyes. He felt unpleasantly through his eyelids that she had turned up the gas. Then she was close to him, and sat down on the edge of the bed. She asked him a question, calmly, as to occurrences since his retirement. He nodded an affirmative.

'Your forehead's all broken out,' she said, moving away.

In a few moments he was aware of the delicious, soothing, heavenly application to his forehead of a handkerchief drenched in eau-de-Cologne and water. The compress descended upon his forehead with the infinite gentleness of an endearment and the sudden solace of a reprieve. He made faint, inarticulate noises.

The light was extinguished for his ease.

He murmured weakly:

'Are you undressed already?'

'No,' she said quietly. 'I can undress all right in the dark.'

He opened his eyes, and could dimly see her moving darkly about, brushing her hair, casting garments. Then she came towards him, a vague whiteness against the gloom, and, bending, felt for his face, and kissed him. She kissed him with superb and passionate violence; she drew his life out of him, and poured in her own. The tremendous kiss seemed to prove that there is no difference between love and hate. It contained everything – surrender, defiance, anger, and tenderness.

Neither of them spoke. The kiss dominated and assuaged him. Its illogicalness overthrew him. He could never have kissed like that under such circumstances. It was a high and bold gesture. It expressed and transmitted confidence. She had explained nothing, justified nothing, made no charge, asked no forgiveness. She had just confronted him with one unarguable fact. And it was the only fact that mattered. His pessimism about marriage lifted. If his spirit was splendidly romantic enough to match hers, marriage remained a feasible state. And he threw away logic and the past, and in a magic vision saw that success in marriage was an affair of goodwill and the right tone. With the whole force of his heart he determined to succeed in marriage. And in the mighty resolve marriage presented itself to him as really rather easy after all.

CHAPTER 10

THE ORGREAVE CALAMITY

I

ON the following Saturday afternoon – that is, six days later –
Edwin had unusually been down to the shop after dinner, and he
returned home about four o'clock. Ada, hearing his entrance,
came into the hall and said:

'Please, sir, missis is over at Miss Orgreave's and wil l ye please
go over?'

'Where's Master George?'

'In missis's own room, sir.'

'All right.'

The 'mistress's own room' was the new nomenclature adopted
by the kitchen, doubtless under suggestion, for the breakfast-
room or boudoir. Edwin opened the door and glanced in. George,
apparently sketching, sat at his mother's desk, with the light falling
over his right shoulder.

He looked up quickly in self-excuse:

'Mother said I could! Mother said I could!'

For the theory of the special sanctity of the boudoir had
mysteriously established itself in the house during the previous
eight or ten days. George was well aware that even Edwin was not
entitled to go in and out as he chose.

'Keep calm, sonny,' said Edwin, teasing him.

With permissible and discreet curiosity he glanced from afar at
the desk, its upper drawers and its pigeon-holes. Obviously it was
very untidy. Its untidiness gave him sardonic pleasure, because
Hilda was ever implying, or even stating, that she was a very tidy
woman. He remembered that many years ago Janet had mentioned orderliness as a trait of the wonderful girl, Hilda Lessways.
But he did not personally consider that she was tidy; assuredly she
by no means reached his standard of tidiness, which standard
indeed she now and then dismissed as old-maidish. Also, he was

sardonically amused by the air of importance and busyness
which she put on when using the desk and the room; her household accounts, beheld at a distance, were his wicked joy. He saw a
bluish envelope lying untidily on the floor between the desk and
the fireplace, and he picked it up. It had been addressed to 'Mrs
George Cannon, 59 Preston Street, Brighton', and readdressed in
a woman's hand to 'Mrs Clayhanger, Trafalgar Road, Bursley'.
Whether the handwriting of the original address was masculine or
feminine he could not decide. The envelope had probably contained only a bill or a circular. Nevertheless he felt at once inimically inquisitive towards the envelope. Without quite knowing it he
was jealous of all Hilda's past life up to her marriage with him.
After a moment, reflecting that she had made no mention of a
letter, he dropped the envelope superciliously, and it floated to
the ground.

'I'm going to Lane End House,' he said.

'Can I come?'

'No.'

II

The same overhanging spirit of a great event which had somehow
justified him in being curt to the boy, rendered him self-conscious
and furtive as he stood in the porch of the Orgreaves, waiting for
the door to open. Along the drive that curved round the oval
lawn under the high trees were wheel marks still surviving from
the previous day. The house also survived; the curtains in all the
windows, and the plants or the pieces of furniture between the
curtains, were exactly as usual. Yet the solid building and its
contents had the air of an illusion.

A servant appeared.

'Good afternoon, Selina.'

He had probably never before called her by name, but today
his self-consciousness impelled him to do uncustomary things.

'Good afternoon, sir,' said Selina, whose changeless attire
ignored even the greatest events. And it was as if she had said:

'Ah, sir! To what have we come!'

She too was self-conscious and furtive.

Aloud she said:

'Miss Orgreave and Mrs Clayhanger are upstairs, sir. I'll tell Miss Orgreave.'

Coughing nervously, he went into the drawing-room, the large obscure room, crowded with old furniture and expensive new furniture, with books, knick-knacks, embroidery, and human history, in which he had first set eyes on Hilda. It was precisely the same as it had been a few days earlier; absolutely nothing had been changed, and yet now it had the archaeological and forlorn aspect of a museum.

He dreaded the appearance of Janet and Hilda. What could he say to Janet, or she to him? But he was a little comforted by the fact that Hilda had left a message for him to join them.

On the previous Tuesday Osmond Orgreave had died, and within twenty-four hours Mrs Orgreave was dead also. On the Friday they were buried together. Today the blinds were up again; the funereal horses with their artificially curved necks had already dragged other corpses to the cemetery; the town existed as usual; and the family of Orgreave was scattered once more. Marian, the eldest daughter, had not been able to come at all, because her husband was seriously ill. Alicia Hesketh, the youngest daughter, far away in her large house in Devonshire, had not been able to come at all, because she was hourly expecting her third child; nor would Harry, her husband, leave her. Charlie, the doctor at Ealing, had only been able to run down for the funeral, because his partner having broken his leg the whole work of the practice was on his shoulders. And today Tom, the solicitor, was in his office exploring the financial side of his father's affairs; Johnnie was in the office of Orgreave and Sons, busy with the professional side of his father's affairs; Jimmie, who had made a sinister marriage, was nobody knew precisely where; Tom's wife had done what she could and gone home; Jimmie's wife had never appeared; Elaine, Marian's child, was shopping at Hanbridge for Janet; and Janet remained among her souvenirs. An epoch was finished, and the episode that concluded it, in its strange features and its swiftness, resembled a vast hallucination.

Certain funerals will obsess a whole town. And the funeral of Mr and Mrs Osmond Orgreave might have been expected to do so. Not only had their deaths been almost simultaneous, but they had been preceded by superficially similar symptoms, though the husband had died of pericarditis following renal disease, and the wife of hyperaemia of the lungs following increasingly frequent attacks of bronchial catarrh. The phenomena had been impressive, and rumour had heightened them. Also Osmond Orgreave for half a century had been an important and celebrated figure in the town; architecturally a large portion of the new parts of it was his creation. Yet the funeral had not been one of the town's great feverish funerals. True, the children would have opposed anything spectacular; but had municipal opinion decided against the children, they would have been compelled to yield. Again and again prominent men in the town had as it were bought their funeral processions in advance by the yard – processions in which their families, willing or not, were reduced to the role of stewards.

Tom and Janet, however, had ordained that nobody whatever beyond the family should be invited to the funeral, and there had been no sincere protest from outside.

The fact was that Osmond Orgreave had never related himself to the crowd. He was not a Freemason; he had never been President of the Society for the Prosecution of Felons; he had never held municipal office; he had never pursued any object but the good of his family. He was a particularist. His charm was kept chiefly for his own home. And beneath the cordiality of his more general connections there had always been a subtle reservation – on both sides. He was admired for his cleverness and his distinction, liked where he chose to be liked, but never loved save by his own kin. Further, he had a name for being 'pretty sharp' in business. Clients had had prolonged difficulties with him – Edwin himself among them. The town had made up its mind about Osmond Orgreave, and the verdict, as with most popular verdicts, was roughly just so far as it went, but unjust in its narrowness. The laudatory three quarters of a column in the *Signal* and the briefer effusive notice in the new halfpenny morning paper, both reflected, for those with perceptions delicate enough to understand, the popular verdict. And though Edwin hated long funerals and the hysteria of a public woe, he had nevertheless a sense of disappointment in the circumstances of the final disappearance of Osmond Orgreave.

The two women entered the room, silently. Hilda looked fierce and protective. Janet Orgreave, pale and in black, seemed very thin. She did not speak. She gave a little nod of greeting.

Edwin, scarcely controlling his voice and his eyes, murmured: 'Good afternoon.'

They would not shake hands; the effort would have broken them. All remained standing, uncertainly. Edwin saw before him two girls aged by the accumulation of experience. Janet, though apparently healthy, with her smooth fair skin, was like an old woman in the shell of a young one. Her eyes were dulled, her glance plaintive, her carriage slack. The conscious wish to please had left her, together with her main excuse for being alive. She was over thirty-seven, and more and more during the last ten years she had lived for her parents. She alone among all the children had remained absolutely faithful to them. To them, and to nobody else, she had been essential – a fountain of vigour and brightness and kindliness from which they drew. To see her in the familiar and historic room which she had humanized and illuminated with her very spirit, was heartrending. In a day she had become unnecessary, and shrunk to the unneeded, undesired virgin which in truth she was. She knew it. Everybody knew it. All the waves of passionate sympathy which Hilda and Edwin in their different ways ardently directed towards her broke in vain upon that fact.

Edwin thought:

'And only the other day she was keen on tennis!'

'Edwin,' said Hilda, 'don't you think she ought to come across to our place for a bit? I'm sure it would be better for her not to sleep here.'

'Most decidedly,' Edwin answered, only too glad to agree heartily with his wife.

'But Johnnie?' Janet objected.

'Pooh! Surely he can stay at Tom's.'

'And Elaine?'

'She can come with you. Heaps of room for two.'

'I couldn't leave the servants all alone. I really couldn't. They wouldn't like it,' Janet persisted. 'Moreover, I've got to give them notice.'

Edwin had to make the motion of swallowing.

'Well,' said Hilda obstinately, 'come along now for the evening, anyhow. We shall be by ourselves.'

'Yes, you must,' said Edwin curtly.

'I – I don't like walking down the street,' Janet faltered, blushing.

'You needn't. You can get over the wall,' said Edwin.

'Of course you can,' Hilda concurred. 'Just as you are now. I'll tell Selina.'

She left the room with decision, and the next instant returned with a telegram in her hand.

'Open it, please. I can't,' said Janet.

Hilda read:

'Mother and boy both doing splendidly. – HARRY.'

Janet dropped on to a chair and burst into tears.

'I'm so glad. I'm so glad,' she spluttered. 'I can't help it.'

Then she jumped up, wiped her eyes, and smiled.

For a few yards the Clayhanger and the Orgreave properties were contiguous, and separated by a fairly new wall, which, after much procrastination on the part of owners, had at last replaced an unsatisfactory thorn hedge. While Selina put a chair in position for the ladies to stand on as a preliminary to climbing the wall, Edwin suddenly remembered that in the days of the untidy thorn hedge Janet had climbed a pair of steps in order to surmount the hedge and visit his garden. He saw her balanced on the steps, and smiling and then jumping, like a child. Now, he preceded her and Hilda on to the wall, and they climbed carefully, and when they were all up Selina handed him the chair and he dropped it on his own side of the wall so that they might descend more easily.

'Be careful, Edwin. Be careful,' cried Hilda, neither pleasantly nor unpleasantly.

And as he tried to read her mood in her voice, the mysterious and changeful ever-flowing undercurrent of their joint life bore rushingly away his sense of Janet's tragedy; and he knew that no events exterior to his marriage could ever overcome for long that constant secret preoccupation of his concerning Hilda's mood.

III

When they came into the house, Ada met them with zest and calamity in her whispering voice:

'Please'm, Mr and Mrs Benbow are here. They're in the drawing-room. They said they'd wait a bit to see if you came back.'

Ada had foreseen that, whatever their superficially indifferent demeanour as members of the powerful ruling caste, her master and mistress would be struck all of a heap by this piece of news. And they were. For the Benbows did not pay chance calls; in the arrangement of their lives every act was neatly planned and fore-ordained. Therefore this call was formal, and behind it was an intention.

'*I* can't see them. I can't possibly, dear,' Janet murmured, as it were intimidated. 'I'll run back home.'

Hilda replied with benevolent firmness:

'No, you won't. Come upstairs with me till they're gone. Edwin, you go and see what they're after.'

Janet faltered and obeyed, and the two women crept swiftly upstairs. They might have been executing a strategic retirement from a bad smell. The instinctive movement, and the manner, were a judgement on the ideals of the Benbows so terrible and final that even the Benbows, could they have seen it, must have winced and doubted for a moment their own moral perfection. It came to this, that the stricken fled from their presence.

'"What they're after"!' Edwin muttered to himself, half-resenting the phrase; because Clara was his sister; and though she bored and exasperated him, he could not class her with exactly similar boring and exasperating women.

And, throwing down his cap, he went with false casual welcoming into the drawing-room.

Young Bert Benbow, prodigiously solemn and uncomfortable in his birthday spectacles, was with his father and mother. Immense satisfaction, tempered by a slight nervousness, gleamed in the eyes of the parents, and the demeanour of all three showed instantly that the occasion was ceremonious. Albert and Clara could not have been more pleased and uplifted had the occasion been a mourning visit of commiseration or even a funeral.

The washed and brushed schoolboy, preoccupied, did not take his share in the greetings with sufficient spontaneity and promptitude.

Clara said, gently shocked:

'Bert, what do you say to your uncle?'

'Good afternoon, uncle.'

'I should think so indeed!'

Clara of course sprang at once to the luscious first topic, as to a fruit:

'How is poor Janet bearing up?'

Edwin was very characteristically of the Five Towns in this – he hated to admit, in the crisis itself, that anything unusual was happening or had just happened. Thus he replied negligently:

'Oh! All right!'

As though his opinion was that Janet had nothing to bear up against.

'I hear it was a *very* quiet funeral,' said Clara, suggesting somehow that there must be something sinister behind the quietness of the funeral.

'Yes,' said Edwin.

'Didn't they ask *you*?'

'No.'

'Well – my word!'

There was a silence, save for faint humming from Albert, and then, just as Clara was mentioning her name, in rushed Hilda.

'What's the matter?' the impulsive Hilda demanded bluntly.

This gambit did not please Edwin, whose instinct was always to pretend that nothing was the matter. He would have maintained as long as anybody that the call was a chance call.

After a few vague exchanges, Clara coughed and said:

'It's really about your George and our Bert ... Haven't you heard? ... Hasn't George said anything?'

'No ... What?'

Clara looked at her husband expectantly, and Albert took the grand male role.

'I gather they had a fight yesterday at school,' said he.

The two boys went to the same school, the new-fangled Higher Grade School at Hanbridge, which had dealt such a blow at the

ancient educational foundations at Oldcastle. That their Bert
should attend the same school as George was secretly a matter of
pride to the Benbows.

'Oh,' said Edwin. 'We've seen no gaping wounds, have we,
Hilda?'

Albert's face did not relax.

'You've only got to look at Bert's chin,' said Clara.

Bert shuffled under the world's sudden gaze. Undeniably there
was a small discoloured lump on his chin.

'I've had it out with Bert,' Albert continued severely. 'I don't
know who was in the wrong – it was about the penknife business,
you know – but I'm quite sure that Bert was not in the right. And
as he's the older we've decided that he must ask George's forgiveness.'

'Yes,' eagerly added Clara, tired of listening. 'Albert says we
can't have quarrels going on like this in the family – they haven't
spoken friendly to each other since that night we were here – and
it's the manly thing for Bert to ask George's forgiveness, and then
they can shake hands.'

'That's what I say.' Albert massively corroborated her.

Edwin thought:

'I suppose these people imagine they're doing something rather
fine.'

Whatever they imagined they were doing, they had made both
Edwin and Hilda sheepish. Either of them would have sacrificed a
vast fortune and the lives of thousands of Sunday-school officers
in order to find a dignified way of ridiculing and crushing the
expedition of Albert and Clara; but they could think of naught
that was effective.

Hilda asked, somewhat curtly, but lamely:

'Where is George?'

'He was in your boudoir a two-three minutes ago, drawing,'
said Edwin.

Clara's neck was elongated at the sound of the word 'boudoir'.

'Boudoir?' said she. And Edwin could in fancy hear her going
down Trafalgar Road and giggling at every house door: 'Did ye
know Mrs Clayhanger has a boudoir? That's the latest.' Still he
had employed the word with intention, out of deliberate bravado.

'Breakfast-room,' he added, explanatory.

'I should suggest,' said Albert, 'that Bert goes to him in the breakfast-room. They'll settle it much better by themselves.' He was very pleased by this last phrase, which proved him a man of the world after all.

'So long as they don't smash too much furniture while they're about it,' murmured Edwin.

'Now, Bert, my boy,' said Albert, in the tone of a father who is also a brother.

And, as Hilda was inactive, Bert stalked forth upon his mission of manliness, smiling awkwardly and blushing. He closed the door after him, and not one of the adults dared to rise and open it.

'Had any luck with missing words lately?' Albert asked, in a detached airy manner, showing that the Bert–George affair was a trifle to him, to be dismissed from the mind at will.

'No,' said Edwin. 'I've been off missing words lately.'

'Of course you have,' Clara agreed with gravity. 'All this must have been very trying to you all ... Albert's done very well of course.'

'I was on "politeness", my boy,' said Albert.

'Didn't you know?' Clara expressed surprise.

'"Politeness"?'

'Sixty-four pounds nineteen shillings per share,' said Albert tremendously.

Edwin appreciatively whistled.

'Had the money?'

'No. Cheques go out on Monday, I believe. Of course,' he added, 'I go in for it scientifically. I leave no chances, I don't. I'm making a capital outlay of over five pounds ten on next week's competition, and I may tell you I shall get it back again, *with* interest.'

At the same moment, Bert re-entered the room.

'He's not there,' said Bert. 'His drawing's there, but he isn't.'

This news was adverse to the cause of manly peace.

'Are you sure?' asked Clara, implying that Bert might not have made a thorough search for George in the boudoir.

Hilda sat grim and silent.

'He may be upstairs,' said the weakly amiable Edwin.

Hilda rang the bell with cold anger.

'Is Master George in the house?' she harshly questioned Ada.

'No'm. He went out a bit since.'

The fact was that George, on hearing from the faithful Ada of the arrival of the Benbows, had retired through the kitchen and through the back door, into the mountainous country towards Bleakridge railway station, where kitefl-ying was practised on immense cinder heaps.

'Ah! Well,' said Albert, undefeated, to Edwin, 'you might tell him Bert's been up specially to apologize to him. Oh, and here's that penknife!' He looked now at Hilda, and producing Tertius Ingpen's knife, he put it with a flourish on the mantelpiece. 'I prefer it to be on your mantelpiece than on ours,' he added, smiling rather grandiosely. His manner as a whole, though compound, indicated with some clearness that while he adhered to his belief in the efficacy of prayer, he could not allow his son to accept from George earthly penknives alleged to have descended from heaven. It was a triumphant hour for Albert Benbow, as he stood there dominating the drawing-room. He perceived that, in addition to silencing and sneaping the elder and richer branch of the family, he was cutting a majestic figure in the eyes of his own son.

In an awful interval, Clara said with a sweet bright smile:

'By the way, Albert, don't forget about what Maggie asked you to ask.'

'Oh, yes! By the way,' said Albert, 'Maggie wants to know how soon you can complete the purchase of this house of yours.'

Edwin moved uneasily.

'I don't know,' he mumbled.

'Can you stump up in a month? Say the end of October anyway, at latest.' Albert persisted, and grew caustic. 'You've only got to sell a few of your famous securities.'

'Certainly. Before the end of October,' Hilda replied, with impulsive and fierce assurance.

Edwin was amazed by this interference on her part. Was she incapable of learning from experience? Let him employ the right tone with absolutely perfect skill, marriage would still be impossible if she meant to carry on in this way! What did she know about the difficulties of completing the purchase? What right had she to put in a word apparently so decisive? Such behaviour was unheard of. She must be mad. Nevertheless he did not yield to anger. He merely said feebly and querulously:

'That's all very well! That's all very well! But I'm not quite so sure as all that. Will she let some of it be on mortgage?'

'No, she won't,' said Albert.

'Why not?'

'Because I've got a new security for the whole amount myself.'

'Oh!'

Edwin glanced at his wife and his resentful eyes said: 'There you are! All through your infernal hurry and cheek Maggie's going to lose eighteen hundred pounds in a rotten investment. I told you Albert would get hold of that money if he heard of it. And just look!'

At this point Albert, who knew fairly well how to draw an advantage from his brother-in-law's characteristic weaknesses, perceived suddenly the value of an immediate departure. And amid loud inquiries of all sorts from Clara, and magnificent generalities from Albert, and gloomy, stiff salutations from uncomfortable Bert, the visit closed.

But destiny lay in wait at the corner of the street for Albert Benbow's pride. Precisely as the Benbows were issuing from the portico, the front door being already closed upon them, the second Swetnam son came swinging down Trafalgar Road. He stopped, raising his hat.

'Hello, Mr Benbow,' he said. 'You've heard the news, I suppose?'

'What about?'

'Missing-word competitions.'

It is a fact that Albert paled.

'What?'

'Injunction in the High Court this morning. All the money's impounded, pending a hearing as to whether the competitions are illegal or not. At the very least half of it will go in costs. It's all over with missing words.'

'Who told you?'

'I've had a wire to stop me from sending in for next week's.'

Albert Benbow gave an oath. His wife ought surely to have been horrorstruck by the word; but she did not blench. Flushing and scowling she said:

'What a shame! We've sent ours in.'

The faithful creature had for days past at odd moments been

assisting her husband in the dictionary and as a clerk . . . And lo! at last, confirmation of those absurd but persistent rumours to the effect that certain busybodies meant if they could to stop missing-word competitions on the ground that they were simply a crude appeal to the famous 'gambling instincts' of mankind and especially of Englishmen! Albert had rebutted the charge with virtuous warmth, insisting on the skill involved in word-choosing, and insisting also on the historical freedom of the institutions of his country. He maintained that it was inconceivable that any English court of justice should ever interfere with a pastime so innocent and so tonic for the tired brain. And though he had had secret fears, and had been disturbed and even hurt by the comments of a religious paper to which he subscribed, he would not waver from his courageous and sensible English attitude. Now the fearful blow had fallen, and Albert knew in his heart that it was heaven's punishment for him. He turned to shut the gate after him, and noticed Bert. It appeared to him that in hearing the paternal oath, Bert had been guilty of a crime, or at least an indiscretion, and he at once began to make Bert suffer.

Meanwhile Swetnam had gone on, to spread the tale which was to bring indignation and affliction into tens of thousands of respectable homes.

IV

Janet came softly and timidly into the drawing-room.

'They are gone?' she questioned. 'I thought I heard the front-door.'

'Yes, thank goodness!' Hilda exclaimed candidly, disdaining the convention (which Edwin still had in respect) that a weakness in family ties should never be referred to, beyond the confines of the family, save in urbane terms of dignity and regret excusing so far as possible the sinner. But in this instance the immense ineptitude of the Benbows had so affected Edwin that, while objecting to his wife's outbreak, he could not help giving a guffaw which supported it. And all the time he kept thinking to himself:

'Imagine that d—d pietistic rascal dragging the miserable shrimp up here to apologize to George!'

He was ashamed, not merely of his relatives, but somehow of all humanity. He could scarcely look even a chair in the face. The Benbows had left behind them desolation, and this desolation affected everything, and could be tasted on the tongue. Janet of course instantly noticed it, and felt that she ought not to witness the shaming of her friends. Moreover, her existence now was chiefly an apology for itself.

She said:

'I really think I ought to go back and see about a meal for Johnnie in case he turns up.'

'Nonsense!' said Hilda sharply. 'With three servants in the house, I suppose Johnnie won't starve! Now just sit down. Sit *down*!' Her tone softened. 'My dear, you're worse than a child . . . Tell Edwin.' She put a cushion behind Janet in the easy-chair. And the gesture made Janet's eyes humid once more.

Edwin had the exciting, disquieting, vitalizing sensation of being shut up in an atmosphere of women. Not two women, but two thousand, seemed to hem him in with their incalculable impulses, standards, inspirations.

'Janet wants to consult you,' Hilda added; and even Hilda appeared to regard him as a strong saviour.

He thought:

'After all, then, I'm not the born idiot she'd like to make out. Now we're getting at her real opinion of me!'

'It's only about father's estate,' said Janet.

'Why? Hasn't he made a will?'

'Oh, yes! He made a will over thirty years ago. He left everything to mother and made her sole executor or whatever you call it. Just like him, wasn't it? . . . D'you know that he and mother never had a quarrel, nor anything near a quarrel?'

'Well,' Edwin, nodding appreciatively, answered with an informed masculine air. 'The law provides for all that. Tom will know. Did your mother make a will?'

'No. Dear thing! She would never have dreamt of it.'

'Then letters of administration will have to be taken out,' said Edwin.

Janet began afresh:

'Father was talking of making a new will two or three months ago. He mentioned it to Tom. He said he should like you to be one of the executors. He said he would sooner have you for an executor than anybody.'

An intense satisfaction permeated Edwin, that he should have been desired as an executor by such an important man as Osmond Orgreave. He felt as though he were receiving compensation for uncounted detractions.

'Really?' said he. 'I expect Tom will take out letters of administration, or Tom and Johnnie together; they'll make better executors than I should.'

'It doesn't seem to make much difference who looks after it and who doesn't,' Hilda sharply interrupted, 'when there's nothing to look after.'

'Nothing to look after?' Edwin repeated.

'Nothing to look after!' said Hilda in a firm and clear tone. 'According to what Janet says.'

'But surely there must be something!'

Janet answered mildly:

'I'm afraid there isn't much.'

It was Hilda who told the tale. The freehold of Lane End House belonged to the estate, but there were first and second mortgages on it, and had been for years. Debts had always beleaguered the Orgreave family. A year ago money had apparently been fairly plentiful, but a great deal had been spent on refurnishing. Jimmie had had money, in connection with his sinister marriage; Charlie had had money in connection with his practice, and Tom had enticed Mr Orgreave into the Palace Porcelain Company. Mr Orgreave had given a guarantee to the bank for an overdraft, in exchange for debentures and shares in that company. The debentures were worthless, and therefore the shares also, and the bank had already given notice under the guarantee. There was an insurance policy – one poor little insurance policy for a thousand pounds – whose capital well invested might produce an income of twelve or fifteen shillings a week; but even that policy was lodged as security for an overdraft on one of Osmond's several private banking accounts. There were many debts, small to middling. The value of the Orgreave architectural connection was excessively dubious, – so much of it had depended upon Osmond Orgreave himself. The estate might prove barely solvent; on the other hand it might prove insolvent; so Johnnie, who had had it from Tom, had told Janet that day, and Janet had told Hilda.

'Your father was let in for the Palace Porcelain Company?' Edwin breathed, with incredulous emphasis on the initial Ps. 'What on earth was Tom thinking of?'

'That's what Johnnie wants to know,' said Janet. 'Johnnie was very angry. They've had some words about it.'

Except for the matter of the Palace Porcelain Company, Edwin was not surprised at the revelations, though he tried to be. The more closely he examined his attitude for years past to the Orgreave household structure, the more clearly he had to admit that a suspicion of secret financial rottenness had never long been absent from his mind – not even at the period of renewed profuseness, a year or two ago, when furniture-dealers, painters, and paperhangers had been enriched. His resentment against the deceased charming Osmond and also against the affectionate and blandly confident mother, was keen and cold. They had existed, morally, on Janet for many years; monopolized her, absorbed her, aged her, worn her out, done everything but finish her, – and they had made no provision for her survival. In addition to being useless, she was defenceless, helpless, penniless, and old; and she shivered now that the warmth of her parents' affection was withdrawn by death.

'You see,' said Janet. 'Father was so transparently honest and generous.'

Edwin said nothing to this sincere outburst.

'Have you got any money at all, Janet?' asked Hilda.

'There's a little household money, and by a miracle I've never spent the ten-pound note poor dad gave me on my last birthday.'

'Well,' said Edwin, sardonically imagining that ten-pound note as a sole defence for Janet against the world. 'Of course Johnnie will have to allow you something out of the business – for one thing.'

'I'm sure he will, if he can,' Janet agreed. 'But he says it's going to be rather tight. He wants us to clear out of the house at once.'

'Take my advice and don't do it,' said Edwin. 'Until the house is let or sold it may as well be occupied by you as stand empty – better in fact because you'll look after it.'

'*That*'s right enough, anyway,' said Hilda, as if to imply that by a marvellous exception a man had for once in a while said something sensible.

'You needn't use all the house,' Edwin proceeded. 'You won't want all the servants.'

'I wish you'd say a word to Johnnie,' breathed Janet.

'I'll say a word to Johnnie, all right,' Edwin answered loudly. 'But it seems to me it's Tom that wants talking to. I can't imagine what he was doing to let your father in for that Palace Porcelain business. It beats me.'

Janet quietly protested:

'I feel sure he thought it was all right.'

'Oh, of course!' said Hilda bitterly. 'Of course! They always do think it's all right. And here's my husband just going into one of those big dangerous affairs, and *he* thinks it's all right, and nothing I can say will stop him from going into it. And he'll keep on thinking it's all right until it's all wrong and we're ruined, and perhaps me left a widow with George.' Her lowered eyes blazed at the carpet.

Janet, troubled, glanced from one to the other, and then, with all the tremendous unconscious persuasive force of her victimhood and her mourning, murmured gently to Edwin:

'Oh! Don't run any risks! Don't run any risks!'

Edwin was staggered by the swift turn of the conversation. Two thousand women hemmed him in more closely than ever. He could do nothing against them except exercise an obstinacy which might be esteemed as merely brutal. They were not accessible to argument – Hilda especially. Argument would be received as an outrage. It would be impossible to convince Hilda that she had taken a mean and disgraceful advantage of him, and that he had every right to resent her behaviour. She was righteousness and injuredness personified. She partook, in that moment, of the victimhood of Janet. And she baffled him.

He bit his lower lip.

'All that's not the business before the meeting,' he said as lightly as he could. 'D'you think if I stepped down now I should catch Johnnie at the office?'

And all the time, while his heart hardened against Hilda, he kept thinking:

'Suppose I *did* come to smash!'

Janet had put a fear in his mind, Janet who in her wistfulness and her desolating ruin seemed to be like only a little pile of dust – all that remained of the magnificent social structure of a united and numerous Orgreave family.

V

Edwin met Tertius Ingpen in the centre of the town outside the offices of Orgreave and Sons, amid the commotion caused by the return of uplifted spectators from a football match in which the team curiously known to the sporting world as 'Bursley Moorthorne' had scored a broken leg and two goals to nil.

'Hello!' Ingpen greeted him. 'I was thinking of looking in at your place tonight.'

'Do!' said Edwin. 'Come up with me now.'

'Can't! . . . Why do these ghastly louts try to walk over you as if they didn't see you?' Then in another tone, very quietly, and nodding in the direction of the Orgreave offices: 'Been in there? . . . What a week, eh! . . . How are things?'

'Bad,' Edwin answered. 'In a word, bad!'

Ingpen lifted his eyebrows.

They turned away out of the crowd, up towards the tranquillity of the Turnhill Road. They were manifestly glad to see each other. Edwin had had a satisfactory interview with Johnnie Orgreave, – satisfactory in the sense that Johnnie had admitted the wisdom of all that Edwin said and promised to act on it.

'I've just been talking to young Johnnie for his own good,' said Edwin.

And in a moment, with eagerness, with that strange, deep satisfaction felt by the carrier of disastrous tidings, he told Ingpen all that he knew of the plight of Janet Orgreave.

'If you ask me,' said he, 'I think it's infamous.'

'Infamous,' Ingpen repeated the word savagely. 'There's no word for it. What'll she do?'

'Well, I suppose she'll have to live with Johnnie.'

'And where will Mrs Chris come in, then?' Ingpen asked in a murmur.

'Mrs Chris Hamson?' exclaimed Edwin, startled. 'Oh! Is that affair still on the carpet? . . . Cheerful outlook!'

Ingpen pulled his beard.

'Anyhow,' said he, 'Johnnie's the most reliable of the crew. Charlie's the most agreeable, but Johnnie's the most reliable. I wouldn't like to count much on Tom, and as for Jimmie, well, of course –!'

'I always look on Johnnie as a kid. Can't help it.'

'There's no law against that, so long as you don't go and blab it out to Mrs Chris,' Ingpen laughed.

'I don't know her.'

'You ought to know her. She's an education, my boy.'

'I've been having a fair amount of education lately,' said Edwin. 'Only this afternoon I was practically told that I ought to give up the idea of my new works because it has risks and the Palace Porcelain Co. was risky and Janet hasn't a cent. See the point?'

He was obliged to talk about the affair, because it was heavily on his mind. A week earlier he had persuaded himself that the success of a marriage depended chiefly on the tone employed to each other by the contracting parties. But in the disturbing scene of the afternoon, his tone had come near perfection, and yet marriage presented itself as even more stupendously difficult than ever. Ingpen's answering words salved and strengthened him. The sensation of being comprehended was delicious. Intimacy progressed.

'I say,' said Edwin, as they parted. 'You'd better not know anything about all this when you come tonight.'

'Right you are, my boy.'

Their friendship seemed once more to be suddenly and surprisingly intensified.

When Edwin returned, Janet had vanished again. Like an animal which fears the hunt and whose shyness nothing can cure, she had fled to cover at the first chance. According to Hilda she had run home because it had occurred to her that she must go through her mother's wardrobe and chest of drawers without a moment's delay.

Edwin's account to his wife of the interview with Johnnie Orgreave was given on a note justifiably triumphant. In brief he had 'talked sense' to Johnnie and Johnnie had been convicted and convinced. Hilda listened with respectful propriety. Edwin said nothing as to his encounter with Tertius Ingpen, partly from prudence and partly from timidity. When Ingpen arrived at the house, much earlier than he might have been expected to arrive, Edwin was upstairs, and on descending he found his wife and his friend chatting in low and intimate voices close together in the drawing-room. The gas had been lighted.

'Here's Mr Ingpen,' said Hilda, announcing a surprise.

'How do, Ingpen?'

'How do, Ed?'

Ingpen did not rise. Nor did they shake hands, but in the Five Towns friends who have reached a certain degree of intimacy proudly omit the ceremony of handshaking when they meet. It was therefore impossible for Hilda to divine that Edwin and Tertius had previously met that day, and apparently Ingpen had not divulged the fact. Edwin felt like a plotter.

The conversation of course never went far away from the subject of the Orgreaves – and Janet in particular. Ingpen's indignation at the negligence which had left Janet in the lurch was more than warm enough to satisfy Hilda, whose grievance against the wicked carelessness of heads of families in general seemed to be approaching expression again. At length she said:

'It's enough to make any woman think seriously of where *she*'d be – if anything happened.'

Ingpen smiled teasingly.

'Now you're getting personal.'

'And what if I am? With my headstrong husband going in for all sorts of schemes!' Hilda's voice was extraordinarily clear and defiant.

Edwin nervously rose.

'I'll just get some cigarettes,' he mumbled.

Hilda and Ingpen scarcely gave him any attention. Already they were exciting themselves. Although he knew that the supply of cigarettes was in the dining-room, he toured half the house before going there; and then lit the gas and with strange deliberation drew the blinds; next he rang the bell for matches, and, having obtained them, lit a cigarette.

When he re-entered the drawing-room, Ingpen was saying with terriffic conviction:

'You're quite wrong, as I've told you before. It's your instinct that's wrong, not your head. Women will do anything to satisfy their instincts, simply anything. They'll ruin your life in order to satisfy their instincts. Yes, even when they know jolly well their instincts are wrong!'

Edwin thought:

'Well, if these two mean to have a row, it's no affair of mine.'

But Hilda, seemingly overfaced, used a very moderate tone to retort:

'You're very outspoken.'

Tertius Ingpen answered firmly:

'I'm only saying aloud what every man thinks . . . Mind – *every* man.'

'And how comes it that *you* know so much about women?'

'I'll tell you some time,' said Ingpen shortly, and then smiled again.

Edwin, advancing, murmured:

'Here. Have a cigarette.'

A few moments later Ingpen was sketching out a Beethoven symphony, unaided, on the piano, and holding his head back to keep the cigarette smoke out of his eyes.

VI

When the hour struck for which Hilda had promised a sandwich supper, Edwin and Tertius Ingpen were alone in the drawing-room, and Ingpen was again at the piano, apparently absorbed in harmonic inventions of his own. No further word had been said upon the subject of the discussion between Ingpen and Hilda. On the whole, despite the reserve of Hilda's demeanour, Edwin considered that marriage at the moment was fairly successful, and the stream of existence running in his favour. At five minutes after the hour, restless, he got up and said:

'I'd better be seeing what's happened to that supper.'

Ingpen nodded, as in a dream.

Edwin glanced into the dining-room, where the complete supper was waiting in illuminated silence and solitude. Then he went to the boudoir. There, the two candlesticks from the mantelpiece had been put side by side on the desk, and the candles lit the figures of Hilda and her son. Hilda, kneeling, held a stamped and addressed letter in her hand, the boy was bent over the desk at his drawing, which his mother regarded. Edwin in his heart affectionately derided them for employing candles when the gas would have been so much more effective; he thought that the use of candles was 'just like' one of Hilda's unforeseeable caprices. But in spite of his secret derision he was strangely affected by the group as revealed by the wavering candle flames in the general darkness of the room. He seldom saw Hilda and George together; neither of them was very expansive; and certainly he had never seen Hilda kneeling by her son's side since a night at the Orgreaves' before her marriage, when George lay in bed unconscious and his spirit hesitated between earth and heaven. He knew that Hilda's love for George had in it something of the savage, but, lacking demonstrations of it, he had been apt to forget its importance in the phenomena of their united existence. Kneeling by her son, Hilda had the look of a girl, and the ingenuousness of her posture touched Edwin. The idea shot through his brain like a star, that life was a marvellous thing.

As the door had been ajar, they scarcely heard him come in. George turned first.

And then Ada was standing at the door.

'Yes'm?'

'Oh! Ada! Just run across with this letter to the pillar, will you?'

'Yes'm.'

'You've missed the post, you know,' said Edwin.

Hilda got up slowly.

'It doesn't matter. Only I want it to be in the post.'

As she gave the letter to Ada he speculated idly as to the address of the letter, and why she wanted it to be in the post. Anyhow, it was characteristic of her to want the thing to be in the post. She would delay writing a letter for days, and then, having written it, be 'on pins' until it was safely taken out of the house; and even when the messenger returned she would ask: 'Did you put that letter in the post?'

Ada had gone.

'What's he drawing, this kid?' asked Edwin genially.

Nobody answered. Standing between his wife and the boy he looked at the paper. The first thing he noticed was some lettering, achieved in an imitation of architect's lettering: '*Plan for proposed new printing works to be erected by Edwin Clayhanger, Esq., upon land at Shawport. George Edwin Clayhanger, Architect.*' And on other parts of the paper, 'Ground-floor plan' and 'Elevation'. The plan at a distance resembled the work of a real architect. Only when closely examined did it reveal itself as a piece of boyish mimicry. The elevation was not finished . . . It was upon this that, with intervals caused by the necessity of escaping from bores, George had been labouring all day. And here was exposed the secret and the result of his chumminess with Johnnie Orgreave. Yet the boy had never said a word to Edwin in explanation of that chumminess; nor had Johnnie himself.

'He's been telling me he's going to be an architect,' said Hilda.

'Is this plan a copy of Johnnie's, or is it his own scheme?' asked Edwin.

'Oh, his own!' Hilda answered, with a rapidity and an earnestness which disclosed all her concealed pride in the boy.

Edwin was thrilled. He pored over the plan, making remarks and putting queries in a dull matter-of-fact tone; but he was so thrilled that he scarcely knew what he was saying or understood the replies to his questions. It seemed to him wondrous, miraculous, overwhelming, that his own disappointed ambition to be an architect should have reflowered in his wife's child who was not his child. He was reconciled to being a printer, and indeed rather liked being a printer, but now all his career presented itself to him as a martyrization. And he passionately swore that such a martyrization should not happen to George. George's ambition should be nourished and forwarded as no boyish ambition had ever been nourished and forwarded before. For a moment he had a genuine conviction that George must be a genius.

Hilda, behind the back of proud, silent George, pulled Edwin's face to hers and kissed it. And as she kissed she gazed at Edwin and her eyes seemed to be saying: 'Have your works; I have yielded. Perhaps it is George's plan that has made me yield, but anyhow I am strong enough to yield. And my strength remains.'

And Edwin thought: 'This woman is unique. What other woman could have done that in just that way?' And in their embrace, intensifying and complicating its significance, were mingled the sensations of their passion, his triumph, her surrender, the mysterious boy's promise, and their grief for Janet's tragedy.

'Old Ingpen's waiting for his supper, you know,' said Edwin tenderly. 'George, you must show that to Mr Ingpen.'

BOOK II
THE PAST

CHAPTER 11

LITHOGRAPHY

I

EDWIN, sitting behind a glazed door with the word 'Private' elaborately patterned on the glass, heard through the open window of his own office the voices of the Benbow children and their mother in the street outside.

'Oh, mother! What a big sign!'

'Yes. Isn't Uncle Edwin a proud man to have such a big sign?'

'Hsh!'

'It wasn't up yesterday.'

'L, i, t, h, o, —'

'My word, Rupy! You are getting on!'

'They're such large letters, aren't they, mother? . . . "Lithographic . . . Lithographic printing. Edwin Clayhanger."'

'Hsh! . . . Bert, how often do you want me to tell you about your shoelace?'

'I wonder if George has come.'

'Mother, can't *I* ring the bell?'

All the children were there, with their screeching voices. Edwin wondered that Rupert should have been brought. Where was the sense of showing a three-year-old infant like Rupert over a printing-works? But Clara was always like that. The difficulty of leaving little Rupert alone at home did not present itself to the august uncle.

Edwin rose, locked a safe that was let into the wall of the room, and dropped the key into his pocket. The fact of the safe being let into the wall gave him as much simple pleasure as any detail of the new works; it was an idea of Johnnie Orgreave's. He put a grey hat carelessly at the back of his head, and, hands in pockets, walked into the next and larger room, which was the clerks' office.

Both these rooms had walls distempered in a green tint, and were fitted and desked in pitch-pine. Their newness was stark, and yet in the clerks' office the irrational habituating processes of time were already at work. On the painted iron mantelpiece lay a dusty white tile, brought as a sample long before the room was finished, and now without the slightest excuse for survival. Nevertheless the perfunctory cleaner lifted the tile on most mornings and dusted underneath it, and replaced it; and Edwin and his staff saw it scores of times daily and never challenged it, and gradually it was acquiring a prescriptive right to exist just where it did. And the day was distant when some inconvenient, reforming person would exclaim:

'What's this old tile doing here?'

What Edwin did notice was that the walls and desks showed marks and even wounds; it seemed to him somehow wrong that the brand new could not remain for ever brand new. He thought he would give a mild reproof or warning to the elder clerk (once the shop clerk in the ancient establishment at the corner of Duck Bank and Wedgwood Street), and then he thought: 'What's the use?' and only murmured:

'I'm not going off the works.'

And he passed out, with his still somewhat gawky gait, to the small entrance hall of the works. On the outer face of the door, which he closed, was painted the word 'Office'. He had meant to have the words 'Counting-house' painted on that door, because they were romantic and fine sounding; but when the moment came to give the order he had quaked before such romance; he was afraid as usual of being sentimental and of 'showing off', and with assumed satire had publicly said: 'Some chaps would stick "Counting-house" as large as life all across the door.' He now regretted his poltroonery. And he regretted sundry other failures in courage connected with the scheme of the works. The works existed, but it looked rather like other new buildings, and not very much like the edifice he had dreamed. It ought to have been grander, more complete, more dashingly expensive, more of an exemplar to the slattern district. He had been (he felt) unduly influenced by the local spirit for half measures. And his life seemed to be a life of half measures, a continual falling short. Once he used to read studiously on Tuesday, Thursday, and Saturday evenings. He seldom read now, and never with regularity. Scarcely a year ago he had formed a beautiful, vague project of being 'musical'. At Hilda's instigation he had bought a book of musical criticism by Hubert Parry, and Hilda had swallowed it in three days, but he had begun it and not finished it. And the musical evenings, after feeble efforts to invigorate them, had fainted and then died on the miserable excuse that circumstances were not entirely favourable to them. And his marriage, so marvellous in its romance during the first days . . .!

Then either his common sense or his self-respect curtly silenced these weak depreciations. He had wanted the woman and he had won her, – he had taken her. There she was, living in his house, bearing his name, spending his money! The world could not get over that fact, and the carper in Edwin's secret soul could not get over it either. He had said that he would have a new works, and, with all its faults and little cowardices, there the new works was! And moreover it had just been assessed for municipal rates at a monstrous figure. He had bought his house (and mortgaged it); he had been stoical to bad debts; he had sold securities – at rather less than they cost him; he had braved his redoubtable wife; and he had got his works! His will, and naught else, was the magic wand that had conjured it into existence.

The black and gold sign that surmounted its blue roofs could be seen from the top of Acre Lane and halfway along Shawport Lane, proclaiming the progress of lithography and steam-printing, and the name of Edwin Clayhanger. Let the borough put that in its pipe and smoke it! He was well aware that the borough felt pride in his works. And he had orders more than sufficient to keep the enterprise handsomely going. Even in the Five Towns initiative seemed to receive its reward.

Life might be as profoundly unsatisfactory as you please, but there was zest in it.

The bell had rung. He opened the main door, and there stood Clara and her brood. And Edwin was the magnificent, wonderful uncle. The children entered, with maternal precautions and recommendations. Every child was clean and spruce: Bert clumsy, Clara minx-like, Amy heavy and benignant, Lucy the pretty little thing, and Rupert simply adorable – each representing a separate and considerable effort of watchful care. The mother came last, worn, still pretty, with a slight dragging movement of the limbs. In her glittering keen eyes were both envy and naïve admiration of her brother. 'What a life!' thought Edwin, meaning what a narrow, stuffy, struggling, conventional, unlovely existence was the Benbows'! He and they lived in different worlds of intelligence. Nevertheless he savoured the surpassing charm of Rupert, the goodness of Amy, the floral elegance of Lucy, and he could appreciate the unending labours of that mother of theirs, malicious though she was. He was bluff and jolly with all of them. The new works being fairly close to the Benbow home, the family had often come *en masse* to witness its gradual mounting, regarding the excursions as a sort of picnic. And now that the imposing place was inaugurated and the signs up, Uncle Edwin had been asked to show them over it in a grand formal visit, and he had amiably consented.

'Has George come, Uncle Edwin?' asked Bert.

George had not come. A reconciliation had occurred between the cousins (though by no means at the time nor in the manner desired by Albert); they were indeed understood by the Benbows to be on the most touching terms of intimacy, which was very satisfactory to the righteousness of Albert and Clara; and George was to have been of the afternoon party; but he had not arrived. Edwin, knowing the unknowableness of George, suspected trouble.

'Machines! Machines!' piped tiny white-frocked Rupert, to whom wondrous tales had been told.

'You'll see machines all right,' said Edwin promisingly. It was not his intention to proceed straight to the machine-room. He would never have admitted it, but his deliberate intention was to display the works dramatically, with the machine-room as a culmination. The truth was, the man was full of secret tricks, contradicting avuncular superior indifference. He was a mere boy – he was almost a school-girl.

He led them through a longish passage, and up steps and down steps – steps which were not yet hallowed, but which would be hallowed – into the stone-polishing shop, which was romantically obscure, with a specially dark corner where a little contraption was revolving all by itself in the process of smoothing a stone. Young Clara stared at the two workmen, while the rest stared at the contraption, and Edwin, feeling ridiculously like a lecturer, mumbled words of exposition. And then next, after climbing some steps, they were in a lofty apartment with a glass roof, sun-shine-drenched and tropical. Here lived two more men, including Karl the German, bent in perspiration over desks, and laboriously drawing. Round about were coloured designs, and stones covered with pencilling, and boards, and all sorts of sheets of paper and cardboard.

'Ooh!' murmured Bert, much impressed by the meticulous cross-hatching of Karl's pencil on a stone.

And Edwin said:

'This is the drawing office.'

'Oh, yes!' murmured Clara vaguely. 'It's very warm, isn't it?'

None of them except Bert was interested. They gazed about dully, uncomprehendingly, absolutely incurious.

'Machines!' Rupert urged again.

'Come on, then,' said Edwin, going out with assumed briskness and gaiety.

At the door stood Tertius Ingpen, preoccupied and alert, with all the mien of a factory inspector in full activity.

'Don't mind me,' said Ingpen. 'I can look after myself In fact, I prefer to.'

At the sight of an important stranger speaking familiarly to Uncle Edwin, all the children save Rupert grew stiff, dismal, and apprehensive, and Clara looked about as though she had sud-denly discovered very interesting phenomena in the corners of the workshop.

'My sister, Mrs Benbow – Mr Ingpen. Mr Ingpen is Her Majesty's Inspector of Factories, so we must mind what we're about,' said Edwin.

Clara gave a bright, quick smile as she limply shook hands. The sinister enchantment which precedes social introduction was broken. And Clara, overcome by the extraordinary chivalry and deference of Ingpen's customary greeting to women, decided that he was a particularly polite man; but she reserved her general judgement on him, having several times heard Albert inveigh against the autocratic unreasonableness of this very inspector, who, according to Albert, forgot that even an employer had to live, and that that which handicapped the employer could not possibly help the workman – 'in the long run'.

'Machines!' Rupert insisted.

They all laughed; the other children laughed suddenly and imitatively, and an instant later than the elders; and Tertius Ingpen, as he grasped the full purport of the remark, laughed more than anyone. He turned sideways and bent slightly in order to give vent to his laughter, which, at first noiseless and imprisoned, gradually grew loud in freedom. When he had recovered, he said thoughtfully, stroking his soft beard:

'Now it would be very interesting to know exactly what that child understands by "machines" – what his mental picture of them is. Very interesting! Has he ever seen any?'

'No,' said Clara.

'Ah! That makes it all the more interesting.' Ingpen added roguishly: 'I suppose you think you *do* know, Mrs Benbow?'

Clara smiled the self-protective, non-committal smile of one who is not certain of having seen the point.

'It's very hot in here, Edwin,' she said, glancing at the door. The family filed out, shepherded by Edwin.

'I'll be back in a sec.,' said he to Clara, on the stairs, and returned to the drawing office.

Ingpen was in apparently close conversation with Karl.

'Yes,' murmured Ingpen, thoughtfully tapping his teeth. 'The whole process is practically a contest between grease and water on the stone.'

'Yes,' said Karl gruffly, but with respect.

And Edwin could almost see the tentacles of Ingpen's mind feeling and tightening round a new subject of knowledge, and greedily possessing it. What a contrast to the vacuous indifference of Clara, who was so narrowed by specialization that she could never apply her brain to anything except the welfare and the aggrandizement of her family! He dwelt sardonically upon the terrible results of family life on the individual, and dreamed of splendid freedoms.

'Mr Clayhanger,' said Ingpen, in his official manner, turning.

The two withdrew to the door. Invisible, at the foot of the stairs, could be heard the family, existing.

'Haven't seen much of lithography, eh?' said Edwin, in a voice discreetly restrained.

Ingpen, ignoring the question, murmured:

'I say, you know, this place is much too hot.'

'Well,' said Edwin. 'What do you expect in August?'

'But what's the object of all that glass roof?'

'I wanted to give 'em plenty of light. At the old shop they hadn't enough, and Karl, the Teuton there, was always grumbling.'

'Why didn't you have some ventilation in the roof?'

'We did think of it. But Johnnie Orgreave said if we did we should never be able to keep it watertight.'

'It certainly isn't right as it is,' said Ingpen, 'and our experience is that these skylighted rooms that are too hot in summer are too cold in winter. How should you like to have your private office in here?'

'Oh!' protested Edwin. 'It isn't so bad as all that.'

Ingpen said quietly:

'I should suggest you think it over – I mean the ventilation.'

'But you don't mean to say that this shop here doesn't comply with your confounded rules?'

Ingpen answered:

'That may or may not be. But we're entitled to make recommendations in any case, and I should like you to think this over, if you don't mind. I haven't any thermometer with me, but I lay it's ninety degrees here, if not more.' In Ingpen's urbane, reasonable tone there was just a hint of the potential might of the whole organized kingdom.

'All serene,' said Edwin, rather ashamed of the temperature after all, and loyally responsive to Ingpen's evident sense of duty, which somehow surprised him; he had not chanced, before, to meet Ingpen at work; earthenware manufactories were inspected once a quarter, but other factories only once a year. The thought of the ameliorating influence that Ingpen must obviously be exerting all day and every day somewhat clashed with and overset his bitter scepticism concerning the real value of departmental administrative government, – a scepticism based less upon experience than upon the persuasive tirades of democratic apostles.

They walked slowly towards the stairs, and Ingpen scribbled in a notebook.

'You seem to take your job seriously,' said Edwin, teasing.

'While I'm at it. Did you imagine that I'd dropped into a sinecure? Considering that I have to keep an eye on three hundred and fifty pot-banks, over a thousand other factories, and over two thousand workshops of sorts, my boy ...! *And* you should see some of 'em. *And* you should listen to the excuses.'

'No wonder,' thought Edwin, 'he hasn't told me what a fine and large factory mine is! ... Still, he might have said something, all the same. Perhaps he will.'

When, after visiting the composing-room, and glancing from afar at the engine-house, the sight-seeing party reached the machine room, Rupert was so affected by the tremendous din and the confusing whir of huge machinery in motion that he began to cry, and, seizing his mother's hand, pressed himself hard against her skirt. The realization of his ambition had overwhelmed him. Amy protectingly took Lucy's hand. Bert and Clara succeeded in being very casual.

In the great lofty room there were five large or fairly large machines, and a number of small ones. The latter had chiefly to do with envelope and bill-head printing and with bookbinding, and only two of them were in use. Of the large machines, three were functioning – the cylinder printing-machine which had been the pride of Edwin's father; the historic 'old machine', also his father's, which had been so called ever since Edwin could remember and which was ageless, and Edwin's latest and most expensive purchase, the 'Smithers' litho-printer. It was on the guarded flank of the 'Smithers', close to the roller racks, that Edwin halted his convoy. The rest of the immense shop, with its complex masses of metal revolving, sliding, or paralysed, its shabby figures of men, boys, and girls shifting mysteriously about, its smell of iron, grease, and humanity, and its fearful racket, was a mere background for the Smithers in its moving might.

The Smithers rose high above the spectators, and at one end of it, higher even than the top parts of the machine, was perched a dirty, frowsy, pretty girl. With a sweeping gesture of her bare arms this girl took a wide sheet of blank paper from a pile of sheets, and lodged it on the receiving rack, whereupon it was whirled off, caught into the clutches of the machine, turned, reversed, hidden away from sight among revolving rollers red and black, and finally thrust out at the other end of the machine, where it was picked up by a dirty, frowsy girl, not pretty, smaller and younger than the high-perched creature, indeed scarcely bigger than Amy. And now on the sheet was printed four times in red the words: 'Knype Mineral Water Mnfg. Co. Best and cheapest. Trade-mark.' Clara screeched a question about the trade-mark, which was so far invisible. Edwin made a sign to the lower dirty, frowsy girl, who respectfully but with extreme rapidity handed him a sheet as it came off the machine, and he shouted through the roar in explanation that the trade-mark, a soda-water syphon in blue, would be printed on the same sheet later from another stone, and the sheets cut into fours, each quarter making a complete poster. 'I thought it must be like that,' replied Clara superiorly. From childhood she had been well accustomed to printing processes, and it was not her intention to be perplexed by 'this lithography'. Edwin made a gesture to hand back the sheet to the machine-girl, but the machine would not pause to allow her to take it. She was the slave of the machine; so long as it functioned, every second of her existence was monopolized, and no variation of conduct permissible. The same law applied to the older girl up near the ceiling. He put the sheet in its place himself, and noticed that to do so required appreciable care and application of the manipulative faculty.

These girls, and the other girls at their greasy task in the great shaking interior which he had created, vaguely worried him. Exactly similar girls were employed in thousands on the pot-banks, and had once been employed also at the pit-heads and even in the pits; but until lately he had not employed girls, nor had his father ever employed girls; and these girls so close to him, so dependent on him, so submissive, so subjugated, so soiled, so vulgar, whose wages would scarcely have kept his wife in boots and gloves, gave rise to strange and disturbing sensations in his heart – not merely in regard to themselves, but in regard to the whole of the work-people. A question obscure and lancinating struck upwards through his industrial triumph and through his importance in the world, a question scarcely articulate, but which seemed to form itself into the words: Is it right?

'Is what right?' his father would have snapped at him. 'Is what right?' would have respectfully demanded Big James, who had now sidled grandiosely to the Smithers, and was fussing among the rollers in the rack. Neither of them would have been capable of comprehending his trouble. To his father an employee was an employee, to be hired as cheaply as possible, and to be exploited as completely as possible. And the attitude of Big James towards the underlings was precisely that of his deceased master. They would not be unduly harsh, they would often be benevolent, but the existence of any problem, and especially any fundamental problem, beyond the direct inter-relation of wages and work could not conceivably have occurred to them. After about three-quarters of a century of taboo, trade unions had now for a dozen years ceased to be regarded as associations of anarchistic criminals. Big James was cautiously in favour of trade unions, and old Darius Clayhanger in late life had not been a quite uncompromising opponent of them. As for Edwin, he had always in secret sympathized with them, and the trade unionists whom he employed had no grievance against him. Yet this unanswerable, persistent question would pierce the complacency of Edwin's prosperity. It seemed to operate in a sort of fourth dimension; few even among trade unionists themselves would have reacted to it. But Edwin lived with it more and more. He was indeed getting used to it. Though he could not answer it, he could parry it, thanks to scientific ideas obtained from Darwin and Spencer, by the reflection that both he and his serfs, whatever their sex, were the almost blind agencies of a vast process of evolution. And this he did, exulting with pride sometimes in the sheer adventure of the affair, and sharing his thoughts with none . . . Strange that once, and not so many years ago either, he had been tempted to sell the business and live inert and ignobly secure on the interest of invested moneys! But even today he felt sudden fears of responsibility; they came and went.

The visitors, having wandered to and fro, staring, trailed out of the machine room, led by Edwin. A wide door swung behind them, and they were in the abrupt, startling peace of another corridor. Clara wiped Rupert's eyes, and he smiled, like a blossom after a storm. The mother and the uncle exchanged awkward glances. They had nothing whatever to say to each other. Edwin could seldom think of anything that he really wanted to say to Clara. The children were very hot and weary of wonders.

'Well,' said Clara, 'I suppose we'd better be moving on now.' She had somewhat the air of a draught animal about to resume the immense labour of dragging a train. 'It's very queer about George. He was to have come with us for tea.'

'Oh! Was he?'

'Of course he was,' Clara replied sharply. 'It was most distinctly arranged.'

At this moment Tertius Ingpen and Hilda appeared together at the other end of the corridor. Hilda's unsmiling face seemed enigmatic. Ingpen was talking with vivacity.

Edwin thought apprehensively:

'What's up now? What's she doing here, and not George?'

And when the sisters-in-law, so strangely contrasting, shook hands, he thought:

'Is it possible that Albert looks on his wife as something unpredictable? Do those two also have moods and altercations, and antagonisms? Are they always preoccupied about what they are thinking of each other? No! It's impossible. Their life must be simply fiendishly monotonous.' And Clara's inferiority before the erect, flashing individuality of Hilda appeared to him despicable. Hilda bent and kissed Rupert, Lucy, Amy, and young Clara, as it were with passion. She was marvellous as she bent over Rupert. She scarcely looked at Edwin. Ingpen stood aside.

'I'm very sorry,' said Hilda perfunctorily. 'I had to send George on an errand to Hanbridge at the last moment.'

Nothing more! No genuine sign of regret! Edwin blamed her severely. 'Send George on an errand to Hanbridge!' That was Hilda all over! Why the devil should she go out of her way to make unpleasantness with Clara? She knew quite well what kind of a woman Clara was, and that the whole of Clara's existence was made up of domestic trifles, each of which was enormous for her.

'Will he be down to tea?' asked Clara.

'I doubt it.'

'Well . . . another day, then.'

Clara, gathering her offspring, took leave at a door in the corridor which gave on to the yard. Mindful to the last of Mr Ingpen's presence (which Hilda apparently now ignored), she smiled sweetly as she went. But behind the smile, Edwin with regret, and Hilda with satisfaction, could perceive her everlasting grudge against their superior splendour. Even had they sunk to indigence Clara could never have forgiven Edwin for having towards the end of their father's life prevented Albert from wheedling a thousand pounds out of old Darius, nor Hilda for her occasional pricking, unanswerable sarcasms . . . Still, Rupert, descending two titanic steps into the yard, clung to his mother as to an angel.

'And *what* errand to Hanbridge?' Edwin asked himself mistrustfully.

II

Scarcely a minute later, when Edwin, with Hilda and Ingpen, was back at the door of the machine room, the office boy could be seen voyaging between roaring machines across the room towards his employer. The office boy made a sign of appeal, and Edwin answered with a curt sign that the office boy was to wait.

'What's that ye say?' Edwin yelled in Ingpen's ear.

Ingpen laughed, and made a trumpet with his hands:

'I was only wondering what your weekly running expenses are.'

Even Ingpen was surprised and impressed by the scene, and Edwin was pleased now, after the flatness of Clara's inspection, that he had specially arranged for two of the machines to be running which strictly need not have been running that afternoon. He had planned a spectacular effect, and it had found a good public.

'Ah!' He hesitated, in reply to Ingpen. Then he saw Hilda's face, and his face showed confusion and he smiled awkwardly.

Hilda had caught Ingpen's question. She said nothing. Her expressive, sarcastic, unappeasable features seemed to say: 'Running expenses! Don't mention them. Can't you see they must be enormous? How can he possibly make this place pay? It's a gigantic folly – and what will be the end of it?'

After all, her secret attitude towards the new enterprise was unchanged. Arguments, facts, figures, persuasions, brutalities had been equally and totally ineffective. And Edwin thought:

'She is the bitterest enemy I have.'

Said Ingpen:

'I like that girl up there on the top of that machine. And doesn't she just know where she is! What a movement of the arms, eh?'

Edwin nodded, appreciative, and then beckoned to the office boy.

'What is it?'

'Please, sir, Mrs 'Amps in the office to see you.'

'All right,' he bawled, casually. But in reality he was taken aback. 'It's Auntie Hamps now!' he said to the other two. 'We shall soon have all Bursley here this afternoon.'

Hilda raised her eyebrows.

'D'you know "Auntie Hamps"?' she grimly asked Ingpen. Her voice, though she scarcely raised it, was plainer than the men's when they shouted. As Ingpen shook his head, she added: 'You ought to.'

Edwin did not altogether care for this public ridicule of a member of the family. Auntie Hamps, though possibly a monster, had her qualities. Hilda, assuming the lead, beckoned with a lift of the head. And Edwin did not care for that either, on his works. Ingpen followed Hilda as though to a menagerie.

Auntie Hamps, in her black attire, which by virtue of its changeless style amounted to a historic uniform, was magnificent in the private office. The three found her standing in wait, tingling with vitality and importance and eagerness. She watched carefully that Edwin shut the door, and kept her eye not only on the door but also on the open window. She received the presentation of Mr Tertius Ingpen with grandeur and with high cordiality, and she could appreciate even better than Clara the polished fealty of his greeting.

'Sit down, Auntie.'

'No, I won't sit down. I thought Clara was here. I told her I might come if I could spare a moment. I must say, Edwin' – she looked around the small office, and seemed to be looking round the whole works in a superb glance – 'you make me proud of you. You make me proud to be your auntie.'

'Well,' said Edwin, 'you can be proud sitting down.'

She smiled. 'No, I won't sit down. I only just popped in to catch Clara. I was going to tea with her and the chicks.' Then she lowered her voice: 'I suppose you've heard about Mr John Orgreave?' Her tone proved, however, that she supposed nothing of the kind.

'No. What about Johnnie?'

'He's run away with Mrs Chris Hamson.'

Her triumph was complete. It was perhaps one of her last triumphs, but it counted among the greatest of her career as a watchdog of society.

The thing was a major event, and the report was convincing. Useless to protest 'Never!' 'Surely not!' 'It can't be true!' It carried truth on its face. Useless to demand sternly: 'Who told you?' The news had reached Auntie Hamps through a curious channel – the stationmaster at Latchett. Heaven alone could say how Auntie Hamps came to have relations with the stationmaster at Latchett. But you might be sure that, if an elopement was to take place from Latchett station, Auntie Hamps would by an instinctive prescience have had relations with the stationmaster for twenty years previously. Latchett was the next station, without the least importance, to Shawport on the line to Crewe. Johnnie Orgreave had got into the train at Shawport, and Mrs Chris had joined it at Latchett, her house being near by. Once on the vast platforms of Crewe, the guilty couple would be safe from curiosity, lost in England, like needles in a haystack.

The Orgreave-Hamson flirtation had been afoot for over two years, but had only been seriously talked about for less than a year. Mrs Chris did not 'move' much in town circles. She was older than Johnnie, but she was one of your blonde, slim, unfruitful women, who under the shade of a suitable hat-brim are ageless. Mr Chris was a heavy man, 'glumpy' as they say down there, a moneymaker in pots, and great on the colonial markets. He made journeys to America and to Australia. His Australian journey occupied usually about four months. He was now on his way back from Sydney, and nearly home. Mrs Chris had not long since inherited a moderate fortune. It must have been the fortune, rendering them independent, that had decided the tragic immoralists to abandon all for love. The time of the abandonment was fixed for them by circumstance, for it had to occur before the husband's return.

Imagine the Orgreave business left in the hands of an incompetent irresponsible like Jimmie Orgreave! And then, what of that martyr, Janet? Janet and Johnnie had been keeping house together – a tiny house. And Janet had had to 'have an operation'. Women, talking together, said exactly what the operation was, but the knowledge was not common. The phrase 'have an operation' was enough in its dread. As a fact the operation, for calculus, was not very serious; it had perfectly succeeded, and Janet, whom Hilda had tenderly visited, was to emerge from the nursing home at Knype Vale within three days. Could not Johnnie and his Mrs Chris have waited until she was re-established? No, for the husband was unpreventibly approaching, and romantic love must not be baulked. Nothing could or should withstand romantic love. Janet had not even been duly warned; Hilda had seen her that very morning, and assuredly she knew nothing then. Perhaps Johnnie would write to her softly from some gay seaside resort where he and his leman were hiding their strong passion. The episode was shocking; it was ruinous. The pair could never return. Even Johnnie alone would never dare to return.

'He was a friend of yours, was he not?' asked Auntie Hamps in bland sorrow of Tertius Ingpen.

He was a friend, and a close friend, of all three of them. And not only had he outraged their feelings – he had shamed them, irretrievably lowered their prestige. They could not look Auntie Hamps in the face. But Auntie Hamps could look them in the face. And her glance, charged with grief and with satisfaction, said: 'How are the mighty fallen, with their jaunty parade of irreligion, and their musical evenings on Sundays, with the windows open while folks are coming home from chapel!' And there could be no retort.

'Another good man ruined by women!' observed Tertius Ingpen, with a sigh, stroking his beard.

Hilda sprang up; and all her passionate sympathy for Janet,

and her disappointment and disgust with Johnnie, the victim of desire, and her dissatisfaction with her husband and her hatred of Auntie Hamps, blazed forth and devastated the unwise Ingpen as she scathingly replied:

'Mr Ingpen, that is a caddish thing to say!'

She despised convention; she was frankly and atrociously rude; and she did not care. Edwin blushed. Tertius Ingpen blushed.

'I'm sorry,' said Ingpen, keeping his temper. 'I think I ought to have left a little earlier. Good-bye Ed. Mrs Hamps –' He bowed with extreme urbanity to the ladies, and departed.

Shortly afterwards Auntie Hamps also departed, saying that she must not be late for tea at dear Clara's. She was secretly panting to disclose the whole situation to dear Clara. What a scene had Clara missed by leaving the works too soon!

CHAPTER 12

DARTMOOR

I

'WHAT was that telegram you had this afternoon, Hilda?'

The question was on Edwin's tongue as he walked up Acre Lane from the works by his wife's side. But it did not achieve utterance. A year had passed since he last walked up Acre Lane with Hilda; and now of course he recalled the anger of that previous promenade. In the interval he had acquired to some extent the habit of containing his curiosity and his criticism. In the interval he had triumphed, but Hilda also had consolidated her position, so that despite the increase of his prestige she was still his equal; she seemed to take strength from him in order to maintain the struggle against him.

During the final half-hour at the works the great, the enormous problem in his mind had been – not whether such and such a plan of action for Janet's welfare in a very grave crisis would be advisable, but whether he should demand an explanation from Hilda of certain disquieting phenomena in her boudoir. In the excitement of his indecision Janet's tragic case scarcely affected his sensibility. For about twelve months Hilda had, he knew, been intermittently carrying on a correspondence as to which she said no word to him; she did not precisely conceal it, but she failed to display it. Lately, so far as his observation went, it had ceased. And then today he had caught sight of an orange telegraph envelope in her waste-paper basket. Alone in the boudoir, and glancing back cautiously and guiltily at the door, he had picked up the little ball of paper and smoothed it out, and read the words: 'Mrs Edwin Clayhanger'. In those days the wives of even prominent business men did not customarily receive such a rain of telegrams that the delivery of a telegram would pass unmentioned and be forgotten. On the contrary, the delivery of a telegram was an event in a woman's life. The telegram which he had detected might have been innocently negligible, in forty different ways. It might, for example, have been from Janet, or about a rehearsal of the Choral Society, or from a tradesman at Oldcastle, or about rooms at the seaside. But supposing that it was not innocently negligible? Supposing that she was keeping a secret? . . . What secret? What conceivable secret? He could conceive no secret. Yes, he could conceive a secret. He had conceived and did conceive a secret, and his private thoughts elaborated it . . .

He had said to himself at the works: 'I may ask her as we go home. I shall see.' But, out in the street, with the disturbing sense of her existence over his shoulder, he knew that he should not ask her. Partly timidity and partly pride kept him from asking. He knew that, as a wise husband, he ought to ask. He knew that common sense was not her strongest quality, and that by diffidence he might be inviting unguessed future trouble; but he would not ask. In the great, passionate war of marriage they would draw thus apart, defensive and watchful, rushing together at intervals either to fight or to kiss. The heat of their kisses had not cooled; but to him at any rate the kisses often seemed intensely illogical; for, though he regarded himself as an improving expert in the science of life, he had not yet begun to perceive that those kisses were the only true logic of their joint career.

He was conscious of grievances against her as they walked up Acre Lane, but instead of being angrily resentful, he was content judicially to register the grievances as further corroboration of his estimate of her character. They were walking up Acre Lane solely because Hilda was Hilda. A year ago they had walked up Acre Lane in order that Edwin might call at the shop. But Acre Lane was by no means on the shortest way from Shawport to Bleakridge. Hilda, however, on emerging from the works, full of trouble concerning Janet, had suddenly had the beautiful idea of buying some fish for tea. In earlier days he would have said: 'How accidental you are! What would have happened to our tea if you hadn't been down here, or if you hadn't by chance thought of fish?' He would have tried to show her that her activities were not based in the principles of reason, and that even the composition of meals ought not to depend upon the hazard of an impulse. Now, wiser, he said not a word. He resigned himself in silence to an extra three quarters of a mile of walking. In such matters, where her deep instinctiveness came into play, she had established over him a definite ascendancy.

Then another grievance was that she had sent George to Hanbridge, knowing that George, according to a solemn family engagement, ought to have been at the works. She was con-scienceless. A third grievance, naturally, was her behaviour to Ingpen. And a fourth came back again to George. Why had she sent George to Hanbridge at all? Was it not to dispatch a telegam which she was afraid to submit to the inquisitiveness of the Post Office at Bursley? A daring supposition, but plausible; and if correct, of what duplicity was she not guilty! The mad, shameful episode of Johnnie Orgreave, the awful dilemma of Janet – colos-sal affairs though they were – interested him less and less as he grew more and more preoccupied with his relations to Hilda. And he thought, not caring:

'Something terrific will occur between us, one of these days.'

And then his bravado would turn to panic.

II

They passed along Wedgwood Street, and Hilda preceded him into the chief poulterer-and-fishmonger's. Here was another slight grievance of Edwin's; for the chief poulterer-and-fishmonger's happened now to be the Clayhanger shop at the corner of Wedgwood Street and Duck Bank. Positively there had been competitors for the old location! Why should Hilda go there and drag him there? Could she not comprehend that he had a certain fine delicacy about entering? . . . The place where the former sign had been was plainly visible on the brickwork above the shop front. Rabbits, fowl, and a few brace of grouse hung in the right-hand window, from which most of the glass had been removed; and in the left, upon newly-embedded slabs of Sicilian marble, lay amid ice the curved forms of many fish, and behind them was the fat white-sleeved figure of the chief poulterer-and-fishmonger's wife with her great, wet hands. He was sad. He seriously thought yet again: 'Things are not what they were in this town, somehow.' For this place had once been a printer's; and he had a conviction that printing was an aristocrat among trades. Indeed, could printing and fishmongering be compared?

The saleswoman greeted them with deference, calling Edwin 'sir', and yet with a certain complacent familiarity, as an occupant to ex-occupants. Edwin casually gave the short shake of the head which in the district may signify 'Good day', and turned, humming, to look at the hanging game. It seemed to him that he could only keep his dignity as a man of the world by looking at the grouse with a connoisseur's eye. Why didn't Hilda buy grouse? The shop was a poor little interior. It smelt ill. He wondered what the upper rooms were like, and what had happened to the decrepit building at the end of the yard. The saleswoman slapped the fish about on the marble, and running water could be heard.

'Edwin,' said Hilda, with enchanting sweetness and simplicity, 'would you like hake or turbot, dear?'

Impossible to divine from her voice that the ruin of their two favourite Orgreaves was complete, that she was conducting a secret correspondence, and that she had knowingly and deliberately offended her husband!

Both women waited, moveless, for the decision, as for an august decree.

When the transaction was finished, the saleswoman handed over the parcel into Hilda's gloved hands; it was a rough-and-ready parcel, not at all like the neat, stiff paper bag of the modern age.

'Very hot, isn't it, ma'am?' said the saleswoman.

And Hilda, utterly distinguished in gesture and tone, replied with calm, impartial urbanity:

'Very. Good afternoon.'

'I'd better take that thing,' said Edwin outside, in spite of himself.

She gave up the parcel to him.

'Tell cook to fry it,' said Hilda. 'She always fries better than she boils.'

He repeated:

'"Tell cook to fry it." What's up now?' His tone challenged.

'I must go over and see Janet at once. I shall take the next car.'

He lifted the end of his nose in disgust. There was no end to the girl's caprices.

'Why at once?' the superior male demanded. Disdain and resentment were in his voice. Hundreds of times, when alone, he had decided that he would never use that voice – first, because it was unworthy of a philosopher; second, because it never achieved any good result; and third, because it often did harm. Yet he would use it. The voice had an existence and volition of its own within his being; he marvelled that the essential mechanism of life should be so clumsy and inefficient. He heard the voice come out, and yet was not displeased, was indeed rather pleasantly excited. A new grievance had been created for him; he might have ignored it, just as he might ignore a solitary cigarette lying in his cigarette case. Both cigarettes and grievances were bad for him. But he could not ignore them. The last cigarette in the case magnetized him. Useless to argue with himself that he had already smoked more than enough, – the cigarette had to emerge from the case and be burnt; and the grievance too was irresistible. In an instant he had it between his teeth and was darkly enjoying it. Of course Hilda's passionate pity for Janet was a fine thing. Granted! But therein was no reason why she should let it run away with her. The worst of these capricious, impulsive creatures was that they could never do anything fine without an enormous fuss and upset. What possible difference would it make whether Hilda went to break the news of disaster to Janet at once or in an hour's time? The mere desire to protect and assuage could not properly furnish an excuse for unnecessarily dislocating a household and depriving oneself of food. On the contrary, it was wiser and more truly kind to take one's meals regularly in a crisis. But Hilda would never appreciate that profound truth – never, never!

Moreover, it was certain that Johnnie had written to Janet.

'I feel I must go at once,' said Hilda.

He spoke with more marked scorn:

'And what about your tea?'

'Oh, it doesn't matter about my tea.'

'Of course it matters about your tea. If you have your tea quietly, you'll find the end of the world won't have come, and you can go and see Janet just the same, and the whole house won't have been turned upside down.'

She put her lips together and smiled mysteriously, saying

nothing. The racket of the Hanbridge and Knype steam-car could be heard behind them. She did not turn her head. The car overtook them, and then stopped a few yards in front. But she did not hail the conductor. The car went onwards.

He had won. His arguments had been so convincing that she could not help being convinced. It was too powerful for even her obstinacy, which as a rule successfully defied any argument whatever.

Did he smile and forgive? Did he extend to her the blessing of his benevolence? No. He could not have brought himself to such a point. After all, she had done nothing to earn approval; she had simply refrained from foolishness. She had had to be reminded of considerations which ought never to have been present in her brain. Doubtless she thought that he was hard, that he was incapable of her divine pity for Janet. But that was only because she could not imagine a combination of emotional generosity and calm common sense; and she never would be able to imagine it. Hence she would always be unjust to him.

When they arrived home, she was still smiling mysteriously to herself. She did not take her hat off – sign of disturbance! He moved with careful tranquillity through the ritual that preceded tea. He could feel her in the house, ordering it, softening it, civilizing it. He could smell the fish. He could detect the subservience of Ada to her mistress's serious mood. He went into the dining-room. Ada followed him with a tray of hot things. Hilda followed Ada. Then George entered, cleaner than ordinary. Edwin savoured deeply the functioning of his home. And his wife had yielded. Her instinct had compelled her not to neglect him; his sagacity had mastered her. In her heart she must admire his sagacity, whatever she said or looked, and her unreasoning passion for him was still the paramount force in her vitality.

'Now, are you two all right?' said Hilda, when she had poured out the tea and Edwin was carving the fish.

Edwin glanced up.

'I don't want any tea,' she said. 'I couldn't touch it.'

She bent and kissed George, took her gloves from the sideboard, and left the house, the mysterious smile still on her face.

III

Edwin controlled his vexation at this dramatic move. It was only slight, and he had to play the serene omniscient to George. Further, the attractive food helped to make him bland.

'Didn't you know your mother had to go out?' said Edwin, with astounding guile.

'Yes, she told me upstairs,' George murmured, 'while she was washing me. She said she had to go and see Auntie Janet again.'

The reply was a blow to Edwin. She had said nothing to him, but she had told the boy. Still, his complacency was not overset. Boy and stepfather began to talk, with the mingled freedom and constraint practised by males accustomed to the presence of a woman, when the woman is absent. Each was aware of the stress of a novel, mysterious, and grave situation. Each also thought of the woman, and each knew that the other was thinking of the woman. Each, over a serious apprehension, seemed to be lightly saying: 'It's rather fun to be without her for a bit. But we must be able to rely on her return.' Nothing stood between them and domestic discomfort. Possible stupidity in the kitchen had no check. As regards the mere household machine, they had a ridiculous and amusing sense of distant danger.

Edwin had to get up in order to pour out more tea. He reckoned that he could both make tea and pour it out with more exactitude than his wife, who often forgot to put the milk in first. But he could not pour it out with the same grace. His brain, not his heart, poured the tea out. He left the tray in disorder. The symmetry of the table was soon wrecked.

'Glad you're going back to school, I suppose?' said Edwin satirically.

George nodded. He was drinking, and he glanced at Edwin over the rim of the cup. He had grown much in twelve months, and was more than twelve months older. Edwin was puzzled by the almost sudden developments of his intelligence. Sometimes the boy was just like a young man; his voice had become a little uncertain. He still showed the greatest contempt for his finger-nails, but he had truly discovered the toothbrush, and was preaching it at school among a population that scoffed yet was impressed.

'No. I'm glad,' he answered.

'Oh! You're glad, are you?'

'Well, I'm glad in a way. A boy does have to go to school, doesn't he, uncle? And the sooner it's over the better. I tell you what I should like – I should like to go to school night and day and have no holidays till it was all done. I sh'd think you could save at least three years with that.'

'A bit hard on the masters, wouldn't it be?'

'I never thought of that. Of course it would *never* be over for them. I expect they'd gradually die.'

'Then you don't like school?'

George shook his head.

'Did you like school, uncle?'

Edwin shook his head. They both laughed.

'Uncle, can I leave school when I'm sixteen?'

'I've told you once.'

'Yes, I know. But did you mean it? People change so.'

'I told you you could leave school when you're sixteen if you pass the London Matric.'

'But what good's the London Matric. to an architect? Mr Orgreave says it isn't any good, anyway.'

'When did he tell you that?'

'Yesterday.'

'But not so long since you were all for being a stock-breeder!'

'Ah! I was only pretending to myself!' George smiled.

'Well, fetch me my cigarettes off the mantelpiece in the drawing-room.'

The boy ran off, eager to serve, and Edwin's glance followed him with affection. George's desire to be an architect had consistently strengthened, save during a brief period when the Show of the North Staffordshire Agricultural Society, held with much splendour at Hanbridge, had put another idea into his noddle – an idea that fed itself richly on glorious bulls and other prize cattle for about a week, and then expired. Indeed, already it had been in a kind of way arranged that the youth should ultimately be articled to Johnnie Orgreave. Among many consequences of Johnnie's defiance to society would probably be the quashing of that arrangement. And there was Johnnie, on the eve of his elopement, chatting to George about the futility of the London Matriculation! Edwin wondered how George would gradually learn what had happened to his friend and inspirer, John Orgreave.

He arrived with the cigarettes and offered them, and lit the match, and offered that.

'And what have you been doing with yourself all afternoon?' Edwin inquired between puffs of smoke.

'Oh, nothing much!'

'I thought you were coming to the works, and then going down to Auntie Clara's for tea?'

'So I was. But mother sent me to Hanbridge.'

'Oh!' murmured Edwin casually. 'So your mother packed you off to Hanbridge, did she?'

'I had to go to the Post Office,' George continued, 'I think it was a telegram, but it was in an envelope and some money.'

'*In*deed!' said Edwin, with a very indifferent air.

He was, however, so affected that he jumped up abruptly from the table, and went into the darkening, chill garden, ignoring George. George, accustomed to these sudden accessions of interest and these sudden forgettings, went unperturbed his ways.

About half past eight Hilda returned. Edwin was closing the curtains in the drawing-room. The gas had been lighted.

'Johnnie has evidently written to Alicia,' she burst out somewhat breathless. 'Because Alicia's telegraphed to Janet that she must positively go straight down there and stay with them when she leaves the Home.'

'What, on Dartmoor?' Edwin muttered, in a strange voice. The very word 'Dartmoor' made him shake.

'It isn't actually on the moor,' said Hilda. 'And so I shall take her down myself. I've told her all about things. She wasn't a bit surprised. They're a strange lot.'

She tried to speak quite naturally, but he knew that she was not succeeding. Their eyes would not meet. Edwin thought:

'How far away we are from this morning!' Hazard and fate, like converging armies, seemed to be closing upon him.

CHAPTER 13

THE DEPARTURE

I

IT was a wet morning. Hilda, already in full street attire, save for her gloves, and with a half-empty cup of tea by her side, sat at the desk in the boudoir. She unlocked the large central drawer immediately below the flap of the desk, with a peculiar, quick, ruthless gesture, which gesture produced a very short snappy click that summed up all the tension spreading from Hilda's mind throughout the house and even into the town. It had been decided that, in order to call for Janet at the Nursing Home and catch the Crewe train at Knype for the Bristol and South-west of England connection, Hilda must leave the house at five minutes to nine.

This great fact was paramount in the minds of various people besides Hilda. Ada upstairs stood bent and flushed over a huge portmanteau into which she was putting the last things, while George hindered her by simultaneously tying to the leather handle a wet label finely directed by himself in architectural characters. The cook in the kitchen was preparing the master's nine o'clock breakfast with new solicitudes caused by a serious sense of responsibility; for Hilda, having informed her in moving tones that the master's welfare in the mistress's absence would depend finally on herself, had solemnly entrusted that welfare to her – had almost passed it to her from hand to hand, with precautions, like a jewel in a casket. Ada, it may be said, had immediately felt the weight of the cook's increased importance. Edwin and the clerks at the works knew that Edwin had to be home for breakfast at a quarter to nine instead of nine, and that he must not be late, as Mrs Clayhanger had a train to catch, and accordingly the morning's routine of the office was modified. And, finally, a short old man in a rainy stable-yard in Acre Parade, between Acre Lane and Oldcastle Street, struggling to force a collar over the head of a cab-horse that towered above his own head, was already blasphemously excited by those pessimistic apprehensions about the flight of time which forty years of train-catching had never sufficed to allay in him. As for Janet, she alone in her weakness and her submissiveness was calm; the nurse and Hilda understood one another, and she was 'leaving it all' to them.

Hilda opened the drawer, half lifting the flap of the desk to disclose its contents. It was full of odd papers, letters, bills, blotting-paper, door-knobs, finger-plates, envelopes, and a small book or two. A prejudiced observer, such as Edwin, might have said that the drawer was extremely untidy. But to Hilda, who had herself put in each item separately, and each for a separate reason, the drawer was not untidy, for her intelligence knew the plan of it, and every item as it caught her eye suggested a justifying reason, and a good one. Nevertheless, she formed an intention to 'tidy out' the drawer (the only drawer in the desk with a safe lock), upon her return home. She felt at the back of the drawer, drew forth the drawer a little farther, and felt again, vainly. A doubt of her own essential orderliness crossed her mind. 'Surely I can't have put those letters anywhere else? Surely I've not mislaid them?' Then she closed the flap of the desk, and pulled the drawer right out, letting it rest on her knees. Yes, the packet was there, hidden, and so was another packet of letters – in the hand-writing of Edwin. She was reassured. She knew she was tidy, had always been tidy. And Edwin's innuendoes to the contrary were inexcusable. Jerking the drawer irregularly back by force into its place, she locked it, reopened the desk, laid the packet on the writing-pad, and took a telegram from her purse to add to the letters in the packet.

The letters were all in the same loose, sloping hand, and on the same tinted notepaper. The signature was plain on one of them, 'Charlotte M. Cannon', and then after it, in brackets, '(Canonges)', – the latter being the real name of George Cannon's French father, and George Cannon's only legal name. The top-most letter began: 'Dear Madam, I think it is my duty to inform you that my husband still declares his innocence of the crime for which he is now in prison. He requests that you shall be informed of this. I ought perhaps to tell you that, since the change in my religious convictions, my feelings –' The first page ended there. Hilda turned the letters over, preoccupied, gazing at them and deciphering chance phrases here and there. The first letter was dated about a year earlier; it constituted the beginning of the resuscitation of just that part of her life which she had thought to be definitely interred in memory.

Hilda had only once – and on a legal occasion – met Mrs Canonges (as with strict correctness she called herself in brackets) – a surprisingly old lady, with quite white hair, and she had thought: 'What a shame for that erotic old woman to have bought and married a man so much younger than herself! No wonder he ran away from her!' She had been positively shocked by the spectacle of the well-dressed, well-behaved, quiet-voiced, prim, decrepit creature with her aristocratic voice. And her knowledge of the possibilities of human nature was thenceforth enlarged. And when George Cannon (known to the law only as Canonges) had received two years' hard labour for going through a ceremony of marriage with herself, she had esteemed, despite all her resentment against him, that his chief sin lay in his real first marriage, not in his false second one, and that for that sin the old woman was the more deserving of punishment. And when the old woman had with strange naïveté written to say that she had become a convert to Roman Catholicism and that her marriage and her imprisoned bigamous husband were henceforth to her sacred, Hilda had reflected sardonically: 'Of course it is always that sort of woman that turns to religion, when she's too old for anything else!' And when the news came that her deceiver had got ten years' penal servitude (and might have got penal servitude for life) for uttering a forged Bank of England note, Hilda had reflected in the same strain: 'Of course, a man who would behave as George behaved to me would be just the man to go about forging bank-notes! I am not in the least astonished. What an inconceivable simpleton I was!'

A very long time had elapsed before the letter arrived bearing the rumour of Cannon's innocence. It had not immediately produced much effect on her mind. She had said not a word to Edwin. The idea of reviving the shames of that early episode in conversation with Edwin was extremely repugnant to her. She would not do it. She had not the right to do it. All her proud independence forbade her to do it. The episode did not concern Edwin. The effect on her of the rumour came gradually. It was increased when Mrs Cannon wrote of evidence, a petition to the Home Secretary, and employing a lawyer. Mrs Cannon's attitude seemed to say to Hilda: 'You and I have shared this man. We alone in all the world.' Mrs Cannon seemed to imagine that Hilda would be interested. She was right. Hilda was interested. Her implacability relented. Her vindictiveness forgave. She pondered with almost intolerable compassion upon the vision of George Cannon suffering unjustly month after long month interminably the horrors of a convict's existence. She read with morbidity the reports of assizes, and picked up from papers and books and from Mrs Cannon pieces of information about prisons. When he was transferred to Parkhurst in the Isle of Wight on account of ill health, she was glad, because she knew that Parkhurst was less awful than Portland; and when from Parkhurst he was sent to Dartmoor she tried to hope that the bracing air would do him good. She no longer thought of him as a criminal at all, but simply as one victim of his passion for herself; she, Hilda, had been the other victim. She raged in secret against the British judicature, its delays, its stoniness, its stupidity. And when the principal witness in support of Cannon's petition died, she raged against fate. The movement for Cannon's release slackened for months. Of late it had been resumed, and with hopefulness. One of Cannon's companions had emerged from confinement (due to an unconnected crime), and was ready to swear affidavits.

Lastly, Mrs Cannon had written stating that she was almost beggared, and suggesting that Hilda should lend her ten pounds towards the expenses of the affair. Hilda had not ten pounds. That very day Hilda, seeing Janet in the Nursing Home, had demanded: 'I say, Jan, I suppose you haven't got ten pounds you can let me have for about a day or so?' and had laughed self-consciously. Janet, flushing with eager pleasure, had replied: 'Of course! I've still got that ten-pound note the poor old dad gave me. I've always kept it in case the worst should happen.' Janet was far too affectionate to display curiosity. Hilda had posted the bank-note late at night. The next day had come a telegram:

'Telegraph if you are sending money.' Not for a great deal would Hilda have dispatched through the hands of the old postmaster at Bursley – who had once been postmaster at Turnhill and known her parents – a telegram such as hers addressed to anybody named 'Cannon'. The fear of chatter and scandal was irrational, but it was a very genuine fear. She had sent her faithful George with the telegram to Hanbridge, – it was just as easy.

Hilda now, after hesitation, put the packet of letters in her handbag, to take with her. It was a precaution of secrecy which she admitted to be unnecessary, for she was quite certain that Edwin never looked into her drawers; much less would he try to open a locked drawer; his incurious confidence in her was in some respects almost touching. Certainly nobody else would invade the drawer. Still, she hid the letters in her handbag. Then, in her fashion, she scribbled a bold-charactered note to Mrs Cannon, giving a temporary address, and this also she put in the handbag.

Her attitude to Mrs Cannon, like her attitude to the bigamist, had slowly changed, and she thought of the old woman now with respect and sympathetic sorrow. Mrs Cannon, before she knew that Hilda was married to Edwin, had addressed her first letter to Hilda 'Mrs Cannon', when she would have been justified in addressing it 'Miss Lessways'. In the days of her boarding-house it had been impossible, owing to business reasons, for Hilda to drop the name to which she was not entitled and to revert to her own. The authentic Mrs Cannon, despite the violence of her grievances, had respected Hilda's difficulty; the act showed kindly forbearance and it had aroused Hilda's imaginative gratitude. Further, Mrs Cannon's pertinacity in the liberation proceedings, and her calm, logical acceptance of all the frightful consequences of being the legal wife of a convict, had little by little impressed Hilda, who had said to herself: 'There is something in this old woman.' And Hilda nowadays never thought of her as an old woman who had been perverse and shameless in desire, but as a victim of passion like George Cannon. She said to herself: 'This old woman still loves George Cannon; her love was the secret of her rancour against him, and it is also the secret of her compassion.' These constant reflections, by their magnanimity, and

their insistence upon the tremendous reality of love, did something to ennoble the clandestine and demoralizing life of the soul
which for a year Hilda had hidden from her husband and from
everybody.

II

It still wanted twenty minutes to nine o'clock. She was too soon.
The night before, Edwin had abraded her sore nerves by warning
her not to be late – in a t one that implied habitual lateness on her
part. Hilda was convinced that she was an exact woman. She
might be late – a little late – six times together, but as there was
a sound explanation of and excuse for each shortcoming, her
essential exactitude remained always unimpaired in her own
mind. But Edwin would not see this. He told her now and then
that she belonged to that large class of people who have the
illusion that a clock stands still at the last moment while last
things are being done. She resented the observation, as she
resented many of Edwin's assumptions concerning her. Edwin
seemed to forget that she had been one of the first women
stenographers in England; that she had been a journalist-
secretary and accustomed to correct the negligences of men of
business, and, finally, that she had been in business by herself
for a number of years. Edwin would sweep all that away, and
treat her like one of your mere brainless butterflies. At any rate,
on the present occasion she was not late. And she took pride,
instead of shame, in her exaggerated earliness. She had the air of
having performed a remarkable feat.

She left the boudoir to go upstairs and superintend Ada,
though she had told the impressed Ada that she should put full
trust in her, and should not superintend her. However, as she
opened the door she heard the sounds of Ada and George direct-
ing each other in the joint enterprise of bringing a very large and
unwieldy portmanteau out of the bedroom. The hour for super-
intendence was therefore past. Hilda went into the drawing-room
idly, nervously, to wait till the portmanteau should have reached
the hall. The French window was ajar, and a wet wind entered
from the garden. The garden was full of rain. Two workmen
were in it, employed by the new inhabitants of the home of the

Orgreaves. Those upstarts had decided that certain branches of the famous Orgreave elms were dangerous and must be cut, and the workmen, shirt-sleeved in the rain, were staying one of the elms with a rope made fast to the swing in the Clayhanger garden. Hilda was unreasonably but sincerely antipathetic to her new neighbours. The white-ended stumps of great elm branches made her feel sick. Useless to insist to her on the notorious treachery of elms! She had an affection for those elms, and, to her, amputation was an outrage. The upstarts had committed other sacrilege upon the house and grounds, not heeding that the abode had been rendered holy by the sacraments of fate. Hilda stared and stared at the rain. And the prospect of the long, jolting, acutely depressing drive through the mud and the rain to Knype Vale, and of the interminable train journey with a tragic convalescent, braced her.

'Mother!'

George stood behind her.

'Well, have you got the luggage down?' She frowned, but George knew her nervous frown and could rightly interpret it.

He nodded.

'Ought I to put "Dartmoor" on the luggage label?'

She gave a negative sign.

Why should he ask such a question? She had never breathed the name of Dartmoor. Why should he mention it? Edwin also had mentioned Dartmoor. 'What, on Dartmoor?' Edwin had said. Did Edwin suspect her correspondence? No. Had he suspected, he would have spoken. She knew him. And even if Edwin had suspected, George could not conceivably have had suspicions, of any sort . . . There he stood, the son of a convict, with no name of his own. He existed – because she and the convict had been unable to keep apart; his ignorance of the past was appalling to think of, the dangers incident to it dreadful; his easy confidence before the world affected her almost intolerably. She felt that she could never atone to him for having borne him.

A faint noise at the front door reached the drawing-room.

'Here's Nunks!' exclaimed George, and ran off eagerly.

This was his new name for his stepfather.

Hilda returned quickly to the boudoir. As she disappeared therein, she heard George descanting to Edwin on the beauties of his luggage label, and Edwin rubbing his feet on the mat and removing his mackintosh.

She came back to the door of the boudoir.

'Edwin.'

'Hello!'

'One moment.'

He came into the boudoir, wiping the rain off his face.

'Shut the door, will you?'

Her earnest, self-conscious tone stirred into activity the dormant, secret antagonisms that seemed ever to lie between them. She saw them animating his eyes, stiffening his pose.

Pointing to the cup and saucer on the desk, Edwin said critically:

'That all you've had?'

'Can you let me have ten pounds?' she asked bluntly, ignoring his implication that in the matter of nourishment she had not behaved sensibly.

'Ten pounds? More?' He was on the defensive, as it were crouching warily behind a screen of his suspicions. She nodded awkwardly. She wanted to be graceful, persuasive, enveloping, but she could not. It was to repay Janet that she had need of the money. She ought to have obtained it before, but she had postponed the demand, and she had been wrong. Janet would not require the money, she would have no immediate use for it, but Hilda could not bear to be in debt to her; to leave the sum outstanding would seem so strange, so sinister, so equivocal; it would mar all their intercourse.

'But look here, child,' said Edwin, protesting, 'I've given you about forty times as much as you can possibly want already.'

He had never squarely refused any demand of hers for money; he had almost always acceded instantly and without inquiry to her demands. Obviously he felt sympathy with the woman who by eternal custom is forced to ask, and had a horror of behaving as the majority of husbands notoriously behaved in such circumstances, obviously he was anxious not to avail himself of the husband's overwhelming economic advantage. Nevertheless, the fact that he earned and she didn't was ever mysteriously present in his relatively admirable attitude. And sometimes – perhaps not without grounds, she admitted – he would hesitate before a request, and in him a hesitation was as humiliating as a refusal would have been from another man. And Hilda resented, not so much his attitude, as the whole social convention upon which it was unassailably based. He earned, she knew. She would not deny that he was the unique source and that without him there would be naught. But still she did not think that she ought to have to ask. On the other hand she had no alternative plan to offer. Her criticism of the convention was destructive, not constructive. And all Edwin's careful regard for a woman's susceptibilities seemed only to intensify her deep-hidden revolt. It was a mere chance that he was thus chivalrous. And whether he was chivalrous or not, she was in his power; and she chafed.

'I should be glad if you could let me have it,' she said grimly.

The appeal, besides being unpersuasive in manner, was too general; it did not particularize. There was no frankness between them. She saw his suspicions multiplying. What did he suspect? What could he suspect? ... Ah! And why was she herself so timorous, so strangely excited, about going even to the edge of Dartmoor? And why did she feel guilty, why was her glance so constrained?

'Well, I can't,' he answered. 'Not now; but if anything unexpected turns up, I can send you a cheque.'

She was beaten.

The cab stopped at the front door, well in advance of time.

'It's for Janet,' she muttered to him desperately.

Edwin's face changed.

'Why in thunder didn't you say so to start with?' he exclaimed. 'I'll see what I can do. Of course I've got a fiver in my pocketbook.'

There were a number of men in the town who made a point of always having a reserve five-pound note and a telegraph form upon their persons. It was the dandyism of well-off prudence.

He sprang out of the room. The door swung to behind him.

In a very few moments he returned.

'Here you are!' he said, taking the note from his pocket-book and adding it to a collection of gold and silver.

Hilda was looking out of the window at the tail of the cab. She did not move.

'I don't want it, thanks,' she replied coldly. And she thought: 'What a fool I am!'

'Oh!' he murmured, with constraint.

'You'd do it for her!' said Hilda, chill and clear, 'but you wouldn't do it for me.' And she thought: 'Why do I say such a thing?'

He slapped all the money crossly down on the desk and left the room. She could hear him instructing Ada and the cabman in the manipulation of the great portmanteau.

'Now, mother!' cried George.

She gazed at the money, and, picking it up, shovelled it into her purse. It was irresistible.

In the hall she kissed George, and nodded with a plaintive smile at Ada. Edwin was in the porch. He held back; she held back. She knew from his face that he would not offer to kiss her. The strange power that had compelled her to alienate him refused to allow her to relent. She passed down the steps out into the rain. They nodded, the theory for George and Ada being that they had made their farewells in the boudoir. But George and Ada none the less had their notions. It appeared to Hilda that instead of going for a holiday with her closest friend, she was going to some recondite disaster that involved the end of marriage. And the fact that she and Edwin had not kissed outweighed all other facts in the universe. Yet what was a kiss? Until the cab laboriously started she hoped for a miracle. It did not happen. If only on the previous night she had not absolutely insisted that nobody from the house should accompany her to Knype! . . . The porch slipped from her vision.

CHAPTER 14
TAVY MANSION

I

HILDA and Harry Hesketh stood together in the soft, warm
Devonshire sunshine bending above the foot-high wire netting
that separated the small ornamental pond from the lawn. By
their side was a St Bernard dog with his great baptizing tongue
hanging out. Two swans, glittering in the strong light, swam
slowly to and fro; one had a black claw tucked up on his back
among downy white feathers; the other hissed at the dog, who
in his vast and shaggy good-nature simply could not understand
this malevolence on the part of a fellow creature. Round about
the elegant haughtiness of the swans clustered a number of
iridescent Muscovy ducks, and a few white Aylesburys with
gamboge beaks that intermittently quacked, all restless and
expectant of blessings to fall over the wire netting that eternally
separated them from the heavenly hunting-ground of the lawn.
Across the pond, looking into a moored dinghy, an enormous
drake with a vermilion top-knot reposed on the balustrade of the
landing-steps. The water reflected everything in a rippled medley –
blue sky, rounded, woolly clouds, birds, shrubs, flowers, grasses,
and browny-olive depths of the plantation beyond the pond,
where tiny children in white were tumbling and shrieking with a
nurse in white.

Harry was extraordinarily hospitable, kind, and agreeable to
his guest. Scarcely thirty, tall and slim, he carried himself with
distinction. His flannels were spotless; his white shirt was spotless; his tennis shoes were spotless; but his blazer, cap, and
necktie (which all had the same multi-coloured pattern of stripes)
were shabby, soiled, and without shape; nevertheless, their dilap-
idation seemed only to adorn his dandyism, for they possessed
a mysterious sacred quality. He had a beautiful moustache, nice
eyes, hands excitingly dark with hair, and no affectations what-

ever. Although he had inherited Tavy Mansion and a fortune from an aunt who had left Oldcastle and the smoke to marry a Devonshire landowner, he was boyish, modest, and ingenuous. Nobody could have guessed from his manner that he had children, nurses, servants, gardeners, grooms, horses, carriages, a rent-roll, and a safe margin at every year's end. He spoke of the Five Towns with a mild affection. Hilda thought, looking at him: 'He has everything, simply everything! And yet he's quite unspoilt!' In spite of the fact that in previous years he had seen Hilda only a few times – and that quite casually at the Orgreaves' – he had assumed and established intimacy at the very moment of meeting her and Janet at Tavistock station the night before, and their friendship might now have been twenty years old instead of twenty hours. Very obviously he belonged to a class superior to Hilda's, but he was apparently quite unconscious of what was still the most deeply-rooted and influential institution of English life. His confiding, confidential tone flattered her.

'How do you think Alicia's looking?' he asked.

'Magnificent,' said Hilda, throwing a last piece of bread into the water.

'So do I,' said he. 'But she's ruined for tennis, you know. This baby business is spiffing, only it puts you right off your game. As a rule she manages to be *hors de combat* bang in the middle of the season. She *has* been able to play a bit this year, but she's not keen – that's what's up with her ladyship – she's not keen now.'

'Well,' said Hilda. 'Even you can't have everything.'

'Why "even" me?' he laughed.

She merely gazed at him with a mysterious smile. She perceived that he was admiring her – probably for her enigmatic quality, so different from Alicia's – and she felt a pleasing self-content.

'Edwin do much tennis nowadays?'

'Edwin?' She repeated the name in astonishment, as though it were the name of somebody who could not possibly be connected with tennis. 'Not he! He's not touched a racket all this season. He's quite otherwise employed.'

'I hear he's a fearful pot in the Five Towns, anyway,' said Harry seriously. 'Making money hand over fist.'

Hilda raised her eyebrows and shook her head deprecatingly.

But the marked repectfulness of Harry's reference to Edwin was agreeable. She thought: 'I do believe I'm becoming a snob!'

'It's hard work making money, even in our small way, in Bursley,' she said – and seemed to indicate the expensive spaciousness of the gardens.

'I should like to see old Edwin again.'

'I never knew you were friends.'

'Well, I used to see him pretty often at Lane End House, after Alicia and I were engaged. In fact once he jolly nearly beat me in a set.'

'Edwin did?' she exclaimed.

'The same ... He had a way of saying things that a feller somehow thought about afterwards.'

'Oh! So you noticed that!'

'Does he still?'

'I – I don't know. But he used to.'

'You ought to have brought him. In fact I quite thought he was coming. Anyhow, I told Alicia to invite him, too, as soon as we knew you were bringing old Jan down.'

'She did mention it, Alicia did. But, oh! He wouldn't hear of it. Works! Works! No holiday all summer.'

'I'll tell you a scheme,' said Harry roguishly. 'Refuse to join the domestic hearth until he comes and fetches you.'

She gave a little laugh. 'Oh, he won't come to fetch me.'

'Well,' said Harry shortly and decisively, 'we shall see what can be done. I may tell you we're rather great at getting people down here ... I wonder where those girls are?' He turned round and Hilda turned round.

The red Georgian house with its windows in octagonal panes, its large pediment hiding the centre of the roof, and its white paint, showed brilliantly across the hoop-studded green, between some cypresses and an ilex; on either side were smooth walls of green – trimmed shrubs forming long alleys whose floors were also green; and here and there a round or oval flower bed, and, at the edges of the garden, curved borders of flowers. Everything was still, save the ship-like birds on the pond, the distant children in the plantation, and the slow-moving, small clouds overhead. The sun's warmth was like an endearment.

Janet and Alicia, their arms round each other's shoulders,

sauntered into view from behind the cypresses. On the more
sheltered lawn nearest the house they were engaged in a quiet
but tremendous palaver; nobody but themselves knew what they
were talking about; it might have been the affair of Johnnie and
Mrs Chris Hamson, as to which not a word had been publicly
said at Tavy Mansion since Janet and Hilda's arrival. Janet still
wore black, and now she carried a red sunshade belonging to
Alicia. Alicia was in white, not very clean white, and rather
tousled. She was only twenty-five. She had grown big and jolly
and downright (even to a certain shamelessness) and careless of
herself. Her body had the curves, and her face the emaciation, of
the young mother. She used abrupt, gawky, kind-hearted gestures.
Her rough affectionateness embraced not merely her children,
but all young living things, and many old. For her children she
had a passion. And she would say openly, as it were, defiantly,
that she meant to be the mother of more children – lots more.

'Hey, lass!' cried out Harry, using the broad Staffordshire
accent for the amusement of Hilda.

The sisters stopped and untwined their arms.

'Hey, lad!' Alicia loudly responded. But instead of looking
at her husband she was looking through him at the babies in the
plantation behind the pond.

Janet smiled, in her everlasting resignation. Hilda, smiling at
her in return from the distance, recalled the tone in which Harry
had said 'old Jan' – a tone at once affectionate and half-
contemptuous. She *was* old Jan, now; destined to be a burden
upon somebody and of very little use to anybody; no longer
necessary. If she disappeared, life would immediately close over
her, and not a relative, not a friend, would be inconvenienced.
Some among them would remark: 'Perhaps it's for the best.'
And Janet knew it. In the years immediately preceding the death
of Mr and Mrs Orgreave, she had hardened a little from her
earlier soft, benevolent self – hardened to everybody save her
father and mother, whom she protected – and now she was
utterly tender again, and her gentle acquiescences seemed to say:
'I am defenceless, and tomorrow I shall be old.'

'I'm going to telegraph to Edwin Clayhanger to come down
for the week-end,' shouted Harry.

And Alicia shouted in reply:

'Oh, spiffing!'

Hilda said nervously:

'You aren't, really?'

She had no intention of agreeing to the pleasant project. A breach definitely existed between Edwin and herself, and the idea of either maintaining it or ending it on foreign ground was inconceivable. Such things could only be done at home. She had telegraphed a safe arrival, but she had not yet written to him nor decided in what tone she should write.

Two gardeners, one pushing a wheeled water-can, appeared from an alley and began silently and assiduously to water a shaded flower bed. Alicia and Harry continued to shout enthusiastically to each other in a manner sufficiently disturbing, but the gardeners gave no sign that anybody except themselves lived in the garden. Alicia, followed by Janet, was slowly advancing towards the croquet lawn, when a parlourmaid tripping from the house overtook her, and with modest deference murmured something to the bawling, jolly mistress. Alicia, still followed by Janet, turned and went into the house, while the parlourmaid with bent head waited discreetly to bring up the rear.

A sudden and terrific envy possessed Hilda as she contrasted the circumstances of these people with her own. These people lived in lovely and cleanly surroundings without a care beyond the apprehension of nursery ailments. They had joyous and kindly dispositions. They were well-bred, and they were attended by servants who, professionally, were even better bred than themselves, and who were rendered happy by smooth words and good pay. They lived at peace with everyone. Full of health, they ate well and slept well. They suffered no strain. They had absolutely no problems, and they did not seek problems. Nor had they any duties, save agreeable ones to each other. Their world was ideal. If you had asked them how their world could be improved for them, they would not have found an easy reply. They could only have demanded less taxes and more fine days ... Whereas Hilda and hers were forced to live among a brutal populace, amid the most horrible surroundings of smoke, dirt, and squalor. In Devonshire the Five Towns was unthinkable; the whiteness of the window curtains at Tavy Mansion almost broke the heart of the housewife in Hilda. And compare – not Hilda's handkerchief-garden, but even the old garden of the Orgreaves, with this elysium, where nothing offended the eye and the soot nowhere lay on the trees, blackening the shiny leaves and stunting the branches. And compare the too mean planning and space-saving of the house in Trafalgar Road with the lavish generosity of space inside Tavy Mansion! . . .

Edwin in the Bursley sense was a successful man, and had consequence in the town, but the most that he had accomplished or could accomplish would not amount to the beginning of appreciable success according to higher standards. Nobody in Bursley really knew the meaning of the word success. And even such local success as Edwin had had – at what peril and with what worry was it won! These Heskeths were safe for ever. Ah! She envied them, and she intensely depreciated everything that was hers. She stood in the Tavy Mansion garden – it seemed to her – like an impostor. Her husband was merely struggling upwards. And moreover she had quarrelled with him, darkly and obscurely; and who could guess what would be the end of marriage? Harry and Alicia never quarrelled; they might have tiffs – nothing worse than that; they had no grounds for quarrelling . . . And supposing Harry and Alicia guessed the link connecting her with Dartmoor prison! . . . No, it could not be supposed. Her envy melted into secret deep dejection amid the beautiful and prosperous scene.

'Evidently someone's called,' said Harry, of his wife's disappearance. 'I hope she's nice.'

'Who?'

'Whoever's called. Shall we knock the balls about a bit?'

They began a mild game of croquet, but after a few minutes Hilda burst out sharply:

'You aren't playing your best, Mr Hesketh. I wish you would.'

He was startled by her eyes and her tone.

'Honest Injun! I am,' he fibbed in answer. 'But I'll try to do better. You must remember croquet isn't my game. Alicia floors me at it five times out of six.'

Then the parlourmaid and another maid came out to lay tea on two tables under the ilex.

'Bowley,' said Harry over his shoulder. 'Bring me a telegraph form next time you come out, will you?'

'Yes, sir,' said the parlourmaid.

Hilda protested:

'No, Mr Hesketh! Really! I assure you –'

The telegraph form came with the tea. Harry knocked a ball against a coloured stick, and both he and Hilda sat down with relief.

'Who's called, Bowley?'

'Mrs Rotherwas, sir.'

Harry counted the cups.

'Isn't she staying for tea?'

'No, sir. I think not, sir.'

Hilda, humming, rose and walked about. At the same moment Alicia, Janet, and a tall young woman in black and yellow emerged from the house. Hilda moved behind a tree. She could hear good-byes. The group vanished round the side of the house, and then came the sound of hoofs and of wheels crunching. An instant later Alicia arrived at the ilex, bounding and jolly; Janet moved more sedately. The St Bernard, who had been reposing near the pond, now smelt the tea and hot cakes and joined the party. The wagging of his powerful tail knocked over a wicker chair, and Alicia gave a squeal. Then Alicia, putting her hands to her mouth, shouted across the lawn and the pond:

'Nursey! Nursey! Take them in!'

And a faint reply came.

'What was the Rotherwas dame after?' asked Harry, sharpening a pencil, when Alicia had ascertained the desires of her guests as to milk and sugar.

'She was after you, of course,' said Alicia. 'Tennis party on Monday. She wants you to balance young Truscott. I just told her so. We shall all go. You'll go, Hilda. She'll be delighted. I should have brought her along only she was in such a hurry.'

Hilda inquired:

'Who is Mrs Rotherwas?'

'Her husband's a big coal owner at Cardiff. But she's a niece or something of the Governor of Dartmoor prison, and she's apparently helping to keep house for dear uncle just now. They'll take us over the prison before tennis. It's awfully interesting. Harry and I have been once.'

'Oh!' murmured Hilda, staggered.

'Now about this 'ere woire,' said Harry. 'What price this?' He handed over the message which he had just composed. It was rather long, and on the form was left space for only two more words.

Hilda could not decipher it. She saw the characters with her eyes, but she was incapable of interpreting them. All the time she thought:

'I shall go to that prison. I can't help it. I shan't be able to keep from going. I shall go to that prison. I must go. Who could have imagined this? I am bound to go, and I shall go.'

But instead of objecting totally to the dispatch of the telegram, she said in a strange voice:

'It's very nice of you.'

'You fill up the rest of the form,' said Harry, offering the pencil.

'What must I put?'

'Well, you'd better put "Countersigned, Hilda". That'll fix it.'

'Will you write it?' she muttered.

He wrote the words.

'Let poor mummy see!' Alicia complained, seizing the telegraph form.

Harry called out:

'Leeks!'

A short-sleeved gardener half hidden by foliage across the garden looked up sharply, saw Harry's beckoning finger, and approached running.

'Have that sent off for me, will you? Tell Jos to take it,' said Harry, and gave Leeks the form and a florin.

'Why, Hilda, you aren't eating anything!' protested Alicia.

'I only want tea,' said Hilda casually, wondering whether they had noticed anything wrong in her face.

II

Edwin, looking curiously out of the carriage window as the train from Plymouth entered Tavistock station early on the Monday, was surprised to perceive Harry Hesketh on the platform. While, in the heavenly air of the September morning, the train was curving through Bickleigh Vale and the valley of the Plym and through the steeper valley of the Meavy, up towards the first fastnesses of the moor, he had felt his body to be almost miraculously well and his soul almost triumphant. But when he saw Harry – the remembered figure, but a little stouter and coarser – he saw a being easily more triumphant than himself.

Harry had great reason for triumph, for he had proved himself to possess a genius for deductive psychological reasoning and for prophecy. Edwin had been characteristically vague about the visit. First he had telegraphed that he could not come, business preventing. Then he had telegraphed that he would come, but only on Sunday, and he had given no particulars of trains. They had all assured one another that this was just like Edwin. 'The man's mad!' said Harry with genial benevolence, and had set himself to one of his favourite studies – Bradshaw. He always handled Bradshaw like a master, accomplishing feats of interpretation that amazed his wife. He had announced, after careful connotations, that Edwin was perhaps after all not such a chump, but that he was in fact a chump, in that, having chosen the Bristol–Plymouth route, he had erred about the Sunday night train from Plymouth to Tavistock. How did he know that Edwin would choose the Bristol–Plymouth route? Well, his knowledge was derived from divination, based upon vast experience of human nature. Edwin would 'get stuck' at Plymouth. He would sleep at Plymouth – staying at the Royal (he hoped) – and would come on by the 8.01 a.m., on Monday, arriving at 8.59 a.m., where he would be met by Harry in the dogcart drawn by Joan. The telegraph office was of course closed after 10 a.m. on Sunday, but if it had been open and he had been receiving hourly dispatches about Edwin's tortuous progress through England, Harry could not have been more sure of his position. And on the Monday Harry had risen up in the very apogee of health, and had driven Joan to the station. 'Mark my words!' he had said, 'I shall bring him back with me for breakfast.' He had offered to take Hilda to the station to witness his triumph; but Hilda had not accepted.

And there Edwin was! Everything had happened according to Harry's prediction, except that, from an unfortunate modesty, Edwin had gone to the wrong hotel at Plymouth.

They shook hands in a glow of mutual pleasure.

'How on earth did you know?' Edwin began.

The careful-casual answer rounded off Harry's triumph. And Edwin thought: 'Why, he's just like a grown-up boy!' But he was distinguished; his club necktie in all its decay was still impressive; and his expansive sincere goodwill was utterly delightful. Also the station, neat, clean, solid – the negation of all gimcrackery – had an aspect of goodwill to man; its advertisements did not flare; and it seemed to be the expression of a sound and self-respecting race. The silvern middle-aged guard greeted Harry with deferential heartiness and saluted Edwin with even more warmth than he had used at Plymouth. On the Sunday Edwin had noticed that in the western country guards were not guards (as in other parts of England), but rather the cordial hosts of their trains. As soon as the doors had banged in a fusillade and the engine whistled, a young porter came and, having exchanged civilities with Harry, picked up Edwin's bag. This porter's face and demeanour showed perfect content. His slight yet eager smile and his quick movements seemed to be saying: 'It is natural and proper that I should salute you and carry your bag while you walk free. You are gentlemen by divine right, and by the same right I am a railway porter and happy.' To watch the man at his job gave positive pleasure, and it was extraordinarily reassuring – reassuring about everything. Outside the station, the groom stood at Joan's head, and a wonderful fox-terrier sat alert under the dogcart. Instantly the dog sprang out and began to superintend the preparations for departure, rushing to and fro and insisting all the time that delay would be monstrous, if not fatal. The dog's excellence as a specimen of breeding was so superlative as to accuse its breeder and owner of a lack of perspective in life. It was as if the entire resources of civilization had been employed towards the perfecting of the points of that dog.

'Balanced the cart, I suppose, Jos?' asked Harry, kindly.

'Yes, sir,' was all that Jos articulated, but his bright face said: 'Sir, your assumption that I have already balanced the cart for three and a bag is benevolent and justified. You trust me. I trust you, sir. All is well.'

The bag was stowed and the porter got threepence and was so happy in his situation that apparently he could not bring himself to leave the scene. Harry climbed up on the right, Edwin on the left. The dog gave one short bark and flew madly forward. Jos loosed Joan's head, and at the same moment Harry gave a click, and the machine started. It did not wait for young Jos. Jos caught the back step as the machine swung by, and levered himself dangerously to the groom's place. And when he had done it he grinned, announcing to beholders that his mission in life was to do just that, and that it was a grand life and he a lucky and enviable fellow.

Harry drove across the Tavy, and through the small grey and brown town, so picturesque, so clean, so solid, so respectable, so content in its historicity. A policeman saluted amiably and firmly, as if saying: 'I am protecting all this, – what a treasure!' Then they passed the Town Hall.

'Town Hall,' said Harry.

'Oh!'

'The Dook's,' said Harry.

He put on a certain facetiousness, but there nevertheless escaped from him the conviction that the ownership of a town hall by a duke was a wondrous rare phenomenon and fine, showing the strength of grand English institutions and traditions, and meet for honest English pride. (And you could say what you liked about progress!) And Edwin had just the same feeling. In another minute they were out of the town. The countryside, though bleak, with its spare hedges and granite walls, was exquisitely beautiful in the morning light; and it was tidy, tended, mature; it was as though it had nothing to learn from the future. Beyond rose the slopes of the moor, tonic and grim. An impression of health, moral and physical, everywhere disengaged itself. The wayfarer, sturdy and benign, invigorated by his mere greeting. The trot of the horse on the smooth winding road, the bounding of the dog, the resilience of the cart springs, the sharp tang of the air on the cheek, all helped to perfect Edwin's sense of pleasure in being alive. He could not deny that he had stood in need of a change.

He had been worrying, perhaps through overwork. Overwork was a mistake. He now saw that there was no reason why he should not be happy always, even with Hilda. He had received a short but nice and almost apologetic letter from Hilda. As for his apprehensions, what on earth did it matter about Dartmoor being so near? Nothing! This district was marvellously reassuring. He thought: 'There simply *is* no social question down here!'

'Had your breakfast?' asked Harry.

'Yes, thanks.'

'Well, you just haven't, then!' said Harry. 'We shall be in the nick of time for it.'

'When do you have breakfast?'

'Nine-thirty.'

'Bit late, isn't it?'

'Oh, no! It suits us . . . I say!' Harry stared straight between the horse's ears.

'What?'

Harry murmured:

'No more news about Johnnie, I suppose?'

(Edwin glanced half round at the groom behind. Harry with a gesture indicated that the groom was negligible.)

'Not that I've heard. Bit stiff, isn't it?' Edwin answered.

'Bit stiff? I should rather say it was. Especially after Jimmie's performance. Rather hard lines on Alicia, don't you think?'

'On all of 'em,' said Edwin, not seeing why Johnnie's escapade should press more on Alicia than, for example, on Janet.

'Yes, of course,' Harry agreed, evidently seeing and accepting the point. 'The less said the better!'

'I'm with you,' said Edwin.

Harry resumed his jolly tone:

'Well, you'd better peck a bit. We've planned a hard day for you.'

'Oh!'

'Yes. Early lunch, and then we're going to drive over to Princetown. Tennis with the Governor of the prison. He'll show us all over the prison. It's worth seeing.'

Impulsively Edwin exclaimed:

'All of you? Is Hilda going?'

'Certainly. Why not?' He raised the whip and pointed:
'Behold our noble towers.'

Edwin, feeling really sick, thought:

'Hilda's mad. She's quite mad . . . Morbid isn't the word!'

He was confounded.

III

At Tavy Mansion Edwin and Harry were told by a maid that
Mrs Hesketh and Miss Orgreave were in the nursery and would
be down in a moment, but that Mrs Clayhanger had a headache
and was remaining in bed for breakfast. The master of the house
himself took Edwin to the door of his wife's bedroom. Edwin's
spirits had risen in an instant, as he perceived the cleverness of
Hilda's headache. There could be no doubt that women were
clever, though perhaps unscrupulously and crudely clever, in a
way beyond the skill of men. By the simple device of suffering
from a headache Hilda had avoided the ordeal of meeting a
somewhat estranged husband in public; she was also preparing
an excuse for not going to Princetown and the prison. Certainly
it was better, in the Dartmoor affair, to escape at the last moment
than to have declined the project from the start.

As he opened the bedroom door, apprehensions and bright
hope were mingled in him. He had a weighty grievance against
Hilda, whose behaviour at parting had been, he considered,
inexcusable; but the warm tone of her curt private telegram to
him and of her almost equally curt letter, re-stating her passionate
love, was really equivalent to an apology, which he accepted with
eagerness. Moreover he had done a lot in coming to Devonshire,
and for this great act he lauded himself and he expected some
gratitude. Nevertheless, despite the pacificism of his feelings, he
could not smile when entering the room. No, he could not!

Hilda was lying in the middle of a very wide bed, and her dark
hair was spread abroad upon the pillow. On the pedestal was a
tea-tray. Squatted comfortably at Hilda's side, with her left arm
as a support, was a baby about a year old, dressed for the day.
This was Cecil, born the day after his grandparents' funeral.
Cecil, with mouth open and outstretched pink hands, of which

the fingers were spread like the rays of half a starfish, from wide eyes gazed at Edwin with a peculiar expression of bland irony. Hilda smiled lovingly; she smiled without reserve. And as soon as she smiled, Edwin could smile, and his heart was suddenly quite light.

Hilda thought:

'That wistful look in his eyes has never changed, and it never will. Imagine him travelling on Sunday when the silly old thing might just as well have come on Saturday, if he'd had anybody to decide him! He's been travelling for twenty-four hours or more, and now he's here! What a shame for me to have dragged him down here in spite of himself! But he would do it for me! He has done it . . . I had to have him, for this afternoon! . . . After all he must be very good at business. Everyone respects him, even here. We may end by being really rich. Have I ever really appreciated him? . . . And now of course he's going to be annoyed again. Poor boy!'

'Hello! Who's this?' cried Edwin.

'This is Cecil. His mummy's left him here with his Auntie Hilda,' said Hilda.

'Another clever dodge of hers!' thought Edwin. He liked the baby being there.

He approached the bed, and, staring nervously about, saw that his bag had already mysteriously reached the bedroom.

'Well, my poor boy! What a journey!' Hilda murmured compassionately. She could not help showing that she was his mother in wisdom and sense.

'Oh, no!' he amiably dismissed this view.

He was standing over her by the bedside. She looked straight up at him timid and expectant. He bent and kissed her. Under his kiss she shifted slightly in the bed, and her arms clung round his neck, and by her arms she lifted herself a little towards him. She shut her eyes. She would not loose him. She seemed again to be drawing the life out of him. At last she let him go, and gave a great sigh. All the past which did not agree with that kiss and that sigh of content was annihilated, and an immense reassurance filled Edwin's mind.

'So you've got a headache?'

She gave a succession of little nods, smiling happily.

'I'm so glad you've come, dearest,' she said, after a pause. She was just like a young girl, like a child, in her relieved satisfaction. 'What about George?'

'Well, as it was left to me to decide, I thought I'd better ask Maggie to come and stay in the house. Much better than packing him off to Auntie Hamps's.'

'And she came?'

'Oh, yes!' said Edwin, indifferently, as if to say: 'Of course she came.'

'Then you did get my letter in time?'

'I shouldn't have got it in time if I'd left Saturday morning as you wanted. Oh! And here's a letter for *you*.'

He pulled a letter from his pocket. The envelope was of the peculiar tinted paper with which he had already been familiarized. Hilda became self-conscious as she took the letter and opened it. Edwin too was self-conscious. To lighten the situation, he put his little finger in the baby's mouth. Cecil much appreciated this form of humour, and as soon as the finger was withdrawn from his toothless gums, he made a bubbling whirring noise, and waved his arms to indicate that the game must continue. Hilda, frowning, read the letter. Edwin sat down, ledging himself cautiously on the brink of the bed, and leaned back a little so as to be able to get at the baby and tickle it among its frills. From the distance, beyond walls, he could hear the powerful, happy cries of older babies, beings fully aware of themselves, who knew their own sentiments and could express them. And he glanced round the long low room with its two small open windows showing sunlit yellow cornfields and high trees, and its monumental furniture, and the disorder of Hilda's clothes and implements humanizing it and individualizing it and making it her abode, her lair. And he glanced prudently at Hilda over the letter-paper. She had no headache; it was obvious that she had no headache. Yet in the most innocent touching way she had nodded an affirmative to his question about the headache. He could not possibly have said to her: 'Look here, you know you haven't got a headache.' She would not have tolerated the truth. The truth would have made her transform herself instantly into a martyr, and him into a brute. She would have stuck to it, even if the seat of eternal judgement had suddenly been installed at the brassy foot of the bed, that she had a headache.

It was with this mentality (he reflected, assuming that his own mentality never loved anything as well as truth) that he had to live till one of them expired. He reminded himself wisely that the woman's code is different from the man's. But the honesty of his intelligence rejected such an explanation, such an excuse. It was not that the woman had a different code, – she had no code except the code of the utter opportunist. To live with her was like living with a marvellous wild animal, full of grace, of cunning, of magnificent passionate gestures, of terrific affection, and of cruelty. She was at once indispensable and intolerable. He felt that to match her he had need of all his force, all his prescience, all his duplicity. The mystery that had lain between him and Hilda for a year was in the letter within two feet of his nose. He could watch her as she read, study her face; he knew that he was the wiser of the two; she was at a disadvantage; as regards the letter, she was fighting on ground chosen by him; and yet he could not in the least foresee the next ten minutes, – whether she would advance, retreat, feint, or surrender.

'Did you bring your dress clothes?' she murmured, while she was reading. She had instructed him in her letter on this point.

'Of course,' he said, manfully, striving to imply the immense untruth that he never stirred from home without his dress clothes.

She continued to read, frowning, and drawing her heavy eyebrows still closer together. Then she said:

'Here!'

And passed him the letter. He could see now that she was becoming excited.

The letter was from the legitimate Mrs George Cannon, and it said that, though nothing official was announced or even breathed, her solicitor had gathered from a permanent and important underling of the Home Office that George Cannon's innocence was supposed to be established, and that the Queen's pardon would, at some time or other, be issued. It was an affecting letter. Edwin, totally ignorant of all that had preceded it, did not immediately understand its significance. At first he did not even grasp what it was about. When he did begin to comprehend he had the sensation of being deprived momentarily of his bearings. He had expected everything but this. That is to say, he had absolutely not known what to expect. The shock was severe.

'*What* is it? *What* is it?' he questioned, as if impatient.

Hilda replied:

'It's about George Cannon. It seems he was quite innocent in that bank-note affair. It's his wife who's been writing to me about it. I don't know why she should. But she did, and of course I had to reply.'

'You never said anything to me about it.'

'I didn't want to worry you, dearest. I knew you'd quite enough on your mind with the works. Besides, I'd no right to worry you with a thing like *that*. But of course I can show you all her letters, – I've kept them.'

Unanswerable! Unanswerable! Insincere, concocted, but unanswerable! The implications in her spoken defence were of the simplest and deepest ingenuity, and withal they hurt him. For example, the implication that the strain of the new works was breaking him! As if he could not support it, and had not supported it, easily! As if the new works meant that he could not fulfil all his duties as a helpmeet! And then the devilishly adroit plea that her concealment was morally necessary since he ought not to be troubled with any result of her preconjugal life! And finally the implication that he would be jealous of the correspondence and might exact the production of it! ... He now callously ignored Cecil's signals for attention ... He knew that he would receive no further enlightenment as to the long secrecy of the past twelve months. His fears and apprehensions and infelicity were to be dismissed with those few words. They would never be paid for, redeemed, atoned. The grand scenic explanation and submission which was his right would never come. Sentimentally, he was cheated, and had no redress. And, as a climax, he had to assume, to pretend, that justice still prevailed on earth.

'Isn't it awful!' Hilda muttered. 'Him in prison all this time!'

He saw that her eyes were wet, and her emotion increasing.

He nodded in sympathy.

He thought:

'She'll want some handling, – I can see that!'

He too, as well as she, imaginatively comprehended the dreadful tragedy of George Cannon's false imprisonment. He had heart enough to be very glad that the innocent man (innocent at any rate of that one thing) was to be released. But at the same time he could not stifle a base foreboding and regret. Looking at his wife, he feared the moment when George Cannon, with all the enormous prestige of a victim in a woman's eyes, should be at large. Yes, the lover in him would have preferred George Cannon to be incarcerated forever. Had he not heard, had he not read, had he not seen on the stage, that a woman never forgets the first man? Nonsense, all that! Invented theatrical psychology! And yet – if it was true! . . . Look at her eyes!

'I suppose he *is* innocent?' he said gruffly, for he mistrusted, or affected to mistrust, the doings of these two women together, – Cannon's wife and Cannon's victim. Might they not somehow have been hoodwinked? He knew nothing, no useful detail, naught that was convincing – and he never would know! Was it not astounding that the bigamist should have both these women on his side, either working for him, or weeping over his woes?

'He must be innocent,' Hilda answered, thoughtfully, in a breaking voice.

'Where is he now, – up yon?'

He indicated the unvisited heights of Dartmoor.

'I believe so.'

'I thought they always shifted 'em back to London before they released 'em.'

'I expect they will do. They may have moved him already.'

His mood grew soft, indulgent. He conceded that her emotion was natural. She had been bound up with the man. Cannon's admitted guilt on the one count, together with all that she had suffered through it, only intensified the poignancy of his innocence on the other count. Contrary to the general assumption, you must be sorrier for an unfortunate rascal than for an unfortunate good man. He could feel all that. He, Edwin, was to be pitied; but nobody save himself would perceive that he was to be pitied.

His own role would be difficult, but all his pride and self-reliance commanded him to play it well, using every resource of his masculine skill, and so prove that he was that which he believed himself to be. The future would be all right, because he would be equal to the emergency. Why should it not be all right? His heart in kindliness and tenderness drew nearer to Hilda's, and he saw, or fancied he saw, that all their guerrilla had been leading up to this, had perhaps been caused by this, and would be nobly ended by it.

Just then a mysterious noise penetrated the room, growing and growing until it became a huge deafening din, and slowly died away.

'I expect that's breakfast,' said Edwin in a casual tone.

The organism of the English household was functioning. Even in the withdrawn calm of the bedroom they could feel it irresistibly functioning. The gong had a physical effect on Cecil; all his disappointment and his sense of being neglected were gathered up in his throat and exploded in a yell. Hilda took him in her right arm and soothed him and called him silly names.

Edwin rose from the bed, and as he did so, Hilda retained him with her left hand, and pulled him very gently towards her, inviting a kiss. He kissed her. She held to him. He could see at a distance of two inches all the dark swimming colour of her wet eyes half veiled by the long lashes. And he could feel the soft limbs of the snuffling baby somewhere close to his head.

'You'd better stick where you are,' he advised her in a casual tone.

Hilda thought:

'Now the time's come. He'll be furious, but I can't help it.'

She said:

'Oh, no! I shall be quite all right soon. I'm going to get up in about half an hour.'

'But then how shall you get out of going to Princetown?'

'Oh! Edwin! I must go! I told them I should go.'

He was astounded. There was no end to her incalculability, – no end! His resentment was violent. He stood right away from her.

'"Told them you should go"!' he exclaimed. 'What in the name of heaven does that matter? Are you absolutely mad?'

She stiffened. Her features hardened. In the midst of her terrible relief as to the fate of George Cannon and of her equal terrible excitement under the enigmatic and irresistible mesmerism of Dartmoor prison, she was desperate, and resentment against Edwin kindled deep within her. She felt the brute in him. She felt that he would never really understand. She felt all her weakness and all his strength, but she was determined. At bottom she knew well that her weakness was the stronger.

'I must go!' she repeated.

'It's nothing but morbidness!' he said savagely. 'Morbidness! . . . Well, I shan't have it. I shan't let you go. And that's flat.'

She kept silent. Frightfully disturbed, cursing women, forgetting utterly in a moment his sublime resolves, Edwin descended to breakfast in the large, strange house. Existence was monstrous.

And before the middle of the morning Hilda came into the garden where everyone else was idling. And Alicia and Janet fondly kissed her. She said her headache had vanished.

'Sure you feel equal to going this afternoon, dearest?' asked Janet.

'Oh, yes!' Hilda replied lightly. 'It will do me good.'

Edwin was helpless. He thought, recalling with vexation his last firm forbidding words to Hilda in the bedroom:

'Nobody *could* be equal to this emergency.'

CHAPTER 15

THE PRISON

I

HARRY had two stout and fast cobs in a light wagonette. He drove himself, and Hilda sat by his side. The driver's boast was that he should accomplish the ten miles, with a rise of a thousand feet, in an hour and a quarter. A hired carriage would have spent two hours over the journey.

It was when they had cleared the town, and were on the long straight rise across the moor towards Longford, that the horses began to prove the faith that was in them, eager, magnanimous, conceiving grandly the splendour of their task in life, and irrepressibly performing it with glory. The stones on the loose-surfaced road flew from under the striding of their hoofs into the soft, dark ling on either hand. Harry's whip hovered in affection over their twin backs, never touching them, and Harry smiled mysteriously to himself. He did not wish to talk. Nor did Hilda. The movement braced and intoxicated her, and rendered thought impossible. She brimmed with emotion, like a vase with some liquid unanalysable and perilous. She was not happy, she was not unhappy; the sensation of her vitality and of the kindred vitality of the earth and the air was overwhelming. She would have prolonged the journey indefinitely, and yet she intensely desired the jail, whatever terrors it might hold for her. At intervals she pulled up the embroidered and monogrammed apron that slipped slowly down over her skirt and over Harry's tennis flannels, disclosing two rackets in a press that lay between them. Perhaps Harry was thinking of certain strokes at tennis.

'Longford!' ejaculated Harry, turning his head slightly towards the body of the vehicle, as they rattled by a hamlet.

Soon afterwards the road mounted steeply, – five hundred feet in little more than a mile, and the horses walked, but they walked in haste, fiercely, clawing at the road with their forefeet and thrusting it behind them. And some of the large tors emerged clearly into view – Cox Tor, the Staple Tors, and Great Mis lifting its granite above them and beyond.

They were now in the midst of the moor, trotting fast again. Behind and before them, and on either side, there was nothing but moor and sky. The sky, a vast hemisphere of cloud and blue and sunshine, with a complex and ever elusive geography of its own, discovered all the tints of heath and granite. It was one of those days when every tint is divided into ten thousand shades, and each is richer and more softly beautiful than the others. On the shoulder of Great Mis rain fell, while little Vixen Tor glittered with mica points in the sun. Nothing could be seen over the whole moor save here and there a long-tailed pony, or a tiny cottage set apart in solitude. And the yellowish road stretched forward, wavily, narrowing, disappeared for a space, reappeared still narrower, disappeared once more, reappeared like a thin meandering line, and was lost on the final verge. It was an endless road. Impossible that the perseverance of horses should cover it yard by yard! But the horses strained onward, seeing naught but the macadam under their noses. Harry checked them at a descent.

'Walkham River!' he announced.

They crossed a pebbly stream by a granite bridge.

'Hut circles!' said Harry laconically.

They were climbing again.

Edwin, in the body of the wagonette with Janet and Alicia, looked for hut circles and saw none; but he did not care. He was content with the knowledge that prehistoric hut circles were somewhere there. He had never seen wild England before, and its primeval sanity awoke in him the primeval man. The healthiness and simplicity and grandiose beauty of it created the sublime illusion that civilization was worthy to be abandoned. The Five Towns seemed intolerable by their dirt and ugliness, and by the tedious intricacy of their existence. Lithography, – you had but to think of the word to perceive the paltriness of the thing! Riches, properties, proprieties, all the safeties, – futile! He could have lived alone with Hilda on the moor, begetting children by her, watching with satisfaction the growing curves of her fecundity – his work, and seeing her with her brood, all their faces beaten by wind and rain and browned with sun. He had a tremendous, a painful longing for such a life. His imagination played round the idea of it with voluptuous and pure pleasure, and he wondered that he had never thought of it before. He felt that he had never before peered into the depths of existence. And though he knew that the dream of such an arcadian career was absurd, yet he seemed to guess that beneath the tiresome surfaces of life in the Five Towns the essence of it might be mystically lived. And he thought that Hilda would be capable of sharing it with him, – nay, he knew she would!

His mood became gravely elated, even optimistic. He saw that he had worried himself about nothing. If she wanted to visit the prison, let her visit it! Why not? At any rate he should not visit it. He had an aversion for morbidity almost as strong as his aversion for sentimentality. But her morbidity could do no harm. She could not possibly meet George Cannon. The chances were utterly against such an encounter. Her morbidity would cure itself. He pitied her, cherished her, and in thought enveloped her fondly with his sympathetic and protective wisdom.

'North Hessary!' said Harry, pointing with his whip to a jutting tor on the right hand. 'We go round by the foot of it. There in a jiff!'

Soon afterwards they swerved away from the main road, obeying a signpost marked 'Princetown'.

'Glorious, isn't it?' murmured Janet, after a long silence which had succeeded the light chatter of herself and Alicia about children, servants, tennis, laundries.

He nodded, with a lively responsive smile, and glanced at Hilda's mysterious back. Only once during the journey had she looked round. Alicia with her coarse kind voice and laugh began to rally him, saying he had dozed.

A town, more granite than the moor itself, gradually revealed its roofs in the heart of the moor. The horses, indefatigable, quickened their speed. Villas, a school, a chapel, a heavy church-tower followed in succession; there were pavements; a brake full of excursionists had halted in front of a hotel; holiday-makers – simple folk who disliked to live in flocks – wandered in ecstatic idleness. Concealed within the warmth of the mountain air, there pricked a certain sharpness. All about, beyond the little town, the tors raised their shaggy flanks surmounted by colossal masses of stone that recalled the youth of the planet. The feel of the world was stimulating like a tremendous tonic. Then the wagon-ette passed a thick grove of trees, hiding a house, and in a moment, like magic, appeared a huge gated archway of brick and stone, and over it the incised words:

PARCERE SUBJECTIS

'Stop! Stop! Harry,' cried Alicia shrilly. 'What are you doing? You'll have to go to the house first.'

'Shall I?' said Harry. 'All right. Two thirty-five, be it noted.'

The vehicle came to a standstill, and instantly clouds of vapour rose from the horses.

'Virgil!' thought Edwin, gazing at the archway, which filled him with sudden horror, like an obscenity misplaced.

II

Less then ten minutes later, he and Hilda and Alicia, together with three strange men, stood under the archway. Events had followed one another quickly, to Edwin's undoing. When the wagonette drew up in the grounds of the Governor's house, Harry Hesketh had politely indicated that for his horses he preferred the stables of a certain inn down the road to any stables that hospitality might offer; and he had driven off, Mrs Rotherwas urging him to return without any delay so that tennis might begin. The Governor had been called from home, and in his absence a high official of the prison was deputed to show the visitors through the establishment. This official was the first of the three strange men; the other two were visitors. Janet had said that she would not go over the prison, because she meant to play tennis and wished not to tire herself. Alicia said kindly that she at any rate would go with Hilda, – though she had seen it all before, it was interesting enough to see again.

Edwin had thereupon said that he should remain with Janet. But immediately Mrs Rotherwas, whose reception of him had been full of the most friendly charm, had shown surprise, if not pain.

What, – come to Princetown without inspecting the wonderful prison, when the chance was there? Inconceivable! Edwin might in his blunt Five Towns way have withstood Mrs Rotherwas, but he could not withstand Hilda, who, frowning, seemed almost ready to risk a public altercation in order to secure his attendance. He had to yield. To make a scene, even a very little one, in the garden full of light dresses and polite suave voices would have been monstrous. He thought of all that he had ever heard of the subjection of men to women. He thought of Johnnie and of Mrs Chris Hamson, who was known for her steely caprices. And he thought also of Jimmie and of the undesirable Mrs Jimmie, who, it was said, had threatened to love Jimmie no more unless he took her once a week without fail to the theatre, whatever the piece, and played cards with her and two of her friends on all the other nights of the week. He thought of men as a sex conquered by the unscrupulous and the implacable, and in this mood, superimposed on his mood of disgust at the mere sight of the archway, he followed the high official and his train. Mrs Rotherwas's last words were that they were not to be long. But the official said privately to the group that they must at any rate approach the precincts of the prison with all ceremony, and he led them proudly, with an air of ownership, round to the main entrance where the wagonette had first stopped.

A turnkey on the other side of the immense gates, using a theatrical gesture, jangled a great bouquet of keys; the portal opened, increasing the pride of the official, and the next moment they were interned in the outer courtyard. The moor and all that it meant lay unattainable beyond that portal. As the group slowly crossed the enclosed space, with the grim façades of yellow-brown buildings on each side and vistas of further gates and buildings in front, the official and the two male visitors began to talk together over the heads of Alicia and Hilda. The women held close to each other, and the official kept upon them a chivalrous eye; the two visitors were friends; Edwin was left out of the social scheme, and lagged somewhat behind, like one who is not wanted but who cannot be abandoned. He walked self-conscious, miserable, resentful, and darkly angry. In one instant the three men had estimated him, decided that he was not of their clan

nor of any related clan, and ignored him. Whereas the official
and the two male visitors, who had never met before, grew more
and more friendly each minute. One said that he did not know
So-and-so of the Scots Greys, but he knew his cousin Trevor of
the Hussars, who had in fact married a niece of his own. And
then another question about somebody else was asked, and
immediately they were engaged in following clues, as explorers
will follow the intricate mouths of a great delta and so unite in
the main stream. They were happy.

Edwin did not seriously mind that; but what he did mind
was their accent – in those days termed throughout the Midlands
'lah-di-dah' (an onomatopoeic description), which, falsifying
every vowel sound in the language, and several consonants,
magically created around them an aura of utter superiority to
the rest of the world. He quite unreasonably hated them, and he
also envied them, because this accent was their native tongue, and
because their clothes were not cut like his, and because they were
entirely at their ease. Useless for the official to throw him an
urbane word now and then; neither his hate nor his constraint
would consent to be alleviated; the urbane words grew less
frequent. Also Edwin despised them because they were seemingly
insensible to the tremendous horror of the jail set there like an
outrage in the midst of primitive and sane Dartmoor. 'Yes,' their
attitude said, 'this is a prison, one of the institutions necessary to
the well-being of society, like a workhouse or an opera house, –
an interesting sight!'

A second pair of iron gates were opened with the same elaborate theatricality as the first, and while the operation was being
done the official, invigorated by the fawning of turnkeys, con-
versed with Alicia, who during her short married life had acquired
some shallow acquaintance with the clans, and he even drew a
reluctant phrase from Hilda. Then, after another open space,
came a third pair of iron gates, final and terrific, and at length
the party was under cover, and even the sky of the moor was lost.
Edwin, bored, disgusted, shamed, and stricken, yielded himself
proudly and submissively to the horror of the experience.

III

Hilda had only one thought – would she catch sight of the innocent prisoner? The party was now deeply engaged in a system of corridors and stairways. The official had said that as the tour of inspection was to be short he would display to them chiefly the modern part of the prison. So far not a prisoner had been seen, and scarcely a warder. The two male visitors were scientifically interested in the question of escapes. Did prisoners ever escape?

'Never!' said the official, with satisfaction.

'Impossible, I suppose. Even when they're working out on the moor? Warders are pretty good shots, eh?'

'Practically impossible,' said the official. 'But there is one way.' He looked up the stairway on whose landing they stood, and down the stairway, and cautiously lowered his voice. 'Of course what I tell you is confidential. If one of our Dartmoor fogs came on suddenly, and kind friends outside had hidden a stock of clothes and food in an arranged spot, then theoretically – I say, theoretically – a man might get away. But nobody ever has done.'

'I suppose you still have the silent system?'

The official nodded.

'Absolutely?'

'Absolutely.'

'How awful it must be!' said Alicia, with a nervous laugh.

The official shrugged his shoulders, and the other two males murmured reassuring axioms about discipline.

They emerged from the stairway into a colossal and resounding iron hall. Round the emptiness of this interior ran galleries of perforated iron protected from the abyss by iron balustrades. The group stood on the second of the galleries from the stony floor, and there were two galleries above them. Far away, opposite, a glint of sunshine had feloniously slipped in, transpiercing the gloom, and it lighted a series of doors. There was a row of these doors along every gallery. Each had a peep-hole, a keyhole, and a number. The longer Hilda regarded, the more nightmarishly numerous seemed the doors. The place was like a huge rabbit-hutch designed for the claustration of countless rabbits. Across the whole width and length of the hall, and at the level of the lowest gallery, was stretched a great net.

'To provide against suicides?' suggested one of the men.

'Yes,' said the official.

'A good idea.'

When the reverberation of the words had ceased, a little silence ensued. The ear listened vainly for the slightest sound. In the silence the implacability of granite walls and iron reticulations reigned over the accursed vision, stultifying the soul.

'Are these cells occupied?' asked Alicia timidly.

'Not yet, Mrs Hesketh. It's too soon. A few are.'

Hilda thought:

'He may be here, – behind one of those doors.' Her heart was liquid with compassion and revolt. 'No,' she assured herself. 'They must have taken him away already. It's impossible he should be here. He's innocent.'

'Perhaps you would like to see one of the cells?' the official suggested.

A warder appeared, and, with the inescapable jangle of keys, opened a door. The party entered the cell, ladies first, then the official and his new acquaintances; then Edwin, trailing. The cell was long and narrow, fairly lofty, bluish-white colour, very dimly lighted by a tiny grimed window high up in a wall of extreme thickness. The bed lay next the long wall; except the bed, a stool, a shelf, and some utensils, there was nothing to furnish the horrible nakedness of the cell. One of the visitors picked up an old book from the shelf. It was a Greek Testament. The party seemed astonished at this evidence of culture among prisoners, of the height from which a criminal may have fallen.

The official smiled.

'They often ask for such things on purpose,' said he. 'They think it's effective. They're very naïve, you know, at bottom.'

'This very cell may be his cell,' thought Hilda. 'He may have been here all these months, years, knowing he was innocent. He may have thought about me in this cell.' She glanced cautiously at Edwin, but Edwin would not catch her eye.

They left. On the way to the workshops, they had a glimpse

of the old parts of the prison, used during the Napoleonic wars, incredibly dark, frowsy, like catacombs.

'We don't use this part – unless we're very full up,' said the official, and he contrasted it with the bright, spacious, healthy excellences of the hall which they had just quitted, to prove that civilization never stood still.

And then suddenly, at the end of a passage, a door opened and they were in the tailor's shop, a large irregular apartment full of a strong stench and of squatted and grotesque human beings. The human beings, for the most part, were clothed in a peculiar brown stuff covered with broad arrows. The dress consisted of a short jacket, baggy knickerbockers, black stockings, and coloured shoes. Their hair was cut so short that they had the appearance of being bald, and their great ears protruded at a startling angle from the sides of those smooth heads. They were of every age, yet they all looked alike, ridiculous, pantomimic, appalling. Some gazed with indifference at the visitors; others seemed oblivious of the entry. They all stitched on their haunches, in the stench, under the surveillance of eight armed warders in blue.

'How many?' asked the official mechanically.

'Forty-nine, sir,' said a warder.

And Hilda searched their loathsome and vapid faces for the face of George Cannon. He was not there. She trembled, – whether with relief or with disappointment she knew not. She was agonized, but in her torture she exulted that she had come.

No comment had been made in the workshop, the official having hinted that silence was usual on such occasions. But in a kind of antechamber – one of those amorphous spaces, serving no purpose and resembling nothing, which are sometimes to be found between definable rooms and corridors in a vast building imperfectly planned – the party halted in the midst of a discussion as to discipline. The male visitors, except Edwin, showed marked intelligence and detachment; they seemed to understand immediately how it was that forty-nine ruffians could be trusted to squat on their thighs and stitch industriously and use scissors and other weapons for hours without being chained to the ground; they certainly knew something of the handling of men. The official, triumphant, stated that every prisoner had the right of personal appeal to the Governor every day.

'They come with their stories of grievances,' said he, tolerant and derisive.

'Which often aren't true?'

'Which are never true,' said the official quietly. 'Never! They are always lies – always! . . . Shows the material we have to deal with!' He gave a short laugh.

'Really!' said one of the men, rather pleased and excited by this report of universal lying.

'I suppose,' Edwin blurted out, 'you can tell for certain when they aren't speaking the truth?'

Everybody looked at him surprised, as though the dumb had spoken. The official's glance showed some suspicion of sarcasm and a tendency to resent it.

'We can,' he answered shortly, commanding his features to a faint smile. 'And now I wonder what Mrs Rotherwas will be saying if I don't restore you to her.' It was agreed that regard must be had for Mrs Rotherwas's hospitable arrangements, though the prison was really very interesting and would repay study.

They entered a wide corridor – one of two that met at right-angles in the amorphous space – leading in the direction of the chief entrance. From the end of this corridor a file of convicts was approaching in charge of two warders with guns. The official offered no remark, but held on. Hilda, falling back near to Edwin in the procession, was divided between a dreadful fear and a hope equally dreadful. Except in the tailor's shop, these were the only prisoners they had seen, and they appeared out of place in the half-freedom of the corridor; for nobody could conceive a prisoner save in a cell or shop, and these were moving in a public corridor, unshackled.

Then she distinguished George Cannon among them. He was the third from the last. She knew him by his nose and the shape of his chin, and by his walk, though there was little left of his proud walk in the desolating, hopeless prison shuffle which was the gait of all six convicts. His hair was iron grey. All these details she could see and be sure of in the distance of the dim corridor. She no longer had a stomach; it had gone, and yet she felt a horrible nausea.

She cried out to herself:

'Why did I come? Why did I come? I am always doing these mad things. Edwin was right. Why do I not listen to him?'

The party of visitors led by the high official, and the file of convicts in charge of armed warders, were gradually approaching one another in the wide corridor. It seemed to Hilda that a fearful collision was imminent, and that something ought to be done. But nobody among the visitors did anything or seemed to be disturbed. Only they had all fallen silent; and in the echoing corridor could be heard the firm steps of the male visitors accompanying the delicate tripping of the women, and the military tramp of the warders with the confused shuffling of the convicts.

'Has he recognized me?' thought Hilda wildly.

She hoped that he had and that he had not. She recalled with the most poignant sorrow the few days of their union, their hours of intimacy, his kisses, her secret realization of her power over him, and of his passion. She wanted to scream:

'That man there is as innocent as any of you, and soon the whole world will know it! He never committed any crime except of loving me too much. He could not do without me, and so I was his ruin. It is horrible that he should be here in this hell. He must be set free at once. The Home Secretary knows he is innocent, but they are so slow. How can anyone bear that he should stop here one instant longer?'

But she made no sound. The tremendous force of an ancient and organized society kept her lips closed and her feet in a line with the others. She thought in despair:

'We are getting nearer, and I cannot meet him. I shall drop.'

She glanced at Edwin, as if for help, but Edwin was looking straight ahead.

Then a warder, stopping, ejaculated with the harsh brevity of a drill-serjeant:

'Halt!'

The file halted.

'Right turn!'

The six captives turned, with their faces close against the wall of the corridor, obedient, humiliated, spiritless, limp, stooping. Their backs presented the most ridiculous aspect; all the calculated grotesquerie of the surpassingly ugly prison uniform was accentuated as they stood thus, a row of living scarecrows, who knew that they had not the right even to look upon free men. Every one of them except George Cannon had large protuberant ears that completed the monstrosity of their appearance.

The official gave his new acquaintances a satisfied glance, as if saying:

'That is the rule by which we manage these chance encounters.'

The visitors went by in silence, instinctively edging away from the captives. And as she passed, Hilda lurched very heavily against Edwin, and recovered herself. Edwin seized her arm near the shoulder, and saw that she was pale. The others were in front.

Behind them they could hear the warder:

'Left turn! March!'

And the shuffling and the tramping recommenced.

IV

In the garden of the Governor's house tennis had already begun when the official brought back his convoy. Young Truscott and Mrs Rotherwas were pitted against Harry Hesketh and a girl of eighteen who possessed a good wrist but could not keep her head. Harry was watching over his partner, quietly advising her upon the ruses of the enemy, taking the more difficult strokes for her, and generally imparting to her the quality which she lacked. Harry was fully engaged; the whole of his brain and body was at strain; he let nothing go by; he missed no chance, and within the laws of the game he hesitated at no stratagem. And he was beating young Truscott and Mrs Rotherwas, while an increasing and polite audience looked on. To the entering party, the withdrawn scene, lit by sunshine, appeared as perfect as a stage show, with its trees, lawn, flowers, toilettes, the flying balls, the grace of the players, and the grey solidity of the Governor's house in the background.

Alicia ran gawkily to Janet, who had got a box of chocolates from somewhere, and one of the men followed her, laughing.

Hilda sat apart; she was less pale. Edwin remained cautiously near her. He had not left her side since she lurched against him in the corridor. He knew; he had divined that that which he most feared had come to pass, – the supreme punishment of Hilda's morbidity. He had not definitely recognized George Cannon, for he was not acquainted with him, and in the past had only once or twice by chance caught sight of him in the streets of Bursley or Turnhill. But he had seen among the six captives one who might be he, and who certainly had something of the Five Towns look. Hilda's lurch told him that by the vindictiveness of fate George Cannon was close to them.

He had ignored his own emotion. The sudden transient weight of Hilda's body had had a strange moral effect upon him. 'This,' he thought, 'is the burden I have to bear. This, and not lithography, nor riches, is my chief concern. She depends on me. I am all she has to stand by.' The burden with its immense and complex responsibilities was sweet to his inmost being; and it braced him and destroyed his resentment against her morbidity. His pity was pure. He felt that he must live more nobly – yes, more heroically – than he had been living; that all irritable pettiness must drop away from him, and that his existence in her regard must have simplicity and grandeur. The sensation of her actual weight stayed with him. He had not spoken to her; he dared not; he had scarcely met her eyes; but he was ready for any emergency. Every now and then, in the garden, Hilda glanced over her shoulder at the house, as though her gaze could pierce the house and see the sinister prison beyond.

The set ended, to Harry Hesketh's satisfaction; and, another set being arranged, he and Mrs Rotherwas, athletic in a short skirt and simple blouse, came walking, rather flushed and breathless, round the garden with one or two others, including Harry's late partner. The conversation turned upon the great South Wales colliery strike against a proposed reduction of wages. Mrs Rotherwas's husband was a colliery proprietor near Monmouth, and she had just received a letter from him. Everyone sympathized with her and her husband, and nobody could comprehend the wrongheadedness of the miners, except upon the supposition that they had been led away by mischievous demagogues. As the group approached, the timid young girl, having regained her nerve, was exclaiming with honest indignation: 'The leaders ought to be shot, and the men who won't go down the pits ought to be *forced* to go down and *made* to work.' And she picked at fluff on her yellow frock. Edwin feared an uprising from Hilda, but naught happened. Mrs Rotherwas spoke about tea, though it was rather early, and they all, Hilda as well, wandered to a large yew tree under which was a table; through the pendent branches of the tree the tennis could be watched as through a screen.

The prison clock tolled the hour over the roofs of the house, and Mrs Rotherwas gave the definite signal for refreshments.

'You're exhausted,' she said teasingly to Harry.

'You'll see,' said Harry.

'No,' Mrs Rotherwas delightfully relented. 'You're a dear, and I love to watch you play. I'm sure you could give Mr Truscott half fifteen.'

'Think so?' said Harry, pleased, and very conscious that he was living fully.

'You see what it is to have an object in life, Hesketh,' Edwin remarked suddenly.

Harry glanced at him doubtfully, and yet with a certain ingenuous admiration. At the same time a white ball rolled near the tree. He ducked under the trailing branches, returned the ball, and moved slowly towards the court.

'Alicia tells me you're very old friends of theirs,' said Mrs Rotherwas, agreeably, to Hilda.

Hilda smiled quietly.

'Yes, we are, both of us.'

Who could have guessed, now, that her condition was not absolutely normal?

'Charming people, aren't they, the Heskeths?' said Mrs Rotherwas. 'Perfectly charming. They're an ideal couple. And I do like their house, it's so deliciously quaint, isn't it, Mary?'

'Lovely,' agreed the young girl.

It was an ideal world, full of ideal beings.

Soon after tea the irresistible magnetism of Alicia's babies drew Alicia off the moor, and with her the champion player,

Janet, Hilda, and Edwin. Mrs Rotherwas let them go with regret, adorably expressed. Harry would have liked to stay, but on the other hand he was delightfully ready to yield to Alicia.

V

On arriving at Tavy Mansion Hilda announced that she should lie down. She told Edwin, in an exhausted but friendly voice, that she needed only rest, and he comprehended, rightly, that he was to leave her. Not a word was said between them as to the events within the prison. He left her, and spent the time before dinner with Harry Hesketh, who had the idea of occupying their leisure with a short game of bowls, for which it was necessary to remove the croquet hoops.

Hilda undressed and got into bed. Soon afterwards both Alicia, with an infant, and Janet came to see her. Had Janet been alone, Hilda might conceivably in her weakness have surrendered the secret to her in exchange for that soft and persuasive sympathy of which Janet was the mistress, but the presence of Alicia made a confidence impossible, and Hilda was glad. She plausibly fibbed to both sisters, and immediately afterwards the household knew that Hilda would not appear at dinner. There was not the slightest alarm or apprehension, for the affair explained itself in the simplest way, – Hilda had had a headache in the morning, and had been wrong to go out; she was now merely paying for the indiscretion. She would be quite recovered the next day. Alicia whispered a word to her husband, who, besides, was not apt easily to get nervous about anything except his form at games. Edwin also, with his Five Towns habit of mind, soberly belittled the indisposition. The household remained natural and gay. When Edwin went upstairs to prepare for dinner, moving very quietly, his wife had her face towards the wall and away from the light. He came round the bed to look at her.

'I'm all right,' she murmured.

'Want nothing at all?' he asked, with nervous gruffness.

She shook her head.

Very impatiently she awaited his departure, exasperated more than she had ever been by his precise deliberation over certain details of his toilet. As soon as he was gone she began to cry; but the tears came so gently from her eyes that the weeping was as passive, as independent of volition, as the escape of blood from a wound.

She had a grievance against Edwin. At the crisis in the prison she had blamed herself for not submitting to his guidance, but now she had reacted against all such accusations, and her grievance amounted to just an indictment of his common sense, his quietude, his talent for keeping out of harm's way, his lack of violent impulses, his formidable respectability. She was a rebel; he was not. He would never do anything wrong, or even perilous. Never, never would he find himself in need of a friend's help. He would always direct his course so that society would protect him. He was a firm part of the structure of society; he was the enemy of impulses. When he foresaw a danger, the danger was always realized; she had noticed that, and she resented it. He was infinitely above the George Cannons of the world. He would be incapable of bigamy, incapable of being caught in circumstances which could bring upon him suspicion of any crime whatever. Yet for her the George Cannons had a quality which he lacked, which he could never possess, and which would have impossibly perfected him – a quality heroic, foolish, martyr-like! She was almost ready to decide that his complete social security was due to cowardice and resulted in self-righteousness! . . . Could he really feel pity as she felt it, for the despised and rejected, and a hatred of injustice equal to hers?

These two emotions were burning her up. Again and again, ceaselessly, her mind ran round the circle of George Cannon's torture and the callousness of society. He had sinned, and she had loathed him; but both his sin and her loathing were the fruit of passion. He had been a proud man, and she had shared his pride; now he was broken, unutterably humiliated, and she partook of his humiliation. The grotesque and beaten animal in the corridor was all that society had left of him who had once inspired her to acts of devotion, who could make her blush, and to satisfy whom she would recklessly spend herself. The situation was intolerable, and yet it had to be borne. But surely it must be ended! Surely at the latest on the morrow the prisoner must be released, and

soothed and reinstated! . . . Pardoned? No! A pardon was an
insult, worse than an insult. She would not listen to the word.
Society might use it for its own purposes; but she would never
use it. Pardon a man after deliberately and fiendishly achieving
his ruin? She could have laughed.

Exhaustion followed, tempering emotion and reducing it to a
profound despairing melancholy that was stirred at intervals by
frantic revolt. The light failed. The windows became vague silver
squares. Outside fowls clucked, a horse's hoof clattered on stones;
servants spoke to each other in their rough, good-natured voices.
The peace of the world had its effect on her, unwilling though she
was. Then there was a faint tap at the door. She made no reply,
and shut her eyes. The door gently opened, and someone tripped
delicately in. She heard movements at the washstand . . . One of
the maids. A match was struck. The blinds were stealthily lowered,
the curtains drawn; garments were gathered together, and at last
the door closed again.

She opened her eyes. The room was very dimly illuminated . A
night-light, under a glass hemisphere of pale rose, stood on the
dressing-table. By magic, order had been restored; a glinting
copper ewer of hot water stood in the whiteness of the basin with
a towel over it; the blue blinds, revealed by the narrowness of
the red curtains, stirred in the depths of the windows; each detail
of the chamber was gradually disclosed, and the chamber was
steeped in the first tranquillity of the night. Not a sound could
be heard. Through the depths of her bitterness, there rose slowly
the sensation of the beauty of existence even in its sadness . . .

A long time afterwards it occurred to her in the obscurity that
the bed was tumbled. She must have turned over and over. The
bed must be arranged before Edwin came. He had to share it.
After all, he had committed no fault; he was entirely innocent.
She and fate between them had inflicted these difficulties and
these solicitudes upon him. He had said little or nothing, but
he was sympathetic. When she had stumbled against him she
had felt his upholding masculine strength. He was dependable,
and would be dependable to the last. The bed must be creaseless
when he came; this was the least she could do. She arose. Very
faintly she could descry her image in the mirror of the great

wardrobe – a dishevelled image. Forgetting the bed, she bathed
her face, and, unusually, took care to leave the washstand as tidy
as the maid had left it. Then, having arranged her hair, she set
about the bed. It was not easy for one person unaided to make
a wide bed. Before she had finished she heard footsteps outside
the door. She stood still. Then she heard Edwin's voice:

'Don't trouble, thanks. I'll take it in myself.'

He entered, carrying a tray, and shut the door, and instantly
she busied herself once more with the bed.

'My poor girl,' he said with quiet kindliness, 'what are you
doing?'

'I'm just putting the bed to rights,' she answered, and almost
with a single movement she slid back into the bed. 'What have
you got there?'

'I thought I'd ask for some tea for you,' he said. 'Nearly the
whole blessed household wanted to come and see you, but I
wouldn't have it.'

She could not say: 'It's very nice of you.' But she said, simply
to please him: 'I should like some tea.'

He put the tray on the dressing-table; then lit three candles,
two on the dressing-table and one on the night-table, and brought
the tray to the night-table.

He himself poured out the tea, and offered the cup. She raised
herself on an elbow.

'Did you recognize him?' she muttered suddenly, after she
had blown on the tea to cool it.

Under ordinary conditions Edwin would have replied to such
an unprepared question with another, petulant and impatient:
'Recognize who?' pretending that he did not understand the
allusion. But now he made no pretences.

'Not quite,' he said. 'But I knew at once. I could see which
of them it must be.'

The subject at last opened between them, Hilda felt an extraordinary solace and relief. He stood by the bedside, in black, with
a great breastplate of white, his hair rough, his hands in his
pockets. She thought he had a fine face; she thought of him as,
at such a time, her superior; she wanted powerfully to adopt his
attitude, to believe in everything he said. They were talking

together in safety, quietly, gravely, amicably, withdrawn and safe in the strange house – he benevolent and assuaging and comprehending, she desiring the balm which he could give. It seemed to her that they had never talked to each other in such tones.

'Isn't it awful – awful!' she exclaimed.

'It is,' said Edwin, and added carefully, tenderly: 'I suppose he *is* innocent.'

She might have flown at him: 'That's just like you – to assume he isn't!' But she replied:

'I'm quite sure of it. I say – I want you to read all the letters I've had from Mrs Cannon. I've got them here. They're in my bag there. Read them now. Of course I always meant to show them to you.'

'All right,' he agreed, drew a chair to the dressing-table where the bag was, found the letters, and read them. She waited, as he read one letter, put it down, read another, laid it precisely upon the first one, with his terrible exactitude and orderliness, and so on through the whole packet.

'Yes,' said he at the end, 'I should say he's innocent this time, right enough.'

'But something ought to be done!' she cried. 'Don't you think something ought to be done, Edwin?'

'Something has been done. Something is being done.'

'But something else!'

He got up and walked about the room.

'There's only one thing to be done,' he said.

He came towards her, and stood over her again, and the candle on the night-table lighted his chin and the space between his eyelashes and his eyebrows. He timidly touched her hair, caressing it. They were absolutely at their ease together in the intimacy of the bedroom. In her brief relations with George Cannon there had not been time to establish anything like such intimacy. With George Cannon she had always had the tremors of the fawn.

'What is it?'

'Wait. That's all. It's not the slightest use trying to hurry these public departments. You can't do it. You only get annoyed for nothing at all. You can take that from me, my child.'

He spoke with such delicate persuasiveness, such an evident desire to be helpful, that Hilda was convinced and grew resigned. It did not occur to her that he had made a tremendous resolve which had raised him above the Edwin she knew. She thought she had hitherto misjudged and underrated him.

'I wanted to explain to you about that ten pounds,' she said.

'That's all right – that's all right,' said he hastily.

'But I *must* tell you. You saw Mrs Cannon's letter asking me for money. Well, I borrowed the ten pounds from Janet. So of course I had to pay it back, hadn't I?'

'How is Janet?' he asked in a new, lighter tone.

'She seems to be going on splendidly, don't you think so?'

'Well then, we'll go home tomorrow.'

'Shall we?'

She lifted her arms and he bent. She was crying. In a moment she was sobbing. She gave him violent kisses amid her sobs, and held him close to her until the fit passed. Then she said, in her voice reduced to that of a child:

'What time's the train?'

CHAPTER 16
THE GHOST

I

IT was six-thirty. The autumn dusk had already begun to fade; and in the damp air, cold, grimy, and vaporous, men with scarves round their necks and girls with shawls over their heads, or hatted and even gloved, were going home from work past the petty shops where sweets, tobacco, fried fish, chitterlings, groceries, and novelettes were sold among enamelled advertisements of magic soaps. In the feeble and patchy illumination of the footpaths, which left the middle of the streets and the upper air all obscure, the chilled, preoccupied people passed each other rapidly like phantoms, emerging out of one mystery and disappearing into another. Everywhere, behind the fanlights and shaded windows of cottages, domesticity was preparing the warm relaxations of the night. Amid the streets of little buildings the lithographic establishment, with a yellow oblong here and there illuminated in its dark façades, stood up high, larger than reality, more important and tyrannic, one of the barracks, one of the prisons, one of the money-works where a single man or a small group of men by brains and vigour and rigour exploited the populace.

Edwin, sitting late in his private office behind those façades, was not unaware of the sensation of being an exploiter. By his side on the large flat desk lay a copy of the afternoon's *Signal* containing an account of the breaking up by police of an open-air meeting of confessed anarchists on the previous day at Manchester. Manchester was, and is still, physically and morally, very close to the Five Towns, which respect it more than they respect London. An anarchist meeting at Manchester was indeed an uncomfortable portent for the Five Towns. Enormous strikes, like civil wars at stalemate, characterized the autumn as they had characterized the spring, affecting directly or indirectly every industry, and weakening the prestige of government, conventions, wealth, and success. Edwin was successful. It was because he was successful that he was staying late and that a clerk in the outer office was staying late and that windows were illuminated here and there in the façades. Holding in his hand the wage-book, he glanced down the long column of names and amounts. Some names conveyed nothing to him; but most of them raised definite images in his mind – of big men, roughs, decent clerks with wristbands, undersized pale machinists, intensely respectable skilled artisans and draughtsmen, thin ragged lads, greasy, slatternly, pale girls, and one or two fat women, – all dirty, and working with indifference in dirt. Most of them kowtowed to him; some did not; some scowled askance. But they were all dependent on him. Not one of them but would be prodigiously alarmed and inconvenienced – to say nothing of going hungry – if he did not pay wages the next morning. The fact was he could distribute ruin with a gesture and nobody could bring him to book . . .

Something wrong! Under the influence of strikes and anarchist meetings he felt with foreboding and even with a little personal alarm that something was wrong. Those greasy, slatternly girls, for instance, with their coarse charm and their sexuality, – they were underpaid. They received as much as other girls, on potbanks, perhaps more, but they were underpaid. What chance had they? He was getting richer every day, and safer (except for the vague menace); yet he could not appreciably improve their lot, partly for business reasons, partly because any attempt to do so would bring the community about his ears, and he would be labelled as a doctrinaire and a fool, and partly because his own common sense was against such a move. Not those girls, not his works, not this industry and that, was wrong. All was wrong. And it was impossible to imagine any future period when all would not be wrong. Perfection was a desolating thought. Nevertheless the struggle towards it was instinctive and had to go on. The danger was (in Edwin's eyes) of letting that particular struggle monopolize one's energy. Well, he would not let it. He did a little here and a little there, and he voted democratically and in his heart was most destructively sarcastic about toryism; and for the rest he relished the adventure of existence, and took the best he conscientiously could, and thought pretty well of himself as a lover of his fellow men. If he was born to be a master, he would be one, and not spend his days in trying to overthrow mastery. He was tired that evening, he had a slight headache, he certainly had worries; but he was not unhappy on the throbbing, tossing steamer of humanity. Nobody could seem less adventurous than he seemed, with his timidities and his love of moderation, comfort, regularity, and security. Yet his nostrils would sniff to the supreme and all-embracing adventure.

He heard Hilda's clear voice in the outer office: 'Mr Clayhanger in there?' and the clerk's somewhat nervously agitated reply, repeating several times an eager affirmative. And he himself, the master, though still all alone in the sanctum, at once pretended to be very busy.

Her presence would thus often produce an excitation in the organism of the business. She was so foreign to it, so unsoiled by it, so aloof from it, so much more gracious, civilized, enigmatic than anything that the business could show! And, fundamentally, she was the cause of the business; it was all for her; it existed with its dirt, noise, crudity, strain, and eternal effort so that she might exist in her elegance, her disturbing femininity, her restricted and deep affections, her irrational capriciousness, and her strange, brusque common sense. The clerks and some of the women felt this; Big James certainly felt it; and Edwin felt it, and denied it to himself, more than anybody. There was no economic justice in the arrangement. She would come in veiled, her face mysterious behind the veil, and after a few minutes she would delicately lift her gloved fingers to the veil, and raise it, and her dark, pale, vivacious face would be disclosed. 'Here I am!' And the balance was even, her debt paid! That was how it was.

In the month that had passed since the visit to Dartmoor, Edwin, despite his resolve to live heroically and philosophically, had sometimes been forced into the secret attitude: 'This woman will kill me, but without her I shouldn't be interested enough to live.' He was sometimes morally above her to the point of priggishness, and sometimes incredibly below her; but for the most part living in a different dimension. She had heard nothing further from Mrs Cannon; she knew nothing of the bigamist's fate, though more than once she had written for news. Her moods were unpredictable and disconcerting, and as her moods constituted the chief object of Edwin's study the effect on him was not tranquillizing. At the start he had risen to the difficulty of the situation; but he could not permanently remain at that height, and the situation had apparently become stationary. His exasperations, both concealed and open, were not merely unworthy of a philosopher, they were unworthy of a common man. 'Why be annoyed?' he would say to himself. But he was annoyed. 'The tone – the right tone!' he would remind himself. Surely he could remember to command his voice to the right tone? But no! He could not. He could infallibly remember to wind up his watch, but he could not remember that. Moreover, he felt, as he had felt before, on occasions, that no amount of right tone would keep their relations smooth, for the reason that principles were opposed. Could she not see? . . . Well, she could not. There she was, entire, unalterable – impossible to chip inconvenient pieces off her – you must take her or leave her; and she could not see, or she would not – which in practice was the same thing.

And yet some of the most exquisite moments of their union had occurred during that feverish and unquiet month – moments of absolute surrender and devotion on her part, of protective love on his; and also long moments of peace. With the early commencement of autumn, all the family had resumed the pursuit of letters with a certain ardour. A startling feminist writer, and the writer whose parentage and whose very name lay in the Five Towns, who had recreated the East and whose vogue was a passion among the lettered – both these had published books whose success was extreme and genuine. And in the curtained gas-lit drawing-room of a night Hilda would sit rejoicing over the triumphant satire of the woman novelist, and Edwin and George would lounge in impossible postures, each mesmerized by a story of the Anglo-Indian; and between chapters Edwin might rouse himself from the enchantment sufficiently to reflect: 'How indescribably agreeable these evenings are!' And ten to one he would say aloud, with false severity: 'George! Bed!' And George, a fine judge of genuineness in severity, would murmur carelessly: 'All right! I'm going!' And not go.

And now Edwin in the office thought:

'She's come to fetch me away.'

He was gratified. But he must not seem to be gratified. The sanctity of business from invasion had to be upheld. He frowned, feigning more diligently than ever to be occupied. She came in, with that air at once apologetic and defiant that wives have in affronting the sacred fastness. Nobody could have guessed that she had ever been a business woman, arriving regularly at just such an office every morning, shorthand-writing, twisting a copying-press, filing, making appointments. Nobody could have guessed that she had ever been in business for herself, and had known how sixpence was added to sixpence and a week's profit lost in an hour. All such knowledge had apparently dropped from her like an excrescence, had vanished like a temporary disfigurement, and she looked upon commerce with the uncomprehending, careless, and yet impressed eyes of a young girl.

'Hello, missis!' he exclaimed casually.

Then George came in. Since the visit to Dartmoor Hilda had much increased her intimacy with George, spending a lot of time with him, walking with him, and exploring in a sisterly and re-assuring manner his most private life. George liked it, but it occasionally irked him and he would give a hint to Edwin that mother needed to be handled at times.

'You needn't come in here, George,' said Hilda.

'Well, can I go into the engine-house?' George suggested. Edwin had always expected that he would prefer the machine room. But the engine-house was his haunt, probably because it was dirty, fiery, and stuffy.

'No, you can't,' said Edwin. 'Pratt's gone by this, and it's shut up.'

'No, it isn't. Pratt's there.'

'All right.'

'Shut the door, dear,' said Hilda.

'Hooray!' George ran off and banged the glass door.

Hilda, glancing by habit at the unsightly details of the deteri-orating room, walked round the desk. With apprehension Edwin saw resolve and perturbation in her face. He was about to say: 'Look here, infant, I'm supposed to be busy.' But he refrained.

Holding out a letter which she nervously snatched from her bag, Hilda said:

'I've just had this – by the afternoon post. Read it.'

He recognized at once the sloping handwriting; but the paper was different; it was a mere torn half sheet of very cheap notepaper. He read:

DEAR MRS CLAYHANGER, – Just a line to say that my husband is at last discharged. It has been weary waiting. We are together, and I'm looking after him. – With renewed thanks for your sympathy and help, Believe me, Sincerely yours, CHARLOTTE M. CANNON

The signature was scarcely legible. There was no address, no date.

Edwin's first flitting despicable masculine thought was: 'She doesn't say anything about that ten pounds!' It fled. He was happy in an intense relief that affected all his being. He said to himself: 'Now that's over, we can begin again.'

'Well,' he murmured. 'That's all right. Didn't I always tell you it would take some time? . . . That's all right.'

He gazed at the paper, waving it in his hand as he held it by one corner. He perceived that it was the letter of a jealous woman, who had got what she wanted and meant to hold it, and entirely to herself; and his mood became somewhat sardonic.

'Very curt, isn't it?' said Hilda strangely. 'And after all this time, too!'

He looked up at her, turning his head sideways to catch her eyes.

'That letter,' he said in a voice as strange as Hilda's, 'that letter is exactly what it ought to be. It could not possibly have been better turned . . . You don't want to keep it, I suppose, do you?'

'No,' she muttered.

He tore it into very small pieces, and dropped them into the waste-paper basket beneath the desk.

'And burn all the others,' he said, in a low tone.

'Edwin,' after a pause.

'Yes?'

'Don't you think George ought to know? Don't you think

one of us ought to tell him, – either you or me? You might tell him.'

'Tell him what?' Edwin demanded sharply, pushing back his chair.

'Well, everything!'

He glowered. He could feel himself glowering; he could feel the justifiable anger animating him.

'Certainly not!' he enunciated resentfully, masterfully, over-poweringly. 'Certainly not!'

'But supposing he hears from outsiders?'

'You needn't begin supposing.'

'But he's bound to have to know some time.'

'Possibly. But he isn't going to know now, any road! Not with my consent. The thing's absolute madness.'

Hilda almost whispered:

'Very well, dear. If you think so.'

'I do think so.'

He suddenly felt very sorry for her. He was ready to excuse her astounding morbidity as a consequence of extreme spiritual tribulation. He added with brusque good nature:

'And so will you, in the morning, my child.'

'Shall you be long?'

'No. I told you I should be late. If you'll run off, my chuck, I'll undertake to be after you in half an hour.'

'Is your headache better?'

'No. On the other hand, it isn't worse.'

He gazed fiercely at the wages-book.

She bent down.

'Kiss me,' she murmured tearfully.

As he kissed her, and as she pressed against him, he absorbed and understood all the emotions through which she had passed and was passing, and from him to her was transmitted an unimaginable tenderness that shamed and atoned for the inclemency of his refusals. He was very happy. He knew that he would not do another stroke of work that night, but still he must pretend to do some. Playfully, without rising, he drew down her veil, smacked her gently on the back, and indicated the door.

'I have to call at Clara's about that wool for Maggie,' she said,

with courage. His fingering of her veil had given her extreme
pleasure.

'I'll bring the kid up,' he said.

'Will you?'

She departed, leaving the door unlatched.

II

A draught from the outer door swung wide open the unlatched
door of Edwin's room.

'What are doors for?' he muttered, pleasantly impatient; then
he called aloud:

'Simpson. Shut the outer door – and this one, too.'

There was no answer. He arose and went to the outer office.
Hilda had passed through it like an arrow. Simpson was not
there. But a man stood leaning against the mantelpiece; he held
at full spread a copy of the *Signal*, which concealed all the upper
part of him except his fingers and the crown of his head. Though
the gas had been lighted in the middle of the room, it must have
been impossible for him to read by it, since it shone through the
paper. He lowered the newspaper with a rustle and looked at
Edwin. He was a big, well-dressed man, wearing a dark grey suit,
a blue Melton overcoat, and a quite new glossy 'boiler-end' felt
hat. He had a straight, prominent nose, and dark, restless eyes,
set back; his short hair was getting grey, but not his short black
moustache.

'Were you waiting to see me?' Edwin said, in a defensive, half-
hostile tone. The man might be a belated commercial traveller
of a big house – some of those fellows considered themselves
above all laws; on the other hand he might be a new customer
in a hurry.

'Yes,' was the reply, in a deep, full and yet uncertain voice.
'The clerk said you couldn't be disturbed, and asked me to wait.
Then he went out.'

'What can I do for you? It's really after hours, but some of
us are working a bit late.'

The man glanced at the outer door, which Edwin was shutting,
and then at the inner door, which exposed Edwin's room.

'I'm George Cannon,' he said, advancing a step, as it were defiantly.

For an instant Edwin was frightened by the sudden melodrama of the situation. Then he thought:

'I'm up against this man. This is a crisis.'

And he became almost agreeably aware of his own being. The man stood close to him, under the gas, with all the enigmatic quality of another being. He could perceive now – at any rate he could believe – that it was George Cannon. Forgetful of what the man had suffered, Edwin felt for him nothing but the instinctive inimical distrust of the individual who has never got at loggerheads with society for the individual who once and for always has. To this feeling was added a powerful resentment of the man's act in coming – especially unannounced – to just *him*, the husband of the woman he had dishonoured. It was a monstrous act – and doubtless an act characteristic of the man. It was what might have been expected. The man might have been innocent of a particular crime, might have been falsely imprisoned; but what had he originally been doing, with what rascals had he been consorting, that he should be even suspected of crime? George Cannon's astonishing presence, so suddenly after his release, at the works of Edwin Clayhanger, was unforgiveable. Edwin felt an impulse to say savagely:

'Look here. You clear out. You understand English, don't you? Hook it.'

But he had not the brutality to say it. Moreover, the clerk returned, carrying, full to the brim, the tin water-receptacle used for wetting the damping-brush of the copying-press.

'Will you come in, please?' said Edwin curtly. 'Simpson, I'm engaged.'

The two men went into the inner room.

'Sit down,' said Edwin grimly.

George Cannon, with a firm gesture, planted his hat on the flat desk between them. He looked round behind him at the shut glazed door.

'You needn't be afraid,' said Edwin. 'Nobody can hear – unless you shout.'

He gazed curiously but somewhat surreptitiously at George

Cannon, trying to decide whether it was possible to see in him a released convict. He decided that it was not possible. George Cannon had a shifty, but not a beaten, look; many men had a shifty look. His hair was somewhat short, but so was the hair of many men, if not of most. He was apparently in fair health; assuredly his constitution had not been ruined. And if his large, coarse features were worn, marked with tiny black spots, and seamed and generally ravaged, they were not more ravaged than the features of numerous citizens of Bursley aged about fifty who saved money, earned honours, and incurred the envy of presumably intelligent persons. And as he realized all this, Edwin's retrospective painful alarm as to what might have happened if Hilda had noticed George Cannon in the outer office lessened until he could dismiss it entirely. By chance she had ignored Cannon, perhaps scarcely seeing him in her preoccupied passage, perhaps taking him vaguely for a customer; but supposing she *had* recognized him, what then? There would have been an awkward scene – nothing more. Awkward scenes do not kill; their effect is transient. Hilda would have had to behave, and would have behaved, with severe common sense. He, Edwin himself, would have handled the affair. A demeanour matter-of-fact and impassible was what was needed. After all, a man recently out of prison was not a wild beast, nor yet a freak. Hundreds of men were coming out of prisons every day . . . He should know how to deal with this man – not pharisaically, not cruelly, not unkindly, but still with a clear indication to the man of his reprehensible indiscretion in being where he then was.

'Did she recognize me – down there – Dartmoor?' asked George Cannon, without any preparing of the ground, in a deep, trembling voice; and as he spoke a flush spread slowly over his dark features.

'Er – yes!' answered Edwin, and his voice also trembled.

'I wasn't sure,' said George Cannon. 'We were halted before I could see. And I daren't look round – I should ha' been punished. I've been punished before now for looking up at the sky at exercise.' He spoke more quickly and then brought himself up with a snort. 'However, I've not come all the way here to talk prison, so you needn't be afraid. I'm not one of your reformers.'

In his weak but ungoverned nervous excitement, from which a faint trace of hysteria was not absent, he now seemed rather more like an ex-convict, despite his good clothes. He had become, to Edwin's superior self-control, suddenly wistful. And at the same time, the strange opening question, and its accent, had stirred Edwin, and he saw with remorse how much finer had been Hilda's morbid and violent pity than his own harsh common sense and anxiety to avoid emotion. The man in good clothes moved him more than the convict had moved him. He seemed to have received vision, and he saw not merely the unbearable pathos of George Cannon, but the high and heavenly charitableness of Hilda, which he had constantly douched, and his own common earthliness. He was exceedingly humbled. And he also thought, sadly: 'This chap's still attached to her. Poor devil!'

'What *have* you come for?' he inquired.

George Cannon cleared his throat. Edwin waited, in fear, for the avowal. He could make nothing out of the visitor's face; its expression was anxious and drew sympathy, but there was something in it which chilled the sympathy it invoked and which seemed to say: 'I shall look after myself.' It yielded naught. You could be sorry for the heart within, and yet could neither like nor esteem it. 'Punished for looking up at the sky.'. . Glimpses of prison life presented themselves to Edwin's imagination. He saw George Cannon again halted and turning like a serf to the wall of the corridor. And this man opposite to him, close to him in the familiar room, was the same man as the serf! Was he the same man? . . . Inscrutable, the enigma of that existence whose breathing was faintly audible across the desk.

'You know all about it – about my affair, of course.'

'Well,' said Edwin, 'I expect you know how much I know.'

'I'm an honest man – you know that. I needn't begin by explaining that to you.'

Edwin nerved himself:

'You weren't honest towards Hilda, if it comes to that.'

He used his wife's Christian name, to this man with whom he had never before spoken, naturally, inevitably. He would not say 'my wife'. To have said 'my wife' would somehow have brought some muddiness upon that wife, and by contact upon her husband.

'When I say "honest" I mean – you know what I mean. About Hilda – I don't defend that. Only I couldn't help myself . . . I daresay I should do it again.' Edwin could feel his eyes smarting and he blinked, and yet he was angry with the man, who went on: 'It's no use talking about that. That's over. And I couldn't help it. I had to do it. She's come out of it all right. She's not harmed, and I thank God for it! If there'd been a child living . . . well, it would ha' been different.'

Edwin started. This man didn't know he was a father – and his son was within a few yards of him – might come running in at any moment! (No! Young George would not come in. Nothing but positive orders would get the boy out of the engine-house so long as the engine-man remained there.) Was it possible that Hilda had concealed the existence of her child, or had announced the child's death? If so, she had never done a wiser thing, and such sagacity struck him as heroic. But if Mrs Cannon knew as to the child, then it was Mrs Cannon who, with equal prudence and for a different end, had concealed its existence from George Cannon or lied to him as to its death. Certainly the man was sincere. As he said 'Thank God!' his full voice had vibrated like the voice of an ardent religionist at a prayer meeting.

George Cannon began again:

'All I mean is I'm an honest man. I've been damnably treated. Not that I want to go into that. No! I'm a fatalist. That's over. That's done with. I'm not whining. All I'm insisting on is that I'm not a thief, and I'm not a forger, and I've nothing to hide. Perhaps I brought my difficulties about that bank-note business on myself. But when you've once been in prison, you don't choose your friends – you can't. Perhaps I might have ended by being a thief or a forger, only on this occasion it just happens that I've had a good six years for being innocent. I never did anything wrong, or even silly, except let myself get too fond of somebody. That might happen to anyone. It did happen to me. But there's nothing else. You understand? I never –'

'Yes, yes, certainly!' said Edwin, stopping him as he was about to repeat all the argument afresh. It was a convincing argument.

'No one's got the right to look down on me, I mean,' George Cannon insisted, bringing his face forward over the desk. 'On the contrary this country owes me an apology. However, I don't want to go into that. That's done with. Spilt milk's spilt. I know what the world is.'

'I agree! I agree!' said Edwin.

He did. The honesty of his intelligence admitted almost too eagerly and completely the force of the pleading.

'Well,' said George Cannon, 'to cut it short, I want help. And I've come to you for it.'

'Me!' Edwin feebly exclaimed.

'You, Mr Clayhanger! I've come straight here from London. I haven't a friend in the whole world, not one. It's not everybody can say that. There was a fellow named Dayson at Turnhill – used to work for me – he'd have done something if he could. But he was too big a fool to be able to; and besides, he's gone, no address. I wrote to him.'

'Oh, that chap!' murmured Edwin, trying to find relief in even a momentary turn of the conversation. 'I know who you mean. Shorthand-writer. He died in the Isle of Man on his holiday two years ago. It was in the papers.'

'*That's* his address, is it? Good old Dead Letter Office! Well, he is crossed off the list, then; no mistake!' Cannon snarled bitterly. 'I'm aware you're not a friend of mine. I've no claim on you. You don't know me; but you know about me. When I saw you in Dartmoor I guessed who you were, and I said to myself you looked the sort of man who might help another man ... Why did you come into the prison? Why did you bring her there? You must have known I was there.' He spoke with a sudden change to reproachfulness.

'I didn't bring her there.' Edwin blushed. 'It was – however, we needn't go into that, if you don't mind.'

'Was she upset?'

'Of course.'

Cannon sighed.

'What do you want me to do?' asked Edwin gloomily. In secret he was rather pleased that George Cannon should have deemed him of the sort likely to help. Was it the flattery of a mendicant? No, he did not think it was. He believed implicitly everything the man was saying.

'Money!' said Cannon sharply. 'Money! You won't feel it, but it will save me. After all, Mr Clayhanger, there's a bond between us, if it comes to that. There's a bond between us. And you've had all the luck of it.'

Again Edwin blushed.

'But surely your wife –' he stammered. 'Surely Mrs Cannon isn't without funds. Of course I know she was temporarily rather short a while back, but surely –'

'How do you know she was short?' Cannon grimly interrupted.

'My wife sent her ten pounds – I fancy it was ten pounds – towards expenses, you know.'

Cannon ejaculated, half to himself, savagely:

'Never told me!'

He remained silent.

'But I've always understood she's a woman of property,' Edwin finished.

Cannon put both elbows on the desk, leaned farther forward, and opened his mouth several seconds before speaking.

'Mr Clayhanger. I've left my wife – as you call her. If I'd stayed with her I should have killed her. I've run off. Yes, I know all she's done for me. I know without her I might have been in prison today and for a couple o' years to come. But I'd sooner be in prison or in hell or anywhere you like than with Mrs Cannon. She's an old woman. She always was an old woman. She was nearly forty when she hooked me, and I was twenty-two. And I'm young yet. I'm not middle-aged yet. She's got a clear conscience, Mrs Cannon has. She always does her duty. She'd let me walk over her, she'd never complain, if only she could keep me. She'd just play and smile. Oh, yes, she'd turn the other cheek – and keep on turning it. But she isn't going to have me. And for all she's done I'm not grateful. Hag. That's what she is!' He spoke loudly, excitedly, under considerable emotion.

'Hsh!' Edwin, alarmed, endeavoured gently to soothe him.

'All right! all right!' Cannon proceeded in a lower but still impassioned voice. 'But look here! You're a man. You know what's what. You'll understand what I mean. Believe me when I say that I wouldn't live with that woman for eternal salvation. I couldn't. I couldn't do it. I've taken some of her money, only a little, and run off . . .' He paused, and went on with conscious persuasiveness now: 'I've just got here. I had to ask your whereabouts. I might have been recognized in the streets, but I haven't been. I didn't expect to find you here at this time. I might have had to sleep in the town tonight. I wouldn't have come to your private house. Now I've seen you I shall get along to Crewe tonight. I shall be safer there. And it's on the way to Liverpool and America. I want to go to America. With a bit o' capital I shall be all right in America. It's my one chance; but it's a good one. But I must have some capital. No use landing in New York with empty pockets.'

Said Edwin, still shying at the main issues:

'I was under the impression that you had been to America once.'

'Yes, that's why I know. I hadn't any money. And what's more,' he added with peculiar emphasis, 'I was brought back.'

Edwin thought:

'I shall yield to this man.'

At that instant he saw the shadow of Hilda's head and shoulders on the glass of the door.

'Excuse me a second,' he murmured, bounded with astonishing velocity out of the room, and pulled the door to after him with a bang.

III

Hilda, having observed the strange, excited gesture, paused a moment, in an equally strange tranquillity, before speaking. Edwin fronted her at the very door. Then she said, clearly and deliberately, through her veil:

'Auntie Hamps has had an attack – heart. The doctor says she can't possibly live through the night. It was at Clara's.'

This was the first of Mrs Hamps's fatal heart attacks.

'Ah!' breathed Edwin, with apparently a purely artistic interest in the affair. 'So that's it, is it? Then she's at Clara's?'

'Yes.'

'What doctor?'

'I forget his name. Lives in Acre Lane. They sent for the

nearest. She can't get her breath – has to fight for it. She jumped out of bed struggling to breathe.'

'Have you seen her?'

'Yes. They made me.'

'Albert there?'

'Oh, yes.'

'Well, I suppose I'd better go round. You go back. I'll follow you.'

He was conscious of not the slightest feeling of sorrow at the imminent death of Auntie Hamps. Even the image of the old lady fighting to fetch her breath scarcely moved him, though the death-bed of his father had been harrowing enough. He and Hilda had the same thought: 'At last something has happened to Auntie Hamps!' And it gave zest.

'I must speak to you,' said Hilda, low, and moved towards the inner door.

The clerk Simpson was behind them at his ink-stained desk, stamping letters, and politely pretending to be deaf.

'No,' Edwin stopped her. 'There's someone in there. We can't talk there.'

'A customer?'

'Yes . . . I say, Simpson. Have you done those letters?'

'Yes, sir,' answered Simpson, smiling. He had been recommended as a 'very superior' youth, and had not disappointed, despite a constitutional nervousness.

'Take them to the pillar, and call at Mr Benbow's and tell them that I'll be round in about a quarter of an hour. I don't know as you need come back. Hurry up.'

'Yes, sir.'

Edwin and Hilda watched Simpson go.

'Whatever's the matter?' Hilda demanded in a low, harsh voice, as soon as the outer door had clicked. It was as if something sinister in her had been suddenly released.

'Matter? Nothing. Why?'

'You look so queer.'

'Well – you come along with these shocks.' He gave a short, awkward laugh. He felt and looked guilty, and he knew that he looked guilty.

'You looked queer when you came out.'

'You've upset yourself, my child, that's all.' He now realized the high degree of excitement which he himself, without previously being aware of it, had reached.

'Edwin, who is it in there?'

'Don't I tell you – it's a customer.'

He could see her nostrils twitching through the veil.

'It's George Cannon in there!' she exclaimed.

He laughed again. 'What makes you feel that?' he asked, feeling all the while the complete absurdity of such fencing.

'When I ran out I noticed somebody. He was reading a newspaper and I couldn't see him. But he just moved it a bit, and I seemed to catch sight of the top of his head. And when I got into the street I said to myself, "It looked like George Cannon", and then I said, "Of course it couldn't be". And then with this business about Auntie Hamps the idea went right out of my head.'

'Well, it is, if you want to know.'

Her mysterious body and face seemed to radiate a disastrous emotion that filled the whole office.

'Did you know he was coming?'

'I did not. Hadn't the least notion!' The sensation of criminality began to leave Edwin. As Hilda seemed to move and waver, he added:

'Now you aren't going to see him!'

And his voice menacingly challenged her, and defied her to stir a step. The most important thing in the world, then, was that Hilda should not see George Cannon. He would stop her by force. He would let himself get angry and brutal. He would show her that he was the stronger. He had quite abandoned his earlier attitude of unsentimental callousness which argued that after all it wouldn't ultimately matter whether they encountered each other or not. Far from that, he was, so it appeared to him, standing between them, desperate and determined, and acting instinctively and conventionally. Their separate pasts, each full of grief and tragedy, converged terribly upon him in an effort to meet in just that moment, and he was ferociously resisting.

'What does he want?'

'He wants me to help him to go to America.'

'*You!*'

'He says he hasn't a friend.'

'But what about his wife?'

'That's just what I said ... He's left her. Says he can't live with her.'

There was a silence, in which the tension appreciably lessened.

'Can't live with her! Well, I'm not surprised. But I do think it's strange, him coming to you.'

'So do I,' said Edwin drily, taking the upper hand; for the change in Hilda's tone – her almost childlike satisfaction in the news that Cannon would not live with his wife – seemed to endow him with superiority. 'But there's a lot of strange things in this world. Now listen here. I'm not going to keep him waiting; I can't.' He then spoke very gravely, authoritatively and ominously: 'Find George and take him home at once.'

Hilda, impressed, gave a frown.

'I think it's very wrong that you should be asked to help him.' Her voice shook and nearly broke. 'Shall you help him, Edwin?'

'I shall get him out of this town at once, and out of the country. Do as I say. As things are he doesn't know there is any George, and it's just as well he shouldn't. But if he stays anywhere about, he's bound to know.'

All Hilda's demeanour admitted that George Cannon had never been allowed to know that he had a son; and the simple candour of the admission frightened Edwin by its very simplicity.

'Now! Off you go! George is in the engine-house.'

Hilda moved reluctantly towards the outer door, like a reproved and rebellious schoolgirl. Suddenly she burst into tears, sprang at Edwin, and, putting her arms round his neck, kissed him through the veil.

'Nobody but you would have helped him – in your place!' she murmured passionately, half admiring, half protesting. And with a backward look as she hurried off, her face stern and yet soft seemed to appeal: 'Help him.'

Edwin was at once deeply happy and impregnated with a sense of the frightful sadness that lurks in the hollows of the world. He stood alone with the flaring gas, overcome.

IV

He went back to the private room, self-conscious and rather tongue-tied, with a clear feeling of relief that Hilda was disposed of, removed from the equation – and not unsuccessfully. After the woman, to deal with the man, in the plain language of men, seemed simple and easy. He was astounded, equally, by the grudging tardiness of Mrs Cannon's information to Hilda as to the release, and by the baffling, inflexible detraction of Hilda's words: 'Well, I'm not surprised.' And the flitting image of Auntie Hamps fighting for life still left him untouched. He looked at George Cannon, and George Cannon, with his unreliable eyes, looked at him. He almost expected Cannon to say: 'Was that Hilda you were talking to out there?' But Cannon seemed to have no suspicion that, in either the inner or the outer room, he had been so close to her. No doubt, when he was waiting by the mantelpiece in the outer room, he had lifted the paper as soon as he heard the door unlatched, expressly in order to screen himself from observation. Probably he had not even guessed that the passer was a woman. Had Simpson been there, the polite young man would doubtless have said: 'Good night, Mrs Clay-hanger', but Simpson had happened not to be there.

'Are you going to help me?' asked George Cannon, after a moment, and his heavy voice was so beseeching, so humble, so surprisingly sycophantic, so fearful, that Edwin could scarcely bear to hear it. He hated to hear that one man could be so slavishly dependent on another. Indeed, he much preferred Cannon's defiant, half-bullying tone.

'Yes,' said he. 'I shall do what I can. What do you want?'

'A hundred pounds,' said George Cannon, and, as he named the sum, his glance was hard and steady.

Edwin was startled. But immediately he began to readjust his ideas, persuading himself that after all the man could not prudently have asked for less.

'I can't give it you all now.'

Cannon's face lighted up in relief and joy. His black eyes sparkled feverishly with the impatience of an almost hopeless desire about to be satisfied. Although he did not move, his self-control had for the moment gone completely, and the secrets of his soul were exposed.

'Can you send it me – in notes? I can give you an address in Liverpool.' His voice could hardly utter the words.

'Wait a second,' said Edwin.

He went to the safe let into the wall, of which he was still so naïvely proud, and unlocked it with the owner's gesture. The perfect fitting of the bright key, the ease with which it turned, the silent, heavy swing of the massive door on its hinges – these things gave him physical as well as moral pleasure. He savoured the security of his position and his ability to rescue people from destruction. From the cavern of the safe he took out a bag of gold, part of the money required for wages on the morrow, – he would have to send to the Bank again in the morning. He knew that the bag contained exactly twenty pounds in half-sovereigns, but he shed the lovely twinkling coins on the desk and counted them.

'Here,' he said. 'Here's twenty pounds. Take the bag, too, – it'll be handier,' and he put the money into the bag. Then a foolish, grand idea struck him. 'Write down the address on this envelope, will you, and I'll send you a hundred tomorrow. You can rely on it.'

'Eighty, you mean,' muttered George Cannon.

'No,' said Edwin, with affected nonchalance, blushing. 'A hundred. The twenty will get you over and you'll have a hundred clear when you arrive on the other side.'

'You're very kind,' said Cannon weakly. 'I –'

'Here. Here's the envelope. Here's a bit of pencil.' Edwin stopped him hastily. His fear of being thanked made him harsh.

While Cannon was nervously writing the address, he noticed that the man's clumsy fingers were those of a day-labourer.

'You'll get it all back. You'll see,' said Cannon, as he stood up to leave, holding his glossy felt hat in his left hand.

'Don't worry about that. I don't want it. You owe me nothing.'

'You'll have every penny back, and before long, too.'

Edwin smiled, deprecating the idea.

'Well, good luck!' he said. 'You'll get to Crewe all right. There's a train at Shawport at eight-seven.'

They shook hands, and quitted the inner office. As he traversed the outer office on his way forth, in front of Edwin, Cannon turned his head, as if to say something, but, confused, he said nothing and went on, and at once he disappeared into the darkness outside. And Edwin was left with a memory of his dubious eyes, hard rather than confident, profoundly relieved rather than profoundly grateful.

'By Jove!' Edwin murmured by himself. 'Who'd have thought it? ... They say those chaps always turn up again like bad pennies, but I bet he won't.' Simultaneously he reflected upon the case of Mrs Cannon, deserted; but it did not excite his pity. He fastened the safe, extinguished the lights, shut the office, and prepared his mind for the visit to Auntie Hamps.

V

Hilda and her son were in the dining-room, in which the table, set for a special meal – half-tea, half-supper – made a glittering oblong of white. On the table, among blue-and-white plates, and knives and forks, lay some of George's shabby schoolbooks. In most branches of knowledge George privately knew that he could instruct his parents – especially his mother. Nevertheless that beloved outgrown creature was still occasionally useful at home lessons, as for instance in 'poetry'. George, disdainful, had to learn some verses each week, and now his mother held a book entitled 'The Poetry Reciter', while George mumbled with imperfect verbal accuracy the apparently immortal lines:

> Abou Ben Adhem, may his tribe increase,
> Awoke one night from a deep dream of peace.

His mother, however, scarcely regarded the book. She knew the poem by heart, and had indeed recited it to George, who, though he was much impressed by her fire, could not by any means have been persuaded to imitate the freedom of her delivery. His elocution tonight was unusually bad, for the reason that he had been pleasurably excited by the immense news of Auntie Hamps's illness. Not that he had any grudge against Auntie Hamps! His pleasure would have been as keen in the grave illness of any other important family connection, save his mother and Edwin. Such notable events gave a sensational interest to domestic life which domestic life as a rule lacked.

Then, through the half-open door of the dining-room came the sound of Edwin's latchkey in the front door.

'There's uncle!' exclaimed George, and jumped up.

Hilda stopped him.

'Put your books together,' said she. 'You know uncle likes to go up to the bathroom before he does *anything*!'

It was a fact that the precisian hated even to be greeted, on his return home in the evening, until he came downstairs from the bathroom.

Hilda herself collected the books and put them on the sideboard.

'Shall I tell Ada?' George suggested, champing the bit.

'No. Ada knows.'

With deliberation Hilda tended the fire. Her mind was in a state of emotional flux. Memories and comparisons mournfully and yet agreeably animated it. She thought of the days when she used to recite amid enthusiasm in the old drawing-room of the Orgreaves; and of the days when she was a wanderer, had no home, no support, little security; and of the brief, uncertain days with George Cannon; and of the eternal days when her only assurance was the assurance of disaster. She glanced at George, and saw in him reminders of his tragic secret father now hidden away, forced into the background, like something obscene. Nearly every development of the present out of the past seemed to her, now, to be tragic. Johnnie Orgreave had, of course, not come back from his idyll with the ripping Mrs Chris Hamson; their seclusion was not positively known; but the whole district knew that the husband had begun proceedings and that the Orgreave business was being damaged by the incompetence of Jimmie Orgreave, whose deplorable wife had a few days earlier been seen notoriously drunk in the dress circle of the Hanbridge Theatre Royal. Janet was still at Tavy Mansion because there was no place for her in the Five Towns. Janet had written to

Hilda, sadly, and the letter breathed her sense of her own futility and superfluousness in the social scheme. In one curt phrase, that very afternoon, the taciturn Maggie, who very seldom complained, had disclosed something of what it was to live day and night with Auntie Hamps. Even Clara, the self-sufficient, protected by an almost impermeable armour of conceit, showed signs of the anxiety due to obscure chronic disease and a husband who financially never knew where he was. Finally, the last glories of Auntie Hamps were sinking to ashes. Only Hilda herself was, from nearly every point of view, in a satisfactory and promising situation. She possessed love, health, money, stability. When danger threatened, a quiet and unfailingly sagacious husband was there to meet and destroy it. Surely nothing whatever worth mentioning, save the fact that she was distantly approaching forty, troubled the existence of Hilda now; and her age certainly did not trouble her.

Ada entered with the hot dishes, and went out.

At length Hilda heard the bathroom door. She left the dining-room, shutting the door on George, who could take a hint very well – considering his years. Edwin, brushed and spruce, was coming downstairs, rubbing his clean hands with physical satisfaction. He nodded amiably, but without smiling.

'Has he gone?' said Hilda, in a low voice.

Edwin nodded. He was at the foot of the stairs.

She did not offer to kiss him, having a notion that he would prefer not to be kissed just then.

'How much did you give him?' She knew he would not care for the question, but she could not help putting it.

He smiled, and touched her shoulder. She liked him to touch her shoulder.

'That's all right,' he said, with a faint condescension. 'Don't you worry about that.'

She did not press the point. He could be free enough with information – except when it was demanded. Some time later he would begin of his own accord to talk.

'How was Auntie Hamps?'

'Well, if anything, she's a bit easier. I don't mind betting she gets over it.'

They went into the dining-room almost side by side, and she inquired again about his headache.

The meal was tranquil. After a few moments Edwin opened the subject of Auntie Hamps's illness with some sardonic remarks upon the demeanour of Albert Benbow.

'Is Auntie dying?' asked George with gusto.

Edwin replied:

'What are those schoolbooks doing there on the sideboard? I thought it was clearly understood that you were to do your lessons in your mother's boudoir?'

He spoke without annoyance, but coldly. He was aware that neither Hilda nor her son could comprehend that to a bookman schoolbooks were not books, but merely an eyesore. He did not blame them for their incapacity, but he considered that an arrangement was an arrangement.

'Mother put them there,' said the base George.

'Well, you can take them away,' said Edwin firmly. 'Run along now.'

George rose from his place between Hilda and Edwin, and from his luscious plate, and removed the books. Hilda watched him meekly go. His father, too, had gone. Edwin was in the right; his position could not be assailed. He had not been unpleasant, but he had spoken as one sublimely confident that his order would not be challenged. Within her heart Hilda rebelled. If Edwin had been responsible for some act contrary to one of her decrees, she would never in his presence have used the tone that he used to enforce obedience. She would have laughed or she would have frowned, but she would never have been the polite autocrat. Nor would he have expected her to play the role; he would probably have resented it.

Why? Were they not equals? No, they were not equals. The fundamental unuttered assumption upon which the household life rested was that they were not equals. She might cross him, she might momentarily defy him, she might torture him, she might drive him to fury, and still be safe from any effective reprisals, because his love for her made her necessary to his being; but in spite of all that his will remained the seat of government, and she and George were only the Opposition. In the end, she had to incline. She was the complement of his existence, but he was not the complement of hers. She was just a parasite, though an essential parasite. Why? ... The reason, she judged, was economic, and solely economic. She rebelled. Was she not as individual, as original, as he? Had she not a powerful mind of her own, experience of her own, ideals of her own? Was she not of a nature profoundly and exceptionally independent? ...

Her lot was unalterable. She had, of course, not the slightest desire to leave him; she was devoted to him; what irked her was that, even had she had the desire, she could not have fulfilled it, for she was too old now, and too enamoured of comfort and security, to risk such an enterprise. She was a captive, and she recalled with a gentle pang, less than regret, the days when she was unhappy and free as a man, when she could say, 'I will go to London', 'I will leave London', 'I am deceived and ruined, but I am my own mistress'.

These thoughts in the idyllic tranquillity of the meal, mingled, below her smiling preoccupations of an honoured house-mistress, with the thoughts of her love for her husband and son and of their excellences, of the masculine love which enveloped and shielded her, of her security, of the tragedy of the bribed and dismissed victim and villain, George Cannon, of the sorrows of some of her friends, and of the dead. In her heart was the unquiet whispering: 'I submit, and yet I shall never submit.

BOOK III
EQUILIBRIUM

CHAPTER 17

GEORGE'S EYES

I

HILDA sat alone in the boudoir, before the fire. She had just come out of the kitchen, and she was wearing the white uniform of the kitchen, unsuited for a boudoir; but she wore it with piquancy. The November afternoon had passed into dusk, and through the window, over the roofs of Hulton Street, stars could be seen in the darkening clear sky. After a very sharp fall and rise of the barometer, accounting for heavy rainstorms, the first frosts were announced, and winter was on the doorstep. The hardy inhabitants of the Five Towns, Hilda among them, were bracing themselves to the discipline of winter, with its mud, increased smuts, sleet, and damp, piercing chills; and they were taking pleasure in the tonic prospect of discomfort. The visitation had threatened ever since September. Now it had positively come. Let it come! Build up the fire, stamp the feet, and defy it! Hilda was exhilarated, having been reawakened to the zest and the romance of life, not merely by the onset of winter, but by dramatic events in the kitchen.

A little over three years had elapsed since the closing of the episode of George Cannon, and for two of those years Hilda had had peace in the kitchen. She had been the firm mistress who knows what she wants, and, knowing also how to handle the peculiar inmates of the kitchen, gets it; she had been the mistress who 'won't put up with' all sorts of things, including middle-age and ugliness in servants, and whom heaven has spoilt by too much favour. Then the cook, with the ingratitude of a cherished domestic, had fallen in love and carried her passion into a cottage miles away at Longshaw. And from that moment Hilda had ceased to be the mistress who by firmness commands fate; she had become as other mistresses. In a year she had had five cooks, giving varying degrees of intense dissatisfaction. She had even dismissed the slim and constant Ada once, but, yielding to an outburst of penitent affection, had withdrawn the notice. The last cook, far removed from youthfulness or prettiness, had left suddenly that day, after insolence, after the discovery of secret beer and other vileness in the attic bedroom, after a scene in which Hilda had absolutely silenced her, reducing ribaldry to sobs. Cook and trunk expelled, Hilda had gone about the house like a fumigation, and into the kitchen like the embodiment of calm and gay efficiency. She would do the cooking herself. She would show the kitchen that she was dependent upon nobody. She had quickened the speed of Ada, accused her 'tartly', but not without dry good-humour, of a disloyal secretiveness, and counselled her to mind what she was about if she wanted to get on in the world.

Edwin knew nothing, for all had happened since his departure to the works after midday dinner. He would be back in due course, and George would be back, and Tertius Ingpen (long ago reconciled) was coming for the evening. She would show them all three what a meal was, and incidentally Ada would learn what a meal was. There was nothing like demonstrating to servants that you could beat them easily at their own game.

She had just lived through her thirty-ninth birthday. 'Forty!' she had murmured to herself with a shiver of apprehension, meaning that the next would be the fortieth. It was an unpleasant experience. She had told Edwin not to mention her birthday abroad. Clumsy George had inquired: 'Mother, how old are you?' To which she had replied, 'Lay-ours for meddlers!' a familiar phrase whose origin none of them understood, but George knew that it signified, 'Mind your own business'. No! She had not been happy on that birthday. She had gazed into the glass and decided that she looked old, that she did not look old, that she looked old, endlessly alternating. She was not stout, but her body was solid, too solid; it had no litheness, none whatever; it was absolutely set; the cleft under the chin was quite undeniable, and the olive complexion subtly ravaged. Still, not a hair of her dark head had changed colour. It was perhaps her soul that was greying. Her married life was fairly calm. It had grown monotonous in ease and tranquillity. The sharp, respectful admiration for her husband roused in her by his handling of the Cannon episode, had gradually been dulled. She had nothing against him. Yet she had everything against him, because apart from his grave abiding love for her, he possessed an object and interest in life, and because she was a mere complement and he was not. She had asked herself the most dreadful of questions: 'Why have I lived? Why do I go on living?' and had answered: 'Because of *them*', meaning Edwin and her son. But it was not enough for her, who had once been violently enterprising, pugnacious, endangered, and independent. For after she had watched over them she had energy to spare, and such energy was not being employed and could not be employed. Reading – a diversion! Fancy work – a detestable device for killing time and energy! Social duties – ditto! Charity – hateful! She had slowly descended into marriage as into a lotus valley. And more than half her life was gone. She could never detect that any other married woman in the town felt as she felt. She could never explain herself to Edwin, and indeed had not tried to explain herself.

Now the affair of the alcoholic cook, aided by winter's first fillip, stimulated and brightened her. And while thinking with a glance at the clock of the precise moment when she must return to the kitchen and put a dish down to the fire, she also thought, rather hopefully and then quite hopefully, about the future of her marriage. Her brain seemed to straighten and correct itself, like the brain of one who, waking up in the morning, slowly perceives that the middle-of-the-night apprehensiveness about eventualities was all awry in its pessimism. She saw that everything could and must be improved, that the new life must begin. Edwin needed to be inspired; she must inspire him. He slouched more and more in his walk; he was more and more absorbed in his business, quieter in the evenings, more impatient in the mornings. Moreover, the household machine had been getting slack. A general tonic was required; she would administer it – and to herself also. They should all feel the invigorating ozone that very night. She would organize social distractions; on behalf of the home she would reclaim from the works those odd hours and half-hours of Edwin's which it had imperceptibly filched. She would have some new clothes, and she would send Edwin to the tailor's. She would make him buy a dogcart and a horse.

Oh! She could do it. She had the mastery of him in many things when she chose to be aroused. In a word she would 'branch out'.

She was not sure that she would not prosecute a campaign for putting Edwin on the Town Council, where he certainly ought to be. It was his duty to take a share in public matters, and ultimately to dominate the town. Suggestions had already been made by wire-pullers, and unreflectively repulsed by the too-casual Edwin. She saw him mayor, and herself mayoress. Once, the prospect of any such formal honour, with all that it entailed of ceremoniousness and insincere civilities, would have annoyed if not frightened her. But now she thought, proudly and timidly and desirously, that she would make as good a mayoress as most mayoresses, and that she could set one or two of them an example in tact and dignity. Why not? Of late neither mayors nor mayoresses in the Five Towns had been what they used to be. The grand tradition was apparently in abeyance, the people who ought to carry it on seeming somehow to despise it. She could remember mayors, especially Chief Bailiffs at Turnhill, who imposed themselves upon the imagination of the town. But nowadays the name of a mayor was never a household word. She had even heard Ingpen ask Edwin: 'See, who *is* the new mayor?' and Edwin start his halting answer: 'Let me see –'

And she had still another and perhaps a greater ambition – to possess a country house. In her fancy her country house was very like Alicia Hesketh's house, Tavy Mansion, which she had never ceased to envy. She felt that in a new home, spacious, with space around it, she could really commence the new life. She saw the place perfectly appointed and functioning perfectly – no bother about smuts on white curtains; no half-trained servants; none of the base, confined promiscuity of filthy Trafalgar Road; and the Benbows and Auntie Hamps at least eight or ten miles off! She saw herself driving Edwin to the station in the morning, or perhaps right into Bursley if she wanted to shop . . . No, she would of course shop at Oldcastle . . . She would leave old Darius Clayhanger's miracle-house without one regret. And in the new life she would be always active, busy, dignified, elegant, influential, and kind. And to Edwin she would be absolutely indispensable.

In these imaginings their solid but tarnished love glittered and gleamed again. She saw naught but the charming side of Edwin and the romantic side of their union. She was persuaded that there really was nobody like Edwin, and that no marriage had ever had quite the mysterious, secretly exciting quality of hers. She yearned for him to come home at once, to appear magically in the dusk of the doorway. The mood was marvellous.

II

The door opened.

'Can I speak to you, m'm?'

It was the voice of Ada, somewhat perturbed. She advanced a little and stood darkly in front of the open doorway.

'What is it, Ada?' Hilda asked curtly, without turning to look at her.

'It's –' Ada began and stopped.

Hilda glanced round quickly, recognizing now in the voice a peculiar note with which experience had familiarized her. It was a note between pertness and the beginning of a sob, and it always indicated that Ada was feeling more acutely than usual the vast injustice of the worldly scheme. It might develop into tears; on the other hand it might develop into mere insolence. Hilda discerned that Ada was wearing neither cap nor apron. She thought: 'If this stupid girl wants trouble, she has come to me at exactly and precisely the right moment to get it. I'm not in the humour, after all I've gone through today, to stand any nonsense either from her or from anybody else.'

'What is it, Ada?' she repeated, with restraint, and yet warningly. 'And where's your apron and your cap?'

'In the kitchen, m'm.'

'Well, go and put them on, and then come and say what you have to say,' said Hilda, thinking: 'I don't give any importance to her cap and apron, but she does.'

'I was thinking I'd better give ye notice, m'm,' said Ada, and she said it pertly, ignoring the command.

The two women were alone together in the house. Each felt it; each felt the large dark emptiness of the house behind them, and the solid front and back doors cutting them off from succour; each had to depend entirely upon herself.

Hilda asked quietly:

'What's the matter now?'

She knew that Ada's grievance would prove to be silly. The girl had practically no common sense. Not one servant girl in a hundred had any appreciable common sense. And when girls happened to be 'upset' – as they were all liable to be, and as Ada by the violent departure of the cook no doubt was – even such minute traces of gumption as they possessed were apt to disappear.

'There's no pleasing you, m'm!' said Ada. 'The way you talked to me in the kitchen, saying I was always a-hiding things from ye. I've felt it very much!'

She threw her head back, and the gesture signified: 'I'm younger than you, and young men are always running after me. And I can get a new situation any time. And I've *not* gone back into my kitchen to put my cap and apron on.'

'Ada,' said Hilda. 'Shall I tell you what's wrong with you? You're a little fool. You know you're talking downright nonsense. You know that as well as I do. And you know you'll never get a better place than you have here. But you've taken an idea into your head – and there you are! Now do be sensible. You say you think you'd better give notice. Think it over before you do anything ridiculous. Sleep on it. We'll see how you feel in the morning.'

'I think I'd better give notice, m'm, especially seeing I'm a fool, and silly,' Ada persisted.

Hilda sighed. Her voice hardened slightly:

'So you'd leave me without a maid just at Christmas! And that's all the thanks I get for all I've done for you.'

'Well, m'm, we've had such a queer lot of girls here lately, haven't we?' The pertness was intensified. 'I don't hardly care to stay. I feel we sh'd both be better for a change like.'

It was perhaps Ada's subtly insolent use of the words 'we' and 'both' that definitely brought about a new phase of the interview. Hilda suddenly lost all desire for an amicable examination of the crisis.

'Very well, Ada,' she said shortly. 'But remember I shan't take you back again, whatever happens.'

Ada moved away, and then returned.

'Could I leave at once, m'm, same as cook?'

Hilda was astonished and outraged, despite all her experience and its resulting secret sardonic cynicism in regard to servants. The girl was ready to walk out instantly.

'And may I inquire where you'd go to?' asked Hilda with a sneer. 'At this time of night you couldn't possibly get home to your parents.'

'Oh,' answered Ada brightly. 'I could go to me cousin's up at Toft End. And her could send down a lad with a barrow for me box.'

The plot, then, had been thought out. 'Her cousin's!' thought Hilda, and seemed to be putting her finger on the cause of Ada's disloyalty. 'Her cousin's!' It was a light in a dark mystery. 'Her cousin's!'

'I suppose you know you're forfeiting the wages due to you the day after tomorrow?'

'I shall ask me cousin about that, m'm,' said Ada, as it were menacingly.

'I should!' Hilda sarcastically agreed. 'I certainly should.' And she thought with bitter resignation: 'She'll have to leave anyhow after this. She may as well leave on the spot.'

'There's those as'll see as I have me rights,' said Ada pugnaciously, with another toss of the head.

Hilda had a mind to retort in anger; but she controlled herself. Already that afternoon she had imperilled her dignity in the altercation with the cook. The cook, however, had not Ada's ready tongue, and, while the mistress had come off best against the cook, she might through impulsiveness find herself worsted by Ada's more youthful impudence, were it once unloosed.

'That will do, then, Ada,' she said. 'You can go and pack your box first thing.'

In less than three-quarters of an hour Ada was gone, and her corded trunk lay just within the scullery door, waiting the arrival of the cousin's barrow. She had bumped it down the stairs herself.

All solitary in the house, which had somehow been transformed into a strange and unusual house, Hilda wept. She had only parted with an unfaithful and ungrateful servant, but she wept. She dashed into the kitchen and began to do Ada's work, still weeping, and she was savage against her own tears; yet they continued softly to fall, misting her vision of fire and utensils and earthenware vessels. Ada had left everything in a moment; she had left the kettle on the fire, and the grease in the square tin in which the dinner joint had been cooked, and the ashes in the fender, and tea leaves in the kitchen teapot and a cup and saucer unwashed. She had cared naught for the inconvenience she was causing; had shown not the slightest consideration; had walked off without a pang, smilingly hoity-toity. And all servants were like that. Such conduct might be due as much to want of imagination, to a simple inability to picture to themselves the consequences of certain acts, as to stark ingratitude; but the consequences remained the same; and Hilda held fiercely to the theory of stark ingratitude.

She had made Ada; she had created her. When Hilda engaged her, Ada was little more than an 'oat-cake girl', – that is to say, one of those girls who earn a few pence by delivering oat-cakes fresh from the stove at a halfpenny each before breakfast at the houses of gormandizing superior artisans and the middle classes. True, she had been in one situation prior to Hilda's, but it was a situation where she learnt nothing and could have learnt nothing. Nevertheless, she was very quick to learn, and in a month Hilda had done wonders with her. She had taught her not only her duties, but how to respect herself, to make the best of herself, and favourably to impress others. She had enormously increased Ada's value in the universe. And she had taught her some worldly wisdom, and permitted and even encouraged certain coquetries, and in the bedroom during dressings and undressings had occasionally treated her as a soubrette if not as a confidante; had listened to her at length, and had gone so far as to ask her views on this matter or that – the supreme honour for a menial. Also she had very conscientiously nursed her in sickness. She had really liked Ada, and had developed a sentimental weakness for her. She had taken pleasure in her prettiness, in her natural grace, and in her crude youth. She enjoyed seeing Ada arrange a bedroom, or answer the door, or serve a meal. And Ada's stupidity – that half-cunning stupidity of her class, which immovably underlay her superficial aptitudes – had not sufficed to spoil her affection for the girl. She had been indulgent to Ada's stupidity; she had occasionally in some soft moods hoped that it was curable. And she had argued in moments of discouragement that at any rate stupidity could be faithful. In her heart she had counted Ada as a friend, as a true standby in the more or less tragic emergencies of the household. And now Ada had deserted her. Stupidity had proved to be neither faithful nor grateful. Why had Ada been so silly and so base? Impossible to say! A nothing! A whim! Nerves! Fatuity! The whole affair was horribly absurd. These creatures were incalculable.

Of course Hilda would have been wiser not to upbraid her so soon after the scene with the cook, and to have spoken more smoothly to the chit in the boudoir. Hilda admitted that. But what then? Was that an excuse for the chit's turpitude? There must be a limit to the mistress's humouring. And probably after all the chit had meant to go ... If she had not meant to go she would not have entered the boudoir apronless and capless. Some rankling word, some ridiculous sympathy with the cook, some wild dream of a Christmas holiday – who could tell what might have influenced her? Hilda gave it up – and returned to it a thousand times. One truth emerged – and it was the great truth of house-mistresses – namely, that it never, never, never pays to be too kind to servants. 'Servants do not understand kindness.' You think they do; they themselves think they do; but they don't, – they don't and they don't. Hilda went back into the immensity of her desolating experience as an employer of female domestic servants of all kinds, but chiefly bad – for the landlady of a small boarding-house must take what servants she can get – and she raged at the persistence of the proof that kindness never paid. What did pay was severity and inhuman strictness, and the maintenance of an impassable gulf between employer and employed. Not again would she make the mistake which she had made a hundred times. She hardened herself to the consistency of a slave-driver. And all the time it was the woman in her, not the mistress, that the hasty thoughtless Ada had wounded. To the woman the kitchen was not the same place without Ada – Ada on whom she had utterly relied in the dilemma caused by the departure of the cook. As with angrily wet eyes she went about her new work in the kitchen, she could almost see the graceful ghost of Ada tripping to and fro therein.

And all that the world, and the husband, would know or understand was that a cook had been turned out for drunkenness, and that a quite sober parlourmaid had most preposterously walked after her. Hilda was aware that in Edwin she had a severe, though a taciturn, critic of her activities as employer of servants. She had no hope whatever of his sympathy, and so she closed all her gates against him. She waited for him as for an adversary, and all the lustre faded from her conception of their love.

III

When Edwin approached his home that frosty evening, he was disturbed to perceive that there was no light from the hall gas shining through the panes of the front door, though some light showed at the dining-room window, the blinds of which had not been drawn. 'What next?' he thought crossly. He was tired, and the keenness of the weather, instead of bracing him, merely made him petulant. He was astonished that several women in a house could all forget such an important act as the lighting of the hall gas at nightfall. Never before had the hall gas been forgotten, and the negligence appeared to Edwin as absolutely monstrous. The effect of it on the street, the effect on a possible caller, was bad enough (Edwin while pretending to scorn social opinion, was really very deferential towards it), but what was worse was the revelation of the feminine mentality.

In opening the door with his latchkey he was purposely noisy, partly in order to give expression to his justified annoyance, and partly to warn all peccant women that the male had arrived, threatening.

As his feet fumbled into the interior gloom and he banged the door, he quite expected a rush of at least one apologetic woman with a box of matches. But nobody came. Nevertheless he could

hear sharp movements through the half-open door of the kitchen.
Assuredly women had the irresponsibility of infants. He glanced
for an instant into the dining-room; the white cloth was laid, but
the table was actually not set. With unusual righteous care he
wiped the half-congealed mud off his boots on the mat; then
removed his hat and his overcoat, took a large new piece of
indiarubber from his pocket and put it on the hall table, felt the
radiator (which despite all his injunctions and recommendations
was almost cold), and lastly he lighted the gas himself. This final
act was contrary to his own rule, for he had often told Hilda
that half her trouble with servants arose through her impatiently
doing herself things which they had omitted, instead of ringing
the bell and seeing the things done. But he was not infrequently
inconsistent, both in deed and in thought. For another example,
he would say superiorly that a woman could never manage
women, ignoring that he the all-wise had never been able to
manage Hilda.

He turned to go upstairs. At the same moment somebody
emerged obscurely from the kitchen. It was Hilda, in a white
apron.

'Oh! I'm glad you've lighted it,' said she curtly, without the
least symptom of apology, but rather affrontingly.

He continued his way.

'Have you seen anything of George?' she asked, and her tone
stopped him.

Yet she well knew that he hated to be stopped of an evening
on his way to the bathroom. It could not be sufficiently emphasized that to accost him before he had descended from the bathroom was to transgress one of the most solemn rules of his daily
life.

'Of course I haven't seen George,' he answered. 'How should
I have seen George?'

'Because he's not back from school yet, and I can't help
wondering –'

She was worrying about George as usual.

He grunted and passed on.

'There's no light on the landing, either,' he said, over the
banisters. 'I wish you'd see to those servants of yours.'

'As it happens there aren't any servants.'

Her tone, getting more peculiar with each phrase, stopped him again.

'Aren't any servants? What d'you mean?'

'Well, I found the attic full of beer bottles, so I sent her off on the spot.'

'Sent who off?'

'Eliza.'

'And where's Ada?'

'She's gone too,' said Hilda defiantly, and as though rebutting an accusation before it could be made.

'Why?'

'She seemed to want to. And she was very impertinent over it.'

He snorted and shrugged his shoulders.

'Well, it's your affair,' he muttered, too scornful to ask details.

'It is,' said she, significantly laconic.

In the bathroom, vexed and gloomy as he brushed his nails and splashed in the wash-basin, he mused savagely over the servant problem. The servant problem had been growing acute. He had predicted several times that a crisis would arrive; a crisis had arrived; he was always right; his rightness was positively uncanny. He had liked Ada; he had not disliked the cook. He knew that Hilda was to blame. How should she not be to blame, – losing her entire staff in one afternoon? It was not merely that she lacked the gift of authoritative control, – it was also that she had no feeling for democratic justice as between one human being and another. And yet among his earliest recollections of her was her passionate sympathy with men on strike as against their employers. Totally misleading manifestations! For her a servant was nothing but a 'servant'. She was convinced that all her servants were pampered and spoilt; and as for Edwin's treatment of his workpeople, she considered it to be ridiculously, criminally soft. If she had implied once she had implied a hundred times that the whole lot of them laughed at him behind his back for a sentimental simpleton. Occasionally Edwin was quite outraged by her callousness. The topic of the eight-hour day, of the ten-hour day, and even of the twelve-hour day (the last for tramway-men) had been lately exciting the district. And Edwin was distressed that in his own house a sixteen-hour day for labour was in vogue and that the employer perceived no shame in it. He did not clearly see how the shame was to be abolished, but he thought that it ought to be admitted. It was not admitted. From six in the morning until ten at night these mysterious light-headed young women were the slaves of a bell. They had no surcease except one long weekday evening each week and a short Sunday evening each fortnight. At one period Hilda had had a fad for getting them out of bed at half-past five, to cure them of laziness. He remembered one cook whose family lived at the village of Brindley Edge, five miles off. This cook on her weekday evening would walk to Brindley Edge, spend three-quarters of an hour in her home, and walk back to Bursley, reaching Trafalgar Road just in time to get to bed. Hilda saw nothing very odd in that. She said the girl could always please herself about going to Brindley Edge.

Edwin's democratic sense was gradually growing in force; it disturbed more and more the peace of his inmost mind. He seldom displayed his sympathies (save to Tertius Ingpen, who, though a Tory, was in some ways astoundingly open to ideas, which seemed to interest him as a pretty equation would interest him), but they pursued their secret activity in his being, annoying him at his lithographic works, and still more in his home. He would suppress them, and grin, and repeat his ancient consoling truth that what was, was. The relief, however, was not permanent.

In that year the discovery of Röntgen Rays, the practical invention of the incandescent gas-mantle, the abolition of the man with the red flag in front of self-propelled vehicles, and the fact that Consols stood at 113, had combined to produce in innumerable hearts the illusion that civilization was advancing at a great rate. But Edwin in his soul scarcely thought so. He was worrying not only about Liberal principles, but about the world; in his youth he had never worried about the world. And of his own personal success he would ask and ask: is it right? He said to himself in the bathroom: 'There's a million domestic servants in this blessed country, and not one of them works less than a hundred hours a week, and nobody cares. I don't think I really care myself. But there it is all the same!' And he was darkly resentful against Hilda on account of the entire phenomenon . . . He foresaw, too, a period of upset and discomfort in his house. Would there, indeed, ever be any real tranquillity in his house, with that strange, primeval cave-woman in charge of it?

As he descended the stairs, Hilda came out of the dining-room with an empty tray.

She said:

'I wish you'd go out and look for George.'

Imagine it – going out into the Five Towns to look for one boy!

'Oh! He'll be all right! I suppose you haven't forgotten Ingpen's coming tonight?'

'Of course I haven't. But I want you to go out and look for George.'

He knew what was in her mind, – namely, an absurd vision of George and his new bicycle crushed under a tramcar somewhere between Bleakridge and Hanbridge. In that year everybody with any pretension to youthfulness and modernity rode a bicycle. Both Edwin and Hilda rode occasionally – such was the power of fashion. Maternal apprehensions had not sufficed to keep George from having a bicycle, nor from riding on it unprotected up and down the greasy slopes of Trafalgar Road to and from school. Edwin himself had bought the bicycle, pooh-poohing danger, and asserting that anyhow normal risks must always be accepted with an even mind. He was about to declare that he would certainly not do anything so silly as to go out and look for George, – and then all of a sudden he had the queer sensation of being alone with Hilda in the house made strange and romantic by a domestic calamity. He gazed at Hilda with her apron, and the calamity had made her strange and romantic also. He was vexed, annoyed, despondent, gloomy, fearful of the immediate future; he had immense grievances; he hated Hilda, he loathed giving way to her. He thought: 'What is it binds me to this incomprehensible woman? I will not be bound!' But he felt that he would be compelled (not by her but by something in himself) to commit the folly of going out to look for George. And he felt that though his existence was an exasperating adventure, still it was an adventure.

'Oh! Damn!' he exploded, and reached for a cap.

And then George came into the hall through the kitchen. The boy often preferred to enter by the back, the stalking Indian way.

IV

George wore spectacles. He had grown considerably. He was now between fourteen and fifteen years of age, and he had begun to look his age. His mental outlook and conversation were on the whole in advance of his age. Even when he was younger he had frequently an adult manner of wise talking, but it had appeared unreal, naïve, – it was amusing rather than convincing. Now he imposed himself even on his family as a genuine adolescent, though the idiom he employed was often schoolboyish and his gestures were immaturely rough. The fact was he was not the same boy. Everybody noticed it. His old charm and delicacy seemed to have gone, and his voice was going. He had become harsh, defiant, somewhat brutal, and egotistic if not conceited. He held a very low opinion of all his schoolfellows, and did not conceal it. Yet he was not very high in his form (the lower fifth); his reports were mediocre; and he cut no figure in the playfield. In the home he was charged with idleness, selfishness, and irresolution. It was pointed out to him that he was not making the best of his gifts, and that if he only chose to make the best of them he might easily, etc. etc. Apparently he did not care a bit. He had marked facility on the piano, but he had insisted on giving up his piano lessons and would not open the piano for a fortnight at a time. He still maintained his intention of being an architect, but he had ceased to show any interest in architecture. He would, however, still paint in watercolours; and he read a lot, but gluttonously, without taste. Edwin and Hilda, and especially Hilda, did not hide their discontent. Hilda had outbursts against him. In regard to Hilda he was disobedient. Edwin always spoke quietly to him, and was seldom seriously disobeyed. When disobeyed Edwin would show a taciturn resentment against the boy, who would sulk and then melt.

'Oh! He'll grow out of it,' Edwin would say to Hilda, yet Edwin, like Hilda, thought that the boy was deliberately naughty, and they held themselves towards him as grieved persons of superior righteousness towards a person of inferior righteousness. Not even Edwin reflected that profound molecular changes might be proceeding in George's brain, for which changes he was in no way responsible. Nevertheless, despite the blighting disappointment of George's evolution, the home was by no means deeply engloomed. No! George had an appealing smile, a mere gawky boyishness, a peculiar way of existing, that somehow made joy in the home. Also he was a centre of intense and continual interest, and of this he was very well aware.

In passing through the kitchen George had of course been struck by the astounding absence of the cook; he had noticed further a fancy apron and a cap lying on the window-sill therein. And when he came into the hall, the strange aspect of his mother (in a servant's apron) and his uncle proved to him that something marvellously unusual, exciting, and uplifting was afoot. He was pleased, agog, and he had the additional satisfaction that great events would conveniently divert attention from his lateness. Still he must be discreet, for the adults were evidently at loggerheads, and therefore touchy. He slipped between Edwin and Hilda with a fairly good imitation of innocent casualness, as if saying: 'Whatever has occurred, I am guiltless, and going on just as usual.'

'Ooh! Bags I!' he exclaimed loudly, at the hall table, and seized the indiarubber, which Edwin had promised for him. His school vocabulary comprised an extraordinary number of words ending in *gs*. He would never, for example, say 'first', but 'foggs'; and never 'second', but 'seggs'. That very morning, for example, meeting Hilda on the mat at the foot of the stairs, he had shocked her by saying: 'You go up foggs, mother, and I'll go seggs.'

'George!' Hilda severely protested. Her anxiety concerning him was now turned into resentment. 'Have you had an accident?'

'An accident?' said George, as though at a loss. Yet he knew perfectly that his mother was referring to the bicycle.

Edwin said curtly:

'Now, don't play the fool. Have you fallen off your bike?

Look at your overcoat. Don't leave that satchel there, and hang your coat up properly.'

The overcoat was in a grievous state. A few days earlier it had been new. Besides money, it had cost an enormous amount of deliberation and discussion, like everything else connected with George. Against his will, Edwin himself had been compelled to conduct George to Shillitoe's, the tailor's, and superintend a third trying-on, for further alterations, after the overcoat was supposed to be finished. And lo, now it had no quality left but warmth! Efforts in regard to George were always thus out of proportion to the trifling results obtained. At George's age Edwin doubtless had an overcoat, but he positively could not remember having one, and he was quite sure that no schoolboy overcoat of his had ever preoccupied a whole household for two minutes, to say nothing of a week.

George's face expressed a sense of injury, and hardened.

'Mother made me take my overcoat. You know I can't cycle in my overcoat. I've not been on my bicycle all day. Also my lamp's broken,' he said, with gloomy defiance.

His curiosity about wondrous events in the house was quenched.

And Edwin felt angry with Hilda for having quite unjustifiably assumed that George had gone to school on his bicycle. Ought she not to have had the ordinary gumption to assure herself, before worrying, that the lad's bicycle was not in the shed? Incredible thoughtlessness. All these alarms for nothing!

'Then why are you so late?' Hilda demanded, diverting to George her indignation at Edwin's unuttered but yet conveyed criticism of herself.

'Kept in.'

'All this time?' Hilda questioned, suspiciously.

George sullenly nodded.

'What for?'

'Latin.'

'Homework? Again?' ejaculated Edwin. 'Why hadn't you done it properly?'

'I had a headache last night. And I've got one today.'

'Another of your Latin headaches!' said Edwin sarcastically.

There was nothing, except possibly cod-liver oil, that George detested more than Edwin's serious sarcasm.

The elders glanced at one another and glanced away. Both had the same fear – the dreadful fear that George might be developing the worse characteristics of his father. Both had vividly in mind the fact that this boy was the son of George Cannon. They never mentioned to each other either the fear or the fact; they dared not. But each knew the thoughts of the other. The boy was undoubtedly crafty; he could conceal subtle designs under a simple exterior; he was also undoubtedly secretive. The recent changes in his disposition had put Edwin and Hilda on their guard, and every time young George displayed cunning, or economized the truth, or lied, the fear visited them. 'I hope he'll turn out all right!' Hilda had said once. Edwin had nearly replied: 'What are you worrying about? The sons of honest men are often rascals. Why on earth shouldn't the son of a rascal be an honest man?' But he had only said, with good-humoured impatience: 'Of course he'll turn out all right!' Not that he himself was convinced.

Edwin now attacked the boy gloomily:

'You didn't seem to have much of a headache when you came in just now.'

It was true.

But George suddenly burst into tears. His headaches were absolutely genuine. The emptiness of the kitchen and the general queer look of things in the house had, however, by their promise of adventurous happenings, caused him to forget his headache altogether, and the discovery of the new indiarubber had been like a tonic to a convalescent. The menacing attitude of the elders had now brought about a relapse. The headache established itself as his chief physical sensation. His chief moral sensation was that of a terrible grievance. He did not often cry; he had not indeed cried for about a year. But tonight there was something nervous in the very air, and the sob took him unawares. The first sob having prostrated all resistance, others followed victoriously, and there was no stopping them. He did not quite know why he should have been more liable to cry on this particular occasion than on certain others, and he was rather ashamed; on the other

hand it was with an almost malicious satisfaction that he perceived the troubling effect of his tears on the elders. They were
obviously in a quandary. Serve them right!

'It's my eyes,' he blubbered. 'I told you these specs would
never suit me. But you wouldn't believe me, and the headmaster
won't believe me.'

The discovery that George's eyesight was defective, about two
months earlier, had led to a desperate but of course hopeless
struggle on his part against the wearing of spectacles. It was
curious that in the struggle he had never even mentioned his
strongest objection to spectacles, – namely, the fact that Bert
Benbow wore spectacles.

'Why didn't you tell us?' Edwin demanded.

Between sobs George replied with overwhelming disillusioned
disgust:

'What's the good of telling you anything? You only think I'm
"codding".'

And he passed upstairs, apparently the broken victim of fate
and parents, but in reality triumphant. His triumph was such that
neither Edwin nor Hilda dared even to protest against the use
of such an inexcusable word as 'codding'.

Hilda went into the kitchen, and Edwin rather aimlessly
followed her. He felt incompetent. He could do nothing except
carry trays, and he had no desire to carry trays. Neither spoke.
Hilda was bending over the fire, then she arranged the grid in
front of the fire to hold a tin, and she greased the tin. He thought
she looked very wistful, for all the somewhat bitter sturdiness of
her demeanour. Tertius Ingpen was due for the evening; she had
no servants – through her own fault; and now a new phase had
arrived in the unending responsibility for George's welfare. He
knew that she was blaming him on account of George. He knew
that she believed in the sincerity of George's outburst; he believed
in it himself. The spectacles were wrong; the headache was
genuine. And he, Edwin, was guilty of the spectacles because he
had forced Hilda, by his calm bantering common sense, to consult a small local optician of good reputation. Hilda had wanted
to go to Birmingham or Manchester; but Edwin said that such
an idea was absurd. The best local optician was good enough

for the great majority of the inhabitants of the Five Towns and would be good enough for George. Why not indeed? Why the craze for specialists? There could be nothing uniquely wrong with the boy's eyes, – it was a temporary weakness. And so on and so on, in accordance with Edwin's instinct for denying the existence of a crisis. And the local optician, consulted, had borne him out. The local optician said that every year he dealt with dozens of cases similar to George's. And now both the local optician and Edwin were overthrown by a boy's sobbing tears.

Suddenly Hilda turned round upon her husband.

'I shall take George to London tomorrow about his eyes,' she said, with immense purpose and sincerity, in a kind of fierce challenge.

This was her amends to George for having often disbelieved him, and for having suspected him of taking after his father. She made her amends passionately, and with all the force of her temperament. In her eyes George was now a martyr.

'To London?' exclaimed Edwin weakly.

'Yes. It's no use half doing these things. I shall ask Charlie Orgreave to recommend me a first-class oculist.'

Edwin dared say nothing. Either Manchester or Birmingham would have been just as good as London, perhaps better. Moreover, she had not even consulted him. She had decided by a violent impulse and announced her decision. This was not right; she would have protested against a similar act by Edwin. But he could not argue with her. She was far beyond argument.

'I wouldn't have that boy's eyesight played with for anything!' she said fiercely.

'Well, of course you wouldn't! Who would?' Edwin thought, but he did not say it.

'Go and see what he's doing,' she said.

Edwin slouched off. He was no longer the master of the house. He was only an economic factor and general tool in the house. And as he wandered like a culprit up the stairs of the mysteriously transformed dwelling he thought again: 'What is it that binds me to her?' But he was abashed, and in spite of himself impressed by the intensity of Hilda's formidable emotion. Nevertheless as he began vaguely to perceive all that was involved in her threat

to go to London on the morrow, he stiffened, and said to himself:
'We shall see about that. We shall just see about that!'

V

They were at the meal. Hilda had covered George's portion of
fish with a plate and put it before the fire to keep warm. She was
just returning to the table. Tertius Ingpen, who sat with his back
to the fire, looked at her over his shoulder with an admiring smile
and said:

'Well, I've had some good meals in this house, but this is
certainly the best bit of fish I ever tasted. So that the catastrophe
in the kitchen leaves me unmoved.'

Hilda, with face suddenly transformed by a responsive smile,
insinuated herself between the table and her armchair, drew
forward the chair by its arms, and sat down. Her keen pleasure
in the compliment was obvious. Edwin noted that the meal was
really very well served, the table brighter than usual, the toast
crisper, and the fish – a fine piece of hake white as snow within
its browned exterior – merely perfect. There was no doubt that
Hilda could be extremely efficient when she desired; Edwin's
criticism was that she was too often negligent, and that in her
moods of conscientiousness she gave herself too urgently and
completely, producing an unnecessary disturbance in the atmosphere of the home. Nevertheless Edwin too felt pleasure in the
compliment to Hilda; and he calmly enjoyed the spectacle of his
wife and his friend side by side on such mutually appreciative
terms. The intimacy of the illuminated table in the midst of the
darker room, the warmth and crackling of the fire, the grave
solidity of the furniture, the springiness of the thick carpet, and
the delicate odours of the repast, – all these things satisfied in him
something that was profound. And the two mature, vivacious,
intelligent faces under the shaded gas excited his loyal affection.

'That's right,' Hilda murmured, in her clear enunciation. 'I do
like praise!'

'Now then, you callous brute,' said Ingpen to Edwin. 'What
do you say?'

And Hilda cried with swift, complaining sincerity:

'Oh! Edwin never praises me!'

Her sincerity convinced by its very artlessness. The complaint had come unsought from her heart. And it was so spontaneous and forcible that Tertius Ingpen, as a tactful guest, saw the advisability of easing the situation by laughter.

'Yes, I do!' Edwin protested, and though he was shocked, he laughed, in obedience to Ingpen's cue. It was true; he did praise her; but not frequently, and almost always in order to flatter her rather than to express his own emotion. Edwin did not care for praising people; he would enthusiastically praise a book, but not a human being. His way was to take efficiency for granted. 'Not so bad', was a superlative of laudation with him. He was now shocked as much by the girl's outrageous candour as by the indisputable revelation that she went hungry for praise. Even to a close friend such as Ingpen, surely a wife had not the right to be quite so desperately sincere. Edwin considered that in the presence of a third person husband and wife should always at any cost maintain the convention of perfect conjugal amenity. He knew couples who achieved the feat, Albert and Clara, for example. But Hilda, he surmised, had other ideas, if indeed she had ever consciously reflected upon this branch of social demeanour. Certainly she seemed at moments to lose all regard for appearances.

Moreover, she was polluting by acerbity the pure friendliness of the atmosphere, and endangering cheer.

'He's too wrapped up in the works to think about praising his wife,' Hilda continued, still in the disconcerting vein of sincerity, but with less violence and a more philosophical air. The fact was that, although she had not regained the zest of the mood so rudely dissipated by the scene with Ada, she was kept cheerful by the mere successful exercise of her own energy in proving to these two men that servants were not in the least essential to the continuance of plenary comfort in her house; and she somewhat condescended towards Edwin.

'By the way, Teddie,' said Ingpen, pulling lightly at his short beard, 'I heard a rumour that you were going to stand for the Town Council in the South Ward. Why didn't you?'

Edwin looked a little confused.

'Who told you that tale?'

'It was about.'

'It never came from me,' said Edwin.

Hilda broke in eagerly:

'He was invited to stand. But he wouldn't. I thought he ought to. I begged him to. But no, he wouldn't. And did you know he refused a J.P. ship-too?'

'Oh!' mumbled Edwin. 'That sort o' thing's not my line.'

'Oh, isn't it?' Ingpen exclaimed. 'Then whose line is it?'

'Look at all the rotters in the Council!' said Edwin.

'All the more reason why you should be on it!'

'Well, I've got no time,' Edwin finished gloomily and uneasily.

Ingpen paused, tapping his teeth with his finger, before proceeding, in a judicial, thoughtful manner which in recent years he had been developing:

'I'll tell you what's the matter with you, old man. You don't know it, but you're in a groove. You go about like a shuttle from the house to the works and the works to the house. And you never think beyond the works and the house.'

'Oh, don't I?'

Ingpen went placidly on:

'No, you don't. You've become a good specimen of the genus "domesticated business man". You've forgotten what life is. You fancy you're at full stretch all the time, but you're in a coma. I suppose you'll never see forty again – and have you ever been outside this island? You went to Llandudno this year because you went last year. And you'll go next year because you went this year. If you happen now and then to worry about the failure of your confounded Liberal Party you think you're a blooming broad-minded publicist. Where are your musical evenings? When I asked you to go with me to a concert at Manchester last week but one, you thought I'd gone dotty, simply because it meant your leaving the works early and not getting to bed until the unheard-of time of one-thirty a.m.'

'I was never told anything about any concert,' Hilda interjected sharply.

'Go on! Go on!' said Edwin, raising his eyebrows.

'I will,' said Ingpen with tranquillity, as though discussing impartially and impersonally the conduct of some individual at the Antipodes. 'Where am I? Well, you're always buying books, and I believe you reckon yourself a bit of a reader. What d'you get out of them? I dare say you've got decided views on the transcendent question whether Emily Brontë was a greater writer than Charlotte. That's about what you've got. Why, dash it, you haven't a vice left. A vice would interfere with your lovely litho. There's only one thing that would upset you more than a machinery breakdown at the works –'

'And what's that?'

'What's that? If one of the hinges of your garden gate came off, or you lost your latchkey! Why, just look how you've evidently been struck all of a heap by this servant affair! I expect i t occurred to you your breakfast might be five minutes late in the morning.'

'Stuff!' said Edwin amiably. He regarded Ingpen's observations as fantastically unjust and beside the mark. But his sense of fairness and his admiration of the man's intellectual honesty would not allow him to resent them. Ingpen would discuss and dissect either his friends or himself with equal detachment; the detachment was complete. And his assumption that his friends fully shared his own dispassionate, curious interest in arriving at the truth appealed very strongly to Edwin's loyalty. That Ingpen was liable to preach and even to hector was a drawback which he silently accepted.

'Struck all of a heap indeed!' muttered Edwin.

'Wasn't he, Hilda?'

'I should just say he was! And I know he thinks it's all my fault,' said Hilda.

Tertius Ingpen glanced at her an instant, and gave a short half-cynical laugh, which scarcely concealed his mild scorn of her feminine confusion of the argument.

'It's the usual thing!' said Ingpen, with scorn still more marked. At this stage of a dissertation he was inclined to be less a human being than the trumpet of a sacred message. 'It's the usual thing! I never knew a happy marriage yet that didn't end in the same way.' Then, perceiving that he was growing too earnest, and that his emphasis on the phrase 'happy marriage' had possibly been too sarcastic, he sniggered.

'I really don't see what marriage has to do with it,' said Hilda, frowning.

'No, of course you don't,' Ingpen agreed.

'If you'd said business –' she added.

'Now we've had the diagnosis,' Edwin sardonically remarked, looking at his plate, 'what's the prescription?' He was reflecting: '"Happy marriage", does he call it! . . . Why on earth does she say I think it's all her fault? I've not breathed a word.'

'Well,' replied Ingpen. 'You live much too close to your infernal works. Why don't you get away, right away, and live out in the country like a sensible man, instead of sticking in this filthy hole – among all these new cottages? . . . Barbarian hordes . . .'

'Oh! Hurrah!' cried Hilda. 'At last I've got somebody who takes my side.'

'Of course you say it's impossible. You naturally would –' Ingpen resumed.

He was interrupted by the entrance of George. Soon after Tertius Ingpen's arrival, George had been dispatched to summon urgently Mrs Tams, the charwoman who had already more than once helped to fill a hiatus between two cooks. George showed now no trace of his late martyrdom, nor of a headache. To conquer George in these latter days you had to demand of him a service. It was Edwin who had first discovered the intensity of the boy's desire to take a useful share in any adult operation whatever. He came in red-cheeked, red-handed, rough, defiant, shy, proud, and making a low intermittent 'oo-oo' noise with protruding lips to indicate the sharpness of the frost outside. As he had already greeted Ingpen he was able to go without ceremony straight to his chair.

Confidentially, in the silence, Hilda raised her eyebrows to him interrogatively. In reply he gave one short nod. Thus in two scarcely perceptible gestures the assurance was asked for and given that the mission had been successful, and that Mrs Tams would be coming up at once. George loved these private and laconic signallings, which produced in him the illusion that he was getting nearer to the enigma of life.

As he persisted in the 'oo-oo' manifestation, Hilda amicably murmured:

'Hsh-hsh!'

George pressed his lips swiftly and hermetically together, and raised his eyebrows in protest against his own indecorum. He glanced at his empty place; whereupon Hilda glanced informingly in the direction of the fire, and George, skilled in the interpretation of minute signs, skirted stealthily round the table behind his mother's chair, and snatched his loaded plate from the hearth.

Nobody said a word. The sudden stoppage of the conversation had indeed caused a slight awkwardness among the elders. George, for his part, was quite convinced that they had been discussing his eyesight.

'Furnace all right again, sonny?' asked Edwin, quietly, when the boy had sat down. Hilda was replenishing Ingpen's plate.

'Blop!' muttered George, springing up aghast. This meant that he had forgotten the furnace in the cellar, source of heat to the radiator in the hall. By a recent arrangement he received sixpence a week for stoking the furnace.

'Never mind! It'll do afterwards,' said Edwin.

But George, masticating fish, shook his head. He must be stern with himself, possibly to atone for his tears. And he went off instantly to the cellar.

'Bit chill,' observed Edwin to him as he left the room. 'A bit chilly' was what he meant; but George delighted to chip the end off a word, and when Edwin chose to adopt the same practice, the boy took it as a masonic sign of profound understanding between them.

George nodded and vanished. And both Edwin and Hilda dwelt in secret upon his boyish charm, and affectionate satisfaction mingled with and softened their apprehensions and their brooding responsibility and remorse. They thought: 'He is simply exquisite,' and in their hearts apologized to him.

Tertius Ingpen asked suddenly:

'What's happened to the young man's spectacles?'

'They don't suit him,' said Hilda eagerly. 'They don't suit him at all. They give him headaches. Edwin would have me take him to the local man, what's-his-name at Hanbridge. I was afraid it would be risky, but Edwin would have it. I'm going to take him to London tomorrow. He's been having headaches for some time and never said a word. I only found it out by accident.'

'Surely,' Ingpen smiled, 'it's contrary to George's usual practice to hide his troubles like that, isn't it?'

'Oh!' said Hilda. 'He's rather secretive, you know.'

'I've never noticed,' said Ingpen, 'that he was more secretive than most of us are about a grievance.'

Edwin, secretly agitated, said in a curious light tone:

'If you ask me, he kept it quiet just to pay us out.'

'Pay you out? What for?'

'For making him wear spectacles at all. These kids want a deuce of a lot of understanding; but that's my contribution. He simply said to himself: "Well, if they think they're going to cure my eyesight for me with their beastly specs they just aren't, and I won't tell 'em!"'

'Edwin!' Hilda protested warmly, 'I wonder you can talk like that!'

Tertius Ingpen went off into one of his peculiar long fits of laughter; and Edwin quizzically smiled, feeling as if he was re-paying Hilda for her unnecessary insistence upon the fact that he was responsible for the choosing of an optician. Hilda, sus-pecting that the two men saw something droll which was hidden from her, blushed and then laughed in turn, somewhat self-consciously.

'Don't *you* think it's best to go to London, about an affair like eyesight?' she asked Ingpen pointedly.

'The chief thing in these cases,' said Ingpen solemnly, 'is to satisfy the maternal instinct. Yes, I should certainly go to London. If Teddie disagrees, I'm against him. Who are you going to?'

'You are horrid!' Hilda exclaimed, and added with positive-ness: 'I shall ask Charlie Orgreave first. He'll tell me the best man.'

'You seem to have a great belief in Charlie,' said Ingpen.

'I have,' said Hilda, who had seen Charlie at George's bedside when nobody knew whether George would live or die.

And while they were talking about Charlie and about Janet, who was now living with her brother at Ealing, the sounds of

George stoking the furnace below came dully up through the floorboards.

'If you and George are going away,' asked Ingpen, 'what'll happen to his worship – with not a servant in the house?'

This important point had been occupying Edwin's mind ever since Hilda had first announced her intention to go to London. But he had not mentioned it to her, nor she to him, their relations being rather delicate. It had, for him, only an academic interest, since he had determined that she should not go to London on the morrow. Nevertheless he awaited anxiously the reply.

Hilda answered with composure:

'I'm hoping he'll come with us.'

He had been prepared for anything but this. The proposition was monstrously impossible. Could a man leave his works at a moment's notice? The notion was utterly absurd.

'That's quite out of the question,' he said at once. He was absolutely sincere. The effect of Ingpen's discourse was, however, such as to upset the assured dignity of his pronouncement; for the decision was simply an illustration of Ingpen's theory concerning him. He blushed.

'Why is it out of the question?' demanded Hilda, inimically gazing at him.

She had lost her lenient attitude towards him of the afternoon. Nevertheless, reflecting upon Tertius Ingpen's indictment of the usual happy marriage, she had been planning the expedition to London as a revival of romance in their lives. She saw it as a marvellous rejuvenating experience. When she thought of all that she had suffered and all that Edwin had suffered, in order that they might come together, she was quite desolated by the prosaic flatness of the ultimate result. Was it to attain their present stolid existence that they had endured affliction for a decade? She wanted passionately to break the mysterious bonds that held them both back from ecstasy and romance. And he would not help her. He would not enter into her desire. She had known that he would refuse. He refused everything – he was so set in his own way. Resentment radiated from her.

'I can't,' said Edwin. 'What d'you want to go tomorrow for? What does a day or two matter?'

Then she loosed her tongue. Why tomorrow? Because you couldn't trifle with a child's eyesight. Already the thing had been dragging on for goodness knew how long. Every day might be of importance. And why not tomorrow? They could shut the house up, and go off together and stay at Charlie's. Hadn't Janet asked them many a time? Maggie would look out for new servants. And Mrs Tams would clean the house. It was really the best way out of the servant question too, beside being the best for George.

'And there's another thing,' she went on without a pause, speaking rapidly and clearly. 'Your eyes want seeing to as well. Do you think I don't know?' she sneered.

'Mine!' he exclaimed. 'My eyes are as right as rain.' It was not true. His eyes had been troubling him.

'Then why have you had a double candle-bracket fixed at your bed-head, when a single one's been enough for you all these years?' she demanded.

'I just thought of it, that's all,' said Edwin glumly, and with no attempt to be diplomatic. 'Anyhow I can't go to London tomorrow. And when I want an oculist,' he finished with grimness, 'Hanbridge'll be good enough for me, I'm thinking.'

Strange, she had never before said a word to him about his eyes!

'Then what *shall* you do while I'm away?' she asked implacably.

But if she was implacable, he also could be implacable. If she insisted on leaving him in the lurch, – well, she should leave him in the lurch! Tertius Ingpen was witness of a plain breach between them. It was unfortunate; it was wholly Hilda's fault; but he had to face the fact.

'I don't know,' he replied curtly.

The next moment George returned.

'Hasn't Mrs Tams been quick, mother?' said George. 'She's come.'

VI

In the drawing-room, after the meal, Edwin could hear through the half-open door the sounds of conversation between Hilda

and Mrs Tams, with an occasional word from George, who was
going to help Mrs Tams to 'put the things away' after she had
washed and wiped. The voice of Mrs Tams was very gentle and
comforting. Edwin's indignant pity went out to her. Why should
Mrs Tams thus cheerfully bear the misfortunes of others? Why
should she at a moment's notice leave a cottageful of young
children and a husband liable at any time to get drunk and maim
either them or her, in order to meet a crisis caused by Hilda's
impulsiveness and lack of tact? The answer, as in so many cases,
was of course economic. Mrs Tams could not afford not to be
at Mrs Clayhanger's instant call; also she was born the victim
of her own altruism; her soul was soft like her plump, cushionlike
body, and she lived as naturally in injustice as a fish in water.
But could anything excuse those who took advantage of such an
economic system, and such a devoted nature? Edwin's conscience
uneasily stirred; he could have blushed. However, he was helpless;
and he was basely glad that he was helpless, that it was no affair
of his after all, and that Mrs Tams had thus to work out her
destiny to his own benefit. He saw in her a seraph for the next
world, and yet in this world he contentedly felt himself her
superior. And her voice, soothing, acquiescent, expressive of the
spirit which gathers in extraneous woes as the medieval saint
drew to his breast the swords of the executioners, continued to
murmur in the hall.

Edwin thought:

'I alone in this house feel the real significance of Mrs Tams.
I'm sure she doesn't feel it herself.'

But these reflections were only the vague unimportant background to the great matter in his mind, – the difficulty with
Hilda. When he had entered the house, questions of gaslight and
blinds were enormous to him. The immense general question of
servants had diminished them to a trifle. Then the question of
George's headache and eyesight had taken precedence. And now
the relations of husband and wife were mightily paramount over
everything else. Tertius Ingpen, having as usual opened the piano,
was idly diverting himself with strange chords, while cigarette
smoke rose into his eyes, making him blink. Like Edwin, Ingpen
was a little self-conscious after the open trouble in the dining-

room. It would have been absurd to pretend that trouble did not
exist; on the other hand the trouble was not of the kind that
could be referred to, by even a very intimate friend. The acknow-
ledgment of it had to be mute. But in addition to being self-
conscious, Ingpen was also triumphant. There was a peculiar
sardonic and somewhat disdainful look on his face as he mused
over the chords, trying to keep the cigarette smoke out of his
eyes. His oblique glance seemed to be saying to Edwin: 'What
have I always told you about women? Well, you've married, and
you must take the consequences. Your wife's no worse than other
wives. Here am I, free! And wouldn't you like to be in my place,
my boy! . . . How wise I have been!'

Edwin resented these unspoken observations. The contrast
between Ingpen's specious support and flattery of Hilda when
she was present, and his sardonic glance when she was absent,
was altogether too marked. Himself in revolt against the institution of marriage, Edwin could not bear that Ingpen should
attack it. Edwin had, so far as concerned the outside world,
taken the institution of marriage under his protection. Moreover
Ingpen's glance was a criticism of Hilda such as no husband
ought to permit. And it was also a criticism of the husband –
that slave and dupe! . . . Yet, at bottom what Edwin resented
was Ingpen's contemptuous pity for the slave and the dupe.

'Why London – and why tomorrow?' said Edwin cheerfully,
with a superior philosophical air, as though impartially studying
an argumentative position, as though he could regard the
temporary vagaries of an otherwise fine sensible woman with
bland detachment. He said it because he was obliged to say something, in order to prove that he was neither a slave nor a dupe.

'Ask me another,' replied Ingpen curtly, continuing to produce
chords.

'Well, we shall see,' said Edwin mysteriously, firmly and
loftily; meaning that, if his opinion were invited, his opinion
would be that Hilda would not go away tomorrow and that
whenever she went she would not go to London.

He had decided to have a grand altercation with his wife that
night, when Ingpen and Mrs Tams had departed, and George
was asleep and they had the house to themselves. He knew his

ground and he could force a decisive battle. He felt no doubt as
to the result. The news of his triumph should reach Ingpen.

Ingpen was apparently about to take up the conversation when
George came clumsily and noisily into the drawing-room. All
his charm seemed to have left him.

'I thought you were going to help,' said Edwin.

'So I am,' George challenged him; and, lacking the courage to
stop at that point, added: 'But they aren't ready yet.'

'Let's try those Haydn bits, George,' Ingpen suggested.

'Oh, no!' said George curtly.

Ingpen and the boy had begun to play easy fragments of duets
together.

Edwin said with sternness:

'Sit down to that piano and do as Mr Ingpen asks you.'

George flushed and looked foolish and sat down; and Ingpen
quizzed him. All three knew well that Edwin's fierceness was only
one among sundry consequences of the mood of the house-
mistress. The slow movement and the scherzo from the symphony
were played. And while the music went on, Edwin heard distinctly the opening and shutting of the front door and an arrival
in the hall, and then chattering. Maggie had called. 'What's she
after?' thought Edwin.

'Hoo! There's Auntie Maggie!' George exclaimed, as soon as
the scherzo was finished, and ran off.

'That boy is really musical,' said Ingpen with conviction.

'Yes, I suppose he is,' Edwin agreed casually as though deprecating a talent which however was undeniable. 'But you'd never
guess he's got a bad headache, would you?'

It was a strange kind of social evening, and Hilda – it seemed
to the august Edwin – had a strange notion of the duties of
hostess. Surely, if Mrs Tams was in the kitchen, Hilda ought to
be in the drawing-room with their guest! Surely Maggie ought to
have been brought into the drawing-room, – she was not a school-
girl, she was a woman of over forty, and yet she had quite inexcusably kept her ancient awkwardness and timidities. He could
hear chatterings from the dining-room, scurryings through the
hall, and chatterings from the kitchen; then a smash of crockery,
a slight scream, and girlish gigglings. They were all the same, all

the women he knew, except perhaps Clara, – they had hours when they seemed to forget that they were adult and that their skirts were long. And how was it that Hilda and Maggie were suddenly so intimate, they whose discreet mutual jealousy was an undeniable phenomenon of the family life? With all his majesty he was simpleton enough never to have understood that two women who eternally suspect each other may yet dissolve upon occasion into the most touching playful tenderness. The whole ground-floor was full of the rumour of an apparent alliance between Hilda and Maggie. And as he listened Edwin glanced sternly at the columns of the evening *Signal*, while Tertius Ingpen, absorbed, worked his way bravely through a sonata of Beethoven.

Then George reappeared.

'Mother's going to take me to London tomorrow about my eyes,' said George to Ingpen, stopping the sonata by his mere sense of the terrific importance of such tidings. And he proceeded to describe the projected doings in London, the visit to Charlie and Janet Orgreave, and possibly to the Egyptian Hall.

Edwin did not move. He kept an admirable and complete calm under the blow. Hilda was decided, then, to defy him. In telling the boy, who during the meal had been permitted to learn nothing, she had burnt her boats; she had even burnt Edwin's boats also; which seemed to be contrary to the rules laid down by society for conjugal warfare, – but women never could fight according to rules! The difficulties and dangers of the great pitched battle which Edwin had planned for the close of the evening were swiftly multiplied. He had misgivings.

The chattering, giggling girls entered the drawing-room. But as Maggie came through the doorway her face stiffened; her eyes took on a glaze; and when Ingpen bent over her hand in all the false ardour of his excessive conventional chivalry, the spinster's terrible constraint – scourge of all her social existence – gripped her like a disease. She could not speak.

'Hello, Mag,' Edwin greeted her.

Impossible to divine in this plump, dowdy, fading, dumb creature the participator in all those chatterings and gigglings of a few moments earlier! Nevertheless Edwin, who knew her profoundly, could see beneath the glaze of those eyes the commonsense soul of the sagacious woman protesting against Ingpen's affected manners and deciding that she did not care for Ingpen at all.

'Auntie Hamps is being naughty again,' said Hilda bluntly.

Ingpen, and then Edwin, sniggered.

'*I* can't do anything with her, Edwin,' said Maggie, speaking quickly and eagerly, as she and Hilda sat down. 'She's bound to let herself in for another attack if she doesn't take care of herself. And she won't take care of herself. She won't listen to the doctor or anybody else. She's always on her feet, and she's got sewing meetings on the brain just now. I've got her to bed early tonight – she's frightfully shaky – and I thought I'd come up and tell you. You're the only one that can do anything with her at all, and you really must come and see her tomorrow on your way to the works.'

Maggie spoke as though she had been urging Edwin for months to take the urgent matter in hand and was now arrived at desperation.

'All right! All right!' said he, with amiable impatience; it was the first he had heard of the matter. 'I'll drop in. But I've got no influence over her,' he added, with sincerity.

'Oh, yes, you have!' said Maggie, mildly now. 'I'm very sorry to hear about George's eyes. Seeing it's absolutely necessary for Hilda to take him to London tomorrow, and you've got no servants at all, can't you come and sleep at Auntie's for a night or two? You've no idea what a relief it would be to me.'

In an instant Edwin saw that he was beaten, that Hilda and Maggie, in the intervals of their giggling, had combined to overthrow him. The tone in which Maggie uttered the words, 'George's eyes', 'absolutely necessary', and 'such a relief' precluded argument. His wife would have her capricious, unnecessary way, and he would be turned out of his own house.

'I think you might, dear,' said Hilda, with the angelic persuasiveness of a loving and submissive wife. Nobody could have guessed from that marvellous tone that she had been determined to defeat him and was then, so to speak, standing over his prostrate form.

Maggie, having said what was necessary to be said, fell back into the constraint from which no efforts of her companions

could extricate her. Such was the effect upon her of the presence
of Tertius Ingpen, a stranger. Presently Ingpen was scanning time-
tables for Hilda, and George was finding notepaper for her, and
Maggie was running up and downstairs for her. She was off to
London. 'In that woman's head,' thought Edwin, as, observing
his wife, he tried in vain to penetrate the secrets behind her
demeanour, 'there's only room for one idea at a time.'

VII

Edwin sat alone in the drawing-room, at the end of an evening
which he declined to call an evening at all. His eyes regarded a
book on his knee, but he was not reading it. His mind was engaged upon the enigma of his existence. He had entered his house
without the least apprehension, and brusquely, in a few hours,
everything seemed to be changed for him. Impulse had conquered
common sense; his ejectment was a settled thing; and he was condemned to the hated abode of Auntie Hamps. Events seemed
enormous; they desolated him; his mouth was full of ashes. The
responsibilities connected with George were increasing; his wife,
incalculable and unforeseeable, was getting out of hand; and the
menace of a future removal to another home in the country was
raised again.

He looked about the room, and he imagined all the house,
every object in which was familiar and beloved, and he simply
could not bear to think of the disintegration of these interiors by
furniture removers, and of the endless rasping business of creating
a new home in partnership with a woman whose ideas about
furnishing were as unsound as they were capricious. He utterly
dismissed the fanciful scheme, as he dismissed the urgings towards public activity. He deeply resented all these headstrong
intentions to disturb him in his tranquillity. They were indefensible, and he would not have them. He would die in sullen obstinacy rather than yield. Impulse might conquer common sense, but
not beyond a certain degree. He would never yield.

Ingpen had departed, to sleep in a room in the same building
as his office at Hanbridge. He knew that Ingpen had no comprehension of domestic comfort and a well-disposed day. Nevertheless,

he envied the man his celestial freedom. If he, Edwin, were free, what an ideal life he could make for himself, a life presided over by common sense, regularity, and order! He was not free; he would never be free; and what had he obtained in exchange for freedom? . . . Ingpen's immense criticism smote him. He had a wife and her child; servants – at intervals; a fine works and many workpeople; a house, with books; money; security. The organized machinery of his existence was tremendous; and it was all due to him, made by him in his own interests and to satisfy his own desires. Without him the entire structure would crumble in a week; without him it would have no excuse. And what was the result? Was he ever, in any ideal sense, happy – that is, free from foreboding, from friction, from responsibility, – and withal lightly joyous? Was any quarter of an hour of his day absolutely what he would have wished? He ranged over his day, and concluded that the best part of it was the very last . . . He got into bed, the candles in the sconce were lit, the gas diminished to a blue speck, and most of the room in darkness; he lay down on his left side, took the marker from the volume in his hand, and began to read; the house was silent and enclosed, the rumbling tramcar – to whose sound he had been accustomed from infancy – did not a bit disturb him; it was in another world; over the edge of his book he could see the form of his wife, fast asleep in the other bed, her plaited hair trailing over the pillow; the feel of the sheets to his limbs was exquisite; he read, the book was good; the chill of winter just pleasantly affected the hand that held the book; nothing annoyed; nothing jarred; sleep approached . . . That fifteen minutes, that twenty or thirty minutes, was all that he could show as the result of the tremendous organized machinery of his existence – his house, his works, his workpeople, his servants, his wife with her child . . .

Hilda came with quick determination into the drawing-room. They had not spoken to each other alone since the decision and his defeat. He was aware of his heart beating resentfully.

'I'm going to bed now, dear,' she said in an ordinary tone. 'I've got a frightful headache, and I must sleep. Be sure and wake me up at seven in the morning will you? I shall have such lots to do.'

He thought:

'Has she a frightful headache?'

She bent down and kissed him several times, very fervently; her lips lingered on his. And all the time she frowned ever so little, and it was as if she was conveying to him: 'But – each for himself in marriage, after all.'

In spite of himself, he felt just a little relieved; and he could not understand why! He watched her as she left the room. How had it come about that the still finally mysterious creature was living in his house, imposing her individuality upon him, spoiling his existence? He considered that it was all disconcertingly strange.

He rose, lit a cigarette, and opened the window; and the frosty air, entering, braced him and summoned his self-reliance. The night was wondrous. And when he had shut the window and turned again within, the room, beautiful, withdrawn, peaceful, was wondrous too. He reflected that soon he would be in bed, calmly reading, with his wife unconscious as an infant in the other bed. And then his grievance against Hilda slowly surged up, and he began for the first time to realize how vast it was.

'Confound that woman!' he muttered, meaning Auntie Hamps.

CHAPTER 18

AUNTIE HAMPS SENTENCED

I

ON the next evening it was Maggie who opened Mrs Hamps's front door for Edwin. There was no light in the lobby, but a faint gleam coming through the open door of the sitting-room disclosed the silhouette of Maggie's broad figure.

'I thought you'd call in this morning,' said Maggie discontentedly. 'I asked you to. I've been expecting you all day.'

'Didn't you get my message?'

'No. What message?'

'D'you mean to say a lad hasn't been here with my portmanteau?' demanded Edwin, alarmed and ready to be annoyed.

'Yes. A lad's been with your portmanteau. But he gave no message.'

'D—n him! I told him to tell you I couldn't possibly get here before night.'

'Well, he didn't!' said Maggie stoutly, throwing back the blame upon Edwin and his hirelings. 'I particularly wanted you to come early. I told Auntie you'd be coming.'

'How's she getting on?' Edwin asked with laconic gruffness, dismissing Maggie's grievance without an apology. He might have to stand nonsense from Hilda; but he would not stand it from Maggie, of whose notorious mildness he at once began to take advantage, as in the old days of their housekeeping together. Moreover, his entrance into this abode was a favour, exhibiting the condescension of the only human being who could exercise influence upon Auntie Hamps.

'She's worse,' said Maggie, briefly and significantly.

'In bed?' said Edwin, less casually, marking her tone.

Maggie nodded.

'Had the doctor?'

'I should think so indeed!'

'Hm! Why don't you have a light in this lobby?' he inquired suddenly, on a dryly humorous note, as he groped to suspend his overcoat upon an unstable hat-stand. It seemed to be a very cold lobby, after his own radiator-heated hall.

'She never will have a light here, unless she's doing the grand for someone. Are you going to wash ye?'

'No. I cleaned up at the works.' A presentiment of the damp chilliness of the Hamps's bedroom had suggested this precaution.

Maggie preceded him into the sitting-room, where a hexagonal occasional table was laid for tea.

'Hello! Do you eat here? What's the matter with the dining-room?'

'The chimney always smokes when the wind's in the south-west.'

'Well, why doesn't she have a cowl put on it?'

'You'd better ask her . . . Also she likes to save a fire. She can't bear to have two fires going as well as the kitchen range. I'll bring tea in. It's all ready.'

Maggie went away.

Edwin looked round the shabby Victorian room. A length of featureless linoleum led from the door to the table. This carpet-protecting linoleum exasperated him. It expressed the very spirit of his aunt's house. He glanced at the pictures, the texts, the beady and the woolly embroideries, the harsh chairs, and the magnificent morocco exteriors of the photograph albums in which Auntie Hamps kept the shiny portraits of all her relatives, from grand-nieces back to the third and fourth generation of ancestors. And a feeling of desolation came over him. He thought: 'How many days shall I have to spend in this deadly hole?' It was extremely seldom that he visited King Street, and when he did come the house was brightened to receive him. He had almost forgotten what the house really was. And, suddenly thrown back into it at its most lugubrious and ignoble, after years of the amenities of Trafalgar Road, he was somehow surprised that that sort of thing had continued to exist, and he resented that it should have dared to continue to exist. He had a notion that, since he had left it behind, it ought to have perished.

He cautiously lifted the table and carried it to the hearthrug.

Then he sat down in the easy-chair, whose special property, as he remembered, was slowly and inevitably to slide the sitter forward to the hard edge of the seat; and he put his feet inside the fender. In the grate a small fire burned between two firebricks. He sneezed.

Maggie came in with a tray.

'Are you cold?' she asked, seeing the new situation of the table.

'Am I cold!' Edwin repeated.

'Well,' said Maggie, 'I always think your rooms are so hot.'

Edwin seized the small serviceable tongs which saved the wear of the large tongs matching the poker and the shovel, and he dragged both firebricks out of the grate.

'No coal here, I suppose!' he exclaimed gloomily, opening the black japanned coal-scuttle. 'Oh! Corn in Egypt!' The scuttle was full of coal. He threw on to the fire several profuse shovelfuls of best household nuts which had cost sixteen shillings a ton even in that district of cheap coal.

'Well,' Maggie murmured, aghast. 'It's a good thing it's you. If it had been anybody else –'

'What on earth does she do with her money?' he muttered.

Shrugging her shoulders, Maggie went out again with an empty tray.

'No servant, either?' Edwin asked, when she returned.

'She's sitting with Auntie.'

'Must I go up before I have my tea?'

'No. She won't have heard you come.'

There was a grilled mutton chop and a boiled egg on the crowded small table, with tea, bread-and-butter, two rounds of dry bread, some cakes, and jam.

'Which are you having – egg or chop?' Edwin demanded as Maggie sat down.

'Oh! They're both for you.'

'And what about you?'

'I only have bread-and-butter as a rule.'

Edwin grunted, and started to eat.

'What's supposed to be the matter with her?' he inquired.

'It seems it's congestion of the lung, and thickened arteries. It wouldn't matter so much about the lung being congested, in itself, only it's the strain on her heart.'

'I see.'

'Been in bed all day, I suppose?'

'No, she would get up. But she had to go back to bed at once. She had a collapse.'

'Hm!'

He could not think of anything else to say.

'Haven't got tonight's *Signal*, have you?'

'Oh, no!' said Maggie, astonished at such a strange demand. 'Hilda get off all right?'

'Yes, they went by the nine train.'

'She told me that she should, if she could manage it. I expect Mrs Tams was up there early.'

Edwin nodded, recalling with bitterness certain moments of the early morning. And then silence ensued. The brother and sister could not keep the conversation alive. Edwin thought: 'We know each other intimately, and we respect each other, and yet we cannot even conduct a meal together without awkwardness and constraint. Has civilization down here got no further than that?' He felt sorry for Maggie, and also kindly disdainful of her. He glanced at her furtively and tried to see in her the girl of the far past. She had grown immensely older than himself. She was now at home in the dreadful Hamps environment. True, she had an income, but had she any pleasures? It was impossible to divine what her pleasures might be, what she thought about when she lay in bed, to what hours she looked forward. First his father, then himself, and lastly Auntie Hamps had subjugated her. And of the three Auntie Hamps had most ruthlessly succeeded, and in the shortest time. And yet – Edwin felt – even Auntie Hamps had not quite succeeded, and the original individual still survived in Maggie and was silently critical of all the phenomena which surrounded her and to which she had apparently submitted. Realizing this, Edwin ceased to be kindly disdainful.

Towards the end of the meal a heavy foot was heard on the stairs.

'Minnie!' Maggie called.

After shuffling and hesitation the sitting-room door was pushed ever so little open.

'Yes, miss,' said someone feebly.

'Why have you left Mrs Hamps? Do you need anything?'

'Missis made me go, miss,' came the reply, very loosely articulated.

'Come in and take your bread,' said Maggie, and aside to Edwin: 'Auntie's at it again!'

After another hesitation the door opened wide, and Minnie became visible. She was rather a big girl, quite young, fat, too fair, undecided, obviously always between two minds. Her large apron, badly-fitting over the blue frock, was of a dubious yellow colour. She wore spectacles. Behind her spectacles she seemed to be blinking in confusion at all the subtle complexities of existence. She advanced irregularly to the table with a sort of nervous desperation, as if saying: 'I have to go through this ordeal.' Edwin could not judge whether she was about to smile or about to weep.

'Here's your bread,' said Maggie, indicating the two rounds of dry bread. 'I've left the dripping on the kitchen table for you.'

Edwin, revolted, perceived of course in a flash what the life of Minnie was under the regime of Auntie Hamps.

'Thank ye, miss.'

He noticed that the veiled voice was that of a rather deaf person.

Blushing, Minnie took the bread, and moved away. Just as she reached the door, she gave a great sob, followed by a number of little ones; and the bread fell on to the carpet. She left it there, and vanished, still violently sobbing.

Edwin, spellbound, stopped masticating. A momentary sensation almost of horror seized him. Maggie turned pale, and he was glad that she turned pale. If she had shown by no sign that such happenings were unusual, he would have been afraid of the very house itself, of its mere sinister walls which seemed to shelter sick tyrants, miserable victims, and enchanted captives; he would have begun to wonder whether he himself was safe in it.

'What next?' muttered Maggie, intimidated but plucky, rising and following Minnie. 'Just go up to Auntie, will you?'

she called to Edwin over her shoulder. 'She oughtn't really to be left alone for a minute.'

II

Edwin pushed open the door and crept with precautions into the bedroom. Mrs Hamps was dozing. In the half-light of the lowered gas he looked at her and was alarmed, shocked, for it was at once apparent that she must be very ill. She lay reclining against several crumpled and crushed pillows, with her head on one side and her veined hands limp on the eiderdown, between the heavy brown side-curtains that hung from the carved mahogany tester. The posture seemed to be that of an exhausted animal, surprised by the unconsciousness of final fatigue, shameless in the intense need of repose. Auntie Hamps had ceased to be a Wesleyan, a pillar of society, a champion of the conventions, and a keeper-up of appearances; she was just an utterly wearied and beaten creature, breathing noisily through wide-open mouth. Edwin could not remember ever having seen her when she was not to some extent arrayed for the world's gaze; he had not seen her at the crisis of any of her recent attacks. He knew that more than once she had recovered when good judges had pronounced recovery impossible; but he was quite sure, now, that she would never rise from that bed. He had the sudden dreadful thought: 'She is done for, sentenced, cut off from the rest of us. This is the end for her. She won't be able to pretend any more. All her efforts have come to this.' The thought affected him like a blow. And two somewhat contradictory ideas sprang from it: first, the entire absurdity of her career as revealed by its close, and secondly, the tragic dignity with which its close was endowing her.

At once contemptible and august, she was diminished, even in size. Her scanty grey hair was tousled. Her pink flannel night-dress with its long, loose sleeves was grotesque; the multitude of her patched outer wrappings, from which peeped her head on its withered neck, and safety-pins, and the orifice of a hot-water bag, were equally grotesque. None of the bed-linen was clean, or of good quality. The eiderdown was old, and the needle-points of its small white feathers were piercing it. The table at the bed-head had a strange collection of poor, odd crockery. The whole room, with its distempered walls of an uncomfortable green colour, in spite of several respectable pieces of mahogany furniture, seemed to be the secret retreat of a graceless and mean indigence. And above all it was damply cold; the window stood a little open, and only the tiniest fire burnt in the inefficient grate.

For decades Auntie Hamps, with her erect figure and handsome face, her black silks, jet ornaments, and sealskins, her small regular subscriptions and her spasmodic splendours of golden generosity, her heroic relentless hypocrisies and her absolute self-reliance and independence, had exhibited a glorious front to the world. With her, person and individuality were almost everything, and the environment she had made for herself almost nothing. The ground floor of her house was presentable, especially when titivated for occasional hospitalities, but not more than presentable. The upper floor was never shown. In particular, Auntie Hamps was not one of those women who invite other women to their bedrooms. Her bedroom was guarded like a fastness. In it, unbeheld, lived the other Auntie Hamps, complementary to the grand and massive Mrs Hamps known to mankind. And now the fastness was exposed, defenceless, and its squalid avaricious secrets discovered; and she was too broken to protest. There was something unbearably pitiful in that. Her pose was pitiful and her face was pitiful. Those features were still far from ugly; the contours of the flushed cheeks, the chin, and the convex eyelids were astonishingly soft, and recalled the young girl of about half a century earlier. She was both old and young in her troubled unconsciousness. The reflection was inevitable: 'She was a young girl – and now she is sentenced.' Edwin felt himself desolated by a terrible gloom which questioned the justification of all life. The cold of the room made him shiver. After gazing for a long time at the sufferer, he tiptoed to the fire. On the painted iron mantelpiece were a basalt clock and three photographs; a recent photograph of smirking Clara surrounded by her brood; a faded photograph of Maggie as a young girl, intolerably dowdy; and an equally faded photograph of himself as a young man of twenty, – he remembered the suit and the necktie in which he had been photographed. The simplicity, the ingenuousness, of his own boyish face moved him deeply and at the same time disgusted him. 'Was I like that?' he thought, astounded, and he felt intensely sorry for the raw youth. Above the clock was suspended by a ribbon a new green card, lettered in silver with some verses entitled 'Lean Hard'. This card, he knew, had superseded a booklet of similar tenor that used to lie on the dressing-table when he was an infant. The verses began:

> Child of My love, 'Leanhard',
> And let Me feel the pressure of thy care.

And they ended:

> Thou lovest Me. I knew it. Doubt not then
> But loving Me, LEAN HARD.

All his life he had laughed at the notion of his Auntie leaning hard upon anything whatever. Yet she had lived continually with these verses ever since the year of their first publication; she had never tired of their message. And now Edwin was touched. He seemed to see some sincerity, some beauty in them. He had a vision of their author, unknown to literature, but honoured in a hundred thousand respectable homes. He thought: 'Did Auntie only pretend to believe in them? Or did she think she did believe in them? Or did she really believe in them?' The last seemed a possibility. Supposing she did really believe in them? ... Yes, he was touched. He was ready to admit that spirituality was denied to none. He seemed to come into contact with the universal immanent spirituality.

Then he stooped to put some bits of coal silently on the fire.

'Who's that putting coal on the fire?' said a faint but sharply protesting voice from the bed.

The weakness of the voice gave Edwin a fresh shock. The voice seemed to be drawing on the very last reserves of its owner's vitality. Owing to the height of the foot of the bed, Auntie Hamps could not see anything at the fireplace lower than the mantelpiece. As she withdrew from earth she employed her fading faculties to expostulate against a waste of coal and to identify the unseen criminal.

'I am,' said Edwin cheerfully. 'It was nearly out.'

He stood up, smiling slightly, and faced her.

Auntie Hamps, lifting her head and frowning in surprise, gazed at him for a few moments, as if trying to decide who he was. Then she said, in the same enfeebled tone as before:

'Eh, Edwin! I never heard you come in. This *is* an honour!' And her head dropped back.

'I'm sleeping here,' said Edwin, with determined cheerfulness. 'Did ye know?'

She reflected, and answered deliberately, using her volition to articulate every syllable:

'Yes. Ye're having Maggie's room.'

'Oh, no, Auntie!'

'Yes, you are. I've told her.' The faint voice became harshly obstinate. 'Turn the gas up a bit, Edwin, so that I can see you. Well, this is an honour. Did Maggie give ye a proper tea?'

'Oh, yes, thanks. Splendid.'

He raised the gas. Auntie Hamps blinked.

'You want something to shade this gas,' said Edwin. 'I'll fix ye something.'

The gas-bracket was a little to the right of the fireplace, over the dressing-table, and nearly opposite the bed. Auntie Hamps nodded. Having glanced about, Edwin put a bonnet-box on the dressing-table, and on that, upright and open, the Hamps family Bible from the ottoman. The infirm creation was just lofty enough to come between the light and the old woman's eyes.

'That'll be better,' said he. 'You're not at all well, I hear, Auntie.' He endeavoured to be tactful.

She slowly shook her head as it lay on the pillow.

'This is one of my bad days . . . But I shall pick up . . . Then has Hilda taken George to London?'

Edwin nodded.

'Eh, I do hope and pray it'll be all right. I've had such good eyesight myself, I'm all the more afraid for others. What a blessing it's been to me! . . . Eh, what a good mother dear Hilda is!' She added after a pause: 'I dare say there never was such a mother as Hilda, unless it's Clara.'

'Has Clara been in today?' Edwin demanded, to change the subject of conversation.

'No, she hasn't. But she will, as soon as she has a moment. She'll be popping in. They're such a tie on her, those children are – and how she looks after them! . . . Edwin!' She called him, as though he were receding.

'Yes?'

The frail voice continued, articulating with great carefulness, and achieving each sentence as though it were a miracle, as indeed it was:

'I think no one ever had such nephews and nieces as I have. I've never had children of my own – that was not to be! – but I must say the Lord has made it up to me in my nephews and nieces. You and Hilda . . . and Clara and Albert . . . and the little chicks!' Tears stood in her eyes.

'You're forgetting Maggie,' said Edwin lightly.

'Yes,' Auntie Hamps agreed, but in a quite different tone, reluctant and critical. 'I'm sure Maggie does her best. Oh! I'm sure she does . . . Edwin!' Again she called him.

He approached the tumbled bed, and even sat on the edge of it, his hands in his pockets. Auntie Hamps, though breathing now more rapidly and with more difficulty, seemed to have re-vitalized herself at some mysterious source of energy. She was still preoccupied by the mental concentration and the effort of volition required for the smallest physical acts incident to her continued existence; but she had accumulated power for the furtherance of greater ends.

'D'ye want anything?' Edwin suggested, indicating the contents of the night-table.

She moved her head to signify a negative. Her pink-clad arms did not stir. And her whole being seemed to be suspended while she prepared for an exertion.

'I'm so relieved you've come,' she said at length, slowly and painfully. 'You can't think what a relief it is to me. I've really no one but you . . . It's about that girl.'

'What girl?'

'Minnie.'

'The servant?'

Mrs Hamps inclined her head, and fetched breath through the wide-open mouth. 'I've only just found it out. She's in trouble.

Oh! She admitted it to me a bit ago. I sent her downstairs. I wouldn't have her in my bedroom a minute longer. She's in trouble. I felt sure she was ... She was at class-meeting last Wednesday. And only yesterday I paid her her wages. Only yesterday! Here she lives on the fat of the land, and what does she do for it? I assure you I have to see to everything myself. I'm always after her ... In a month she won't be fit to be seen ... Edwin, I've never been so ashamed ... That I should have to tell such a thing to my own nephew!' She ceased, exhausted.

Edwin was somewhat amused. He could not help feeling amused at such an accident happening in the house of Mrs Hamps.

'Who's the man?' he asked.

'Yes, and that's another thing!' answered Mrs Hamps solemnly, in her extreme weakness. 'It's the barman at the Vaults, of all people. She wouldn't admit it, but I know.'

'What are you going to do?'

'She must leave my house at once.'

'Where does she live – I mean her people?'

'She has no parents.' Auntie Hamps reflected for a few moments. 'She has an aunt at Axe.'

'Well, she can't get to Axe tonight,' said Edwin positively. 'Does Maggie know about it?'

'Maggie!' exclaimed Mrs Hamps scornfully. 'Maggie never notices *anything*.' She added in a graver tone: 'And there's no reason why Maggie should know. It's not the sort of thing that Maggie ought to know about. You can speak to the girl herself. It will come much better from you. I shall simply tell Maggie I've decided the girl must go.'

'She can't go tonight,' Edwin repeated, humouringly, but firmly.

Auntie Hamps proved the sincerity of her regard for him by yielding.

'Well,' she murmured, 'tomorrow morning, then. She can turn out the sitting-room, and clean the silver in the black box, and then she can go – before dinner. I don't see why I should give her her dinner. Nor her extra day's wages either.'

'And what shall you do for a servant? Get a charwoman?'

'Charwoman? No! Maggie will manage.' And then with a

sudden flare of relished violence: 'I always knew that girl was a mopsy slut. And what's more, if you ask me, she brought him into the house – and after eleven o'clock at night too!'

'All right!' Edwin muttered, to soothe the patient.

And Mrs Hamps sadly smiled.

'It's such a relief to me,' she breathed. 'You don't know what a relief to me it is to put it in your hands.'

Her eyelids dropped. She said no more. Having looked back for an instant in a supreme effort on behalf of the conventions upon which society was established, Auntie Hamps turned again exhausted towards the lifting veil of the unknown. And Edwin began to realize the significance of the scene that was ended.

III

'I say,' Edwin began, when he had silently closed the door of the sitting-room. 'Here's a lark, if you like!' And he gave a short laugh. It was under such language and such demeanour that he concealed his real emotion, which was partly solemn, partly pleasurable, and wholly buoyant.

Maggie looked up gloomily. With a bit of pencil held very close to the point in her heavy fingers, she was totting up the figures of household accounts in a penny red-covered cash-book.

Edwin went on:

'It seems the girl yon' – he indicated the kitchen with a jerk of the head – ''s been and got herself into a mess.'

Maggie leaned her chin on her hand.

'Has she been talking to you about it?' With a similar jerk of the head Maggie indicated Mrs Hamps's bedroom.

'Yes.'

'I suppose she's only just found it out?'

'Who? Auntie? Yes. Did you know about it?'

'Did I know about it?' Maggie repeated with mild disdainful impatience. 'Of course I knew about it. I've known for weeks. But I wasn't going to tell *her*.' She finished bitterly.

Edwin regarded his sister with new respect and not without astonishment. Never before in their lives had they discussed any inconvenient sexual phenomenon. Save for vague and very careful occasional reference to Clara's motherhood, Maggie had never given any evidence to her brother that she was acquainted with what are called in Anglo-Saxon countries 'the facts of life', and he had somehow thought of her as not having emerged, at the age of forty-four or so, from the naïve ignorance of the young girl. Now her perfectly phlegmatic attitude in front of the Minnie episode seemed to betoken a familiarity that approached cynicism. And she was not at all tongue-tied; she was at her ease. She had become a woman of the world. Edwin liked her; he liked her manner and her tone. His interest in the episode even increased.

'She was for turning her out tonight,' said he. 'I stopped that.'

'I should think so indeed!'

'I've got her as far as tomorrow morning.'

'The girl won't go tomorrow morning either!' said Maggie. 'At least, if she goes, I go.' She spoke with tranquillity, adding: 'But we needn't bother about that. Auntie'll be past worrying about Minnie tomorrow morning . . . I'd better go up to her. She can't possibly be left alone.'

Maggie shut the account book, and rose.

'I only came down for a sec. to tell you. She was dozing,' said Edwin apologetically. 'She's awfully ill. I'd no idea.'

'Yes, she's ill right enough.'

'Who'll sit up with her?'

'I shall.'

'Did you sit up with her last night?'

'No – only part of the night.'

'We ought to get a nurse.'

'Well, we can't get one tonight.'

'And what about Clara? Can't she take a turn? Surely in a case like this she can chuck her eternal kids for a bit.'

'I expect she could. But she doesn't know.'

'Haven't you sent round?' He expressed surprise.

'I couldn't,' said Maggie with undisturbed equanimity. 'Who could I send? I couldn't spare Minnie. The thing didn't seem at all serious until this morning. Since then I've had my hands full.'

'Yes, I can see you have,' Edwin agreed appreciatively.

'It was lucky the doctor called on his own. He does sometimes, you know, since she began to have her attacks.'

'Well, I'll go round to Clara's myself,' said Edwin.

'I shouldn't,' said Maggie. 'At least not tonight.'

'Why not?' He might have put the question angrily, over-bearingly; but Maggie was so friendly, suave, confidential, persuasive, and so sure of herself, that with pleasure he copied her accents. He enjoyed thus talking to her intimately in the ugly dark house, with the life-bearing, foolish Minnie on the one hand, and the dying old woman on the other. He thought: 'There's something splendid about Mag. In fact I always knew there was.' And he forgot her terrible social shortcomings, her utter lack of the feminine seductiveness that for him ought to be in every woman, and her invincible stolidity. Her sturdy and yet scarcely articulate championship of Minnie delighted him and quickened his pulse.

'I'd sooner not have her here tonight,' said Maggie. 'You knew they'd had a tremendous rumpus, didn't you?'

'Who? Auntie and Clara?'

'Yes.'

'I didn't. What about? When? Nobody ever said anything to me.'

'Oh, it must have been two or three months ago. Auntie said something about Albert not paying me my interest on my money he's got. And then Clara flared up, and the fat was in the fire.'

'D'you mean to say he's not paying you your interest? Why didn't you tell me?'

'Oh! It doesn't matter. I didn't want to bother you.'

'Well, you ought to have bothered me,' said Edwin, with a trace of benevolent severity. He was astounded, and somewhat hurt, that this great family event should have been successfully concealed from him. He felt furious against Albert and Clara, and at the same time proud that his prognostication about the investment with Albert had proved correct.

'Did Hilda know?'

'Oh, yes. Hilda knew.'

'Well, I'm dashed!' The exclamation showed naïveté. His impression of the chicanery of women was deepened, so that it actually disquieted him. 'But I suppose,' he went on, 'I suppose this row isn't going to stop Clara from coming here, seeing the state Auntie's in?'

'No, certainly not. Clara would come like a shot if she knew, and Albert as well. She's a good nurse – in some ways.'

'Well, if they aren't told, and anything happens to Auntie in the night, there'll be a fine to-do afterwards, – don't forget that.'

'Nothing'll happen to Auntie in the night,' said Maggie, with tranquil reassurance. 'And I don't think I could stand 'em to-night.'

The hint of her nervous susceptibility, beneath that stolid exterior, appealed to him.

Maggie, since closing the account book, had moved foot by foot anxiously towards the door, and had only been kept in the room by the imperative urgency of the conversation. She now had her hand on the door.

'I say!' He held her yet another moment. 'What's this about me taking your room? I don't want to turn you out of your room.'

'That's all right,' she said, with a kind smile. 'It's easiest, really. Moreover, I dare say there won't be such a lot of sleeping . . . I must go up at once. She can't possibly be left alone.'

Maggie opened the door, and she had scarcely stepped forth when Minnie from the kitchen rushed into the lobby and dropped, intentionally or unintentionally, on her knees before her. Edwin, unobserved by Minnie, witnessed the scene through the doorway. Minnie, agitated almost to the point of hysteria, was crying violently, and as she breathed her shoulders lifted and fell and the sound of her sobbing rose periodically to a shriek and sank to a groan. She knelt with her body and thighs upright and her head erect, making no attempt to stem the tears or to hide her face. In her extreme desolation she was perhaps as unconscious of herself as she had ever been. Her cap was awry on her head, and her hair disarranged; the blinking spectacles made her ridiculous; only the blue print uniform, and the sinister yellowish apron drawn down tight under her knees, gave a certain respectable regularity to her extraordinary and grotesque appearance.

To Edwin she seemed excessively young and yet far too large and too developed for her age. The girl was obviously a fool.

Edwin could perceive in her no charm whatever, except that of
her innocence; and it was not easy to imagine that any man, even
the barman at the Vaults, could have mistaken her, even momentarily, for the ideal. And then some glance of her spectacled eyes,
or some gesture of the great red hand, showed him his own
blindness and mysteriously made him realize the immensity of
the illusion and the disillusion through which she had passed in
her foolish and incontinent simplicity. What had happened to
her was miraculous, exquisite, and terrible. He felt the magic of
her illusion and the terror of her disillusion. Already in her
girlishness and her stupidity she had lived through supreme hours.
'Compared to her,' he thought, 'I don't know what life is. No
man does.' And he not only suffered for her sorrow, he gave her
a sacred quality. It seemed to him that heaven itself ought to
endow her with beauty, grace, and wisdom, so that she might
meet with triumphant dignity the ordeals that awaited her; and
that mankind should supplement the work of heaven by clothing
her richly and housing her in secluded splendour, and offering her
the service which only victims merit. Surely her caprices ought to
be indulged and honoured! . . . Edwin was indignant; indignation
positively burnt his body. She was helpless and defenceless and she
had been exploited by Auntie Hamps. And after having been
exploited she had been driven out by ukase on week-night to
class-meeting and on Sunday night to chapel, to find Christ,
with the result that she had found the barman at the Vaults. The
consequences were inevitable. She was definitely ruined, unless
the child should bereave her by dying; and even then she might
still be ruined. And what about the child, if the child lived? And
although Edwin had never seen the silly girl before, he said to
himself while noticing that a crumb or two of the bread dropped
by her still remained on the floor: 'I'll see that girl through whatever it costs!' He was not indignant against Auntie Hamps.
How could he be indignant against an expiring old creature
already desperate in the final dilemma? He felt nearly as sorry
for Auntie Hamps as for Minnie. He was indignant against destiny, of which Auntie Hamps was only the miserable, unimagina-
tive instrument.

'I'd better go tonight, miss. Let me go tonight!' cried Minnie.

And she cried so loudly that Edwin was afraid Auntie Hamps
might hear and might make an apparition at the head of the
stairs and curse Minnie with fearful Biblical names. And the
old woman in the curtained bed upstairs was almost as present
to him as the girl kneeling before his eyes on the linoleum of
the lobby.

'Minnie! Minnie! Don't be foolish!' said Maggie, standing
over her and soothing her, not with her hands but with her voice.

Maggie had shown no perturbation or even surprise at
Minnie's behaviour. She stood looking down at her benevolent,
deprecating, and calm. And by contrast with Minnie she seemed
to be quite middle-aged. Her tone was exactly right. It reminded
Edwin of the tone which she would use to himself when she was
sixteen and the housekeeper, and he was twelve. Maggie had long
since lost authority over him; she had lost everything; she would
die without having lived; she had never begun to live – (No,
perhaps once she had just begun to live!) – Minnie had prime
knowledge far exceeding hers. And yet she had power over
Minnie and could exercise it with skill.

Minnie, hesitating, sobbed more slowly, and then ceased to
sob.

'Go back into the kitchen and have something to eat, and then
you can go to bed. You'll feel differently in the morning,' said
Maggie with the same gentle blandness.

And Minnie, as though fascinated, rose from her knees.

Edwin, surmising what had passed between the two in the
kitchen while he was in the bedroom, was aware of a fresh,
intense admiration for Maggie. She might be dowdy, narrow, dull,
obstinate, virgin, – but she was superb. She had terrific reserves.
He was proud of her. The tone merely of her voice as she spoke
to the girl seemed to prove the greatness of her deeply hidden soul.

Suddenly Minnie caught sight of Edwin through the doorway,
flushed red, had the air of slavishly apologizing to the un-
approachable male for having disturbed him by her insect woes,
and vanished. Maggie hurried upstairs to the departing. Edwin
was alone with the chill draught from the lobby into the room,
and with the wonder of life.

IV

In the middle of the night Edwin kept watch over Auntie Hamps, who was asleep. He sat in a rocking-chair, with his back to the window and the right side of his face to the glow of the fire. The fire was as effective as the size and form of the grate would allow; it burnt richly red; but its influence did not seem to extend beyond a radius of four feet outwards from its centre. The terrible damp chill of the Five Towns winter hung in the bedroom like an invisible miasma. He could feel the cold from the window, which was nevertheless shut, through the shawl with which he had closed the interstices of the back of the chair, and, though he had another thick shawl over his knees, the whole of his left side felt the creeping attack of the insidious miasma. A thermometer which he had found and which lay on the night-table five yards from the fire registered only fifty-two degrees. His expelled breath showed in the air. It was as if he were fighting with all resources against frigidity, and barely holding his own.

In the half-light of the gas, still screened from the bed by the bonnet-box and the Bible, he glanced round amid the dark shadows at the mean and sinister ugliness of the historic chamber, the secret nest and withdrawing place of Auntie Hamps; and the real asceticism of her life and of the life of all her generation almost smote him. Half a century earlier such a room had represented comfort; in some details, as for instance in its bed, it represented luxury; and in half a century Auntie Hamps had learnt nothing from the material progress of civilization but the use of the hot-water bag; her vanished and forgotten parents would have looked askance at the enervating luxuriousness of her hot-water bag – unknown even to the crude wistful boy Edwin on the mantelpiece. And Auntie Hamps herself was wont, as it were, to atone for it by using the still tepid water therefrom for her morning toilet instead of having truly hot water brought up from the kitchen. Edwin thought: 'Are we happier for these changes brought about by the mysterious force of evolution?' And answered very emphatically: 'Yes, we are.' He would not for anything have gone back to the austerities of his boyhood.

He rocked gently to and fro in the chair, excited by events and by the novel situation, and he was not dissatisfied with himself. Indeed he was aware of a certain calm complacency, for his common sense had triumphed over Maggie's devoted silly womanishness. Maggie was for sitting up through the night; she was anxious to wear herself out for no reason whatever; but he had sent her to bed until three o'clock, promising to call her if she should be needed. The exhausted girl was full of sagacity save on that one point of martyrdom to the fullest – apparently with her a point of honour. For the sake of the sensation of having martyrized herself utterly she was ready to imperil her fitness for the morrow. She secretly thought it was unfair to call upon him, a man, to share her fatigues. He regarded himself as her superior in wisdom, and he was relieved that anyone so wise and balanced as Edwin Clayhanger had taken supreme charge of the household organism.

Restless, he got up from the chair and looked at the bed. He had heard no unusual sound therefrom, but to excuse his restlessness he had said: 'Suppose some change had occurred and I didn't notice it!' No change had occurred. Auntie Hamps lay like a mite, like a baby forlorn, senile and defenceless, amid the heaped pillows and coverings of the bed. Within the deep gloom of the canopy and the over-arching curtains only her small, soft face was alive; even her hair was hidden in the indentation made by the weight of her head in the pillows. She was unconscious, either in sleep or otherwise, – he could not tell how. And in her unconsciousness the losing but obstinate fight against the power which was dragging her over the edge of eternity still went on. It showed in the apprehensive character of her breathing, which made a little momentary periodic cloud above her face, and in the uneasy muscular movements of the lips and jaws, and in the vague noises in her throat. A tremendous pity for her re-entered his heart, almost breaking it, because she was so beaten, and so fallen from the gorgeousness of her splendour. Even Minnie could have imposed her will upon Auntie Hamps now; each hour she weakened.

He had no more resentment against her on account of Minnie, no accusation to formulate. He was merely grieved, with a compassionate grief, that Auntie Hamps had learnt so little while living so long. He knew that she was cruel only because she was incapable of imagining what it was to be Minnie. He understood. She worshipped God under the form of respectability, but she did worship God. Like all religious votaries she placed religion above morality; hence her chicane, her inveterate deceit and self-deceit. It was with a religious aim that she had concealed from him the estrangement between herself and Clara. The unity of the family was one of her major canons (as indeed it was one of Edwin's). She had a passion for her nephew and nieces. It was a grand passion. Her pride in them must have been as terrific as her longing that they and all theirs should conform to the sole ideal that she comprehended. Undeniably there was something magnificent in her religion – her unscrupulousness in the practice of it, and the mighty consistency of her career. She had lived. He ceased to pity her, for she towered above pity. She was dying, but only for an instant. He would smile at his aunt's primeval notions of a future life, yet he had to admit that his own notions, though far less precise, could not be appreciably less crude. He and she were anyhow at one in the profound and staggering conviction of immortality. Enlightened by that conviction, he was able to reduce the physical and mental tragedy of the death-bed to its right proportions as a transiency between the heroic past and the inconceivable future. And in the stillness of the room and the stillness of the house, perfumed by the abnegation of Maggie and the desolate woe of the ruined Minnie whom the Clayhangers would save, and in the outer stillness of the little street with the Norman church-tower sticking up out of history at the bottom of its slope, Edwin felt uplifted and serene.

He returned to the rocking-chair.

'She's asleep now in some room I've never seen!' he reflected.

He was suddenly thinking of his wife. During the previous night, lying sleepless close to her while she slept soundly, he had reflected long and with increasing pessimism. The solace of Hilda's kiss had proved fleeting. She had not realized – he himself was then only realizing little by little – the enormity of the thing she had done. What she had deliberately and obstinately done was to turn him out of his house. No injury that she might have chosen could have touched him more closely, more painfully, – for his house to him was sacred. Her blundering with the servants might be condoned, but what excuse was it possible to find for this precipitate flight to London involving the summary ejectment from the home of him who had created the home and for and by whom the home chiefly existed? True, the astounding feat of wrong-headedness had been aided by the mere chance of Maggie's calling (capricious women were always thus lucky!) – Maggie's suggestion and request had given some afterglow of reason to the mad project. But the justification was still far from sufficient. And the odious idea haunted him that, even if Maggie had not called with her tale, Hilda would have persisted in her scheme all the same. Yes, she was capable of that! The argument that George's eyes (of whose condition she had learnt by mere hazard) could not wait until domestic affairs were arranged, was too grotesque to deserve an answer.

Lying thus close to his wife in the dark, he had perceived that the conflict between his individuality and hers could never cease. No diplomatic devices of manner could put an end to it. And he had seen also that as they both grew older and developed more fully, the conflict was becoming more serious. He assumed that he had faults, but he was solemnly convinced that the faults of Hilda were tremendous, essential, and ineradicable. She had a faculty for acting contrary to justice and contrary to sense which was simply monstrous. And it had always been so. Her whole life had been made up of impulsiveness and contumacy in that impulsiveness. Witness the incredible scenes of the strange Dartmoor episode – all due to her stubborn irrationality! The perspective of his marriage was plain to him in the night, – and it ended in a rupture. He had been resolutely blind to Hilda's peculiarities, dismissing incident after incident as an isolated misfortune. But he could be blind no more. His marriage was all of a piece, and he must and would recognise the fact . . . The sequel would be a scandal! . . . Well, let it be a scandal! As the minutes and hours passed in grim meditation, the more attractive grew the lost freedom of the bachelor and the more ready he felt to face any ordeal that lay between him and it . . . And, just as it was occurring to him that his proper course was to have fought a terrific open decisive battle with her in front of both Maggie and Ingpen, he had fallen asleep.

Upon awaking, barely in time to arouse Hilda, he knew that the mood of the night had not melted away as such moods are apt to melt when the window begins to show a square of silver-grey. The mood was even intensified. Hilda had divined nothing. She never did divine the tortures which she inflicted in his heart. She did not possess the gumption to divine. Her demeanour had been amazing. She averred that she had not slept at all. Instead of cajoling, she bullied. Instead of tacitly admitting that she was infamously wronging him, she had assumed a grievance of her own – without stating it. Once she had said discontentedly about some trifle: 'You might *at any rate* –' as though the victim should caress the executioner. She had kissed him at departure, but not as usual effusively, and he had suffered the kiss in enmity; and after an unimaginable general upset and confusion, in which George had shown himself strangely querulous, she had driven off with her son, – unconscious, stupidly unaware, that she was leaving a disaster behind her. And last of all Edwin, solitary, had been forced to perform the final symbolic act, that of locking him out of his own sacred home! The affair had transcended belief.

All day at the works his bitterness and melancholy had been terrible, and the works had been shaken with apprehension, for no angry menaces are more disconcerting than those of a man habitually mild. Before evening he had decided to write to his wife from Auntie Hamps's, – a letter cold, unanswerable, crushing, that would confront her unescapably with the alternatives of complete submission or complete separation. The phrases of the letter came into his mind . . . He would see who was master . . . He had been full of the letter when he entered Auntie Hamps's lobby. But the strange tone in which Maggie had answered his questions about the sick woman had thrust the letter and the crisis right to the back of his mind, where they had uneasily remained throughout the evening.

And now in the rocking-chair he was reflecting:

'She's asleep in some room I've never seen!'

He smiled, such a smile, candid, generous, and affectionate, as was Hilda's joy, such a smile as Hilda dwelt on in memory when she was alone. The mood of resentment passed away, vanished like a nightmare at dawn, and like one of his liverish headaches dispersed suddenly after the evening meal. He saw everything differently. He saw that he had been entirely wrong in his estimate of the situation, and of Hilda. Hilda was a mother. She had the protective passion of maternity. She was carried away by her passions; but her passions were noble, marvellous, unique. He himself could never – he thought, humbled – attain to her emotional heights. He was incapable of feeling about anything or anybody as she felt about George. The revelation concerning George's eyesight had shocked her, overwhelmed her with remorse, driven every other idea out of her head. She must atone to George instantly; instantly she must take measures – the most drastic and certain – to secure him from the threatened danger. She could not count the cost till afterwards. She was not a woman in such moments, – she was an instinct, a desire, a ruthless purpose. And as she felt towards George, so she must feel, in other circumstances, towards himself. Her kisses proved it, and her soothing hand when he was unwell. Mrs Hamps had said: 'Eh, dear! What a good mother dear Hilda is!' A sentimental outcry! But there was profound truth in it, truth which the old woman had seen better than he had seen it. 'I daresay there never was such a mother – unless it's Clara!' Hyperbole! And yet he himself now began to think that there never could have been such a mother as Hilda. Clara too in her way was wonderful . . . Smile as you might, these mothers were tremendous. The mysterious sheen of their narrow and deep lives dazzled him. For the first time, perhaps, he bowed his head to Clara.

But Hilda was far beyond Clara. She was not only a mother but a lover. Would he cut himself off from her loving? Why? For what? To live alone in the arid and futile freedom of a Tertius Ingpen? Such a notion was fatuous. Where lay the difficulty between himself and Hilda? There was no difficulty. How had she harmed him? She had not harmed him. Everything was all right. He had only to understand. He understood. As for her impulsiveness, her wrongheadedness, her bizarre ratiocination, – he knew how to accept them, for was he not a philosopher? They were indeed part of the incomparable romance of existence with these prodigious and tantalizing creatures. He admitted that Hilda in some aspects transcended him, but in others he was comfortably confident of his own steady, conquering superiority. He thought of her with the most exquisite devotion. He pictured the secret tenderness of their reunion amid the conventional gloom of Auntie Hamps's death-bed . . . He was confident of his ability to manage Hilda, at any rate in the big things, – for example the disputed points of his entry into public activity and their removal from Trafalgar Road into the country. The sturdiness of the male inspired him. At the same time the thought of the dark mood from which he had emerged obscurely perturbed him, like a fearful danger passed; and he argued to himself with satisfaction, and yet not quite with conviction, that he had yielded to Maggie, and not to Hilda, in the affair of the journey to London, and that therefore his masculine marital dignity was intact.

And then he started at a strange sound below, which somehow recalled him to the nervous tension of the house. It was a knocking at the front door. His heart thumped at the formidable muffled noise in the middle of the night. He jumped up, and glanced at the bed. Auntie Hamps was not wakened. He went downstairs where the gas which he had lighted was keeping watch.

CHAPTER 19

DEATH AND BURIAL

I

ALBERT BENBOW was at the front door. Edwin curbed the expression of his astonishment.

'Hello, Albert!'

'Oh! You aren't gone to bed?'

'Not likely. Come in. What's up?'

Albert, with the habit of one instructed never to tread actually on a doorstep lest it should be newly whitened, stepped straight on to the inner mat. He seemed excited, and Edwin feared that he had just learnt of Auntie Hamps's illness and had come in the middle of the night ostensibly to make inquiries, but really to make a grievance of the fact that the Benbows had been 'kept in ignorance'. He could already hear Albert demanding: 'Why have you kept us in ignorance?' It was quite a Benbow phrase.

Edwin shut the door and shut out the dark and windy glimpse of the outer world which had emphasized for a moment the tense seclusion of the house.

'You've heard, of course, about the accident to Ingpen?' said Albert. His hands were deep in his overcoat pockets; the collar of the thin, rather shabby overcoat was turned up; an old cap adhered to the back of his head. While talking he slowly lifted his feet one after the other, as though desiring to get warmth by stamping but afraid to stamp in the night.

'No, I haven't,' said Edwin, with false calmness. 'What accident?'

The perspective of events seemed to change; Auntie Hamps's illness to recede, and a definite and familiar apprehension to be supplanted by a fear more formidable because it was a fear of the unknown.

'It was all in the late special *Signal*!' Benbow protested, as if his pride had been affronted.

'Well, I haven't seen the *Signal*. What is it?' And Edwin thought: 'Is somebody else dying too?'

'Fly-wheel broke. Ingpen was inspecting the slip-house next to the engine-house. Part of the fly-wheel came through and knocked a loose nut off the blunger right into his groin.'

'Whose works?'

Albert answered in a light tone:

'Mine.'

'And how's he going on?'

'Well, he's had an operation and Stirling's got the nut out. Of course they didn't know what it was till they got it out. And now Ingpen wants to see you at once. That's why I've come.'

'Where is he?'

'At the hospital.'

'Pirehill?'

'No. The Clowes – Moorthorne Road, you know.'

'Is he going on all right?'

'He's very weak. He can scarcely whisper. But he wants you. I've been up there all the time, practically.'

Edwin seized his overcoat from the rack.

'I had a rare job finding ye,' Benbow went on. 'I'd no idea you weren't all at home. I wakened most of Hulton Street over it. It was Smiths next door came out at last and told me missis and George had gone to London and you were over here.'

'I wonder who told *them*!' Edwin mumbled as Albert helped him with the overcoat. 'I must tell Maggie. We've got some illness here, you know.'

'Oh?'

'Yes. Auntie. Very sudden. Seemed to get worse tonight. Fact is I was sitting up while Maggie has a bit of sleep. She was going to send round for Clara in the morning. I'll just run up to Mag.'

Having thus by judicious misrepresentation deprived the Benbows of a grievance, Edwin moved towards the stairs. Maggie, dressed, already stood at the top of them, alert, anxious, adequate.

'Albert, is that you?'

After a few seconds of quick murmured explanation, Edwin and Albert departed, and as they went Maggie, in a voice doubly harassed but cheerful and oily, called out after them how glad she would be, and what a help it would be, if Clara could come round early in the morning.

The small Clowes Hospital was high up in the town opposite the Park, near the station and the railway cutting and not far from the Moorthorne ridge. Behind its bushes, through which the wet night-wind swished and rustled, it looked still very new and red in the fitful moonlight. And indeed it was scarcely older than the Park and swimming-baths close by, and Bursley had not yet lost its naïve pride in the possession of a hospital of its own. Not much earlier in the decade this town of thirty-five thousand inhabitants had had to send all its 'cases' five miles in cabs to Pirehill Infirmary. Albert Benbow, with the satisfaction of a habitué, led Edwin round through an aisle of bushes to the side entrance for out-patients. He pushed open a dark door, walked into a gaslit vestibule, and with the assured gestures of a proprietor invited Edwin to follow. A fat woman who looked like a charwoman made tidy sat in a windsor chair in the vestibule, close to a radiator. She signed to Albert as an old acquaintance to go forward, and Albert nodded in the manner of one conspirator to another. What struck Edwin was that this middle-aged woman showed no sign of being in the midst of the unusual. She was utterly casual and matter-of-fact. And Edwin had the sensation of moving in a strange nocturnal world – a world which had always co-existed with his own, but of which he had been till then most curiously ignorant. His passage through the town listening absently to Albert's descriptions of the structural damage to Ingpen and to the works, and Albert's defence against unbrought accusations, had shown him that the silent streets lived long after midnight in many a lighted window here and there and in the movements of mysterious but not furtive frequenters. And he seemed to have been impinging upon half-veiled enigmas of misfortune or of love. At the other end of the thread of adventure was his aunt's harsh bedroom with Maggie stolidly watching the last ebb of senile vitality, and at this end was the hospital, full of novel and disturbing vibrations and Tertius Ingpen waiting to impose upon him some charge or secret.

At the top of the naked stairs which came after a dark corridor was a long naked resounding passage lighted by a tiny jet at either end. A cough from behind a half-open door came echoing out and filled the night and the passage. And then at another door appeared a tall, thin, fair nurse in blue and white, with thin lips and a slight smile, hard and disdainful.

'Here's Mr Clayhanger, nurse!' muttered Albert Benbow, taking off his cap, with a grimace at once sycophantic and grandiose.

Edwin imagined that he knew by sight everybody in the town above a certain social level, but he had no memory of the face of the nurse.

'How is he?' he asked awkwardly, fingering his hat.

The girl merely raised her eyebrows.

'You mustn't stay,' said she, in a mincing but rather loud voice that matched her lips.

'Oh, no, I won't!'

'I suppose *I'd* better stop outside!' said Benbow.

Edwin followed the nurse into a darkened room, of which the chief article of furniture appeared to be a screen. Behind the screen was a bed, and on the bed in the deep obscurity lay a form under creaseless bedclothes. Edwin first recognized Ingpen's beard, then his visage, very pale and solemn, and without the customary spectacles. Of the whole body only the eyes moved. As Edwin approached the bed he cast across Ingpen a shadow from the distant gas.

'Well, old chap!' he began with constraint. 'This is a nice state of affairs! How are you getting on?'

Ingpen's inquiring apprehensive dumb glance silenced the clumsy greeting. It was just as if he had been rebuked: 'This is no time for how d'ye dos.' When he had apparently made sure that Edwin was Edwin, Ingpen turned his eyes to the nurse.

'Water!' he whispered.

The nurse shook her head.

'Not yet,' she replied, with tepid indifference.

Ingpen's eyes remained on her a moment and then went back to Edwin.

'Ed,' he whispered, and gazed once more at the nurse, who, looking away from the bed, did not move.

Edwin bent over the bed.

'Ed,' Ingpen recommenced, speaking very deliberately. 'Go to my office. In the top drawer of the desk in the bedroom there's some photos and letters ... Burn them ... Before morning ... Understand?'

Edwin was profoundly stirred. In his emotion was pride at Ingpen's trust, astonishment at the sudden, utterly unexpected revelation, and the thrill of romance.

He thought:

'The man is dying!'

And the tragic sensation of the vigil of the nocturnal world almost overcame him.

'Yes,' he said. 'Anything else?'

'No.'

'What about keys?'

Ingpen gave him another long glance.

'Trousers.'

'Where are his clothes?' Edwin asked the nurse, whose lips were ironic.

'Oh! They'll tell you downstairs. You'd better go now.'

As he went from the room he could feel Ingpen's glance following him. He raged inwardly against the callousness of the nurse. It seemed monstrous that he should abandon Ingpen for the rest of the night, defenceless, to the cold tyranny of the nurse, whose power over the sufferer was as absolute as that of an eastern monarch, who had never heard of public opinion, over the meanest slave. He could not bear to picture to himself Ingpen and the nurse alone together.

'Isn't he allowed to drink?' he could not help murmuring, at the door.

'Yes, at intervals.'

He wanted to chastise the nurse. He imagined an endless succession of sufferers under her appalling, inimical nonchalance. Who had allowed her to be a nurse? Had she become a nurse in order to take some needed revenge against mankind? And then he thought of Hilda's passionate, succouring tenderness when he himself was unwell, – he had not been really ill for years. What was happening to Ingpen could never happen to him, because

Hilda stood everlastingly between him and such a horror. He considered that a bachelor was the most pathetic creature on the earth. He was drenched in the fearful, wistful sadness of all life . . . The sleeping town; Auntie Hamps on the edge of eternity; Minnie trembling at the menaces of her own body; Hilda lying in some room that he had never seen; and Ingpen . . .!

'Soon over!' observed Albert Benbow in the corridor.

Edwin could have winced at the words.

'How do you think he is?' asked Albert.

'Don't know!' Edwin replied. 'Look here, I've got to get hold of his clothes – downstairs.'

'Oh! That's it, is it? Pocket-book! Keys! Eh?'

II

Edwin had once been in Tertius Ingpen's office at the bottom of Crown Square, Hanbridge, but never in the bedroom which Ingpen rented on the top floor of the same building. It had been for seventy or eighty years a building of four squat storeys; but a new landlord, seeing the architectural development of the town as a local metropolis and determined to join in it at a minimum of expense, had knocked the two lower storeys into one, fronted them with fawn-coloured terracotta, and produced a lofty shop whose rent exceeded the previous rent of the entire house.

The landlord knew that passers-by would not look higher up the façade than the ground floor, and that therefore any magnificence above that level was merely wasted. The shop was in the occupation of a tea dealer who gave away beautiful objects such as vases and useful objects such as tea-trays to all purchasers. Ingpen's office, and a solicitor's office, were on the first floor, formerly the second; the third floor was the headquarters of the Hanbridge and District Ethical Society; the top floor was temporarily unlet, save for Ingpen's room. Nobody except Ingpen slept in the building, and he very irregularly.

The latchkey for the side-door was easy to choose in the glittering light of the latest triple-jetted and reflectored gas-lamps which the corporation, to match the glories of the new town hall, had placed in Crown Square. The lock, strange to say, worked easily. Edwin entered somewhat furtively, and as it were guiltily, though in Crown Square and the streets and the other squares visible therefrom, not a soul could be seen. The illuminated clock of the Old Town Hall at the top of the square showed twenty-five minutes to four. Immediately within the door began a new, very long and rather mean staircase, with which Edwin was acquainted. He closed the door, shutting out the light and the town, and struck a match in the empty building. He had walked into Hanbridge from Bursley, and as soon as he began to climb the stairs he was aware of great fatigue, both physical and mental. The calamity to Ingpen had almost driven Auntie Hamps out of his mind; it had not, however, driven Minnie out of his mind. He was gloomy and indignant on behalf of both Ingpen and Minnie. They were both victims. Minnie was undoubtedly a fool, and he was about to learn, perhaps, to what extent Ingpen had been a fool.

Each footstep sounded loud on the boards of the deserted house. Having used several matches and arrived at the final staircase, Edwin wondered how he was to distinguish Ingpen's room there from the others without trying keys in all of them till he got to the right one. But on the top landing he had no difficulty, for Ingpen's card was fastened with a drawing-pin on to the first door he saw. A match burnt his fingers and expired just as he was shaking out a likely key from Ingpen's bunch. And then, in the black darkness, he perceived a line of light under the door in front of which he stood. He forgot his fatigue in an instant. His heart leaped. A burglar? Or had Ingpen left the gas burning? Ingpen could not have left the gas burning since, according to Albert Benbow, he had been in Bursley all the afternoon. With precautions, and feeling very desperate and yet also craven, he lit a fresh match and managed quietly to open the door, which was not locked.

As soon as he beheld the illuminated interior of the room, all his skin crept and flushed as though he had taken a powerful stimulant. A girl reclined asleep in a small basket lounge-chair by the gas-fire. He could not see her face, which was turned towards the wall and away from the gas-jet that hung from the ceiling over an old desk; but she seemed slim and graceful, and there was something in the abandonment of unconsciousness that made her marvellously alluring. Her hat and gloves had been thrown on the desk, and a cloak lay on a chair. These coloured and intimate objects – extensions of the veritable personality of the girl – had the effect of delightfully completing the furniture of a room which was in fact rather bare. A narrow bed in the far corner, disguised under a green rug as a sofa; a green square of carpet, showing the unpolished boards at the sides; the desk, and three chairs; a primitive hanging wardrobe in another corner, hidden by a bulging linen curtain; a portmanteau; a few un-framed prints on the walls; an alarm-clock on the mantelpiece, – there was nothing else in the chamber where Ingpen slept when it was too late, or he was too slack, to go to his proper home. But nothing else was needed. The scene was perfect; the girl rendered it so. An immense envy of, and admiration for, Ingpen surged through Edwin, who saw here the realization of a dream that was to marriage what poetry is to prose. Ingpen might rail against women and against marriage in a manner exaggerated and in-defensible; but he had at any rate known how to arrange his life and how to keep his own counsel. He had all the careless mascu-line freedom of his condition, – and in the background this ex-quisite phenomenon! The girl, her trustfulness, her abandonment, her secrecy, that white ear peeping out of her hair, – were his! It was staggering that such romance could exist in the Five Towns, of all places – for Edwin had the vague notion, common to all natives, that his own particular district fell short of full human nature in certain characteristics. For example, he could credit a human nature dying for love in Manchester, but never in the Five Towns. Even the occasional divorces that gave piquancy to life in the Five Towns seemed to lack the mysterious glamour of all other divorces.

He thought:

'Was it because he was expecting her that he sent me? Perhaps the desk was only a blind – and he couldn't tell me any more. Anyhow I shall have to break it to her.'

He felt exceedingly awkward and unequal to the situation so startling in its novelty. Yet he did not wish himself away.

As timidly, hat in hand, he went forward into the room, the girl stirred and woke up, to the creaking of the chair.

'Oh! Tert!' she murmured between sleeping and waking.

Edwin did not like her voice. It reminded him of the voice of the nurse whom he had just left.

The girl, looking round, perceived that it was not Tertius Ingpen who had come in. She gave a short, faint scream, then gathered herself together and with a single movement stood up, perfectly collected and on the defensive.

'It's all right! It's all right!' said Edwin. 'Mr Ingpen gave me his keys and asked me to come over and get some papers he wants . . . I hope I didn't frighten you. I'd no idea –'

She was old! She was old! That is to say, she was not the girl he had seen asleep. Before his marriage he would have put her age at thirty-two, but now he knew enough to be sure that she must be more than that. She was not graceful in movement. The expression of her pale face was not agreeable. Her gestures were not distinguished. And she could not act her part in the idyll. Moreover her frock was shabby and untidy. But chiefly she was old. Had she been young, Edwin would have excused all the rest. Romance was not entirely destroyed, but very little remained.

He thought, disdainfully, and as if resenting a deception:

'Is this the best he can do?'

And the Five Towns sank back to its ancient humble place in his esteem.

The woman said with a silly nervous giggle:

'I called to see Mr Ingpen. He wasn't expecting me. And I suppose while I was waiting I must have dropped off to sleep.'

It might have been true, but to Edwin it was inexpressibly inane. She seized her hat and then her cloak.

'I'm sorry to say Mr Ingpen's had an accident,' said Edwin.

She stopped, both hands above her head fingering her hat.

'An accident? Nothing serious?'

'Oh, no! I don't think so,' he lied. 'A machinery accident. They had to take him to the Clowes Hospital at Bursley. I've just come from there.'

She asked one or two more questions, all the time hurrying

her preparations to leave. But Edwin judged with disgust that she was not deeply interested in the accident. True, he had minimized it, but she ought not to have allowed him to minimize it. She ought to have obstinately believed that it was very grave.

'I do hope he'll soon be all right,' she said, snatching at her gloves and going to the door. 'Good night!' She gave another silly giggle, preposterous in a woman of her age. Then she stopped. 'I think you're gentleman enough not to say anything about me being here,' she said, rather nastily. 'It was quite an accident. I could easily explain it, but you know what people are!'

What a phrase – 'I think you're gentleman enough'!

He blushed and offered the required assurance.

'Can I let you out?' he started forward.

'No thanks!'

'But you can't open the door.'

'Yes, I can.'

'The stairs are all dark.'

'Please don't trouble yourself,' she said dryly, in the tone of a woman who sees offence in the courtesy of a male travelling companion on the railway.

He heard her steps *diminuendo* down the stairs.

Closing the door, he went to the window, and drew aside the blind. Perhaps she would pass up the Square. But she did not pass up the Square, which was peopled by nothing but meek gas-lamps under the empire of the glowing clock in the pediment of the Old Town Hall. Where had she gone? Where did she come from? Her accent had no noticeable peculiarity. Was she married, or single, or a widow? Perhaps there was hidden in her some strange and seductive quality which he had missed . . . He saw the slim girl again reclining in the basket chair . . . After all, she was a woman, and she had been in Ingpen's room, waiting for him!

Later, seated in front of the open drawer in the old desk, gathering together letters and photographs – photographs of her in adroitly managed poses, taken at Oldham; letters in a woman's hand – he was penetrated to the marrow by the disastrous and yet beautiful infelicity of things. The mere sight of the letters (of which he forbore to decipher a single word, even a signature)

nearly made him cry; the photographs were tragic with the intolerable evanescence of life. By the will of Tertius Ingpen helpless
on the bed in the hospital, these documents of a passion or of a
fancy were to be burnt. Why? Was it true that Ingpen was dying?
Better to keep them. No, they must be burnt. He rose, and, with
difficulty, burnt them by instalments in a shovel over the tiny
fender that enclosed the gas-stove, – the room was soon half full
of smoke . . . Why had he deceived the woman as to the seriousness of Ingpen's accident? To simplify and mitigate the interview,
to save himself trouble; that was all! Well, she would learn soon
enough!

His eye caught a print on the wall above the bed, – a classic
example of the sentimentality of Marcus Stone: departing
cavalier, drooping maiden, terraced garden. It was a dreadful
indictment of the Tertius Ingpen who talked so well, with such
intellectual aplomb, with such detachment and exceptional
cynicism. It was like a ray exposing some secret sinister corner
in the man's soul. He had hung up that print because it gave him
pleasure! Poor chap! But Edwin loved him. He decided that he
would call again at the hospital before returning to Auntie
Hamps's. Impossible that the man was dying! If the doctor or
the matron had thought he was in danger they would have
summoned his relatives. He might be dying. He might be dead.
He must have immediately feared death, or he would not have
imposed upon Edwin such an errand . . . What simple, touching,
admirable trust in a friend's loyalty the man had displayed!

Edwin put out the gas-stove, which exploded, lit a match,
gave a great yawn, put out the gas, and began the enterprise of
leaving the house.

III

'Look here! I must have some tea, *now*!' said Edwin curtly and
yet appealingly to Maggie, who opened the door for him at
Auntie Hamps's.

It was nearly eight o'clock. He had been to the hospital again,
and, having reported in three words to Ingpen, whose condition
was unchanged, had remained there some time. But he had said

nothing to Ingpen about the woman. At six o'clock the matron had come into the room, and the nurse thenceforward until seven o'clock, when she went off duty, was a changed girl. Edwin slightly knew the matron, who was sympathetic but strangely pessimistic – considering her healthy, full figure.

'The water's boiling,' answered Maggie, in a comforting tone, and disappeared instantly into the kitchen.

Edwin thought:

'There are some things that girl understands!'

She had shown no curiosity, no desire to impart news, because she had immediately comprehended that Edwin was, or imagined himself to be, at the end of his endurance. Maggie, with simple and surpassing wisdom, had just said to herself: 'He's been out all night, and he's not used to it.' For a moment he felt that Maggie was wiser, and more intimately close to him, than anybody else in the world.

'In the dining-room,' she called out from the kitchen.

And in the small dining-room there was a fire! It was like a living welcoming creature. The cloth was laid, the gas was lighted. On the table was beautiful fresh bread-and-butter. A word, a tone, a glance of his on the previous evening had been enough to bring back the dining-room into use! Happily the wind suited the chimney. He had scarcely sat down in front of the fire when Maggie entered with the teapot. And at the sight of the teapot Edwin felt that he was saved. Before the tea was out of the teapot it had already magically alleviated the desperate sensations of physical fatigue and moral weariness which had almost overcome him on the way from the hospital in the chill and muddy dawn.

'What will you have to eat?' said Maggie.

'Nothing. I couldn't eat to save my life.'

'Perhaps you'll have a bit of bread-and-butter later,' said Maggie blandly.

He shook his head.

'How is she?'

'Worse,' said Maggie. 'But she's slept.'

'Who's up with her now? Minnie?'

'No. Clara.'

'Oh! She's come?'

'She came at seven.'

Edwin was drinking the divine tea. After a few gulps he told Maggie briefly about Tertius Ingpen, saying that he had had to go 'on business' for Ingpen to Hanbridge.

'Are you all right for the present?' she asked after a few moments.

He nodded. He was eating bread-and-butter.

'You had any sleep at all?' he mumbled, munching.

'Oh, yes! A little,' she answered cheerfully, leaving the room.

He poured out more tea, and then sat down in the sole easy-chair for a minute's reflection before going upstairs and thence to the works.

Not until he woke up did he realize that there had been any danger of his going to sleep. The earthenware clock on the mantelpiece (a birthday gift from Clara and Albert) showed five minutes past eleven. Putting no reliance on the cheap, horrible clock, he looked at his watch, which had stopped for lack of winding up. The fire was very low. His chief thought was: 'It can't possibly be eleven o'clock, because I haven't been down to the works, and I haven't sent word I'm not coming either!' He got up hurriedly and had reached the door when the sound of a voice on the stairs held him still like an enchantment. It seemed to be the voice, eloquent, and indeed somewhat Church-of-England, of the Rev. Christian Flowerdew, the new superintendent of the Bursley Wesleyan Methodist Circuit. The voice said: 'I do hope so!' and then offered a resounding remark about the weather being the kind of weather that, bad as it was, people must expect in view of the time of year. Maggie's voice concurred. As soon as the front door closed, Edwin peeped cautiously out of the dining-room.

'Who was that?' he murmured.

'Mr Flowerdew. She wanted him. Albert sent for him early this morning.'

Maggie came into the room and shut the door.

'I've been to sleep,' said Edwin.

'Yes, I know. I wasn't going to have you disturbed. They're all here.'

'Who are all here?'

'Clara and the children. Auntie asked to see all of them. They waited in the drawing-room for Mr Flowerdew to go. Bert didn't go to school this morning, in case – because it was so far off. Clara fetched the others out of school, except Rupy of course – he doesn't go.'

'Good heavens! I never came across such a morbid lot in my life. I believe they like it.'

Clara could be heard marshalling the brood up the stairs.

'You'd better go up,' said Maggie persuasively.

'I'd better go to the works – I'm no use here. What time is it?'

'After eleven. I think you'd better go up.'

'Does she ask for me?'

'Oh, yes. All the time sometimes. But she forgets for a bit.'

'Well, anyhow I must wash myself and change my collar.'

'All right. Wash yourself, then.'

'How is she now?'

'She isn't taking anything.'

When Edwin nervously pushed open the bedroom door, the room seemed to be crowded. Over the heads of clustering children towered Clara and Albert. As soon as the watchful Albert caught sight of Edwin, he made a conspiratorial sign and hurried to the door, driving Edwin out again.

'Didn't know you were here,' Edwin muttered.

'I say,' Albert whispered. 'Has she made a will?'

'I don't know.'

The bedroom door half opened, and Clara in her shabby morning dress glidingly joined them.

'He doesn't know,' said Albert to Clara.

Clara's pretty face scowled a little as she asked sharply and resentfully:

'Then who does know?'

'I should ha' thought *you'd* know,' said Edwin.

'Me! I like that! She hasn't spoken to me for months, has she, Albert? And she was always frightfully close about all these things.'

'About what things?'

'Well, you know.'

It was a fact. Auntie Hamps had never discussed her own finance, or her testamentary dispositions, with anybody. And
nobody had ever dared to mention such subjects to her.

'Don't you think you'd better ask her?' said Clara. 'Albert
thinks you ought.'

'No, I don't,' said Edwin, with curt disdain.

'Well then, I shall,' Albert decided.

'So long as you don't do it while I'm there!' Edwin said
menacingly. 'If you want to ask people about their wills you
ought to ask them before they're actually dying. Can't you see
you can't worry her about her will now?'

He was intensely disgusted. He thought of Mrs Hamps's bed,
and of Tertius Ingpen's bed, and of the woman at dead of night
in Ingpen's room, and of Minnie's case; and the base insensibility
of Albert and Clara made him feel sick. He wondered whether any
occasion would ever have solemnity enough for them to make
them behave with some distinction, some grandeur. For himself,
if he could have secured a fortune by breathing one business
word to Auntie Hamps just then, he would have let the fortune
go.

'There's nothing more to be said,' Clara murmured.

In the glance of both Clara and Albert Edwin saw hatred and
envy. Clara especially had never forgiven him for preventing their
father from pouring money into that sieve, her husband, nor for
Hilda's wounding tongue, nor for his worldly success. And
they both suspected that either Maggie or Auntie Hamps had
told him of Albert's default in the payment of interest, and so fear
was added to their hatred and envy.

They all entered the bedroom, the children having been left
alone only a few seconds. Rupert, wearing a new blue overcoat
with gilt buttons, had partially scrambled on to the bed; the pale
veined hands of Auntie Hamps could be seen round his right
hand; Rupert had grown enormous, and had already utterly
forgotten the time when he was two years old. The others, equally
altered, stood two on either side of the bed, – Bert and young
Clara to the right, and Amy and Lucy to the left. Lucy was crying
and Amy was benignantly wiping her eyes. Bert, a great lump of
a boy, was to leave school at Christmas, but he was still ranked

with the other children as a child. Young Clara sharply and
Bert heavily turned round to witness the entrance of their elders.

'Oh! Here's Uncle Edwin!'

'Edwin!'

'Yes, Auntie!'

The moral values of the room were instantly changed by the
tone in which Auntie Hamps had murmured 'Edwin'. All the
Benbows knew, and Edwin himself knew, that a personage of
supreme importance in Auntie Hamps's eyes had come into the
scene. The Benbows became secondary, and even Auntie Hamps's
grasp of Rupert's hand loosened, and, having already kissed her,
the child slipped off the bed. Edwin approached, and over the
heads of the children, and between the great darkening curtains,
he could at last see the face of the dying woman like a senile doll's
face amid the confusion of wrappings and bedclothes. The deep-
set eyes seemed to burn beneath the white forehead and sparse
grey hair; the cheeks, still rounded, were highly flushed over a
very small part of their surface; the mouth, always open, was
drawn in, and the chin, still rounded like the cheeks, protruded.
The manner of Auntie Hamps's noisy breathing, like the puzzled
gaze of her eyes, indicated apprehension of the profoundest,
acutest sort.

'Eh!' said she, in a somewhat falsetto voice, jerky and excessively feeble. 'I thought – I'd – lost you.' Her hand was groping
about.

'No, no,' said Edwin, leaning over between young Clara and
Rupert.

'She's feeling for your hand, Edwin,' said Clara.

He quickly took her hot, brittle fingers; they seemed to cling
to his for essential support.

'Have you – been to the works?' Auntie Hamps asked the
question as though the answer to it would end all trouble.

'No,' he said. 'Not yet.'

'Eh! That's right! That's right!' she murmured, apparently
much impressed by a new proof of Edwin's wisdom.

'I've had a sleep.'

'What?'

'I've been having a sleep,' he repeated more loudly.

'Eh! That's right! That's right . . . I'm so glad – the children have been to see me . . . Amy – did you kiss me?' Auntie Hamps looked at Amy hard, as if for the first time.

'Yes, Auntie.'

And then Amy began to cry.

'Better take them away,' Edwin suggested aside to Albert. 'It's as much as she can stand. The parson's only just gone, you know.'

Albert, obedient, gave the word of command, and the room was full of movement.

'Eh, children, children!' Auntie Hamps appealed.

Everybody stood stockstill, gazing attendant.

'Eh, children – bless you all for coming! If you grow up – as good as your mother – it's all I ask – all I ask – your mother and I – have never had a cross word – have we, mother?'

'No, Auntie,' said Clara, with a sweet, touching smile that accentuated the fragile charm of her face.

'Never – since mother was – as tiny as you are.'

Auntie Hamps looked up at the ceiling during a few strained breaths, and then smiled for an instant at the departing children, who filed out of the room. Rupert loitered behind, gazing at his mother. The mere contrast between the infant so healthy and the dying old woman was pathetic to Edwin. Clara, with an exquisite reassuring gesture and smile, picked up the stout Rupert and kissed him and carried him to the door, while Auntie Hamps looked at mother and son, ecstatic.

'Edwin!'

'Yes, Auntie?'

They were alone now. She had not loosed his hand. Her voice was very faint, and he bent over her still lower in the alcove of the curtains, which seemed to stretch very high above them.

'Have you heard from Hilda?'

'Not yet. By the second post, perhaps.'

'It's about George's eyes – isn't it?'

'Yes.'

'She's done quite right – quite right. It's just – like Hilda. I do hope – and pray – the boy's eyesight – is safe.'

'Oh, yes!' said Edwin. 'Safe enough.'

'You really think so?' She had the air of hanging on his words.

He nodded.

'What a blessing!' She sighed deeply with relief.

Edwin thought:

'I believe her relations must have been her passion.' And he was impressed by the intensity of that passion.

'Edwin!'

'Yes, Auntie?'

'Has – that girl – gone yet?'

'Who?' he questioned, and added more softly: 'Minnie, d'you mean?' His own voice sounded too powerful, too healthy and dominating, in comparison with her failing murmurs.

Auntie Hamps nodded. 'Yes – Minnie.'

'Not yet.'

'She's going?'

'Yes.'

'Because I can't trust – Maggie – to see to it.'

'I'll see to it.'

'Has she done – the silvers – d'you know?'

'She's doing them,' answered Edwin, who thought it would be best to carry out the deception with artistic completeness.

'She needn't have her dinner before she goes.'

'No?'

'No.' Auntie Hamps's face and tone hardened. 'Why should she?'

'All right.'

'And if she asks – for her wages – tell her – I say there's nothing due – under the circumstances.'

'All right, Auntie,' Edwin agreed, desperate.

Maggie, followed by Clara, softly entered the room. Auntie Hamps glanced at them with a certain cautious suspicion, as though one or other of them was capable of thwarting her in the matter of Minnie. Then her eyes closed, and Edwin was aware of a slackening of her hold on his hand. The doctor, who called half an hour later, said that she might never speak again, and she never did. Her last conscious moments were moments of satisfaction.

Edwin slowly released his hand.

'Where's Albert?' he asked Clara, merely for the sake of saying something.

'He's taking the children home, and then he's going to the works. He ought to have gone long ago. There's a dreadful upset there.'

'I suppose there is,' said Edwin, who had forgotten that the fly-wheel accident must have almost brought Albert's manufactory to a standstill. And he wondered whether it was the family instinct, or anxiety about Auntie Hamps's will, that had caused Albert to absent himself from business on such a critical morning.

'I ought to go too,' he muttered, as a full picture of a lithographic establishment masterless swept into his mind.

'Have you telegraphed to Hilda?' Clara demanded.

'No.'

'Haven't you!'

'What's the use?'

'Well, I should have thought you would.'

'Oh, no!' he said, falsely mild. 'I shall write.' He was immensely glad that Hilda was not present in the house to complicate still further the human equation.

Maggie was silently examining the face obscured in the gloom of the curtains.

Instead of remaining late that night at the works, Edwin came back to the house before six o'clock. He had had word that the condition of Tertius Ingpen was still unchanged. Clara had gone home to see to her children's evening meal. Maggie sat alone in the darkened bedroom, where Auntie Hamps, her features a mere pale blur between the over-arching curtains, still withheld the secret of her soul's reality from the world. Even in the final unconsciousness there was something grandiose which lingered from her crowning magnificent deceptions and obstinate effort to safeguard the structure of society. The sublime obstinacy of the woman had transformed hypocrisy into a virtue, and not the imminence of the infinite unknown had sufficed to make her apostate to the steadfast principles of her mortal career.

'What about tonight?' Edwin asked.

'Oh! Clara and I will manage.'

There was a tap at the door. Edwin opened it. Minnie, abashed but already taking courage, stood there blinking with a letter in her hand.

'Ah!' he breathed. Hilda's great scrawling caligraphy was on the envelope.

The letter read: 'Darling boy, George has influenza, Charlie says. Temp. 102 anyway. So of course he can't go out tomorrow. I knew this morning there was something wrong with him. Janet and Charlie send their love. – Your ever loving wife, HILDA'

He was exceedingly uplifted and happy and exhausted. Hilda's handwriting moved him. The whole missive was like a personal emanation from her. It lived with her vitality. It fought for the mastery of the household interior against the mysterious, far-reaching spell of the dying woman. 'Your loving wife'. Never before, during their marriage, had she written a phrase so comforting and exciting. He thought: 'My faith in her is never worthy of her.' And his faith leaped up and became worthy of her.

'George has got influenza,' he said indifferently.

'George! But influenza's very serious for him, isn't it?' Maggie showed alarm.

'Why should it be?'

'Considering he nearly died of it at Orgreaves'!'

'Oh! *Then*! . . . He'll be all right.'

But Maggie had put fear into Edwin, – a superstitious fear. Influenza indeed might be serious for George. Suppose he died of it. People did die of influenza. Auntie Hamps – Tertius Ingpen – and now George! . . . All these anxieties mingling with his joy in the thought of Hilda! And all the brooding rooms of the house waiting in light or in darkness for a decisive event!

'I must go and lie down,' he said. He could contain no more sensations.

'Do,' said Maggie.

IV

At two o'clock in the afternoon of Auntie Hamps's funeral, a procession consisting of the following people moved out of the small, stuffy dining-room of her house across the lobby into the drawing-room: The Rev. Christian Flowerdew, the Rev. Guy Cliffe (second minister), the aged Rev. Josiah Higginbotham (supernumerary minister), the chapel and the circuit stewards, the doctor, Edwin, Maggie, Clara, Bert and young Clara (being respectively the eldest nephew and the eldest niece of the deceased), and finally Albert Benbow; Albert came last because he had constituted himself the marshal of the ceremonies. In the drawing-room the coffin with its hideous brass plate and handles lay upon two chairs, and was covered with white wreaths. At the head of the coffin was placed a small table with a white cloth; on the cloth a large inlaid box (in which Auntie Hamps had kept odd photographs), and on the box a black book. The drawn blinds created a beautiful soft silver gloom which solemnized everything and made even the clumsy carving on the coffin seem like the finest antique work. The three ministers ranged themselves round the small table; the others stood in an irregular horseshoe about the coffin, nervous, constrained, and in dread of catching each other's glances. Mr Higginbotham, by virtue of his age, began to read the service, and Auntie Hamps became 'she', 'her', and 'our sister' – nameless. In the dining-room she had been the paragon of all excellences, – in the drawing-room, packed securely and neatly in the coffin, she was a sinner snatched from the consequences of sin by a miracle of divine sacrifice.

The interment thus commenced was the result of a compromise between two schools of funebrial manners sharply divergent. Edwin, immediately after the demise, had become aware of influences far stronger than those which had shaped the already half-forgotten interment of old Darius Clayhanger into a form repugnant to him. Both Albert and Clara, but especially Albert, had assumed an elaborate funeral, with a choral service at the Wesleyan Chapel, numerous guests, a superb procession, and a substantial and costly meal in the drawing-room to conclude. Edwin had at once and somewhat domineeringly decided: no guests whatever outside the family, no service at the chapel, every rite reduced to its simplest. When asked why, he had no logical answer. He soon saw that it would be impossible not to invite a minister and the doctor. He yielded, intimidated by the sacredness of custom. Then not only the Wesleyan Chapel but its Sunday school sent dignified emissaries, who so little expected a No to their honorific suggestions that the No was unuttered and unutterable. Certain other invitations were agreed upon. The Sunday school announced that it would 'walk', and prepared to 'walk'.

All the emissaries spoke of Auntie Hamps as a saint; they all averred with restrained passion that her death was an absolutely irreparable loss to the circuit; and their apparent conviction was such that Edwin's whole estimate of Auntie Hamps and of mankind was momentarily shaken. Was it conceivable that none of these respectable people had arrived at the truth concerning Auntie Hamps? Had she deceived them all? Or were they simply rewarding her in memory for her ceaseless efforts on behalf of the safety of society?

Edwin stood like a rock against a service in the Wesleyan Chapel. Clara cunningly pointed out to him that the Wesleyan Chapel would be heated for the occasion, whereas the chapel at the cemetery, where scores of persons had caught their deaths in the few years of its existence, was never heated. His reply showed genius. He would have the service at the house itself. The decision of the chief mourner might be regretted, and was regretted, but none could impugn its correctitude nor its social distinction; some said approvingly that it was 'just like' Edwin. Thenceforward the arrangements went more smoothly, the only serious difficulty being about the route to the cemetery. Edwin was met by a saying that 'the last journey must be the longest': which meant that the cortège must go up St Luke's Square and along the Market Place past the Town Hall and the Shambles, encountering the largest number of sightseers, instead of taking the nearest way along Wedgwood Street. Edwin chose Wedgwood Street.

In the discussions, Maggie was neutral, thus losing part of the very little prestige which she possessed. Clara and Albert considered Edwin to be excessively high-handed. But they were remarkably moderate in criticism, for the reason that no will had been found. Maggie and Clara had searched the most secret places of the house for a will, in vain. All that they had found was a brass and copper paper-knife wrapped in tissue-paper and labelled 'For Edwin, with Auntie's love', and a set of tortoise-shell combs equally wrapped in tissue-paper and labelled 'For Maggie, with Auntie's love.' Naught for Clara! Naught for the chicks!

Albert (who did all the running about) had been to see Mr Julian Pidduck, the Wesleyan solicitor, who had a pew at the back of the chapel and was famous for invariably arriving at morning service half an hour late. Mr Pidduck knew of no will. Albert had also been to the Bank – that is to say, *the* Bank, at the top of St Luke's Square, whose former manager had been a buttress of Wesleyanism. The new manager (after nearly eight years he was still called the 'new' manager, because the previous manager, old Lovatt, had been in control for nearly thirty years), Mr Breeze, was ill upstairs on the residential floor with one of his periodic attacks of boils; the cashier, however, had told Albert that certain securities, but no testament, were deposited at the Bank; he had offered to produce the securities, but only to Edwin, as the nearest relative. Albert had then secretly looked up the pages entitled 'Intestates' Estates' in *Whitaker's Almanack* and had discovered that whereas Auntie Hamps being intestate, her personal property would be divided equally between Edwin, Maggie, and Clara, her real property would go entirely to Edwin. (Edwin also had secretly looked up the same pages.) This gross injustice nearly turned Albert from a Tory into a Land Laws reformer. It accounted for the comparative submissiveness of Clara and Albert before Edwin's arrogance as the arbiter of funerals. They hoped that, if he was humoured, he might forego his rights. They could not credit, and Edwin maliciously did not tell them, that no matter what they did he was incapable of insisting on such rights.

While the ministers succeeded each other in the conduct of the service, each after his different manner, Edwin scrutinized the coffin, and the wreaths, and the cards inscribed with mournful ecstatic affection that nestled amid the flowers, and the faces of the audience, and his thought was: 'This will soon be over now!' Beneath his gloomy and wearied expression he was unhappy, but rather hopeful and buoyant, looking forward to approaching felicity. His reflections upon the career of Auntie Hamps were kind, and utterly uncritical; he wondered what her spirit was doing in that moment. The mystery ennobled his mind. Yet he wondered also whether the ministers believed all they were saying, why the superintendent minister read so well and prayed with such a lack of distinction, how much the wreaths cost, whether the Sunday-school deputation had silently arrived in the street, and why men in overcoats and hatless looked so grotesque in a room, and why, when men and women were assembled on a formal occasion, the women always clung together.

Probing his left-hand pocket, he felt a letter. He had received it that morning from Hilda. George was progressing very well, and Charlie Orgreave had actually brought the oculist with his apparatus to see him at Charlie's house. Charlie would always do impossibilities for Hilda. It was Charlie who had once saved George's life – so Hilda was convinced. The oculist had said that George's vision was normal, and that he must not wear glasses, but that on account of a slight weakness he ought to wear a shade at night in rooms which were lighted from the top. In a few days Hilda and George would return. Edwin anticipated their arrival with an impatience almost gleeful, so anxious was he to begin the new life with Hilda. Her letters had steadily excited him. He pictured the intimacies of their reunion. He saw her ideally. His mind rose to the finest manifestations of her individuality, and the inconveniences of that individuality grew negligible. Withal, he was relieved that George's illness had kept her out of Bursley during the illness, death, and burial of Auntie Hamps. Had she been there, he would have had three persons to manage instead of two, and he could not have asserted himself with the same freedom.

And then there was a sound of sobbing outside the door. Minnie, sharing humbly but obstinately in the service according to her station, had broken down in irrational grief at the funeral of the woman whose dying words amounted to an order for her execution. Edwin, though touched, could have smiled; and he felt abashed before the lofty and incomprehensible marvels of human nature. Several outraged bent heads twisted round in the direction of the door, but the minister intrepidly continued with the final prayer. Maggie slipped out, the door closed, and the sound of sobbing receded.

After the benediction Albert resumed full activity, while the remainder of the company stared and cleared their throats without exchanging a word. The news that the hearse and coaches had not arrived helped them to talk a little. The fault was not that of the undertaker, but Edwin's. The service had finished too soon, because in response to Mr Flowerdew's official question: 'How much time do you give me?' he had replied: 'Oh! A quarter of an hour,' whereas Albert the organizer had calculated upon half an hour. The representatives of the Sunday school were already lined up on the pavement, and on the opposite pavement and in the roadway were knots of ragged, callously inquisitive spectators. The vehicles could at length be descried on the brow of Church Street. They descended the slope in haste. The four mutes nipped down with agility from the hammercloths, hung their greasy top hats on the ornamental spikes of the hearse, and sneaked grimly into the house. In a second the flowers were shifted from the coffin, and with startling accomplished swiftness the coffin was darted out of the room without its fraudulent brass handles even being touched, and down the steps into the hearse, and the flowers replaced. The one hitch was due to Edwin attempting to get into the first coach instead of waiting for the last one. Albert, putting on his new black gloves, checked him. The ministers and the doctor had to go first, the chapel officials next, and the chief mourners – Edwin, Albert, and Bert – had the third coach. The women stayed behind at the door, frowning at the murmurous crowd of shabby idlers. Albert gave a supreme glance at the vehicles and the walkers, made a signal, and joined Edwin and Bert in the last coach, buttoning his left-hand glove. Edwin would only hold his gloves in his hand. The cortège moved. Rain was threatening, and the street was muddy.

At the cemetery it was raining, and the walkers made a string of glistening umbrellas; only the paid mutes had no umbrellas. Near the gates, under an umbrella, stood a man with a protruding chin and a wiry grey moustache. He came straight to Edwin and shook hands. It was Mr Breeze, the bank manager. His neck, enveloped in a white muffler, showed a large excrescence behind, and he kept his head very carefully in one position.

He said, in his defiant voice:

'I only had the news this morning, and I felt that I should pay the last tribute of respect to the deceased. I had known her in business and privately for many years.'

His greeting of Albert was extremely reserved, and Albert showed him a meek face. Albert's overdraft impaired the cordiality of their relations.

'Sorry to hear you've got your old complaint!' said Edwin, astounded at this act of presence by the terrible bank manager.

Vehicles, by some municipal caprice, were forbidden to enter the cemetery. And in the rain, between the stone-perpetuated great names of the town's history – the Boultons, the Lawtons, the Blackshaws, the Beardmores, the Dunns, the Longsons, the Hulmes, the Suttons, the Greenes, the Gardiners, the Calverts, the Dawsons, the Brindleys, the Baineses, and the Woods – the long procession preceded by Auntie Hamps tramped for a third of a mile along the asphalted path winding past the chapel to the graveside. And all the way Mr Breeze, between Edwin and Albert, with Bert a yard to the rear, talked about boils, and Edwin said Yes and No, and Albert said nothing. And at the graveside the three ministers removed their flat round hats and put on skull-caps, while skilfully holding their umbrellas aloft.

And while Mr Flowerdew was reading from a little book in the midst of the large, encircling bare-headed crowd with umbrellas, and the gravedigger with absolute precision accompanied his words with three castings of earth into the hollow of the grave, Edwin scanned an adjoining tombstone, which marked the family vault of Isaac Plant, a renowned citizen. He read, chased in gilt letters on the Aberdeen granite, the following lines: 'Sacred to the memory of Adelaide Susan, wife of Isaac Plant, died 27th June, 1886, aged 47 years. And of Mary, wife of Isaac Plant, died 11th December, 1890, aged 33 years. And of Effie Harriet, wife of Isaac Plant, died 9th December, 1893, aged 27 years. *The Flower Fadeth*. And of Isaac Plant, died 9th February, 1894, aged 79 years. *I know that my Redeemer Liveth*.' And the passionate career of the aged and always respectable rip seemed to Edwin to have been a wondrous thing. The love of life was in Isaac Plant. He had risen above death again and again. After having detested him, Edwin now liked him on the tombstone.

And even in that hilly and bleak burial-ground, with melan-choly sepulchral parties and white wind-blown surplices dotted about the sodden slopes, and the stiff antipathetic multitude around the pit which held Auntie Hamps, and the terrible seared, harsh, grey-and-brown industrial landscape of the great smoking amphitheatre below, Edwin felt happy in the sensation of being alive and of having to contend with circumstance. He was in-spired by the legend of Isaac Plant and of Auntie Hamps, who in very different ways had intensely lived. And he thought in the same mood of Tertius Ingpen, who was now understood to be past hope. If he died – well, he also had intensely lived! And he thought too of Hilda, whose terrific vitality of emotion had caused him such hours of apprehension and exasperation. He exulted in all those hours. It seemed almost a pity that, by reason of his new-found understanding of Hilda, such hours would not recur. His heart flew impatiently forward into the future, to take up existence with her again.

When the ministers pocketed their skull-caps and resumed their hats, everybody except Edwin appeared to feel relief in turning away from the grave. Faces brightened; footsteps were more alert. In the drawing-room Edwin had thought: 'It will soon be over', and every face near him was saying, 'It is over'; but now that it was over Edwin had a pang of depression at the eagerness with which all the mourners abandoned Auntie Hamps to her strange and desolate grave amid the sinister population of corpses.

He lingered, glancing about. Mr Breeze also lingered, and then in his downright manner squarely approached Edwin.

'I'll walk down with ye to the gates,' said he.

'Yes,' said Edwin.

Mr Breeze moved his head round with care. Their umbrellas touched. In front of them the broken units of a procession tramped in disorder, chatting.

'I've got that will for you,' said Mr Breeze in a confidential tone.

'What will?'

'Mrs Hamps's.'

'But your cashier said there was no will at your place!'

'My cashier doesn't know everything,' remarked Mr Breeze.
And in his voice was the satisfied grimness of a true native of
the district, and a Longshaw man. 'Mrs Hamps deposited her
will with me as much as a friend as anything else. The fact is, I
had it in my private safe. I should have called with it this morning,
but I knew that you'd be busy, and what's more, I can't go paying
calls of a morning. Here it is.'

Mr Breeze drew an endorsed foolscap envelope from the breast
pocket of his overcoat, and handed it to Edwin.

'Thanks,' said Edwin very curtly. He could be as native as any
native. But beneath the careful imperturbability of his demeanour
he was not unagitated.

'I've got a receipt for you to sign,' said Mr Breeze. 'It's slipped
into the envelope. Here's an ink-pencil.'

Edwin comprehended that he must stand still in the rain and
sign a receipt for the will as best he could under an umbrella. He
complied. Mr Breeze said no more.

'Good-bye, Mr Breeze,' said Edwin at the gates.

'Good day to you, Mr Clayhanger.'

The coaches trotted down the first part of the hill into Bursley,
but as soon as the road became a street, with observant houses
on either side, the pace was reduced to a proper solemnity.
Edwin was amused and even uplifted by the thought of the will
in his pocket; his own curiosity concerning it diverted him; he
anticipated complications with a light heart. To Albert he said
nothing on the subject, which somehow he could not bring himself to force bluntly into the conversation. Albert talked about
his misfortunes at the works, including the last straw of the engine
accident; and all the time he was vaguely indicating reasons –
the presence of Bert in the carriage necessitated reticence – for
his default in the interest-paying to Maggie. At intervals he gave
out that he was expecting much from Bert, who at the New Year
was to leave school for the works – and Bert, taciturn behind his
spectacles, had to seem loyal, earnest, and promising.

As they approached the Clowes Hospital Edwin saw a nurse
in a bonnet, white bow, and fluent blue robe emerging from the
shrubbery and putting up an umbrella. She looked delightful,
– at once modest and piquant, until he saw that she was the

night-nurse; and even then she still looked delightful. He thought:
'I'd no idea she could look like that!' and began to admit to
himself that perhaps in his encounters with her in the obscurity of
the night he had not envisaged the whole of her personality. Involuntarily he leaned forward. Her eyes were scintillant and
active, and they caught his. He saluted; she bowed, with a most
inviting, challenging, and human smile.

'There's Nurse Faulkner!' he exclaimed to Albert. 'I must just
ask her how Ingpen is. I haven't heard today.' He made as if to
lean out of the window.

'But you can't stop the procession!' Albert protested in horror,
unable to conceive such an enormity.

'I'll just slip out!' said Edwin guiltily.

He spoke to the coachman, and the coach halted.

In an instant he was on the pavement.

'Drive on,' he instructed the coachman; and to the outraged
Albert: 'I'll walk down.'

Nurse Faulkner, apparently flattered by the proof of her
attractiveness, stopped and smiled upon the visitor. She had a
letter in one hand.

'Good afternoon, nurse.'

'Good morning, Mr Clayhanger. I'm just going out for my
morning walk before breakfast,' said she.

She had dimples. These dimples quite ignored Edwin's
mourning and the fact that he had quitted a funeral in order to
speak to her.

'How is Mr Ingpen today?' Edwin asked. He could read on
the envelope in her hand the words 'The Rev'.

She grew serious, and said in a low, cheerful tone: 'I think
he's going on pretty well.'

Edwin was startled.

'D'you mean he's getting better?'

'Slowly. He's taking food more easily. He was undoubtedly
better this morning. I haven't seen him since, of course.'

'But the matron seemed to think –' He stopped, for the dimples
began to reappear.

'Matron always fears the worst, you know,' said Nurse
Faulkner, not without irony.

'Does she?'

The matron had never held out hope to Edwin, and he had unquestioningly accepted her opinion. It had not occurred to him that the matron of a hospital could be led astray by her instinctive, unconscious appetite for gloom and disaster.

The nurse nodded.

'Then you think he'll pull through?'

'I'm pretty sure he will. But of course I've not seen the doctor – I mean since the first night.'

'I'm awfully glad.'

'His brother came over from Darlington to see him yesterday evening, you know.'

'Yes. I just missed him.'

The nurse gave a little bow as she moved up the road.

'Just going to the pillar-box,' she explained. 'Dreadful weather we're having!'

He left her, feeling that he had made a new acquaintance.

'She's in love with a parson, I bet,' he said to himself. And he had to admit that she had charm -- when off duty.

The news about Ingpen filled him with bright joy. Everything was going well. Hilda would soon be home; George's eyes were not seriously wrong; the awful funeral was over; and his friend was out of danger – marvellously restored to him. Then he thought of the will. He glanced about to see whether anybody of importance was observing him. There was nobody. The coaches were a hundred yards in front. He drew out the envelope containing the will, managed to extract the will from the envelope, and opened the document, – not very easily because he was holding his umbrella. A small printed slip fluttered to the muddy pavement. He picked it up; it was a printed form of attestation clause, seemingly cut from *Whitaker's Almanack*: 'Signed by the testator (or testatrix as the case may be) in the presence of us, both present at the same time', etc.

'She's got that right, anyhow,' he murmured.

Then, walking along, he read the will of Auntie Hamps. It was quickly spotted with raindrops.

At the house the blinds were drawn up, and the women sedately cheerful. Maggie was actually teasing Bert about his new hat, and young Clara, active among the preparations for tea for six, was intensely and seriously proud at being included in the ceremonial party of adults. She did not suspect that the adults themselves had a novel sensation of being genuinely adult, and that the last representative of the older generation was gone, and that this common sensation drew them together rather wistfully.

'Oh! By the way, there's a telegram for you,' said Maggie, as Minnie left the dining-room after serving the last trayful of hot dishes and pots.

Edwin took the telegram. It was from Hilda, to say that she and George would return on the morrow.

'But what about the house being cleaned, and what about servants?' cried Edwin, affecting, in order to conceal his pleasure, an annoyance which he did not in the least feel.

'Oh! Mrs Tams has been looking after the house – I shall go round and see her after tea. I've got one servant for Hilda.'

'You never told me anything about it,' said Edwin, who was struck, by no means for the first time, by the concealment which all the women practised.

'Didn't I?' Maggie innocently murmured. 'And then Minnie can go and help if necessary until you're all settled again. Hadn't we better have the gas lighted before we begin?'

And in the warm cosiness of the small, ugly dining-room shortly to be profaned by auctioneers and furniture-removers, amid the odours of tea and hot tea-cakes, and surrounded by the family faces intimate, beloved, and disdained, Edwin had an exciting vision of the new life with Hilda, and the vision was shot through with sharp flitting thoughts of the once gorgeous Auntie Hamps forlorn in the cemetery and already passing into oblivion.

After tea, immediately the children had been sent home, he said, self-consciously, to Albert:

'I've got something for you.'

And offered the will. Maggie and Clara were upstairs.

'What is it?'

'It's Auntie's will. Breeze had it. He gave it to me in the cemetery. It seems he only knew this morning Auntie was dead. I think that was why he came up.'

'Well, I'm –!' Albert muttered.

His hand trembled as he opened the paper.

Auntie Hamps had made Edwin sole executor, and had left all her property in trust for Clara's children. Evidently she had reasoned that Edwin and Maggie had all they needed, and that the children of such a father as Albert could only be effectually helped in one way, which way she had chosen. The will was seven years old, and the astounding thing was that she had drawn it herself, having probably copied some of the wording from some source unknown. It was a wise if a rather ruthless will; and its provisions, like the manner of making it, were absolutely characteristic of the testatrix. Too mean to employ a lawyer, she had yet had a magnificent gesture of generosity towards that Benbow brood which she adored in her grandiose way. And further she had been clever enough not to invalidate the will by some negligent informality. It was as tight as if Julian Pidduck himself had drawn it.

And she had managed to put Albert in a position highly exasperating. For he was both very pleased and very vexed. In slighting him, she had aggrandized his children.

'What of it?' he asked nervously.

'It's all right so far as I'm concerned,' said Edwin, with a short laugh. And he was sincere, for he had no desire whatever to take a share of his aunt's modest wealth. He shrank from the trustee-ship, but he knew that he could not avoid it, and he was getting accustomed to power and dominion. Albert would have to knuckle down to him, and Clara too.

Maggie and Clara came back together into the room, notice-ably sisterly. They perceived at once from the men's faces that they were in the presence of a historic event.

'I say, Clary,' Albert began; his voice quavered.

CHAPTER 20

THE DISCOVERY

I

HILDA showed her smiling, flattering face at the door of Edwin's private office at a few minutes to one on Saturday morning, and she said:

'I had to go to the dressmaker's after my shopping, so I thought I might as well call for you.' She added with deference: 'But I can wait if you're busy.'

True that the question of mourning had taken her to the dressmaker's, and that the dressmaker lived in Shawport Lane, not four minutes from the works; but such accidents had nothing to do with her call, which, being part of a scheme of Hilda's, would have occurred in any case.

'I'm ready,' said Edwin, pleased by the vision of his wife in the stylish wide-sleeved black jacket and black hat which she had bought in London. 'What have you got in that parcel?'

'It's your new office coat,' Hilda replied, depositing on the desk the parcel which had been partly concealed behind her muff. 'I've mended the sleeves.'

'Aha!' Edwin lightly murmured. 'Let's have a look at it.'

His benevolent attitude towards the new office coat surprised and charmed her. Before her journey to London with George he would have jealously resented any interfering hand among his apparel, but since her return he had been exquisitely amenable. She thought, proud of herself:

'It's really quite easy to manage him. I never used to go quite the right way about it.'

Her new system, which was one of the results of contact with London and which had been inaugurated a week earlier on the platform of Knype station when she stepped down from the London train, consisted chiefly in smiles, voice control, and other devices to make Edwin believe in any discussion that she fully

appreciated his point of view. Often (she was startled to find) this
simulation had the unexpected result of causing her actually to
appreciate his point of view. Which was very curious.

London indeed had had its effect on Hilda. She had seen the
Five Towns from a distance, and as something definitely provincial. Having lived for years at Brighton, which is almost a
suburb of London, and also for a short time in London itself, she
could not think of herself as a provincial, in the full sense in which
Edwin, for example, was a provincial. She had gone to London
with her son, not like a staring and intimidated provincial, but
with the confidence of an initiate returning to the scene of
initiation. And once she was there, all her old condescensions
towards the dirty and primitive ingenuous Five Towns had very
quickly revived. She discovered Charlie Orgreave, the fairly
successful doctor in Ealing (a suburb rich in doctors), to be the
perfect Londoner, and Janet, no longer useless and forlorn,
scarcely less so. These two, indeed, had the air of having at length
reached their proper home after being born in exile. The same
was true of Johnnie Orgreave, now safely through the matrimonial court and married to his blonde Adela (formerly the
ripping Mrs Chris Hamson), whose money had bought him a
junior partnership in an important architectural firm in Russell
Square. Johnnie and Adela had come over from Bedford Park to
Ealing to see Hilda, and Hilda had dined with them at Bedford
Park at a table illuminated by crimson-shaded night-lights, – a
repast utterly different in its appointments and atmosphere from
anything conceivable in Trafalgar Road. The current Five Towns
notion of Johnnie and his wife as two morally ruined creatures
hiding for the rest of their lives in shame from an outraged public
opinion, seemed merely comic in Ealing and Bedford Park. These
people referred to the Five Towns with negligent affection, but
with disdain, as to a community that, with all its good qualities,
had not yet emerged from barbarism. They assumed that their
attitude was also Hilda's, and Hilda, after a moment's secret
resentment, had indeed made their attitude her own. When she
mentioned that she hoped soon to move Edwin into a country
house, they applauded and implied that no other course was
possible. Withal, their respect, to say nothing of their regard, for

Edwin, the astute and successful man of business, was obvious and genuine. The two brothers Orgreave, amid their possibly superficial splendours of professional men, hinted envy of the stability of Edwin's trade position. And both Janet and Adela, shopping with Hilda, showed her, by those inflections and eyebrowliftings of which women possess the secret, that the wife of a solid and generous husband had quite as much economic importance in London as in the Five Towns.

Thus when Hilda got into the train at Euston, she had in her head a plan of campaign compared to which the schemes entertained by her on the afternoon of the disastrous servants episode seemed amateurish and incomplete. And also she was like a returning adventurer, carrying back to this savage land the sacred torch of civilization. She had perceived, as never before, the superior value of the suave and refined social methods of the metropolitan middle classes, compared with the manners of the Five Towns, and it seemed to her, in her new enthusiasm for the art of life, that if she had ever had a difficulty with Edwin, her own clumsiness was to blame. She saw Edwin as an instrument to be played upon, and herself as a virtuoso. In such an attitude was necessarily a condescension. Yet this condescension somehow did not in the least affect the tenderness and the fever of her longing for Edwin. Her excitement grew as the train passed across the dusky December plain towards him. She thought of the honesty of his handshake and of his wistful glance. She knew that he was better than any of the people she had left, – either more capable, or more reliable, or more charitable, or all three. She knew that most of the people she had left were at heart snobs. 'Am I getting a snob?' she asked herself. She had asked herself the question before. 'I don't care if it is snobbishness. I want certain things, and I will have them, and they can call it what they like.' Like the majority of women, she was incapable of being frightened by the names of her desires. She might be snobbish in one part of her, but in another she had the fiercest scorn for all that Ealing stood for. And in Edwin she admired nothing more than the fact that success had not modified his politics, which were as downright as they had ever been; she could not honestly say the same for herself; and assuredly the Orgreaves could not say the same for themselves. In politics, Edwin was an inspiration to her.

And when the train entered the fiery zone of industry, and slackened speed amid the squalid twilit streets, and stopped at Knype station in front of a crowd of local lowering faces and mackintoshed and gaitered forms, and the damp chill of the Five Towns came in through the opened door of the compartment, her heart fell, and she regretted the elegance of Ealing. But simultaneously her heart was beating with ecstatic expectation. She saw Edwin's face. It was a local face. He wore mourning. He saw her; his eye lighted; his wistful smile appeared. 'Yes,' she thought, 'he is the same as my image of him. He is better than any of them. I am safe. What a shame to have left him all alone! He was quite right – there was no need for it. But I am so impulsive. He must have suffered terribly with those Benbows, and shut out of his own house too.'. . His hand thrilled her. In the terrible sincerity and outpouring of her kiss she sought to compensate him for all wrongs past and future. Her joy in being near him again made her tingle. His matter-of-fact calmness pleased her. She thought: 'I know him, with his matter-of-fact calmness!' 'Hello, kid,' Edwin addressed George with man-to-man negligence. 'Been looking after your mother?' George answered like a Londoner. She had them side by side. It was the fact that George had looked after her. London had matured him; he had picked up a little Ealing. He was past Edwin's shoulder. Indeed he was surprisingly near to being a man. She had both of them. On the platform they surrounded her with their masculine protection. George's secret deep respect for Edwin was not hidden from her.

And yet, all the time, in her joy, reliance, love, admiration, eating him with her eyes, she was condescending to Edwin, – because she had plans for his good. She knew better than he did what would be for his good. And he was a provincial and didn't suspect it. 'My poor boy!' she had said gleefully in the cab, pulling suddenly at a loose button of the old grey coat which he wore surreptitiously under his new black overcoat. 'My poor boy, what a state you are in!' implying in her tone of affectionate raillery that without her he was a lost man. Through this loose button, she was his mother, his good angel, his saviour. The trifle had led to a general visitation of his wardrobe, conducted by her with metropolitan skill in humouring his susceptibilities.

Edwin now tried on the new office coat with the self-consciousness that none but an odious dandy can avoid on such occasions. 'It seems warmer than it used to be,' he said, pleased to have her beholding him and interesting herself in him, especially in his office. Her presence there, unless it happened to arouse his jealousy for his business independence, always pleasurably excited him. Her muff on the desk had the air of being the muff of a woman who was amorously interested in him, but his relations with whom were not regularized by the law or the church.

'Yes,' said she. 'I've put some wash-leather inside the lining at the back.'

'Why?'

'Well, didn't you say you felt the cold from the window, and it's bad for your liver?'

Her glance said:

'Am I not a clever woman?'

And his replied:

'You are.'

'That's the end of that, I hope, darling,' she remarked, picking up the old office coat and dropping it with charming affected disgust into the waste-paper basket.

He shouted for the clerk, who entered with some letters for signature. Under the eyes of his wife Edwin signed them with the demeanour of a secretary of state signing the destiny of provinces, while the clerk respectfully waited.

'I've asked Maggie to come up for the week-end,' said Hilda carelessly, when they were alone together, and Edwin was straightening the desk preparatory to departure.

Since her return she had become far more friendly with Maggie than ever before, – not because Maggie had revealed any new charm, but because she saw in Maggie a victim of injustice. Nothing during the week had more severely tested Hilda's new methods of intercourse with Edwin than the disclosure of the provisions of Auntie Hamps's will, which she had at once and definitely set down as monstrous. She simply could not comprehend Edwin's calm acceptance of them, and a month earlier she

THE DISCOVERY

would have been bitter about it. It was not (she was convinced)
that she coveted money, but that she hated unfairness. Why
should the Benbows have all Auntie Hamps's possessions, and
Edwin and Maggie, who had done a thousand times more for her
than the Benbows, nothing? Hilda's conversation implied that the
Benbows ought to be ashamed of themselves, and when Edwin
pointed out that their good luck was not their fault, only a miracle
of self-control had enabled her to say nicely: 'That's quite true',
instead of sneering: 'That's you all over, Edwin!' When she learnt
that Edwin would receive not a penny for his labours as executor
and trustee for the Benbow children, she was speechless. Perceiving that he did not care for her to discourse upon what she considered to be the wrong done to him, she discoursed upon the
wrong done to Maggie – Maggie who was already being deprived
by the wicked Albert of interest due to her. And Edwin had to
agree with her about Maggie's case. It appeared that Maggie
also agreed with her about Maggie's case. As for the Benbows,
Hilda had not deigned to say one word to them on the matter.
A look, a tone, a silence, had sufficed to express the whole of
Hilda's mind to those Benbows.

'Oh!' said Edwin. 'So Maggie's coming for the week-end, is
she? Well, that's not a bad scheme.' He knew that Maggie had
been very helpful about servants, and that, the second servant
having not yet arrived, she would certainly do much more work
in the house than she 'made'. He pictured her and Hilda
becoming still more intimate as they turned sheets and blankets
and shook pillows on opposite sides of beds, and he was glad.

'Yes,' said Hilda. 'I've called there this morning.'

'And what's she doing with Minnie?'

'We've settled all that,' said Hilda proudly. Edwin had told
her in detail the whole story of Minnie, and she had behaved
exactly as he had anticipated. Her championship of Minnie had
been as passionate as her ruthless verdict upon Minnie's dead
mistress. 'The girl's aunt was there when I called. We've settled
she is to go to Stone, and Maggie and I shall do something for
her, and when it's all over I may take her on as housemaid.
Maggie says she probably wouldn't make a bad housemaid.
Anyhow it's all arranged for the present.'

'Then Maggie'll be without a servant?'

'No, she won't. We shall manage that. Besides, I suppose Maggie won't stay on in that house all by herself for ever! . . . It's just the right size, I see.'

'Just!' said Edwin.

He was spreading over his desk a dust sheet with a red scalloped edging which Hilda had presented to him three days earlier.

She gazed at him with composed and justifiable self-satisfaction, as if saying: 'Leave absolutely to me everything in my department, and see how smooth your life will be!'

He would never praise her, and she had a very healthy appetite for praise, which appetite always went hungry. But now, instead of resenting his niggardly reserve, she said to herself: 'Poor boy! He can't bring himself to pay compliments; that's it. But his eyes are full of delicious compliments.' She was happy, even if apprehensive for the immediate future. There she was, established and respected in his office, which was his church and the successful rival of her boudoir. Her plans were progressing.

She approached the real business of her call:

'I was thinking we might have gone over to see Ingpen this afternoon.'

'Well, let's.'

Ingpen, convalescent, had insisted, two days earlier, on being removed to his own house, near the village of Stockbrook, a few miles south of Axe. The departure was a surprising example of the mere power of volition on the part of a patient. The routine of hospital life had exasperated the recovering soul of this priest of freedom to such a point that doctor, matron, and friends had had to yield to a mere instinct.

'There's no decent train to go, and none at all to come back until nearly nine o'clock. And we can't cycle in this weather – at least I can't, especially in the dark.'

'Well, what about Sunday?'

'The Sunday trains are worse.'

'What a ghastly line!' said Edwin. 'And they have the cheek to pay five per cent! I remember Ingpen telling me there was one fairish train into Knype in the morning, and one out in the afternoon. And there wouldn't be that if the Locomotive Superintendent didn't happen to live at Axe.'

'It's a pity you haven't got a dogcart, isn't it?' said Hilda, lightly smiling. 'Because then we could use the works horse now and then, and it wouldn't really cost anything extra, would it?'

Her heart was beating perceptibly.

Edwin shook his head, agreeably, but with firmness.

'Can't mix up two different things like that!' he said.

She knew it. She was aware of the whole theory of horse-owning among the upper trading class in the Five Towns. A butcher might use his cob for pleasure on Sundays – he never used it for pleasure on any other day – but traders on a higher plane than butchers drew between the works and the house a line which a works horse was not permitted to cross. One or two, perhaps, – but not the most solid – would put a carter into a livery overcoat and a shabby top hat and describe him as a coachman while on rare afternoons he drove a landau or a victoria picked up cheap at Axe or Market Drayton. But the majority had no pretensions to the owning of private carriages. The community was not in fact a carriage community. Even the Orgreaves had never dreamed of a carriage. Old Darius Clayhanger would have been staggered into profanity by the suggestion of such a thing. Indeed, until some time after old Clayhanger's death the printing business had been content to deliver all its orders in a boy-pushed handcart. Only when Edwin discovered that, for instance, two thousand catalogues on faced clay paper could not be respectably delivered in a handcart, had he steeled himself to the prodigious move of setting up a stable. He had found an entirely trustworthy ostler-carter with the comfortable name of Unchpin, and, an animal and a tradesman's covered cart having been bought, he had left the affair to Unchpin. Naturally he had never essayed to drive the tradesman's cart. An Edwin Clayhanger could not be seen on the insecure box of a tradesman's cart. He had learnt nothing about horses except that a horse should be watered before, and not after, being fed, that shoeing cost a shilling a week and fodder a shilling a day, and that a horse driven over a hundred and fifty miles a week was likely to get 'a bit over' at the knees. At home the horse and cart had always been regarded as being just as exclusively a works item as the printing-machines or the steam-engine.

'I suppose,' said Hilda carefully, 'you've got all the work one horse can do?'

'*And* more.'

'Well, then, why don't you buy another one?' She tried to speak carelessly, without genuine interest.

'Yes, no doubt!' Edwin answered dryly. 'And build fresh stables, too.'

'Haven't you got room for two?'

'Come along and look, and then perhaps you'll be satisfied.'

Buzzers, syrens, and whistles began to sound in the neighbourhood. It was one o'clock.

'Shall I? . . . Your overcoat collar's turned up behind. Let me do it.'

She straightened the collar.

They went out, through the clerk's office. Edwin gave a sideways nod to Simpson. In the passage some girls and a few men were already hurrying forth. None of them took notice of Edwin and Hilda. They all plunged for the street as though the works had been on fire.

'They are in a hurry, my word!' Hilda murmured, with irony.

'And why shouldn't they be?' the employer protested almost angrily.

In the small yard stood the horseless cart, with 'Edwin Clayhanger, Lithographer and Steam Printer, Bursley' on both its sides. The stable and cart-shed were in one penthouse, and to get to the stable it was necessary to pass through the cart-shed. Unchpin, a fat man of forty with a face marked by black seams, was bending over a chaff-cutter in the cart-shed. He ignored the intruders. The stable consisted of one large loosebox, in which a grey animal was restlessly moving.

'You see!' Edwin muttered curtly.

'Oh! What a beautiful horse! I've never seen him before.'

'Her,' Edwin corrected.

'Is it a mare?'

'So they say.'

'I never knew you'd got a fresh one.'

'I haven't – yet. I've taken this one for a fortnight's trial, from Chawner . . . How's she doing, Unchpin?' he called to the cart-shed.

Unchpin looked round and stared.

'Bit light,' he growled and turned back to the chaff-cutter, which he seemed to be repairing.

'I thought so,' said Edwin.

'But her's a good 'un,' he added.

'But where's the old horse?' asked Hilda.

'With God,' Edwin replied. 'Dropped down dead last week.'

'What of?'

Edwin shook his head.

'It's a privilege of horses to do that sort of thing,' he said. 'They're always doing it.'

'You never told me.'

'Well, you weren't here, for one thing.'

The mare inquisitively but cautiously put her muzzle over the door of the box. Hilda stroked her. The animal's mysterious eyes, her beautiful coat, her broad back, her general bigness relatively to Hilda, the sound of her feet among the litter on the paving stones, the smell of the stable, – these things enchanted Hilda.

'I should adore horses!' she breathed, half to herself, ecstatic-ally; and wondered whether she would ever be able to work her will on Edwin in the matter of a dog cart. She pictured herself driving the grey mare, who had learnt to love her, in a flashing dogcart, Edwin by her side on the front seat. Her mind went back enviously to Tavy Mansion and Dartmoor. But she felt that Edwin had not enough elasticity to comprehend the rapture of her dream. She foresaw nearly endless trouble and altercation and chicane before she could achieve her end. She was ready to despair, but she remembered her resolutions and took heart.

'I say, Unchpin,' said Edwin. 'I suppose this box couldn't be made into two stalls?'

Unchpin on his gaitered legs clumped towards the stable, and gazed gloomily into the box. When he had gazed for some time, he touched his cap to Hilda.

'It could,' he announced.

'Could you get a trap into the shed as well as the cart?'

'Ay! If ye dropped th' shafts o' th' trap under th' cart. What of it, mester?'

'Nothing. Only missis is going to have this mare.'

After a pause, Unchpin muttered:

'Missis, eh!'

Hilda had moved a little away into the yard. Edwin approached her, flushing slightly, and with a self-consciousness which he tried to dissipate with one wink. Hilda's face was set hard.

'I must just go back to the office,' she said, in a queer voice.

She walked quickly, Edwin following. Simpson beheld their return with gentle surprise. In the private office Hilda shut the door. She then ran to the puzzled Edwin, and kissed him with the most startling vehemence, clasping her arms – in one hand she still held the muff – round his neck. She loved him for being exactly as he was. She preferred his strange, uncouth method of granting a request, of yielding, of flattering her caprice, to any politer, more conventional methods of the metropolis. She thought that no other man could be as deeply romantic as Edwin. She despised herself for ever having been misled by the surface of him. And even the surface of him she saw now as it were, through the prism of passionate affection, to be edged with the blending colours of the rainbow. And when they came again out of the office, after the sacred rite, and Edwin, as uplifted as she, glanced back nevertheless at the sheeted desk and the safe and the other objects in the room with the half-mechanical habitual solicitude of a man from whom the weight of responsibility is never lifted, she felt saddened because she could not enter utterly into his impenetrable soul, and live through all his emotions, and comprehend like a creator the always baffling wistfulness of his eyes. This sadness was joy; it was the aura of her tremendous satisfaction in his individuality and in her triumph and in the thought: 'I alone stand between him and desolation.'

II

'Wo!' exclaimed Hilda broadly, bringing the mare and the vehicle to a standstill in front of the 'Live and Let Live' inn in the main street of the village of Stockbrook, which lay about a mile and a half off the high road from the Five Towns to Axe. And immediately the mare stopped she was enveloped in her own vapour.

'Ha!' exclaimed Edwin, with faint benevolent irony. 'And no bones broken!'

A man came out from the stable-yard.

The village of Stockbrook gave the illusion that hundreds of English villages were giving that Christmas morning, – the illusion that its name was Arcadia, that finality had been reached, and that the forces of civilization could go no further. More suave than a Dutch village, incomparably neater and cleaner and more delicately finished than a French village, it presented, in the still, complacent atmosphere of long tradition, a picturesque medley of tiny architectures nearly every aspect of which was beautiful. And if seven people of different ages and sexes lived in a two-roomed cottage under a thatched roof hollowed by the weight of years, without drains and without water, and also without freedom, the beholder was yet bound to conclude that by some mysterious virtue their existence must be gracious, happy, and in fact ideal – especially on Christmas Day, though Christmas Day was also quarter-day – and that they would not on any account have it altered in the slightest degree. Who could believe that fathers of families drank away their children's bread in the quaint taproom of that creeper-clad hostel – a public house fit to produce ecstasy in the heart of every American traveller – 'The Live and Let Live'? Who could have believed that the Weslyan Methodists already singing a Christmas hymn inside the dwarf Georgian conventicle, and their fellow-Christians straggling under the lych into the churchyard, scorned one another with an immortal detestation, each claiming a monopoly in knowledge of the unknowable? But after all the illusion of Arcadia was not entirely an illusion. In this calm, rime-decked, Christmas-imbued village, with its motionless trees enchanted beneath a vast grey impenetrable cloud, a sort of relative finality had indeed been reached, – the end of an epoch that was awaiting dissolution.

Edwin had not easily agreed to the project of shutting up house for the day and eating the Christmas dinner with Tertius Ingpen.

Although customarily regarding the ritual of Christmas, with its family visits, its exchange of presents, its feverish kitchen activity, its somewhat insincere gaiety, its hours of boredom, and its stomachic regrets, as an ordeal rather than a delight, he nevertheless abandoned it with reluctance and a sense of being disloyal to something sacred. But the situation of Ingpen, Hilda's strong desire and her teasing promise of a surprise, and the still continuing dearth of servants had been good arguments to persuade him.

And though he had left Trafalgar Road moody and captious, thinking all the time of the deserted and cold home, he had arrived in Stockbrook tingling and happy, and proud of Hilda, – proud of her verve, her persistency, and her success. She had carried him very far on the wave of her new enthusiasm for horse-traction. She had beguiled him into immediately spending mighty sums on a dog cart, new harness, rugs, a driving-apron, and a fancy whip. She had exhausted Unchpin, upset the routine of the lithographic business, and gravely overworked the mare, in her determination to learn to drive. She had had the equipage out at night for her lessons. On the other hand she had not in the least troubled herself about the purchase of a second horse for mercantile purposes, and a second horse had not yet been bought.

When she had announced that she would herself drive her husband and son over to Stockbrook, Edwin had absolutely negatived the idea; but Unchpin had been on her side; she had done the double journey with Unchpin, who judged her capable and the mare (eight years old) quite reliable, and who moreover wanted Christmas as much as possible to himself. And Hilda had triumphed. Walking the mare uphill – and also downhill – she had achieved Stockbrook in safety; and the conquering air with which she drew up at the 'Live and Let Live' was delicious. The chit's happiness and pride radiated out from her. It seemed to Edwin that by the mere strength of volition she had actually created the dog cart and its appointments, and the mare too! And he thought that he himself had not lived in vain if he could procure her such sensations as her glowing face then displayed. Her occasionally overbearing tenacity, and the little jars which good resolutions several weeks old had naturally not been powerful enough to prevent, were forgotten and forgiven.

He would have given all his savings to please her caprice, and been glad. A horse and trap, or even a pair of horses and a landau, were a trifling price to pay for her girlish joy and for his own tranquillity in his beloved house and business.

'Catch me, both of you!' cried Hilda.

Edwin had got down, and walked round behind the vehicle to the footpath, where George stood grinning. The stableman, in classic attitude, was at the mare's head.

Hilda jumped rather wildly. It was Edwin who countered the shock of her descent. The edge of her velvet hat knocked against his forehead, disarranging his cap. He could smell the velvet, as for an instant he held his wife – strangely acquiescent and yielding – in his arms, and there was something intimately feminine in the faint odour. All Hilda's happiness seemed to pass into him, and that felicity sufficed for him. He did not desire any happiness personal to himself. He wanted only to live in her. His contentment was profound, complete, rapturous.

And yet in the same moment, reflecting that Hilda would certainly have neglected the well-being of the mare, he could say to the stableman:

'Put the rug over her, will you?'

'Hello! Here's Mr Ingpen!' announced George, as he threw the coloured rug on the mare.

Ingpen, pale and thickly enveloped, came slowly round the bend of the road, waving and smiling. He had had a relapse, after a too early sortie, and was recovering from it.

'I made sure you'd be about here,' he said, shaking hands. 'Merry Christmas, all!'

'Ought you to be out, my lad?' Edwin asked heartily.

'Out? Yes. I'm as fit as a fiddle. And I've been ordered mild exercise.' He squared off gaily against George and hit the stout adolescent in the chest.

'What about all your parcels, Hilda?' Edwin inquired.

'Oh! We'll call for them afterwards.'

'Afterwards?'

'Yes. Come along – before you catch a chill.' She winked openly at Ingpen, who returned the wink. 'Come along, dear. It's not far. We have to walk across the fields.'

'Put her up, sir?' the stableman demanded of Edwin.

'Yes. And give her a bit of a rub down,' he replied absently, remembering various references of Hilda's to a surprise. His heart misgave him. Ingpen and Hilda looked like plotters, very intimate and mischievous. He had a notion that living with a woman was comparable to living with a volcano – you never knew when a dangerous eruption might not occur.

Within three minutes the first and minor catastrophe had occurred.

'Bit sticky, this field path of yours,' said Edwin uneasily.

They were all four slithering about in brown clay under a ragged hedge in which a few red berries glowed.

'It was as hard as iron the day before yesterday,' said Hilda.

'Oh! So you where here the day before yesterday, were you? . . . What's that house there?' Edwin turned to Ingpen.

'He's guessed it in one!' Ingpen murmured, and then went off into his characteristic *crescendo* laugh.

The upper part of a late-eighteenth-century house, squat and square, with yellow walls, black uncurtained windows, high slim chimneys, and a blue slate roof, showed like a gigantic and mysterious fruit in a clump of variegated trees, some of which were evergreen.

'Ladderedge Hall, my boy,' said Ingpen. 'Seat of the Beechinors for about a hundred years.'

' "Seat", eh!' Edwin murmured sarcastically.

'It's been empty for two years,' remarked Hilda brightly. 'So we thought we'd have a look at it.'

And Edwin said to himself that he had divined all along what the surprise was. It was astounding that a man could pass with such rapidity as Edwin from vivid joy to black and desolate gloom. She well knew that the idea of living in the country was extremely repugnant to him, and that nothing would ever induce him to consent to it. And yet she must needs lay this trap for him, prepare this infantile surprise, and thereby spoil his Christmas, she who a few moments earlier had been the embodiment of surrender in his arms! He said no word. He hummed a few notes and glanced airily to right and left with an effort after unconcern. The presence of Ingpen and the boy, and the fact of Christmas, forbade him to speak freely. He could not suddenly stop and drive his stick into the earth and say savagely:

'Now listen to me! Once for all, I won't have this country house idea! So let it be understood, – if you want a row, you know how to get it.'

The appearance of amity – and the more high-spirited the better – must be kept up throughout the day. Nevertheless in his heart he challenged Hilda desperately. All her good qualities became insignificant, all his benevolent estimates of her seemed ridiculous. She was the impossible woman. He saw a tremendous vista of unpleasantness, for her obstinacy in warfare was known to him, together with her perfect lack of scruple, of common sense, and of social decency. He had made her a present of a horse and trap – solely to please her – and this was his reward! The more rope you gave these creatures, the more they wanted! But he would give no more rope. Compromise was at an end . . . The battle would be joined that night . . . In his grim and resolute dejection there was something almost voluptuous. He continued to glance airily about, and at intervals to hum a few notes.

Over a stile they dropped into a rutty side road, and opposite was the worn iron gate of Ladderedge Hall, with a house-agent's board on it. A short curved gravel drive, filmed with green, led to the front door of the house. In front were a lawn and a flower-garden, beyond a paddock, and behind a vegetable garden and a glimpse of stabling; a compact property! Ingpen drew a great key from his pocket. The plotters were all prepared; they took their victim for a simpleton, a ninny, a lamb.

In the damp echoing interior Edwin gazed without seeing, and heard as in a dream without listening. This was the hall, this the dining-room, this the drawing-room, this the morning-room . . . White marble mantelpieces, prehistoric grates, wall paper hanging in strips, cobwebs, uneven floors, scaly ceilings, the invisible vapour of human memories! This was the kitchen, enormous, then the larder, enormous, and the scullery still more enormous (with a pump-handle flanking the slopstone)! No water. No gas. And what was this room opening out of the kitchen? Oh! That must be the servants' hall . . . Servants' hall indeed! Imagine Edwin Clayhanger living in a 'Hall', with a servants' hall therein! Snobbishness unthinkable! He would not be able to look his friends in the face . . . On the first floor, endless bedrooms, but no bathroom. Here, though, was a small bedroom that would make a splendid bathroom . . . Ingpen, the ever expert, conceived a tank-room in the roof, and traced routes for plumber's pipes. George, excited, and comprehending that he must conduct himself as behoved an architect, ran up to the attic floor to study on the spot the problem of the tank-room, and Ingpen followed. Edwin stared out of a window at the prospect of the Arcadian village lying a little below across the sloping fields.

'Come along, Edwin,' Hilda coaxed.

Yes, she had pretended a deep concern for the welfare of the suffering, feckless bachelor, Tertius Ingpen. She had paid visit after visit in order to watch over his convalescence. Choosing to ignore his scorn for all her sex, she had grown more friendly with him than even Edwin had ever been. Indeed by her sympathetic attentions she had made Edwin seem callous in comparison. And all the time she had been merely pursuing a private design – with what girlish deceitfulness!

In the emptiness of the house the voices of Ingpen and George echoed from above down the second flight of stairs.

'No good going to the attics,' muttered Edwin, on the landing.

Hilda, half cajoling, half fretful, protested:

'Now, Edwin, don't be disagreeable.'

He followed her on high, martyrized. The front wall of the house rose nearly to the top of the attic windows, screening and darkening them.

'Cheerful view!' Edwin growled.

He heard Ingpen saying that the place could be had on a repairing lease for sixty-five pounds a year, and that perhaps one thousand two hundred pounds would buy it. Dirt cheap.

'Ah!' Edwin murmured. 'I know those repairing leases. One thousand pounds wouldn't make this barn fit to live in.'

He knew that Ingpen and Hilda exchanged glances.

'It's larger than Tavy Mansion,' said Hilda.

Tavy Mansion! There was the secret! Tavy Mansion was at the

bottom of her scheme. Alicia Hesketh had a fine house, and Hilda must have a finer. She, Hilda, of all people, was a snob. He had long suspected it.

He rejoined sharply:

'Of course it isn't larger than Tavy Mansion! It isn't as large.'

'Oh, Edwin. How can you say such things!'

In the portico, as Ingpen was relocking the door, the husband said negligently, superiorly, cheerfully:

'It's not so bad. I expect there's hundreds of places like this up and down the country – going cheap.'

The walk back to the 'Live and Let Live' was irked by constraint, against which everyone fought nobly, smiling, laughing, making remarks about cock robins, the sky, the Christmas dinner.

'So I hear it's settled you're going to London when you leave school, kiddie,' said Tertius Ingpen, to bridge over a fearful hiatus in the prittle-prattle.

George, so big now and so mannishly dressed as to be amused and not a bit hurt by the appellation 'kiddie', confirmed the statement in his deepening voice.

Edwin thought:

'It's more than *I* hear, anyway!'

Hilda had told him that during the visit to London the project for articling George to Johnnie Orgreave had been revived, but she had not said that a decision had been taken. Though Edwin from careful pride had not spoken freely – George being Hilda's affair and not his – he had shown no enthusiasm. Johnnie Orgreave had sunk permanently in his esteem – scarcely less so that Jimmie, whose conjugal eccentricities had scandalized the Five Towns and were achieving the ruin of the Orgreave practice; or than Tom, who was developing into a miser. Moreover, he did not at all care for George going to London. Why should it be thought necessary for George to go to London? The sagacious and successful provincial in Edwin was darkly jealous of London, as a rival superficial and brilliant. And now he learnt from Ingpen that George's destiny was fixed . . . A matter of small importance, however!

Did 'they' seriously expect him to travel from Ladderedge

Hall to his works, and from his works to Ladderedge Hall every weekday of his life? He laughed sardonically to himself.

Out came the sun, which George greeted with a cheer. And Edwin, to his own surprise, began to feel hungry.

III

'I shan't take that house, you know,' said Edwin, casually and yet confidentially, in a pause which followed a long analysis, by Ingpen, of Ingpen's sensations in hospital before he was out of danger.

They sat on opposite sides of a splendid extravagant fire in Ingpen's dining-room.

Ingpen, sprawling in a shabby, uncomfortable easy-chair, and flushed with the activity of digestion, raised his eyebrows, squinted down at the cigarette between his lips, and answered impartially:

'No. So I gather. Of course you must understand it was Hilda's plan to go up there. I merely fell in with it, – simplest thing to do in these cases!'

'Certainly.'

Thus they both condescended to the feather-headed capricious woman, dismissed her, and felt a marked access of sincere intimacy on a plane of civilization exclusively masculine.

In the succeeding silence of satisfaction and relief could be heard George, in the drawing-room above, practising again the piano part of a Haydn violin sonata which he had very nervously tried over with Ingpen while they were awaiting dinner.

Ingpen said suddenly:

'I say, old chap! Why have you never mentioned that you happened to meet a certain person in my room at Hanbridge that night you went over there for me?' He frowned.

Edwin had a thrill, pleasurable and apprehensive, at the prospect of a supreme confidence.

'It was no earthly business of mine,' he answered lightly. But his tone conveyed: 'You surely ought to be aware that my loyalty and my discretion are complete.'

And Ingpen, replying to Edwin's tone, said with a simple directness that flattered Edwin to the heart:

'Naturally I knew I was quite safe in your hands ... I've reassured the lady.' Ingpen smiled slightly.

Edwin was too proud to tell Ingpen that he had not said a word to Hilda, and Ingpen was too proud to tell Edwin that he assumed as much.

At that moment Hilda came into the room, murmuring a carol that some children of Stockbrook had sung on the doorstep during dinner.

'Don't be afraid – I'm not going to interrupt. I know you're in the thick of it,' said she archly, not guessing how exactly truthful she was.

Ingpen, keeping his presence of mind in the most admirable manner, rejoined with irony:

'You don't mean to say you've finished already explaining to Mrs Dummer how she ought to run my house for me?'

'How soon do you mean to have this table cleared?' said Hilda.

The Christmas dinner, served by a raw girl in a large bluish-white pinafore, temporarily hired to assist Mrs Dummer the housekeeper, had been a good one. Its only real fault was that it had had a little too much the air of being a special and mighty effort; and although it owed something to Hilda's parcels, Ingpen was justified in the self-satisfaction which he did not quite conceal as a bachelor host. But now, under Hilda's quizzing gaze, not merely the table but the room and the house sank to the tenth rate. The coarse imperfections of the linen and the cutlery grew very apparent; the disorder of bottles and glasses and cups re-called the refectory of an inferior club. And the untidiness of the room, heaped with accumulations of newspapers, magazines, documents, books, boxes, and musical-instrument cases, loudly accused the solitary despot whose daily caprices of arrangement were perpetuated and rendered sacred by the ukase that nothing was to be disturbed. Hilda's glinting eyes seemed to challenge each corner and dark place to confess its shameful dirt, and the malicious poise of her head mysteriously communicated the fact that in the past fortnight she had spied out every sinister secret in the whole graceless, primitive wigwam.

'This table,' retorted Ingpen bravely, 'is going to be cleared when it won't disturb me to have it cleared.'

'All right,' said Hilda. 'But Mrs Dummer does want to get on with her washing-up.'

'Look here, madam,' Ingpen replied. 'You're a little ray of sunshine, and all that, and I'm the first to say so; but I'm not your husband.' He made a warning gesture. 'Now don't say you'd be sorry for any woman I was the husband of. Think of something more original.' He burst out laughing.

Hilda went to the window and looked out at the fading day.

'Please, I only popped in to say it's nearly a quarter to three, and George and I will go down to the inn and bring the dogcart up here. I want a little walk. We shan't get home till dark as it is.'

'Oh! Chance it and stop for tea, and all will be forgiven.'

'Drive home in the dark? Not much!' Edwin murmured.

'He's afraid of my driving,' said Hilda.

When Edwin and Ingpen were alone together once more, Ingpen's expression changed back instantly to that which Hilda had disturbed, and Edwin's impatience, which had uneasily simmered during the interruption, began to boil.

'Her husband's in a lunatic asylum, I may tell you,' said Ingpen.

'Whose?'

'The young woman's in question.'

For Edwin, it was as if a door had opened in a wall and disclosed a vast unsuspected garden of romance.

'Really!'

'Yes, my boy,' Ingpen went on quietly, with restraint, but not without a naïve and healthy pride in the sudden display of the marvellous garden. 'And I didn't meet her at a concert, or on the Grand Canal, or anything of that sort. I met her in a mill at Oldham while I was doing my job. He was the boss of the mill. I walked into an office and he was lying on the floor on the flat of his back, and she was wiping her feet on his chest. He was saying in a very anxious tone: "You aren't half wiping them. Harder! Harder!" That was his little weakness, you see. He happened to be convinced that he was a doormat. She had been hiding the thing for weeks, coming with him to the works, and so on, to calm him.' Ingpen spoke more quickly and excitedly: 'I never saw a more awful thing in my life! I never saw a more awful thing in my life! And coming across it suddenly, you see . . . There was something absolutely odious in him lying down like that, and her trying to soothe him in the way he wanted. You should have seen the serious expression of his face, simply bursting with anxiety for her to wipe her boots properly on him. And her face when she caught sight of me. Oh! Dreadful! Dreadful!' Ingpen paused, and then continued calmly: 'Of course I soon tumbled to it. For the matter of that, it didn't want much tumbling to. He went raving mad the same afternoon. And he's been more or less raving mad ever since.'

'What a ghastly business . . . Any children?'

'No, thank God!' Ingpen answered with fresh emotion. 'But don't you forget that she's still the wife of that lunatic, and he'll probably live for ever. She's tied up to him just as if she was tied up to a post. Those are our divorce laws! Isn't it appalling? Isn't it inconceivable? Just think of the situation of that woman!' Ingpen positively glared at Edwin in the intensity of his indignation.

'Awful!' Edwin murmured.

'Quite alone in the world, you know!' said Ingpen. 'I'm hanged if I know what she'd have done without me. She hadn't a friend – at any rate she hadn't a friend with a grain of sense. Astonishing how solitary some couples are! . . . It aged her frightfully. She's much younger than she looks. Happily there was a bit of money – enough in fact.'

Deeply as Edwin had been impressed by his romantic discovery of a woman in Ingpen's room at Hanbridge, he was still more impressed by it now. He saw the whole scene again, and saw it far more poetically. He accused himself of blindness, and also of a a certain harshness of attitude towards the woman. He endowed her now with wondrous qualities. The adventure, in its tragical-ness and its clandestine tenderness, was enchanting. How exquisite must be the relations between Ingpen and the woman if without warning she could go to his lair at night and wait confidently for his return! How divine the surprise for him, how ardent the welcome! He envied Ingpen. And also he admired him, for Ingpen had obviously conducted the affair with worthy expertise. And he had known how to win devotion.

With an air of impartiality Ingpen proceeded:

'You wouldn't see her quite at her best, I'm afraid. She's very shy – and naturally she'd be more shy than ever when you saw her. She's quite a different woman when the shyness has worn off. The first two or three times I met her I must say I didn't think she was anything more than a nice well-meaning creature – you know what I mean. But she's much more than that. Can't play, but I believe she has a real feeling for music. She has time for reading, and she does read. And she has a more masculine understanding than nearly any other woman I've ever come across.'

'You wait a bit!' thought Edwin. This simplicity on the part of a notable man of the world pleased him and gave him a comfortable sense of superiority.

Aloud he responded sympathetically:

'Good! ... Do I understand she's living in the Five Towns now?'

'Yes,' said Ingpen, after a hesitation. He spoke in a peculiar, significant voice, carefully modest. The single monosyllable conveyed to Edwin: 'I cannot deny it. I was necessary to this woman, and in the end she followed me!'

Edwin was impressed anew by the full revelation of romance which had concealed itself in the squalid dailiness of the Five Towns.

'In fact,' said Ingpen, 'you never know your luck. If she'd been free I might have been fool enough to get married.'

'Why do you say a thing like that?'

'Because I think I should be a fool to marry.' Ingpen tapping his front teeth with his fingernail, spoke reflectively, persuasively, and with calm detachment.

'Why?' asked Edwin, persuasively also, but nervously, as though the spirit of adventure in the search for truth was pushing him to fatal dangers.

'Marriage isn't worth the price – for me, that is. I dare say I'm peculiar.' Ingpen said this quite seriously, prepared to consider impartially the proposition that he was peculiar. 'The fact is, my boy, I think my freedom is worth a bit more than I could get out of any marriage.'

'That's all very well,' said Edwin, trying to speak with the same dispassionate conviction as Ingpen, and scarcely succeeding. 'But look what you miss! Look how you live!' Almost involuntarily he glanced with self-complacence round the unlovely, unseemly room, and his glance seemed to penetrate ceilings and walls, and to discover and condemn the whole charmless house from top to bottom.

'Why? What's the matter with it?' Ingpen replied uneasily; a slight flush came into his cheeks. 'Nobody has a more comfortable bed or more comfortable boots than I have. How many women can make coffee as good as mine? No woman ever born can make first-class tea. I have all I want.'

'No, you don't. And what's the good of talking about coffee, and tea, and beds?'

'Well, what else is there I want that I haven't got? If you mean fancy cushions and draperies, no thanks!'

'You know what I mean all right . . . And then "freedom" as you say. What do you mean by freedom?'

'I don't specially mean,' said Ingpen, tranquil and benevolent, 'what I may call physical freedom. I'd give that up. I like a certain amount of untidiness, for instance, and I don't think an absence of dust is the greatest thing in the world; but I wouldn't in the least mind giving all that up. It wouldn't really matter to me. What I won't give up is my intellectual freedom. Perhaps I mean intellectual honesty. I'd give up even my intellectual freedom if I could be deprived of it fairly and honestly. But I shouldn't be. There's almost no intellectual honesty in marriage. There can't be. The entire affair is a series of compromises, chiefly base, on the part of the man. The alternative is absolute subjection of the woman, which is offensive. No woman not absolutely a slave ever hears the truth except in anger. You can't say the same about men, and you know it. I'm not blaming; I'm stating. Even assuming a married man gets a few advantages that I miss, they're all purely physical –'

'Oh, no! Not at all.'

'My boy,' Ingpen insisted, sitting up, and gazing earnestly at Edwin. 'Analyse them down, and they're all physical – all! And I tell you I won't pay the price for them. I won't. I've no grievance against women; I can enjoy being with women as much as anybody, but I won't – I will not – live permanently on their level. That's why I say I might have been fool enough to get married. It's quite simple.'

'Hm!'

Edwin, although indubitably one of those who had committed the vast folly of marriage, and therefore subject to Ingpen's indictment, felt not the least constraint, nor any need to offer an individual defence. Ingpen's demeanour seemed to have lifted the argument above the personal. His assumption that Edwin could not be offended was positively inspiring to Edwin. The fear of truth was exorcized. Freedom of thought existed in that room in England. Edwin reflected: 'If he's right and I'm condemned accordingly, – well, I can't help it. Facts are facts, and they're extremely interesting.'

He also reflected:

'Why on earth can't Hilda and I discuss like that?'

He did not know why, but he profoundly and sadly knew that such discussion would be quite impossible with Hilda.

The red-hot coals in the grate subsided together.

'And I'll tell you another thing –' Ingpen commenced.

He was stopped by the entrance of Mrs Dummer, a fat woman, with an old japanned tray. Mrs Dummer came in like a desperate forlorn hope. Her aged, grim, and yet somewhat hysterical face seemed to say: 'I'm going to clear this table and get on with my work, even if I die for it at the hands of a brutal tyrant.' Her gestures as she made a space for the tray and set it down on the table were the formidable gestures of the persecuted at bay.

'Mrs Dummer,' said Ingpen, in a weak voice, leaning back in his chair. 'Would you mind fetching me my tonic off my dressing-table? I've forgotten it.'

'Bless us!' exclaimed Mrs Dummer.

As she had hurried out, Ingpen winked placidly at Edwin in the room in which the shadows were already falling.

Nevertheless, when the dogcart arrived at the front door, Ingpen did seem to show some signs of exhaustion. Hilda would not get down. She sent word into the house by George that the departure must occur at once. Ingpen went out with Edwin, plaintively teased Hilda about the insufferable pride of those who, sit in driving seats, and took leave of her with the most puncti-lious and chivalrous ceremonial, while Hilda inscrutably smiling bent down to him with condescension from her perch.

'I'll sit behind going home, I think,' said Edwin. 'George, you can sit with your mother.'

'Tchik! Tchik!' Hilda signalled.

The mare with a jerk started off down the misty and darkening road.

IV

The second and major catastrophe occurred very soon after the arrival in Trafalgar Road. It was three-quarters of an hour after sunset and the street-lamps were lighted. Unchpin, with gloomy fatalism, shivered obscurely in the dark porch, waiting to drive the dogcart down to the stable. Hilda had requested his presence; it was she also who had got him to bring the equipage up to the house in the morning. She had implied, but not asserted, that to harness the mare and trot up to Bleakridge was the work of a few minutes, and that a few minutes' light labour could make no real difference to Unchpin's Christmas Day. Edwin, descrying Unchpin in the porch, saw merely a defenceless man who had been robbed of the most sacred holiday of the year in order to gratify the selfish caprice of an overbearing woman. When asked how long he had been in the porch, Unchpin firmly answered that he had been there since three o'clock, the hour appointed by Mrs Clayhanger. Edwin knew nothing of this appointment, and in it he saw more evidence of Hilda's thoughtless egotism. He perceived that he would be compelled to stop her from using his employees as her private servants, and that the prohibition would probably cause trouble. Hilda demanded curtly of Unchpin why he had not waited in the warm kitchen, according to instruc-tions, instead of catching his death of cold in the porch. The reply was that he had rung and knocked fifteen times without getting a response.

At this Hilda became angry, not only with Emmie, the default-ing servant, but with the entire servant class and with the world. Emmie, the new cook, and temporarily the sole resident servant, was to have gone to Maggie's for her Christmas dinner, and to have returned at half past two without fail in order to light the drawing-room fire and prepare for tea-making. But, Maggie at the last moment having decided to go to Clara's for the middle of the day, Emmie was told to go with her and be as useful as she could at Mrs Benbow's until a quarter past two.

'I hope you've got your latchkey, Edwin,' said Hilda threateningly, as if ready to assume that with characteristic and inexcusable negligence he had left his latchkey at home.

'I have,' he said dryly, drawing the key from his pocket.

'Oh!' she muttered, as if saying: 'Well, after all, you're no better than you ought to be.' And took the key.

When she opened the door, Edwin surreptitiously gave half a crown to Unchpin, who was lighting the carriage-lamps.

George, with the marvellous self-preserving instinct of a small animal unprotected against irritated prowling monsters, had become invisible.

The front doorway yawned black like the portal of a tomb. The place was a terrible negation of Christmas. Edwin felt for the radiator; it was as cold to the touch as a dead hand. He lit the hall lamp, and the decorations of holly and mistletoe contrived by Hilda and George with smiles and laughter on Christmas Eve stood revealed as the very symbol of insincerity. Without taking off his hat and coat, he went into the unlighted glacial drawing-room, where Hilda was kneeling at the grate and striking matches. A fragment of newspaper blazed, and then the flame expired. The fire was badly laid.

'I'm sick of servants!' Hilda exclaimed with fury. 'Sick! They're all alike!' Her tone furiously blamed Edwin and everybody.

And Edwin knew that the day was a pyramid of which this moment was the dreadful apex. At intervals during the drive home Hilda had talked confidentially to George of the wondrous things he and she could do if they only resided in the country – things connected with flowers, vegetables, cocks, hens, ducks, cows, rabbits, horses. She had sketched out the life of a mistress of Ladderedge Hall, and she had sketched it out for the benefit of the dull, hard man sitting behind. Her voice, so persuasive and caressing to George, had been charged with all sorts of accusations against the silent fellow whose back now and then collided with hers. She had exasperated him. She had wilfully and deliberately exasperated him ... Her treatment of Unchpin, her childish outburst concerning servants, her acutely disagreeable demeanour, all combined now to exhaust the poor remainder of Edwin's patience. Not one word had been said about Ladderedge Hall, but Ladderedge Hall loomed always between them. Deadly war was imminent. Let it come! He would prefer war to a peace which meant for him nothing but insults and injustice. He would welcome war. He turned brusquely and lit the chandelier. On the table beneath it lay the writing-case that Hilda had given to George, and the edition of Matthew Arnold that she had given to Edwin, for a Christmas present. One of Edwin's Christmas presents to her, an ermine stole, she was wearing round her neck. Tragic absurdities, these false tokens of love ... There they were, both of them in full street attire, she kneeling at the grate and he standing at the table, in the dank drawing-room which now had no resemblance to a home.

Edwin said with frigid and disdainful malevolence:

'I wish you could control yourself, Hilda. The fact that a servant's a bit late on Christmas Day is no reason for you to behave like a spoilt child. You're offensive.'

His words, righteously and almost murderously resentful, seemed to startle and frighten the very furniture, which had the air of waiting, enchanted, for disaster.

Hilda turned her head and glared at Edwin. She threw back her shoulders, and her thick eyebrows seemed to meet in a passionate frown.

'Yes,' she said, with her clear, stinging articulation. 'That's just like you, that is! I lend my servant to your sister. She doesn't send her back, – and it's my fault! I should have thought the Benbows twisted you round their little finger enough, without you having to insult me because of them. Goodness knows what tricks they didn't play to get your aunt's money – every penny of it! And now they make you do all the work of the estate, for their benefit, and of course you do it like a lamb! You can never spare a minute from the works for me, but you can spare hours and hours for Auntie Hamps's estate and the Benbows! It's always like that.' She paused and spoke more thickly: 'But I don't see why you should insult me on the top of it!'

Her features went awry. She sobbed.

'You make me ill!' said Edwin savagely.

He walked out of the room and pulled the door to.

George was descending the stairs.

'Where are you going to, uncle?' demanded George, as Edwin opened the front door.

'I'm going down to see Auntie Maggie,' Edwin answered, forcing himself to speak very gently. 'Tell your mother if she asks.' The boy guessed the situation. It was humiliating that he should guess it, and still more humiliating to be compelled to make use of him in the fatal affair.

                              V

He walked at a moderate pace down Trafalgar Road. He did not know where he was going. Certainly he was not going to see Maggie. He had invented the visit to Maggie instantly in answer to George's question, and he could not understand why he had invented it. Maggie would be at Clara's; and, in a misfortune, he would never go to Clara's; only when he was successful and triumphant could he expose himself to the Benbows.

The weather was damp and chill without rain. The chilliness was rather tonic and agreeable to his body, and he felt quite warm, though on getting down from the dogcart a few minutes earlier he had been cold almost to the point of numbness. He could not remember how, nor when, the change had occurred.

Every street-lamp was the centre of a greenish-grey sphere, which presaged rain as though the street-lamp were the moon. The pavements were greasy with black slime, the road deep in lamp-reflecting mire through which the tram-lines ran straight and gleaming. Far down the slope a cage of light moving obscurely between the glittering avenue of lamps indicated the steam-tram as it lifted towards the farther hill into the heart of the town. Where the lamps merged together and vanished, but a little to the left, the illuminated dial of the clock in the Town Hall tower glowed in the dark heavens. The street was deserted; no *Signal* boys, no ragged girls staring into sweet shops, no artisans returning from work, no rattling carts, no vehicles of any kind save the distant tram. All the little shops were shut; even the little greengrocer's shop, which never closed, was shut now, and its customary winter smell of oranges and apples withdrawn. The little inns, not yet open, showed through their lettered plate windows one watching jet of gas amid blue-and-red paper festoons and bunches of holly. The gloomy fronts of nearly all the houses were pierced with oblongs of light on which sometimes appeared transient shadows of human beings. A very few other human beings, equally mysterious, passed furtive and baffling up and down the slope. Melancholy, familiar, inexplicable, and piteous – the melancholy of existence itself – rose like a vapour out of the sodden ground, ennobling all the scene. The lofty disc of the Town Hall clock solitary in the sky was somehow so heartrending, and the lives of the people both within and without the houses seemed to be so woven of futility and sorrow, that the menace of eternity grew intolerable.

Edwin's brain throbbed and shook like an engine-house in which the machinery was his violent thoughts. He no longer saw his marriage as a chain of disconnected episodes; he saw it as a drama the true meaning of which was at last revealed by the climax now upon him. He had had many misgivings about it, and had put them away, and they all swept back presenting themselves as a series of signs that pointed to inevitable disaster. He had been blind, from wilfulness or cowardice. He now had vision. He had arrived at honesty. He said to himself, as millions of men and women have said to themselves, with awestruck calm: 'My marriage was a mistake.' And he began to face the consequences of the admission. He was not such a fool as to attach too much importance to the immediate quarrel, nor even to the half-suppressed but supreme dissension concerning a place of residence. He assumed, even, that the present difficulties would somehow, with more or less satisfaction, be adjusted. What, however, would not and could not be adjusted was the temperament that produced them. Those difficulties, which had been preceded by smaller difficulties, would be followed by greater. It was inevitable. To hope otherwise would be weakly sentimental, as his optimism during the vigil in Auntie Hamps's bedroom had been weakly sentimental. He must face the truth: 'She won't alter her ways – and I shan't stand them.' No matter what their relations might in future superficially appear to be, their union was over. Or, if it was not actually over, it soon would be over, for the forces to shatter it were incontrollable and increasing in strength.

'Of course she can't help being herself!' he said impartially. 'But what's that got to do with me?'

His indictment of his wife was terrific and not to be answered. She had always been a queer girl. On the first night he ever saw her, she had run after him into his father's garden, and stood with him in the garden porch that he had since done away with, and spoken to him in the strangest manner. She was abnormal. The dismal and perilous adventure with George Cannon could not have happened to a normal woman. She could not see reason, and her sense of justice was non-existent. If she wanted a thing she must have it. In reality she was a fierce and unscrupulous egotist, incapable of understanding a point of view other than her own. Imagine her bursting out like that about Auntie Hamps's will! It showed how her mind ran. That Auntie Hamps had an absolute right to dispose of her goods as she pleased; that there was a great deal to be said for Auntie Hamps's arrangements; that in any case the Benbows were not to blame; that jealousy was despicable and the mark of a mean mind; that the only dignified course for himself was to execute the trust imposed upon him without complaining, – these things were obvious; but not to her! No human skill could ever induce her to grant them. She did not argue – she felt; and the disaster was that she did not feel rightly ... Imagine her trying to influence Ingpen's housekeeping, to worry the man, – she the guest and he the host! What would she say if anybody played the same game on her? ...

She could not be moderate. She expected every consideration from others, but she would yield none. She had desired a horse and trap. She had received it. And how had she used the gift? She had used it in defiance of the needs of the works. She had upset everybody and everything, and assuredly Unchpin had a very

legitimate grievance . . . She had said that she could not feel at
home in her own house while the house belonged to Maggie.
Edwin had obediently bought the house, – and now she wanted
another house. She scorned her husband's convenience and
preferences, and she wanted a house that was preposterously
inaccessible. The satisfaction of her caprice for a dogcart had
not in the slightest degree appeased her egotism. On the contrary
it had further excited her egotism and sharpened its aggressive-
ness. And by what strange infantile paths had she gone about the
enterprise of shifting Edwin into the country! Not a frank word
to Edwin of the house she had found and decided upon! Silly
rumours of a 'surprise'! And she had counted upon the presence
of Ingpen to disarm Edwin and to tie his hands. The conspiracy
was simply childish. And because Edwin had at once shown his
distaste for her scheme, she had taken offence. Her acrimony had
gradually increased throughout the day, hiding for a time under
malicious silences and enigmatic demeanours, darting out in
remarks to third persons and drawing back, and at last displaying
itself openly, cruelly, monstrously. The injustice of it all passed
belief. There was no excuse for Hilda, and there never would be
any excuse for her. She was impossible; she would be still more
impossible. He did not make her responsible; he admitted that
she was not responsible. But at the same time, with a disdainful
and cold resentment, he condemned and hated her.

He recalled Ingpen's: 'I won't pay the price.'

'And I won't!' he said. 'The end has come!'

He envied Ingpen.

And there flitted through his mind the dream of liberty – not
the liberty of ignorant youth, but liberty with experience and
knowledge to use it. Ravishing prospect! Marriage had advantages. But he could retain those advantages in freedom. He knew
what a home ought to be; he had the instinct of the interior; he
considered that he could keep house as well as any woman, and
better than most; he was not, in that respect, at all like Ingpen,
who suffered from his inability to produce and maintain comfort
. . . He remembered Ingpen's historic habitual phrase about the
proper place for women, – 'behind the veil'. It was a phrase
which intensely annoyed women; but nevertheless how true!

And Ingpen had put it into practice. Ingpen, even in the banal
Five Towns, had shown the way . . . He saw the existence of males,
with its rationality and its dependableness, its simplicity, its
directness, its honesty, as something ideal. And as he pictured
such an existence – with or without the romance of mysterious
and interesting creatures ever modestly waiting for attention
behind the veil – further souvenirs of Hilda's wilful naughtiness
and injustice rushed into his mind by thousands; in formulating
to himself his indictment against her, he had overlooked ninety
per cent of them; they were endless, innumerable. He marshalled
them again and again, with the fiercest virulence, the most
sombre gloom, with sardonic, bitter pleasure.

In the hollow where Trafalgar Road begins to be known as
Duck Bank, he turned to the left and, crossing the foot of
Woodisun Bank, arrived at one of the oldest quarters of the town,
where St Luke's Church stands in its churchyard amid a triangle
of little ancient houses. By the light of a new and improved gas-
lamp at the churchyard gates could be seen the dark silhouette
of the Norman tower and the occasional white gleam of grave-
stones.

One solitary couple, arm-in-arm, and bending slightly towards
each other, came sauntering in the mud past the historic National
Schools towards the illumination of the lamp. The man was a
volunteer, with a brilliant vermilion tunic, white belt, and black
trousers; he wore his hat jauntily and carried a diminutive cane;
pride was his warm overcoat. The girl was stout and short, with
a heavily flowered hat and a dark amorphous cloak; under her
left arm she carried a parcel. They were absorbed in themselves.
Edwin discerned first the man's face, in which was a gentle and
harmless coxcombry, and then the girl's face, ecstatic, upward-
gazing, seeing absolutely naught but the youth . . . It was
Emmie's face, as Edwin perceived after a momentary doubt due
to his unfamiliarity with the inhabitants of his own house.
Emmie, so impatiently and angrily awaited by her mistress, had
lost her head about a uniform. Emmie, whose place was in the
kitchen among saucepans and crockery, dish-clouts and brushes,
had escaped into another realm, where time is not. That she had
no immediate intention of returning to her kitchen was shown

by the fact that she was moving deliberately in a direction away from it. She was not pretty, for Hilda had perforce long since ceased to insist upon physical charm in her servants; she was not even young, – she was probably older than the adored soldier. But her rapt ecstasy, her fearful bliss, made a marvellous sight, rendered touching by the girl's coarse gawkiness.

It seemed lamentable, pathetic, to Edwin that destiny should not permit her to remain for ever in that dream. 'Can it be possible,' he thought, 'that a creature capable of such surpassing emotion is compelled to cook my bacon and black my boots?'

The couple, wordless, strolled onwards, sticking close to the railings. The churchyard was locked, but Emmie and the soldier were doing the best they could to satisfy that instinct which in the Five Towns seems to drive lovers to graves for their pleasure. The little houses cast here and there a blind yellow eye on the silent and tranquil scene. Edwin turned abruptly back into Woodisun Bank, feeling that he was a disturber of the peace.

Suddenly deciding to walk up to Hillport 'for the sake of exercise', he quickened his pace. After a mile and a half, when he had crossed the railway at Shawport and was on the Hillport rise, and the Five Towns had begun to spread out in a map behind him, he noticed that he was perspiring. He very seldom perspired, and therefore he had the conviction that the walk was 'doing him good'. He felt exhilarated, and moved still faster.

His mood was now changed. The spectacle of Emmie and the soldier had thrown him violently out of resentment into wonder. His indignation was somewhat exhausted, and though he tried again and again to flick it back into full heat and activity, he could not. He kept thinking of the moment in the morning when, standing ready to jump from the dogcart, his wife had said: 'Catch me, both of you', and he recalled vividly the sensation of her acquiescence, her momentary yielding – imperceptible yet unforgettable – as he supported her strongly in his arms; and with this memory was mingled the smell of velvet. Strange that a woman so harsh, selfish, and overbearing, could thus contradict her whole character in an instant of surrender! Was she in that gesture confiding to him the deepest secret? . . . Rubbish! But now he no longer looked down on her disdainfully. Honesty made

him admit that it was puerile to affect disdain of an individuality
so powerful and so mysterious. If she was a foe, she was at any
rate a dangerous fighter, and not to be played with. And yet she
could be a trifle, a wisp of fragile flesh in his arms!

He saw the beatific face of Emmie against the churchyard gates
under the lamp ... Why not humour Hilda? Why not let her
plant their home according to her caprice? ... Certainly not!
Never would he do it! Why should he? Time after time he angrily
rejected the idea. Time after time it returned. What did it matter
to Hilda where she lived? And had he not bought their present
house solely in order to please her? The first consideration in
choosing a home ought to be and must be the consideration of
business convenience ... Yet, what did it matter to him where
his home was? (He remembered a phrase of Ingpen's: 'I don't
live on that plane.') Could he not adapt himself? He dreamt of
very rapid transit between Ladderedge Hall and the works.
Motor-cars had just become lawful; but he had never happened
to see one, though he had heard of several in the district, or
passing through. His imagination could not rise so high as a
motor-car. That he could ever use or possess one did not even
occur to him. He thought only of a fast-trotting horse, and a trap
with indiarubber tyres; himself the driver; sometimes Hilda the
driver ... an equipage to earn renown in the district. 'Clayhanger's trap,' – 'He drives in from Ladderedge in thirty-five
minutes. The horse simply won't walk; doesn't know how to!'
And so on. He had heard such talk of others. Why should not
others hear it of him? ... Then, the pleasure, the mere pleasure –
call it sensual or what you like – of granting a caprice to the
capricious creature! If a thing afforded her joy, why not give it?
... To see her in the role of mistress of a country house, delicately horsey, excited about charitable schemes, protecting the
poor, working her will upon gardeners and grooms, stamping
her foot in the violence of her resolution to have her own way,
offering sugar to a horse, nursing a sick dog! Amusing! Agreeable! ... And all that activity of hers a mere dependence of his
own! Flattering to his pride! ... He could afford it easily, for he
was richer even than his wife supposed. To let the present house
ought not to be difficult. To sell it advantageously ought not to be

impossible ... In this connection he thought, though not seriously, of Tom Swetnam, who had at last got himself engaged to one of those Scandinavian women about whom he had been chaffed for years. Tom would be wanting an abode, and probably a good one.

He was carried away by his own dream. To realize that dream he had only to yield, to nod negligently, to murmur with benevolent tolerance: 'All right. Do as you please.' He would have nothing to withdraw, for he had uttered no refusal. Not a word had passed between them as to Ladderedge Hall since they had quitted it. He had merely said that he did not like it, – 'poured cold water on it' as the phrase was. True, his demeanour had plainly intimated that he was still opposed in principle to the entire project of living in the country; but a demeanour need not be formally retracted; it could be negatived without any humiliation ...

No, he would never yield, though yielding seemed to open up a pleasant, a delicious prospect. He could not yield. It would be wrong, and it would be dangerous, to yield. Had he not already quite clearly argued out with himself the whole position? And yet why not yield? ... He was afraid as before a temptation.

He re-crossed the railway, and crossed Fowlea Brook, a boundary, back into the borough. The dark path lay parallel with the canal, but below it. He had gone right through Hillport and round Hillport Marsh and returned down the flank of the great ridge that protects the Five Towns on the west. He could not recollect the details of the walk; he only knew that he had done it all, that time and the miles had passed with miraculous rapidity, and that his boots were very muddy. A change in the consistency of the mud caused him to look up at the sky, which was clearing and showed patches of faint stars. A frost had set in, despite the rainy prophecy of street-lamps. In a few moments he had climbed the short steep curving slope on to the canal bridge. He was breathless and very hot.

He stopped and sat on the parapet. In his schooldays he had crossed this bridge twice a day on the journey to and from Oldcastle. Many times he had lingered on it. But he had forgotten the little episodes of his schooldays, which seemed now almost to belong to another incarnation. He did, however, recall that as a boy he could not sit on the parapet unless he vaulted up to it. He thought he must have been ridiculously small and boyish. The lights of Bursley, Bleakridge, Hanbridge, and Cauldon hung round the eastern horizon in an arc. To the north presided the clock of Bursley Town Hall, and to the south the clock of Cauldon Church; but both were much too far off to be deciphered. Below and around the church clock the vague fires of Cauldon Bar Ironworks played, and the tremendous respiration of the blast-furnaces filled the evening. Beneath him gleamed the foul water of the canal . . . He trembled with the fever that precedes a supreme decision. He trembled as though he was about to decide whether or not he would throw himself into the canal. Should he accept the country-house scheme? Ought he to accept it? The question was not simply that of a place of residence, – it concerned all his life.

He admitted that marriage must be a mutual accommodation. He was, and always had been, ready to accommodate. But Hilda was unjust, monstrously unjust. Of that he was definitely convinced . . . Well, perhaps not monstrously unjust, but very unjust. How could he excuse such injustice as hers? He obviously could not excuse it . . . On previous occasions he had invented excuses for her conduct, but they were not convincing excuses. They were compromises between his intellectual honesty and his desire for peace. They were, at bottom, sentimentalism.

And then there flashed into his mind, complete, the great discovery of all his career. It was banal; it was commonplace; it was what everyone knew. Yet it was the great discovery of all his career. If Hilda had not been unjust in the assertion of her own individuality, there could be no merit in yielding to her. To yield to a just claim was not meritorious, though to withstand it would be wicked. He was objecting to injustice as a child objects to rain on a holiday. Injustice was a tremendous actuality! It had to be faced and accepted. (He himself was unjust. At any rate he intellectually conceived that he must be unjust, though honestly he could remember no instance of injustice on his part.) To reconcile oneself to injustice was the master achievement. He had read it; he had been aware of it; but he had never really felt it till that moment on the dark canal bridge. He was awed, thrilled by the realization. He longed ardently to put it to the test. He did put it to the test. He yielded on the canal bridge. And in yielding, it seemed to him that he was victorious.

He thought confidently and joyously:

'I'm not going to be beaten by Hilda! And I'm not going to be beaten by marriage. Dashed if I am! A nice thing if I had to admit that I wasn't clever enough to be a husband!'

He was happy, but somewhat timorously so. He had the sense to suspect that his discovery would scarcely transform marriage into an everlasting Eden, and that serious trouble would not improbably recur. 'Marriage keeps on all the time till you're dead!' he said to himself. But he profoundly knew that he had advanced a stage, that he had acquired new wisdom and new power, and that no danger in the future could equal the danger that was past.

He thought:

'I know where I am!'

It had taken him years to discover where he was. Why should the discovery occur just then? He could only suppose that the cumulative battering of experience had at length knocked a hole through his thick head, and let saving wisdom in. The length of time necessary for the operation depended upon the thickness of the head. Some heads were impenetrable and their owners came necessarily to disaster. His head was probably of an average thickness.

When he got into Trafalgar Road, at the summit of Bleak-ridge, he hesitated to enter his own house, on account of the acute social difficulties that awaited him there, and passed it like a beggar who is afraid. One by one he went by all the new little streets of cottages with drawing-rooms – Millett Street, Wilcox Street, Paul Street, Oak Street, Hulton Street, – and the two old little streets, already partly changed – Manor Street and Higgin-botham Street. Those mysterious newcoming families from no-where were driving him out – through the agency of his wife! The Orgreaves had gone, and been succeeded by excellent people with whom it was impossible to fraternize. There were rumours that in view of Tom Swetnam's imminent defection the

Swetnam household might be broken up and the home abandoned. The Suttons, now that Beatrice Sutton had left the district,
talked seriously of going. Only Dr Stirling was left on that side
of the road, and he stayed because he must. The once exclusive
Terraces on the other side were losing their quality. Old Darius
Clayhanger had risen out of the mass, but he was fiercely
exceptional. Now the whole mass seemed to be rising, under the
action of some strange leaven, and those few who by intelligence,
by manners, or by money counted themselves select were fleeing
as from an inundation. Edwin had not meant to join in the exo-
dus. But he too would join it. Destiny had seized him. Let him be
as democratic in spirit as he would, his fate was to be cut off from
the democracy, with which, for the rest, he had very little of
speech or thought or emotion in common, but in which, from an
implacable sense of justice, he was religiously and unchangeably
determined to put his trust.

He braced himself, and, mounting the steps of the porch, felt
in his pocket for his latchkey. It was not there. Hilda had taken it
and not returned it. She never did return it when she borrowed it,
and probably she never would. He had intended to slip quietly
into the house, and prepare if possible an astute opening to
minimize the difficulty of the scenes which must inevitably occur.
For his dignity would need some protection. In the matter of his
dignity, he wished that he had not said quite so certainly to
Ingpen: 'I shan't take that house.'

With every prim formality, Emmie answered his ring. She was
wearing the mask and the black frock and the white apron and
cap of her vocation. Not the slightest trace of the beatified
woman in the flowered hat under the lamp at the gates of the
churchyard! No sign of a heart or of passion or of ecstasy!
Incredible creatures – they were all incredible!

He thought, nervous:

'I shall meet Hilda in half a second.'

George ran into the hall, wearing his new green shade over his
eyes.

'Here he is, mother!' cried George. 'I say, nunks, Emmie
brought up a parcel for you from Uncle Albert and Auntie
Clara. Here it is. It wasn't addressed outside, so I opened it.'

He indicated the hall table, on which, in a bed of tissue-paper and brown paper, lay a dreadful flat inkstand of blue glass and bronze, with a card: 'Best wishes to Edwin from Albert and Clara.'

George and Edwin gazed at each other with understanding.

'Just my luck, isn't it, sonny?' said Edwin. 'It's worse than last year's.'

'You poor dear!' said Hilda, appearing, all smiles and caressing glances. She was in a pale grey dress. 'Whatever shall you do with it? You know you'll have to put it on view when they come up. Emmie' – to the maid vanishing into the kitchen – 'we'll have supper now.'

'Yes,' said Edwin to himself, with light but sardonic tolerance. 'Yes, my lady. You're all smiles because you're bent on getting Ladderedge Hall out of me. But you don't know what a near shave you've had of getting something else.'

He was elated. The welcome of his familiar home was beautiful to him. And the incalculable woman with a single gesture had most unexpectedly annihilated the unpleasant past and its consequences. He could yield upon the grand contention how and when he chose. He had his acquiescence waiting like a delightful surprise for Hilda. As he looked at her lovingly, with all her crimes of injustice thick upon her, he clearly realized that he saw her as no other person saw her, and that because it was so she in her entirety was indispensable to him. And when he tried to argue impartially and aloofly with himself about rights and wrongs, asinine reason was swamped by an entirely irrational and wise joy in the simple fact of the criminal's existence.

VI

In the early spring of 1897 there was an evening party at the Clayhangers'. But it was not called a party; it was not even called a reception. The theory of the affair was that Hilda had 'just asked a few people to come in, without any fuss'. The inhabitants of the Five Towns had, and still have, an aversion for every sort of formal hospitality, or indeed for any hospitality other than the impulsive and the haphazard. One or two fathers with forceful daughters agitated by newly revealed appetites in themselves, might hire a board schoolroom in January, and give a dance at which sharp exercise and hot drinks alone kept bodies warm in the icy atmosphere. Also musical and dramatic societies and games clubs would have annual conversaziones and dances, which however were enterprises of cooperation rather than of hospitality. Beyond these semi-public entertainments there was almost nothing, in the evening, save card-parties and the small regular reunions of old friends who had forgathered on a certain night of the week for whisky or tea and gossip ever since the beginning of time, and would continue to do so till some coffin or other was ordered. Every prearranged assemblage comprising more than two persons beyond the family was a 'function' – a term implying both contempt and respect for ceremonial; and no function could be allowed to occur without an excuse for it, – such as an anniversary. The notion of deliberately cultivating human intercourse for its own sake would have been regarded as an affectation approaching snobbishness. Hundreds of well-to-do and socially unimpeachable citizens never gave or received an invitation to a meal. The reason of all this was not meanness, for no community outside America has more generous instincts than the Five Towns; it was merely a primitive self-consciousness striving to conceal itself beneath breezy disdain for those more highly developed manners which it read about with industry and joy in the weekly papers, but which it lacked the courage to imitate.

The break-up of the Orgreave household had been a hard blow to the cult of hospitality in Bleakridge. Lane End House in the old days was a creative centre of hospitality; for the force of example, the desire to emulate, and the necessity of paying in kind for what one has permitted oneself to receive will make hosts of those who, by their own initiative, would never have sent out an invitation. When the Orgreaves vanished, sundry persons in Bleakridge were discouraged, – and particularly Edwin and Hilda, whose musical evenings had never recovered from the effect of the circumstances of the first one. They entertained only by fits and starts, when Hilda happened to remember that she held a high position in the suburb. Hilda was handicapped by the fact that she could not easily strike up friendships with other women. She had had one friend, and after Janet's departure she had fully confided in no woman. Moreover it was only at intervals that Hilda felt the need of companionship. Her present party was due chiefly to what Edwin in his more bitter moods would have called snobbishness, – to wit, partly a sudden resolve not to be outshone by the Swetnams, who in recent years, as the younger generation of the family grew up, had beyond doubt increased their ascendancy; and partly the desire to render memorable the last months of her residence in Bleakridge.

The list of Hilda's guests, and the names absent from it, gave an indication of the trend of social history. The Benbows were not asked; the relations of the two families remained as friendly as ever they were, but the real breach between them, caused by profound differences of taste and intelligence, was now complete. Maggie would have been asked, had she not refused in advance, from a motive of shyness. In all essential respects Maggie had been annexed by Clara and Albert. She had given up Auntie Hamps's house (of which the furniture had been either appropriated or sold) and gone to live with the Benbows as a working aunt, – this in spite of Albert's default in the matter of interest; she forewent her rights, slept in a small room with Amy, paid a share of the household expenses, and did the work of a nurse-maid and servant combined – simply because she was Maggie. She might, had she chosen, have lived in magnificence with the Clayhangers, but she would not face the intellectual and social strain of doing so. Jim Orgreave was not invited; briefly he had become impossible, though he was still well-dressed. More strange – Tom Orgreave and his wife had only been invited after some discussion, and had declined! Tom was growing extra-ordinarily secretive, solitary, and mysterious. It was reported that Mrs Tom had neither servant nor nursemaid, and that she dared not ask her husband for money to buy clothes. Yet Edwin and Tom when they met in the street always stopped for a talk, generally about books. Daisy Marrion, who said openly that Tom and Mrs Tom were a huge disappointment to everybody, was invited and she accepted. Janet Orgreave had arrived in Bursley on a visit to the Clayhangers on the very day of the party.

The Cheswardines were asked, mainly on account of Stephen, whose bluff, utterly unintellectual, profound good-nature, and whose adoration of his wife, were gradually endearing him to the perceptive. Mr and Mrs Fearns were requested to bring their daughter Annunciata, now almost marriageable, and also Mademoiselle Renée Souchon, the French governess, newly arrived in the district, of the Fearns's younger children. Folks hinted their astonishment that Alma Fearns should have been imprudent enough to put so exotic a woman under the same roof with her husband. Ingpen needed no invitation; nothing could occur at the Clayhangers' without him. Doctor Stirling was the other mature bachelor. Finally in the catalogue were four Swetnams, the vigorous and acute Sarah (who was a mere acquaintance), aged twenty-five, Tom Swetnam, and two younger brothers. Tom had to bring with him the prime excuse for the party, – namely, Miss Manna Höst of Copenhagen, to whom Hilda intended to show that the Swetnams were not the only people on earth. There were thus eight women, eight men (who had put on evening dress out of respect for the foreigner), and George.

At eleven o'clock, when the musical part of the entertainment was over, Miss Höst had already fully secured for herself the position which later she was to hold as the wife of Tom Swetnam. Bleakridge had been asked to meet her and inspect her, and the opinion of Bleakridge was soon formed that Copenhagen must be a wondrous and a romantic place and that Tom Swetnam knew his way about. In the earliest years when the tourist agencies first discovered the advertising value of the phrase 'Land of the Midnight Sun', Tom the adventurous had made the Scandinavian round trip, and each subsequent summer he had gone off again in the same direction. The serpents of the Hanbridge and the Bursley Conservative clubs, and of the bar of the Five Towns Hotel, had wagered that there was a woman at the bottom of it. There was. He had met her at Marienlyst, the watering-place near Helsingör (called by the tourist agencies Elsinore). Manna Höst was twenty-three, tall and athletically slim, and more blonde than any girl ever before seen in the Five Towns. She had golden hair and she wore white. It was understood that she spoke

Danish, Swedish, and Norwegian. She talked French with facility to Renée Souchon. And Tom said that her knowledge of German surpassed her knowledge of either French or English. She spoke English excellently, with a quaint, endearing accent, but with correctness. Sometimes she would use an idiom (picked up from the Swetnam boys), exquisitely unaware that it was not quite suited to the lips of a young woman in a strange drawing-room; her innocence, however, purified it.

She sang classical songs in German, with dramatic force, and she could play accompaniments. She was thoroughly familiar with all the music haltingly performed by Ingpen, Janet, Annunciata, and young George. Ingpen was very seriously interested in her views thereon. She knew about the French authors from whose works Renée Souchon chose her recitations. And standing up at the buffet-table in the dining-room, she had fabricated astounding sandwiches in the Danish style. She stated that Danish cooks reckoned ninety-three sorts of sandwiches. She said in her light, eager voice, apropos of cooking: 'There is one thing I cannot understand. I cannot understand why you English throw your potatoes to melt in cold water for an hour before you boil them.' 'Nor I!' interjected Renée Souchon. No other woman standing round the table had ever conceived the propriety of boiling potatoes without first soaking them in cold water, and Manna was requested to explain. 'Because,' she said, 'it – it lets go the salts of potassium which are so necessary for the pheesical development of the body.' Whereupon Tertius Ingpen had been taken by one of his long *crescendo* laughs, a laugh that ended by his being bent nearly double below the level of the table. Everybody was much impressed, and Ingpen himself not the least. Ingpen wondered what a girl so complex could see in a man like Tom Swetnam, who, although he could talk freely about the arts, had no real feeling for any of them.

But what impressed the company even more than Miss Höst's accomplishments was the candid fervour of her comprehensive interest in life, which was absolutely without self-consciousness or fear. She talked with the same disarming ingenuous eager directness to hard-faced Charles Fearns, the secret rake; to his wife, the ageing and sweetly-sad mother of a family; to Renée

Souchon, who despite her plainness and her rumoured bigotry seemed to attract all the men in the room by something provocative in her eye and the carriage of her hips; to the simple and powerful Stephen Cheswardine; to Vera, the delicious and elegant cat; to Doctor Stirling with his Scotch mysticism; and to Tertius Ingpen the connoisseur and avowed bachelor. She spoke to Hilda, Janet, and Daisy Marrion as one member of a secret sisterhood to other members, to Annunciata as a young girl, and to George as an initiated sister. She left them to turn to Edwin with a trustful glance as to one whose special reliability she had divined from the first. 'Have a liqueur, Miss Höst,' Edwin enjoined her. In a moment she was sipping Chartreuse. 'I love it!' she murmured.

But somehow beneath all such freedoms and frankness she did not cease to be a maiden with reserves of mystery. Her assumption that nobody could misinterpret her demeanour was remarkable to the English observers, and far more so to Renée Souchon. All gazed at her piquant blonde face, scarcely pretty, with its ardent restless eyes, and felt the startling compliment of her quick, searching sympathy. And she, tinglingly aware of her success, proved easily equal to the ordeal of it. Only at rare intervals did she give a look at the betrothed, as if for confirmation of her security. As for Tom, he was positively somewhat unnerved by the brilliance of the performance. He left her alone, without guidance, as a ring-master who should stand aside during a turn and say: 'See this marvel! I am no longer necessary.' When people glanced at him after one of her effects, he would glance modestly away, striving to hide from them his illusion that he himself had created the bewitching girl. At half past eleven, when the entire assemblage passed into the drawing-room, she dropped on to the piano-stool and began a Waldteufel waltz with irresistible seductiveness. Hilda's heart leaped. In a minute the carpet was up, and the night, which all had supposed to be at an end, began.

At nearly one o'clock in the morning the party was moving strongly by its own acquired momentum and needed neither the invigoration nor the guidance which hosts often are compelled to give. Hilda, having finished a schottische with Doctor Stirling, missed Janet from the drawing-room. Leaving the room in search of her, she saw Edwin with Tom Swetnam and the glowing Manna at the top of the stairs.

'Hello!' she called out. 'What are you folks doing?'

Manna's light laugh descended like a shower of crystals.

'Just taking a constitutional,' Edwin answered.

Hilda waved to them in passing. She was extremely elated. Among other agreeable incidents was the success of her new black lace frock. Edwin's voice pleased her, – it was so calm, wise, and kind, and at the same time mysteriously ironical. She occasionally admitted, at the sound of that voice when Edwin was in high spirits, that she had never been able to explore completely the more withdrawn arcana of his nature. He had behaved with perfection that evening. She admitted that he was the basis of the evening, that without him she could never have such triumphs. It was strange that a man by spending so many hours per day at a works could create the complicated ease and luxury of a home. She perceived how steadily and surely he had progressed since their marriage, and how his cautiousness always justified itself, and how he had done all that he had said he would do. And she had a vision of that same miraculous creative force of his at work, by her volition, in the near future upon Ladderedge Hall. Her mood became a strange compound of humility before him and of self-confident pride in her own power to influence him.

In the boudoir Janet was reclining in the sole easy-chair. Dressed in grey (she had abandoned white), she was as slim as ever, and did not look her age. With face flushed, eyes glinting under drooping lids, and bosom heaving rather quickly, she might have passed in the half-light for a young married woman still under the excitement of matrimony, instead of a virgin of forty.

'I was so done up I had to come and hide myself!' she murmured in a dreamy tone.

'Well, of course you've had the journey today and everything . . .'

'I never did come across such a dancer as Charles Fearns!' Janet went on.

'Yes,' said Hilda, standing with her back to the fire, with one hand on the mantelpiece. 'He's a great dancer – or at least he makes you think so. But I'm sure he's a bad man.'

'Yes, I suppose he is!' Janet agreed with a sigh.

Neither of the women spoke for a moment, and each looked away.

Through the closed door came the muffled sound of the piano, played by Annunciata. No melody was distinguishable, – only the percussion of the bass chords beating out the time of a new mazurka. It was as if the whole house faintly but passionately pulsed in the fever of the dance.

'I see you've got a Rossetti,' said Janet at last, fingering a blue volume that lay on the desk.

'Edwin gave it me,' Hilda replied. 'He's gradually giving me all my private poets. But somehow I haven't been able to read much lately. I expect it's the idea of moving into the country that makes me restless.'

'But is it settled, all that?'

'Of course it's settled, my dear. I'm determined to take him away' – Hilda spoke of her husband as of a parcel or an intelligent bear on a chain, as loving wives may – 'right out of all this. I'm sure it will be a good thing for him. He doesn't mind, really. He's promised me. Only he wants to make sure of either selling or letting this house first. He's always very cautious, Edwin is. He simply hates doing a thing straight off.'

'Yes, he is rather that way inclined,' said Janet.

'I wanted him to take Ladderedge at once, even if we didn't move into it. Anyhow we couldn't move into it immediately because of the repairs and things. They'll take a fine time, I know. We can get it for sixty pounds a year. And what's sixty pounds more or less to Edwin? It's no more than what the rent of this house would be. But no, he wouldn't! He must see where he stands with this house before he does anything else! You can't alter him, you know!'

The door was cautiously pushed, and Ingpen entered.

'So you're discussing her!' he said, low, with a satiric grin.

'Discussing who?' Hilda sharply demanded.

'You know.'

'Tertius,' said Hilda. 'You're worse than a woman.'

He giggled with delight.

'I suppose you mean that to be very severe.'

'If you want to know, we were talking about Ladderedge.'

'So apologize!' said Janet, sitting up.

Ingpen's face straightened, and he began to tap his teeth with his thumb.

'Curious! That's just what I came in about. I've been trying to get a chance to tell you all the evening. There's somebody else after Ladderedge, a man from Axe. He's been to look over it twice this week. I thought I'd tip you the wink.'

Hilda stood erect, putting her shoulders back.

'Have you told Edwin?' she asked very curtly.

'Yes.'

'What did he say?'

'He said it was only a dodge of the house-agent's to quicken things up.'

'And do you think it is?'

'Well, I doubt it,' Ingpen answered apprehensively. 'That's why I wanted to warn you – his lordship being what he is.'

Voices, including Edwin's, could be heard in the hall.

'Here, I'm not going to be caught conspiring with you!' Ingpen whispered. 'It's more than my place is worth.' And he departed.

The voices receded, and Hilda noiselessly shut the door. Everything was now changed for her by a tremendous revulsion. The beating of the measure of the mazurka seemed horrible and maddening. Her thought was directed upon Edwin with the cold fury of which only love is capable. It was not his fault that some rival was nibbling at Ladderedge, but it was his fault that Ladderedge should still be in peril. She saw all her grandiose plan ruined. She felt sure that the rival was powerful and determined, and that Edwin would let him win, either by failing to bid against him, or by mere shilly-shallying. Ladderedge was not the only suitable country residence in the county; there were doubtless many others; but Ladderedge was just what she wanted, and – more important with her – it had become a symbol. She had a misgiving that if they did not get Ladderedge they would remain in Trafalgar Road, Bursley, for ever and ever. Yet, angry and desperate though she was, she somehow did not accuse and arraign Edwin – any more than she would have accused and arraigned a climate. He was in fact the climate in which she lived. A moment ago she had said: 'You can't alter him!' But now all the energy of her volition cried out that he must be altered.

'My girl,' she said, turning to Janet. 'Do you think you can stand a scene tomorrow?'

'A scene?' Janet repeated the words guardedly. The look on Hilda's face somewhat alarmed her.

'Between Edwin and me. I'm absolutely determined that we shall take Ladderedge, and I don't care how much of a row we have over it.'

'It isn't as bad as all that?' Janet softly murmured, with her skill to soothe.

'Yes, it is!' said Hilda violently.

'I was wondering the other day, after one of your letters,' Janet proceeded gently, 'why after all you were so anxious to go into the country. I thought you wanted Edwin to be on the Town Council or something of that kind. How can he do that if you're right away at a place like Stockbrook?'

'So I should like him to be on the Town Council! But all I really want is to get him away from his business. You don't know, Janet!' she spoke bitterly, and with emotion. 'Nobody knows except me. He'll soon be the slave of his business if he keeps on. Oh, I don't mean he stays at nights at it. He scarcely ever does. But he's always thinking about it. He simply can't bear being a minute late for it, everything must give way to it, – he takes that as a matter of course, and that's what annoys me, especially as there's no reason for it, seeing how much he trusts Big James and Simpson. I believe he'd do anything for Big James. He'd listen to Big James far sooner than he'd listen to me . . . Disagreeable fawning old man, and quite stupid! Simpson isn't so bad. I tell you Edwin only looks on his home as a nice place to be quiet in when he isn't at the works. I've never told him so, and I don't think he suspects it, but I will tell him one of these days. He's very good, Edwin is, in all the little things. He always tries to be just. But he isn't just, in the big things. He's most frightfully unjust. I sometimes wonder where he imagines I come in. Of course he'd do any mortal thing for me – except spare half a minute from the works . . . What do I care about money? I don't care *that* much about money. When there's money I can spend it, that's all. But I'd prefer to be poor, and him to be rude and cross and impatient – which he scarcely ever is – than have this feeling all the time that it's the works first, and everything else second. I don't mind for myself – no, really I don't, at least very little! But I do mind for him. I call it humiliating for a man to get like that. It puts everything upside down. Look at Stephen Cheswardine, for instance. There's a pretty specimen! And Edwin'll be as bad as him soon.'

'But everyone says how fond Stephen is of his wife!'

'And isn't Edwin fond of me? Stephen Cheswardine despises his wife – only he can't do without her. That's all. And he treats her accordingly. And I shall be the same.'

'Oh! Hilda!'

'Yes, I shall. Yes, I shall. But I won't have it. I'd as lief be married to a man like Charles Fearns. He isn't a slave to his business anyhow. I shall get Edwin farther away. And when I've got him away I shall see he doesn't go to the works on Saturdays, too. I've quite made up my mind about that. And if he isn't on the Town Council he can be on the County Council – that's quite as good, I hope!'

Never before had Hilda spoken so freely to anyone, not even to Janet. Fierce pride had always kept her self-contained. But now she had no feeling of shame at her outburst. Tears stood in her eyes – and yet she faced Janet, making no effort to hide them.

'My dear!' breathed the deprecating Janet, shocked out of her tepid virginal calm by a revelation of conjugal misery such as had never been vouchsafed to her. She was thinking: 'How can the poor thing face her guests after this? Everybody will see that something's happened – it will be awful! She really ought to think of her position.'

There was a silence.

The door opened with a sharp sound, and Hilda turned away her head as from the suddenly visible mouth of a cannon. The music could be heard plainly, and beneath it the dull shuffling of feet on the bare boards of the drawing-room. Manna Höst came in radiant, followed by Edwin and Tom Swetnam.

'Well, Hilda,' said Edwin, with a slight timid constraint. 'I've got rid of your house for you. Here are the deluded victims.'

'We have seen every corner of it, Mrs Clayhanger,' said Manna Höst enthusiastically. 'It is lovely. But how can you wish to leave it? It is so practical!'

Perceiving the agitation of Hilda's face, Edwin added in a lower voice to his wife:

'I thought I wouldn't say anything until it was settled, for fear you might be let in for a disappointment. He'll buy it if I leave fifteen hundred on mortgage. So I shall. But of course he wanted her to have a good look at it first.'

'How unfair I am!' thought Hilda, as she made some banal remark to Miss Höst. 'Don't I know I can always rely on him?'

'Mr Clayhanger made us promise not to –' Miss Höst began to explain.

'It was just like him!' Hilda interrupted, smiling.

She had a strong desire to jump at Edwin and kiss him. She was saved. Her grandiose plan would proceed. The house sold, Edwin was bound to secure Ladderedge Hall against no matter what rival; and he would do it. But it was the realization of her power over her husband that gave her the profoundest joy.

About an hour later, when everyone felt that the party was over, the guests, reluctant to leave, and excited afresh by the news that the house had changed hands during the revel, were all assembled in the drawing-room. A few were seated on the chairs which, with the tables, had been pushed against the walls. George had squatted on the carpet rolled up into the hearth, where the fire was extinct; he was not wearing his green shade. The rest were grouped around Manna Höst in the middle of the room.

Miss Höst, the future mistress of the abode, was now more than ever the centre of regard. Apparently as fresh as at the start, and picking delicately at a sweet biscuit, the flushed blonde stood answering questions about her views on England and especially on the Five Towns. She was quite sure of herself, and utterly charming in her confidence. Annunciata Fearns envied her acutely. The other women were a little saddened by the thought of

all the disillusions that inevitably lay before her. It was touching
to see her glance at Tom Swetnam, convinced that she understood
him to the core, and in him all the psychology of his sex.

'Everybody knows,' she was saying, 'that the English are the
finest nation, and I think the Five Towns are much more English
than London. That's why I adore the Five Towns. You do not
know how English you are here. It makes me laugh because you
are so English, and you do not know it. I love you.'

'You're flattering us,' said Stephen Cheswardine, enchanted
with the girl.

Everybody waited in eager delight for her next words. Such tit-
bits of attention and laudation did not often fall to the district. It
occurred to people that after all the local self-conceit might not be
entirely unjustified.

'Ah!' Manna pouted. 'But you have spots!'

'Spots!' repeated young Paul Swetnam, amid a general laugh.

She turned to him: 'You said there were no spots on Knype
Football Club, did you not? Well, there is a spot on you English.
You are dreadfully exasperating to us Danes. Oh, I mean it!
You are exasperating because you will not show your feelings!'

'Tom, that must be one for you,' said Charlie Fearns.

'We're too proud,' said Doctor Stirling.

'No,' replied Manna maliciously. 'It is not pride. You are
afraid to show your feelings. It is because you are cowards – in
that!'

'We aren't!' cried Hilda, inspired. And yielding to the temptation which had troubled her incessantly ever since she left the
boudoir, she put her arms round Edwin and kissed him. 'So
there!'

'Loud applause!' said young George on the roll of carpet.
He said it kindly, but with a certain superiority, perhaps due to
the facts that he was wearing a man's 'long trousers' for the first
time that night, and that he regarded himself as already almost a
Londoner. There was some handclapping.

Edwin's eyes had seduced Hilda. Looking at them surreptitiously, she had suddenly recalled another of his tricks, – tricks
of goodness. When she had told him one evening that Minnie
was prematurely the mother of a girl, he had said: 'Well, we'll put

£130 in the savings bank for the kid.' '£130? Whatever are you talking about?' '£130. I received it from America this very morning as ever is.' And he showed her a draft on Brown, Shipley, & Co. He said 'from America'. He was too delicate to say 'from George Cannon'. It had been a triumphant moment for him. And now, as before them all Hilda held him to her, the delicious thought that she had power over him, that she was shaping the large contours of his existence, made her feel solemn in her bliss. And yet simultaneously she was reflecting with a scarcely perceptible hardness: 'It's each for himself in marriage after all, and I've got my own way.' And then she noticed the whiteness of his shirt-front under her chin, and that reminded her of his mania for arranging his linen according to his own ideas, in his own drawer, and the absurd tidiness of his linen; and she wanted to laugh.

'What a romance she has made of my life!' thought Edwin, confused and blushing, as she loosed him. And though he looked round with affection at the walls which would soon no longer be his, the greatness of the adventure of existence with this creature, to him unique, and the eternal expectation of some new ecstasy, left no room in his heart for a regret,

He caught sight of Ingpen alone in a corner by the piano, nervously stroking his silky beard. The memory of the secret woman in Ingpen's room came back to him. Without any process of reasoning, he felt very sorry for both of them, and he was aware of a certain condescension in himself towards Ingpen.

MORE ABOUT PENGUINS
AND PELICANS

Penguinews, which appears every month, contains details of all the new books issued by Penguins as they are published. From time to time it is supplemented by *Penguins in Print*, which is a complete list of all titles available. (There are some five thousand of these.)

A specimen copy of *Penguinews* will be sent to you free on request. For a year's issues (including the complete lists) please send 50p if you live in the British Isles, or 75p if you live elsewhere. Just write to Dept EP, Penguin Books Ltd, Harmondsworth, Middlesex, enclosing a cheque or postal order, and your name will be added to the mailing list.

In the U.S.A.: For a complete list of books available from Penguin in the United States write to Dept CS, Penguin Books Inc., 7110 Ambassador Road, Baltimore, Maryland 21207.

In Canada: For a complete list of books available from Penguin in Canada write to Penguin Books Canada Ltd, 41 Steelcase Road West, Markham, Ontario.